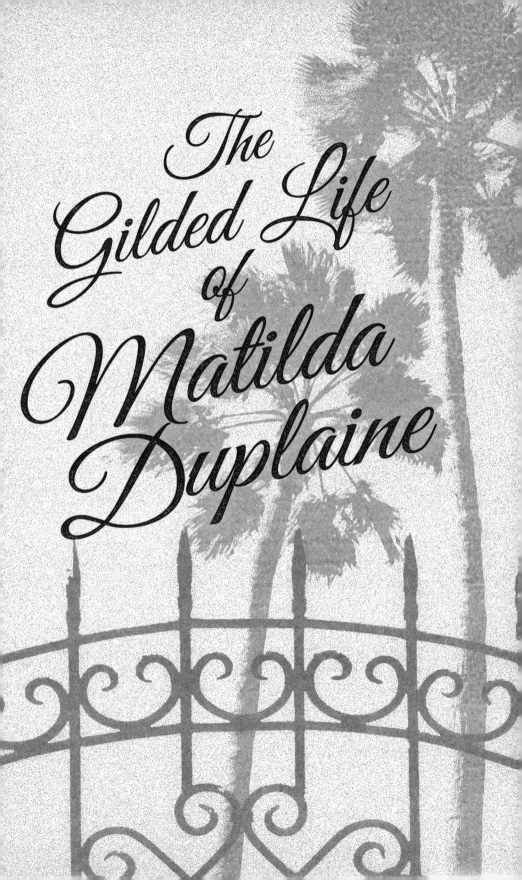

The Gilded Life
of
Matilda Duplaine

ALEX BRUNKHORST

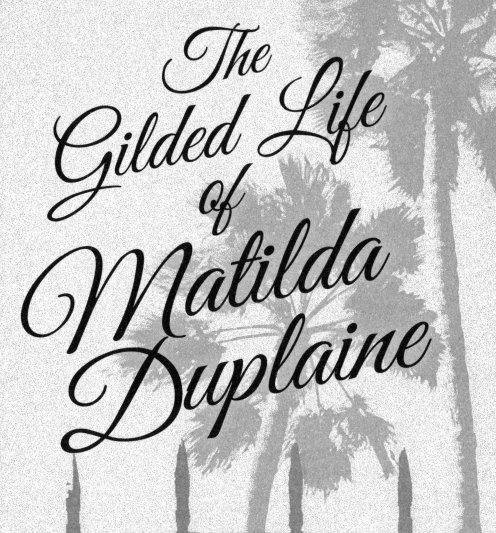

The Gilded Life of Matilda Duplaine

MIRA

ISBN-13: 978-0-7783-1753-1

The Gilded Life of Matilda Duplaine

Printed in U.S.A.

First printing: October 2015
10 9 8 7 6 5 4 3 2 1

To John

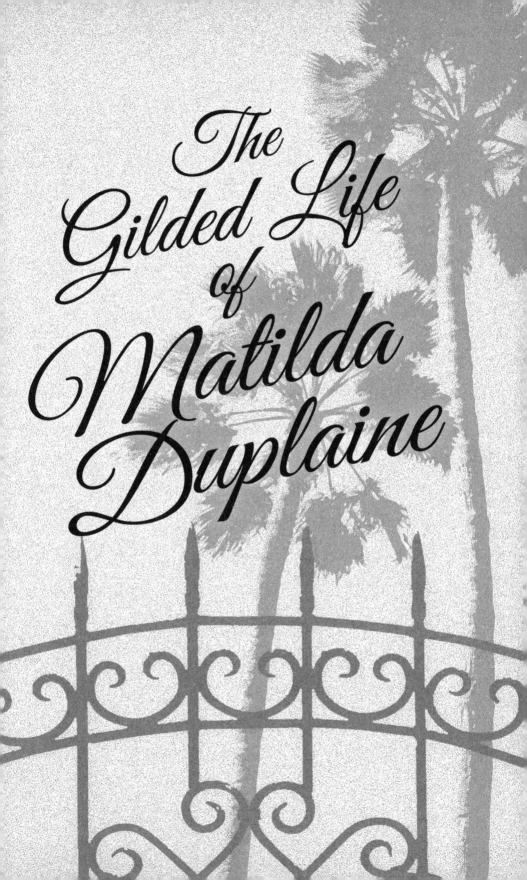

The Gilded Life of Matilda Duplaine

One

The tinkle of an antique servant bell announced my arrival.

The shop was so cluttered with priceless art and centuries-old furniture that maneuvering among them was impossible. I stood in place, hoping someone would come to my rescue. Sixty seconds later, she did. I did not hear the opening or closing of a door, and there was nothing to indicate how she had entered the room. Had she been watching me from behind the ceiling-height Asian room divider she would have seen me grasping for distractions—my cell phone, my reporter's notebook, a feigned interest in a chalk drawing that hung on the wall.

Nothing I had read could do Lily Goldman justice. She was in her midfifties, but she could have passed for forty-five. Her eyebrows were tweezed in an arched manner, and her blond hair was expertly coiffed in a tame bouffant that looked as if she had come from a salon. Her face was small and refined save for a prominent nose that belonged on a woman twice her size. It was her most striking feature, one that a less self-confident woman of means would have done away with years ago through plastic surgery.

"May I help you?" Lily asked. Her voice was surprisingly low, and it had a hint of a lady who smoked too much—though I was certain Lily had never picked up a cigarette in her life. Her breeding was too fine for that.

I discreetly rubbed my right hand on my pant leg, hoping to dry it. I reached over an antique oak writing desk, where my proffered hand hung in the air. She looked at it blankly.

"Yes, I'm Thomas Cleary. I'm a reporter, for the *Times*."

For the first time she made eye contact, and I thought I detected a slightly favorable response, but then:

"I hate reporters. I never speak to the press," she said.

"You must be Ms. Goldman." Phil Rubenstein, my editor, had warned me about Lily Goldman's disdain for journalists before sending me on this mission. I got the distinct impression he thought it would be fruitless.

She looked away, focusing on a bronze candlestick in the shape of a bird. She rotated the bird one hundred eighty degrees.

"Birds don't migrate north, they migrate south. It is autumn, after all. This place is such a mess. I need to speak to the staff. Where did you go to school, Mr. Cleary?"

"You can call me Thomas. I went to Harvard."

"At Harvard I bet they taught you that birds migrate south for the winter, north for the summer."

"I recall picking up that tidbit at St. Mary's, my grade school in Milwaukee."

"A Catholic boy," she said with a wry smile.

She waited for me to respond, but I didn't. I was nervous because I was on what I hoped was my big-break assignment. It was my first and only story on the entertainment beat—a short retrospective on Joel Goldman, who had just passed away.

Despite the fact that we were only steps away from one of Los Angeles's most bustling intersections, it was strangely quiet in Lily's shop. I had come here straight from the paper, which was alive with phones ringing, keyboards clicking and frantic deadlines being met. Here, there hadn't been a single phone call, not a single customer. No car had passed. There was a formal

English garden in front, but its chaises were bare, and its bird-bath and trees were devoid of birds.

"Were you taught by nuns in Milwaukee? I hear they can be terrible on the self-confidence," Lily said.

"I was," I said, nervously shifting my position. The reclaimed wood beneath me creaked. "It was Harvard that wiped away the self-confidence, though. The nuns weren't so bad in comparison."

"Milwaukee to Harvard. Quite the journey. Let's just hope it was a one-way ticket out."

"That's still uncertain," I replied—a gross understatement.

"And Los Angeles? Is this another layover or your final destination?"

"Yet to be determined, as well."

Lily fixed her eyes directly on me. They were deep set and an extraordinary shade of green.

"Do your parents miss you?"

"My mother passed away a year ago." The memory was still fresh and I forced down the lump that formed in my throat. "And, yes, my dad misses me. I'm an only child. He wants me to come home and work for the local paper. But a hundred thousand in student loans later I can't bear to take a U-turn like that."

"I'm sorry to hear about your mother…and the student loans."

I detected no judgment in Lily Goldman's words, but I suddenly felt embarrassed by the fact that I had referenced the death of my mother and my student loans in the same sentence.

"How old are you?" she asked.

"Twenty-six."

"She died young, then?"

"She was forty-eight. Pancreatic cancer."

"It must have been devastating."

Few people had taken this level of interest in my life since my mom had died, and I almost forgot why I was there to see her. I wanted to sit down in the distressed leather chair to my right, light a cigarette and tell Lily Goldman everything—about my mother, who shriveled into a skeleton while I toiled on inconsequential stories thousands of miles away in Los Angeles, a city I hated; about my grade school piano teacher, Sister Cecilia, who whacked my knuckles with an iron ruler; about the kids who used to pick me last for Red Rover.

And I wanted to tell her about Manhattan. What had happened there.

Professor Grandy's Journalism Rule Number One: Never let your subject change the subject.

"Enough about my situation. I apologize for taking so much of your time," I said. Even as a young boy I had always shunned attention, particularly from strangers, and here I was escorting Lily into the dark corners of my life rather than visiting hers. "I'm very sorry to hear of your father's passing. We're doing a piece on him, and I was hoping you could give me a quote or an anecdote, something that will make the reader know him better—something to remember him by."

"Ah, yes, my father."

At first that was all she said. I didn't blame her, because he was that kind of man. Joel Goldman's story was as legendary and epic as the movies he had brought to the screen. He had grown up in Nazi-occupied Poland, escaped the gas chamber, passed through Ellis Island as a boy with only a nickel in his pocket and within ten years catapulted his way from reading scripts in RKO's story department to creating one of the big movie studios.

According to Joel Goldman's former business associates, Joel had been known for his micromanagement, and that was putting it kindly. When he stepped on set—which he did almost daily—he practiced lines with his leading ladies, he whispered in his directors' ears, he berated craft services for everything from dry strudel to weak coffee. In the age of typewriters, Joel had been known to tear up entire first acts and shred them to the floor while horrified scriptwriters looked on. He scoured

expenses to the penny and had been a ruthless negotiator. As a former studio chairman had anonymously told me over the phone that afternoon, "If Joel Goldman sat across from you and you dropped a penny on the floor, he would pick it up and put it in his own pocket and consider himself the luckier for it."

My strongest trait as a journalist was not in asking, but in listening. So I waited.

"A hell of a man, my father," Lily finally said. "The first man to produce a movie that made a hundred million dollars. Can you believe it? He started a movie studio when he was only twenty-eight years old. That's unimaginable. Nowadays boys your age are pushing mail carts at talent agencies, not winning Academy Awards. That was the golden age of the cinema, of Hollywood. Bogie and Bacall used to come to our house in Cap d'Antibes for tea."

She smiled at the memory, and then I lost her behind the Asian screen. "Have you been to Antibes?" she called.

"I can't say I have."

Lily reemerged. She stared at an imaginary point in the distance through heavily leaded antique glass that distorted the outside garden. "We used to sit on the veranda, watch the boats and sip tea with rum. I know it sounds awful, but it's the most delightful drink. It was there that Bette Davis auditioned for *What Ever Happened to Baby Jane?* The sea there is incredible, so green—so different than the sea in Los Angeles."

"It sounds wonderful," I said.

"The most exciting time of my life. I often think—well, it sounds silly—but I often think that if we go to Heaven we'll be allowed to live our lives again, fast-forwarding through the bad times, of course." She looked away, as if she might have revealed too much to a stranger. "I would go back there. To those times with my father in the South of France. I have no use for Hollywood. I only care for what it bought us."

She glanced at the notebook, unopened in my hand. I hadn't

written a thing. It might have been nerves, or maybe Lily's personal memories were like coins she had dropped to the ground by accident. Unlike her father, I could not pick them up while she was steps away from me. It would be stealing.

"Is that the sort of thing you're looking for?" she asked.

"What?"

"The quote."

"Yes, that's perfect." I scribbled to catch up.

"I figured as much. Intimacy—it's what we're all looking for."

She focused squarely on me again, this time homing in on my clothes. I had picked up the shirt several years earlier in Cambridge at a discount store and had ironed the shirt and pants myself that morning. The result was deep creasing that was worse than if I had let the dryer have its way with them.

"How does the paper allow its reporters to dress like they just came from a late night of too much drink?"

Lily wore all brown—sweater, knee-length skirt and two-inch pumps. But even in its singular color and simplicity the outfit bled money. The ensemble brought to mind a Parisian tailor on hands and knees with pins in her teeth. The only pizazz in the outfit was a substantial ivory necklace. I had only known Lily for a few minutes, but it already made sense. Diamonds could still be bought on the open market; elephant tusks could not.

Lily made a small adjustment to my collar, and her hands rested on my upper spine. It had been a long time since a woman had touched me, and I tightened.

As a reporter I was trained to see the tiniest of clues—those fragments and fingerprints others could only see under a microscope. There was, at that moment, a brief spark in Lily's green eyes. And then, just as quickly as her eyes bloomed, they withered and went almost black.

I had thought that Lily had been the one to bare her soul in this interview, but instead she had set the course so I would be the subject who revealed too much.

"You're a very handsome young man. Don't let poor clothing choices get in the way of that," she said, before calling out to the other room, "Ethan, come here."

A few seconds later a slight man around my age entered through the French doors in the back.

"Yes, Ms. Goldman." He spoke in little more than a whisper, and if his slim-fitting attire was off-the-rack it was off an expensive one.

"Thomas here is going to be attending dinner this evening. Please arrange with Kurt to pick him up."

"Thank you for the invitation," I interjected. "But I have a deadline, and I'm not exactly the fastest typist."

"That's one thing you'd think the nuns would have done right," Lily said. "It's a fabulous group—some of the guests worked with my father and are quite newsworthy in their own rights. I promise you won't be disappointed."

In truth, I generally would have forgone a dinner party invitation, but if there was any opportunity for this dinner to beef up my story on Joel Goldman I knew I had to attend. I gave Ethan my address in Silver Lake, an area on the east side of Los Angeles known as a bastion for artists—all of them hipper than I. Ethan arranged for me to be picked up at seven o'clock sharp.

"Good. It's decided, then," Lily said. "Thomas, I'll see you soon. Ethan, make sure everything goes smoothly."

Lily would soon disappear behind the Asian screen, but just before she did, she turned around and set her eyes on me one more time.

"Once again, I'm sorry about your mother, Thomas. You must be terribly lonely."

Before I could respond, Lily had vanished among the antiques.

Two

And so that was how it began. Simply, without the fanfare one comes to expect from an evening that turns life's course from left to right. I called Phil Rubenstein to let him know I would be late with the story. Rubenstein hated slipped deadlines, but once I informed him that I would be joining Lily and a "newsworthy" cast for dinner, he let this one slide a few hours to accommodate the extra research. He then shocked me by changing the story from a one-column to two.

I had only one sport coat—a sales-rack special from a big-and-tall store in Milwaukee. I was tall and broad in the way Midwestern Germanic men are, but I was not big enough to fill out the coat properly, and its fit had always been loose. I was hoping Lily wouldn't notice. I splashed on some aftershave I had got for college graduation, and I slid my notebook and tape recorder into my jacket's interior pocket.

At precisely seven o'clock, my building's downstairs buzzer rang. An Asian man of about fifty, with an expression stern as his handshake, stood at the door.

"I'm Kurt," he said in the same manner one might use to greet a girl not attractive enough to sleep with.

"I'm Thomas, from the *Times*." I added that last part as an afterthought, as if it somehow legitimized me.

Kurt opened the back door of a silver Mercedes sedan and I slid in. It smelled of new leather. I suspected Lily was the type of woman whose cars always smelled of new leather. An Evian water and, coincidentally or not, today's *Los Angeles Times* rested in the seat pocket. I opened the paper to the Local section. My one-column article on the proposed 405 Freeway expansion was on page three.

I put the paper back in the seat pocket as we headed west down Sunset Boulevard, toward the sea, as Lily Goldman had called it. I had never been driven by a private driver before and I didn't know if I was meant to make conversation or sit in silence. I decided to take Kurt's cue. He didn't address me once during the hour-long journey; he listened to classical music on the radio and never glanced into the rearview mirror unless it was to change lanes.

Finally, after our long sinuous trip across town, Kurt put on his blinker, preparing for a sharp right into a narrow road that traveled between colossal white walls. A filigree black-iron signpost announced where we were going. The words *Bel-Air* lit up the twilight in a curious shade of blue-white, the color of an ice-skating rink. The words were written in an old-fashioned glitzy font embellished with curlicues and arcs. It was a font from the days when more meant more.

Bel-Air wasn't gated, as some Los Angeles communities were. Instead, it was simply known as a place that commoners like me didn't visit.

We took a soft left and then a sharp right, and then we drove through the winding hills. I opened the tinted window halfway. We were a mere thirteen miles away from my apartment, but the air felt as if it had rolled in from another lifetime. It was foggy and cool, and it smelled of smoke from real chimneys, of lawns freshly cut, of hedges just pruned and of autumn-blooming flowers. Silver Lake reeked of the pavement and the people who slept on it.

The few street signs I made out from the window had regal

names, and if you were looking from the street you would think there were no houses here, only thirty-foot hedges, iron gates and video cameras. The tight streets, two-acre parcels and light traffic had the makings of a neighborhood, but there were no sidewalks. From what I could tell, people here didn't borrow sugar—they sent their drivers to the store for it.

Flowers hung from heavy vines and wept into the narrow streets, squeezing them even tighter. We didn't have foliage like this in the rest of Los Angeles, and I wondered if the flowers were indigenous to only these six square miles. Perhaps the rain here was different, or maybe even the sun preferred Bel-Air. I reached out my window, and I plucked one of the dew-swept flowers off its vine, allowing it to wither between my thumb and index finger before placing it in my interior jacket pocket beside my tape recorder.

Even as a little boy I had always been fascinated by wealth. I grew up in a working-class family, and while my teenage friends were content playing in the streets in Milwaukee's rough inner city, I chose my running path along Lake Michigan, where behemoth mansions reminded one of another era, an era when the industry of the Midwest made millionaires. I dreamed of living in those manors with owners who didn't have a care in the world. At fifteen, when it came time for employment, I eschewed fast food or gas stations. Instead, I worked for an older, wealthy gentleman by the name of Mr. Wayne. I had always been mechanically inclined, so in the evenings my head would be bent over the guts of his expensive hot-rod collection bringing dead cars back to life. In summers, I was a golf caddy at Milwaukee's most expensive country club, even though it required multiple bus transfers to get to work. And then at Harvard, I was surrounded by wealth unimaginable for a boy from the working class of the heartland. For the first time in my life, money seemed accessible, something I could get. All I had to do was work in the world of investments, as most of my college buddies had done. When it came down to it, though, I had chosen a different path—one that would keep me firmly in the lot of the middle class for the rest of my life.

Old iron gates opened. We hadn't announced ourselves, but tiny video cameras blinked red in the eyes of the stone lions.

The steep, narrow driveway ended at a cobblestone motor court with an ornate fountain depicting sea nymphs at play. Prehistoric-looking foliage surrounded an old stone Spanish-style mansion. The cacti were ten feet tall and blue lights illuminated trees with spiky leaves and exotic flowers.

I tapped the front door's heavy knocker. I heard the clackety-clack of heels on a tile floor and the door opened. A house cat with spots like a leopard sprinted across the foyer.

The woman was in her late thirties and dressed for a rococo costume party, not an intimate dinner. Her outfit featured a tortoise-and-feather headpiece, white fur shawl, snakeskin pants so tight they might have been painted on and six-inch ostrich heels. I thought of Lily's ivory necklace. I wondered if wearing endangered species was a status symbol in all of Los Angeles's social stratosphere or just this specific circle of it.

"You must be Thomas. Come in. You're pale. It looks like you could use a drink. And a trip to Tahiti. But we can take care of that later."

We stood in a two-story entry the size of a ballroom. Red wax candles served as wall sconces and the only man-made light came from an overhead chandelier adorned with dragons and crystals. Juliet balconies above us were empty, but I got the sense that during grander parties violinists played there and during more intimate ones men and women did.

"Everyone, this is Thomas, Lily's friend," the woman who answered the door said, leading me from the foyer to a smaller room.

She did not bother introducing herself, but her manner was as theatrical as her attire and her words echoed on the stone. The four other people in the room hushed on cue, and I was embarrassed by their silence, their undeserved stares. In order to divert my eyes, I took in the room's zebra chairs, antlered sconces and mirrored ceilings, wondering if I had fallen down the rabbit hole.

"Thomas, darling, what are you drinking?" the oddly dressed woman asked.

I scanned the group with the corners of my eyes. There was no Lily. My heart quickened, and I was so nervous I briefly and irrationally thought that I had shown up to the wrong party.

"Sweetheart. Is everything okay?" the woman pressed me, after her question had gone unanswered.

She stood beside the type of formal mirrored bar you would've found in a 1920s Art Deco speakeasy in Manhattan. There were no off-the-shelf bottles; liquor was kept in heavy crystal decanters. Sterling silver–framed snapshots surrounded the crystal on all sides. It was then that I realized Lily Goldman had invited me to a dinner party at someone else's house.

I paused for a moment. I needed to choose a drink that was both elegant and available in one of those anonymous bottles. I thought of my ex-girlfriend—she had been a girl who would have known what to order in a scene like this. A gimlet. That had been her drink of choice.

"Yes. Sorry. A gimlet, please. On the rocks."

"A gimlet—how old-fashioned and moneyed of you. I'll have to remember that," she said. "I love anything old-fashioned. Right, George?"

"And moneyed, which is the only reason you fell in love with me," George said with a glint in his eye, as if he knew it was true but was also flattered by it.

"Fell in love maybe, but stayed in love no. California's a community property state. Even half your money would've kept me in couture and a G5," she said as she squeezed three slices of lime into the drink she had prepared.

George walked over and preemptively sandwiched my hand

in both of his. His squeeze was more appropriate for a long-lost high school chum than a random dinner-party crasher, and I immediately liked him for it.

"George Bloom. My wife, Emma, has many wonderful traits—I love her dearly—but introductions aren't one of them. Welcome to our humble abode."

So this was why Rubenstein had so easily moved my deadline.

Everyone knew George Bloom as the most powerful man in the music business. He grinned, and his large-toothed smile was as wide as his jaw was formidable. It was easy to imagine him bestowing that same charming grin on musicians he wanted to sign to his record label—with great success. Unlike his wife, whose outfit must have been the result of vintage binge shopping and weeks of planning, George wore a golf shirt and khakis more appropriate for a round of links than a dinner party. I was sure his casual attire was neither picked nor approved by Emma, so George's message was clear: he was boss of this castle.

"Nice to meet you," I said. "Thanks for having me."

"It's our pleasure, truly. Lily's on her way. In the meantime, come in. Meet the rest of the group."

George placed his hand on my back, nudging me deeper into the drawing room.

A gimlet magically appeared in my hand, and I studied it, not knowing if I was supposed to wait for a toast. George saw my hesitation. His eyes said, "Go ahead, drink, young man."

I took a hurried sip of my drink. In the corner, I caught a glimpse of David Duplaine, undisputedly Hollywood's most powerful man. He leaned back in his chair, tips of his fingers together so his hands formed a pyramid, his legs crossed. I diverted my eyes from his and focused on the sofa.

"Carole, Charles, David...everyone, this is Thomas. Thomas is a close friend of Lily's."

Carole Partridge was one of the most famous actresses in the world, and here she was, within ten feet of me, lounging on a purple velvet sofa, stroking the leopard cat. She balanced herself on a bony elbow and a curvy hip, and her pale bare feet were the equivalent of George's golf shirt—proof she was important enough to do whatever she damn well pleased.

Reality and fantasy briefly merged and I felt as if I was looking at Carole on-screen from the first row in a movie theater. Her retro-hourglass figure was the stuff of *Playboy*. Her arms and legs were lean and muscular. Her hazel eyes were sleepy in a seductive way, and her flawless, milky-white skin seemed as if it belonged in a black-and-white film—Technicolor, or real life, made it appear almost fake.

"Would you like me to get up?" Carole asked in a bored manner, as if after three minutes in the room my presence was already growing old.

"Not necessary," I declared.

Carole's husband, Charles, stood up in her stead.

"Thomas, nice to meet you," Charles said. "Sit down, join us. We were thrilled when Lily said she invited you. We need some new blood around here."

Charles had the general aura of someone for whom work had always been optional. His speech was tinted with a rarified East Coast accent that was most likely cultivated with lacrosse buddies at Choate or a place like it. At Harvard I knew plenty of guys who were born into a lifetime of financial security, and they, like Charles, always seemed to have a general calm about them, as if their money was a superpower.

"Thanks," I said, settling into a chair and taking a long sip of my gimlet.

"Lily tells us you're a reporter," George said.

"That's correct." I focused intensely on my drink, experiencing a bit of stage fright. At the mention of the word *reporter* the tape recorder felt heavier in my interior pocket, reminding me of my second-class and gauche life.

"A friend of mine—may he rest in peace—always said that

the difference between journalists and reporters is that journalists lie, reporters just make shit up," George said.

"In that case I'm a journalist. I've never had a good imagination. If I did I would have been a novelist or written for the movies," I replied.

"Charles just wrote a screenplay DreamWorks bought for seven figures," George said genially. There was a ring of pride in his voice.

Something about George reminded me of Mr. Wayne, the gentleman with the hot-rod collection I had worked for in high school. They both oozed charm and seemed inclined to grab your hand, squeeze it and escort you to that glorious and splendid place where they had ended up.

Charles smiled good-naturedly. "The stock market was flat so I was bored. I copied one of Spielberg's movies scene by scene, inserting different names and monsters."

There was a hearty round of laughs from the group.

Though I had only just met Charles, I could already imagine him alone in a plush home office, sitting at an old-fashioned typewriter, a heavy glass of Macallan 21 beside him, and the rest of the bottle close enough to be in eyesight but too far for a refill. The television on the wall would be paused on a scene from *Close Encounters of the Third Kind*.

I cast a sideways glance at Carole. Her fingertips were so deeply burrowed in the leopard cat's neck folds they disappeared to the knuckle. She hadn't joined the group in laughter, hadn't cracked a smile.

"How did you meet Lily, Thomas?" Carole was thirty-eight, but her voice was forty-eight and smooth as cognac. It was more of a purr than a voice.

"I'm doing a story on her father."

The question didn't seem like small talk, and I hoped I answered correctly. I had never been in the close presence of someone so famous, and I had yet to find that gray area between feigned ignorance and asking for an autograph.

"A great man, Joel Goldman," Emma said, as she adjusted a feather in her hair and gave a peripheral glance to her husband. "George did the music for many of Joel's films. Right, love?"

"David and I both worked for him. Were it not for Joel we wouldn't be sitting here, or it would have had to happen some other way."

An imaginary breeze rolled in. David Duplaine was still sitting, silently, in the corner, and now the group shifted their attention his way. Even the leopard cat gave a lazy glance in David's direction before settling back under Carole's palm.

David Duplaine was the chairman of a movie studio—the pinnacle of off-camera stardom in Los Angeles. But that wasn't all. In addition to producing many of the world's top-grossing movies, David had grown the studio's subsidiary television network from infancy to its presently dominant state. He was now in the process of gobbling up major market newspapers and technology companies to create a media empire across all platforms. David was the most powerful media titan in the world.

My job at the *Times* wasn't as much writing as it was reading—people. And I knew from the moment I saw him that David Duplaine would be a difficult man to read.

I avoided eye contact at first, homing in on his sneakers, which in any other city would be too young for a man of fifty. He wore a white T-shirt that might have been Hanes or Gucci but whatever the case fit perfectly. He was small of stature and build, and his head was shaved in the manner fashionable for men who are balding. His brown eyes were heavily lidded and bored looking, his eyebrows lively and interested and his strong nose as crooked as if it had survived a few street fights along the way. Yet the combination came together to form someone who was quite interesting looking and, in fact, he was always included in eligible-bachelor lists throughout the globe.

David hadn't bothered to acknowledge me in any manner, but I felt his presence the way a gazelle feels a cheetah in the depths of night on the plains—he was there, waiting, and whatever my next move was it wouldn't matter.

"Hello, everyone," announced a woman's voice.

I felt an extraordinary sense of relief when I saw Lily in the doorway. She was draped in black silk and her ivory necklace was gone in favor of wide cuffs that covered half her forearms in gold webs of pearls and emeralds.

"Lily!" Emma stood up and handed Lily a drink. "How are you, sweetheart? Those cuffs… I hate you for them."

"Oh these—they're terribly old and I never think to wear them. You can have them, in fact. I'll messenger them to you tomorrow." Lily smiled at me. "Most important, has everyone met Thomas?"

"Yes, yes. He's lovely, absolutely lovely. And *so* good-looking," Emma said, as if I weren't in earshot. "Now let's eat. I'm bloody famished."

We passed through an arch to a saffron-colored formal dining room prepped to comfortably seat seven, though it could do the same for forty if larger-scale entertaining were in order. The first thing I noticed were the flowers—gothic, untamed arrangements of twigs, branches, berries and deeply colored, oversize, drooping roses.

The rectangular table was set with heavy gold plates, glass goblets and a tall candelabra that held so many candles the room seemed on fire. Emma was not one for fine china and dainty centerpieces.

I almost made the mistake of sitting down before seeing the place card with my name written in a medieval font.

"Thomas, you're sitting next to me. I never seat couples beside each other. I figure we have enough time together as it is. Not that I don't love my husband, because I do. Ridiculously so." Emma blew George an air-kiss as she sat down at the head of the table.

Emma sat to my left, Carole my right. While the first course was served, my presence was still new and exciting. Lily and Emma shelled me with rapid-fire questions—"Do tell. What was it like to grow up in a town like Milwaukee?"—and Charles and George interjected here and there. They dropped plenty of names—movie stars, studio heads, political figures. Just hearing those names gave me a rush. I felt as if I was a part of it. Had I chosen to whip out my notebook or betray confidences, I would have had enough fodder for ten juicy stories. Instead I kept quiet, hoping an off-the-record meal would create more on-the-record content later.

The novelty of a stranger at the table had grown thin by the time we reached the entrée, and as I ate my Alaskan salmon theatrically drizzled with an exotic sauce and accompanied by a vegetable I didn't recognize, I was generally ignored.

I didn't mind being left out—situations like this were exactly why I had become a reporter in the first place. Although I could've chosen more lucrative occupations to be sure, my fascination with people had led me to the world of journalism. It was my job to observe behavior and collect information. For example, over the span of entrée to dessert wine, I noticed that Emma picked up a call from someone she later called her "stylist" and I saw George shoot his wife a "Don't be rude" look when she did so. It was obvious that Lily didn't care for Emma's choice of heavy goblets by the way she lifted her glass a quarter inch off the table and then immediately put it back down, as if the sip of wine wasn't worth the exertion. Charles and George seemed to be best friends—this was clear by the way they knew the minutiae of each other's lives. Charles, for example, asked about the weekly Billboard numbers for one of George's albums, and George in turn expressed concern for Charles's pet pigeon that had mysteriously disappeared three mornings earlier.

Despite the odd pigeon comment, if I were to home in on

the two most interesting characters at the table it would have been Carole and David. I say this because introverted people intrigue me. I always think they have something to hide or, at the very least, want people to believe they do. It was too early for me to say if this was the case here, but there was something about these two that made me want to know more.

I watched each of them closely, searching for clues. In the span of an entire dinner there was only one: just after our main course, David's cell phone vibrated, indicating a text message. He pulled out his phone and glanced at it. Carole watched discreetly, and then she made eye contact with him.

"Is everything okay?" Carole asked, voice low but concerned.

"Work thing," David responded. "Never sleeps."

"How was your dinner, Thomas?" Charles asked, changing the subject.

"Delicious. You're a wonderful cook, Emma."

"I can't take credit for it. But I can take credit for hiring the chef. Cordon Bleu, Paris. I went there personally and dipped my spoon into all of their kettles. I liked Francois's the best."

Charles raised his glass in toast and everyone went back to their side conversations. The dessert wine went on for another half hour or so, and I found myself staring through a large picture window at a majestic date palm covered in blue lights. That tree had to be a hundred years old. I looked at the lights intently until they blurred together into a filmy blue that saturated the air. To my right, I noticed Carole gazed at the same blue air. She seemed lost in it. When she finally tore her eyes away, she stood up from the table. She took her drink with her and never returned to the room.

Twenty minutes later the group congregated for a postdinner brandy in what Emma called "the card room." I had never been to a house with a room dedicated to cards before, but it made sense since Emma had specifically said that she loved "anything old-fashioned," and cards would have certainly fallen into that category.

The glass room was lined in lattice more suitable for the outdoors than an interior space, and its plants had been allowed to run wild. Two oversize square tables were illuminated by massive pagoda-shaped chandeliers, their crystals generously casting off light.

Admittedly, I had never been a card guy—in fact, I didn't even know how to play simple games like bridge or poker—so I excused myself to make a phone call, but instead slipped outside to have a stealth cigarette, a habit I had picked up a few years earlier and never quit. I settled into a lounge chair next to a grass-bordered body of water that resembled a swamp. Its water was green and murky and my eye caught an occasional minnow swimming beneath its lily pads. Were it not for the diving board at the northwest end, I wouldn't have even known it was a swimmable pool.

I lit a match and put it to the tip of my cigarette. What a night it had been. I was here in Bel-Air with some of the most important people in a city full of important people. I was so high I never wanted to come down. I knew Lily's motive for the invitation, and it had nothing to do with feeding a sweet Midwestern kid a home-cooked meal. Over crème brûlée, Lily had insisted everyone at the table give me quotes about her father. She was no fool, and she knew that favorable quotes from some of the most important people in the industry carried heavy weight.

But then I reflected on a scene from that afternoon—of Lily's fingers on my neck. I wondered if there had been some other reason for Lily's invitation.

I took a puff of my cigarette. I watched its golden tip light the clear, starry Bel-Air sky. We were in the middle of the city, but the quiet sky belonged in a countryside somewhere. It made me feel vaguely existential, as if above and beyond us there was nothing—nothing to hope for, no afterlife, nothing to make us choose one course of action over another.

The leopard cat jumped onto my lap and snapped me out of my reverie. Just then I heard a slight rustle from a dark spot in the corner of the property.

I saw a single shadow, but then it divided in half—into two separate shadows. The gestures of their hands and their body contact indicated a familiarity, and I was certain they were two of the dinner guests who had slipped outside for a side conversation. But despite my journalist's curiosity, I instinctually turned away. I had always felt uncomfortable intruding on others' privacy, so I looked at the swimming pool instead. An orange minnow slithered against the pool's muddy edge, and the leopard cat's eyes grew large, but he didn't pounce.

Then, as quickly as they had appeared, the shadows were gone.

I finished my cigarette and headed back into the house.

"Wanna come in, big guy?" I asked the leopard cat, whose eyes shone like green lights. I held the door open for him, but he darted away into the deep black night.

I found the card room on my second try. I opened the huge wooden doors, expecting to find two of the dinner guests absent. They were all there, though, engaged in a six-person game of poker. I shouldn't have finished the cigarette.

"Thomas, where did you disappear to?" Lily said.

"I fold." Carole threw in her cards.

"I fold," George repeated.

"The swimming pool," I said.

"Would you like to borrow a bathing suit?" Emma asked. "We usually swim in the buff, but we have extras in the pool house."

"No, thank you. I went outside for a cigarette."

"I fold," David said.

"You're so silly, Thomas." Emma presented me with a gold ashtray in the shape of a lion. "I bought this at the Duquette sale and I have been absolutely *dying* to use it. Besides, smoke makes the house feel lived-in. That was my goal with all this—" She spread her arms out wide. "Can't you tell?"

I almost started to laugh, but then caught the seriousness in her eyes.

"Well, you've done a good job of it," I said, lifting a brandy— a drink I hated—in toast.

Emma smiled before returning to her card game. There was nothing about this mansion that would indicate Emma Bloom's desire to make it feel lived-in—not the cold stone floors that echoed conversation, not the swampy swimming pool, nor the stiff-backed zebra-covered chairs in the drawing room.

I sat on the outskirts of the game, watching as Emma shuffled with the expertise of a Vegas casino dealer. I thought again of the shadows outside, of Carole and David's exchange at dinner. Sure, I was here to pull some quotes on the recently departed Joel Goldman. But something told me the real story was much bigger and more far-reaching than that.

Professor Grandy's Journalism Rule Number Two: The dead are only interesting in the context of the lives they left behind.

"I hope you don't mind—we're going to drop David off. His driver fell ill unexpectedly, poor thing," Lily said, as Kurt helped her into her champagne mink shrug, which seemed too warm for the weather. "He only lives around the corner. It won't be much out of our way."

"Of course," I said.

Kurt opened the car doors for us. David sat in the front, Lily and I in the back.

While Kurt had listened to classical music on our long drive, now the station was tuned to the radio affiliate of David's cable news network.

It was only a block away, and we drove it in silence. The radio commentator was the only one who spoke. He pontificated, with left-wing conviction, about the upcoming presidential election. In the Midwest this one block would have been a nice after-dinner walk, but there were no pedestrians in Bel-Air. The streets were too narrow and the people too rich for that.

We took one turn before stopping in front of an impressive barricade of palatial gray iron gates. They were simple and unadorned, and they opened like magic.

We passed through the gates into the grandest estate I had ever seen. We had just come from a property so magnificent it took my breath away, but compared to David's estate, Emma and George's felt humble. The long driveway meandered through acres of gently rolling hills sparsely dotted with trees. At the end of the driveway was a grand old Palladian manse. The first floor was glowing. Upstairs, only one room was lit, its curtain closed.

My first reaction was to notice how impersonal David's estate seemed. The regal house was surrounded by carefully pruned formal gardens and thirty-foot hedges.

We stopped in the octagonal motor court.

"Thanks for the ride, Kurt," David said. "Lily, I'll call you in the morning." He looked at me intensely, with that incongruous combination of bored eyes and lively eyebrows. I was captivated. "And, Thomas—" David let the name sit by itself for a moment. "I look forward to reading the article on Joel. And I wish you the best of luck at the *Times*."

They were the first words David had said to me all night.

A valet attendant in his midtwenties dressed in starched whites opened David's door for him.

"Welcome home, Mr. Duplaine," he said.

Before I could say thank-you or good-night, the valet had already closed David's door behind him. Kurt turned off the radio. I watched through the tinted glass as David was briskly escorted through the front door by a butler. Soon after, the upstairs light went dark.

Three

It was one of those magical nights I didn't want to end. So when Lily invited me over for a nightcap I accepted.

Once we left David's manor, it was a turn, a turn and another quick turn before we arrived at the end of a cul-de-sac. Kurt pointed a clicker at a gate covered by flowers. We drove up the cobblestone driveway slowly, arriving at a large stucco manor with ivy crawling up its walls so densely the windows were mostly covered with leaves. Like Lily, the refined and glamorous place seemed as if it belonged more in the South of France than in Los Angeles. I guessed the property to be an acre or so—smaller than the Blooms' and tiny compared to David's. But it was lusher than both; the house was nested in the most stunning flowers and trees I had ever seen.

Kurt opened the thick antique front door and we walked into a small foyer that was too diminutive for a house of this magnitude. Moments later I understood: the foyer was meant to set expectations low, to make the fifty-foot-long living room appear even grander.

The house was furnished in the same manner as Lily's shop. Heavy antiques rested beside modern chalk art; bookcases were filled to the brim with rare books that were wrapped in cellophane to fight off dust. Almost miraculously, ivy grew along the leaded glass doors and crawled up the interior walls to the ceiling.

"What are you drinking?" Lily asked, as she walked to a smaller version of the Blooms' bar.

"Water's great. Thanks."

Lily poured Evian water into a glass made of tortoise shell.

"The ivy—how does it live?" I asked.

"It doesn't," Lily said. "With no sunlight or fresh air it dies." Lily pointed to the ceiling, to ivy that was brown and petrified.

Lily picked up a lemon but then couldn't find a paring knife. Her eyes briefly searched for Kurt, before she abandoned the idea of sliced lemon altogether and gave me my room-temperature water as is.

It struck me as odd how Lily and her friends employed house-fuls of servants but then did random things for themselves. For example, Lily had referenced "the staff" in her shop, but she had busied herself moving antiques. Likewise, Emma had person-ally answered the door and prepared my gimlet, but the staff-to-dinner-party-guest ratio in that household appeared around two to one. And David: in the span of a three-hour dinner, had his driver really fallen too ill to drive one block?

Lily sat on the couch, her bare feet curled beneath her. She unclasped her cuffs, and she placed them on the table beside her as if they were handcuffs she had been eager to unshackle. She then shivered, though two wood-burning fireplaces taller than me flanked the room, with fire reaching to their brims. Kurt must have stoked the embers for hours before Lily had re-turned home.

Kurt walked in with a cup of hot tea on a silver tray.

"Did you have a nice time?" Lily asked.

"Yes, thank you so much for the invitation."

"It can be a bit difficult being the seventh. Some say it's un-lucky, but I think you handled it very well. And it was delightful to have someone under the age of thirty around. I so rarely rub shoulders with youth anymore."

Lily smiled approvingly, and I again noticed how attractive she was. It wasn't that in-your-face kind of beauty Carole possessed. Lily's father had been rich, so her mother had probably been pretty. That was how the world worked.

As if reading my mind, Lily leaned to her left and picked up a silver-framed black-and-white photo.

"If you haven't decided on a photo for your story yet, this would be a delightful choice. My father adored my mother, absolutely adored her, and it would paint a much fuller picture of him than some snapshot of him at his desk running the studio."

I studied the photo. Joel Goldman and his wife were walking down steps from a jet. Lily's mother was so beautiful she could have been one of Joel's starlets. She wore a raincoat and gloves, and a loose printed scarf knotted below her chin covered her head so only a bit of her blond hair showed. Oversize earrings dangled three inches below her ears. They were incongruous with the rest of the outfit, as if her jewels were a form of rebellion.

And her husband, he was big all over—big face, big blond hair, big eyes, big crooked nose, big presence and two hundred pounds of stone for a body. The only things wiry about Joel Goldman were his glasses. Despite his wife's beauty, it was Joel who was the center of the photo.

In the background, behind the couple, was a guy I recognized as a much younger David Duplaine.

"When was this photo taken?" I asked.

"Eighteen years ago—give or take a year. When you're my age they all blur. I only remember the really good or really bad ones—and sometimes not even those."

"Is that David?" I asked, pointing at the figure in the background. David seemed to be onstage, but positioning himself just beyond the spotlight.

"Yes." Lily smiled.

"You've known him a long time, then."

"Over a quarter of a century. David was a hustler. He grew up in Queens and lied his way into a talent agency. He told them he graduated from college but he didn't. In fact, David never much believed in the value of school. Education—that he believed in. David is the most educated man I know, but not through formal schooling." Lily sipped her tea. "The agency found out, and he would have been fired had my father not made a phone call. David would have done well anyways, but he always thought that phone call saved his life. He can be so melodramatic—David."

In fact, in a city that thrived on the theatrical, David was never portrayed as the dramatic sort. One of his films could bomb, a newspaper could win a Pulitzer, a television show could sweep the Emmys, and David would handle all three scenarios with the same stoicism.

For the first time I wondered if Lily was what we in journalism would call a reliable source. Or, conversely, perhaps Lily was right. Maybe David and the rest of them were always smiling for the cameras, but their real lives—the ones that took place in the dressing rooms of very expensive real estate—had nothing to do with their public personas.

To avoid Lily's eyes I looked at the ivy. It was spotlighted, and its shadows played on the ceiling.

Lily, for her part, studied her tea. Its exotic scent combined with the smell of burned wood made me think of the Orient.

Lily took a sip of her tea before continuing, "David worked at the talent agency for a few years, and then my father gave him two million dollars to start his own production company. He had the magic touch, as they say in the movies, and a few years later the company was rolled into the studio—and David made the transition to running it. And the rest is history."

"That was quite the gamble. For your father, I mean."

"All great businessmen are gamblers in one way or another.

35

My father was no exception. Many of his leading ladies had never been in a picture before. He'd take a chance on a girl if she had je ne sais quoi. He optioned a screenplay from his driver that became one of his highest-grossing films." Lily's green eyes traveled far away. "In fact, my father loved to gamble, but his vice wasn't the stock market or the horses. It was people."

"It doesn't sound like a vice if he won."

"Generally, but not always. Sometimes the house wins," Lily said distantly. "And how about you, Thomas Cleary, are you a gambler?"

I hadn't thought of it before. But now I considered Harvard—how I had got there. And Los Angeles—how I had crawled out of the rubble of my life to end up at one of the most prestigious papers in the country. And then there was Willa. By pedigree I should have been a member of her staff, but instead I had spent years with her heart resting—precariously, it would turn out—in my palm.

"Yes, I guess you could say I am—a gambler."

"I could tell, the moment I met you. Midwesterners are typically horribly risk averse, but I pegged you for the type to throw your chips down," Lily said with what might have been a glint in her eye. "What was your biggest bet?"

"I gambled on a girl." I thought again of Willa, who even years later never traveled far from my thoughts. I pictured her vividly the afternoon we had first met in Boston, propped on her elbow on a blanket beside the Charles River.

"And you lost, I'm assuming." Lily raised an eyebrow while blatantly looking at my ring finger and bringing me back to the present.

"You could say that."

"Was she a Harvard girl?"

"Yes, originally from Manhattan."

"Which part?"

"Fifth Avenue."

Lily smiled wryly. "Girls like that are trained from a very young age to break the hearts of sweet men like you."

"You should have told me earlier. It was an expensive lesson," I said. "It drained my emotional bank account."

"At least your financial bank account is still intact. It could be worse."

"I'm a reporter. My emotional bank account will always be more plentiful than my financial one, and if it's not, then I have a problem."

Lily smiled. "Don't take it personally, love. You're a tremendous catch, but even the biggest bass isn't a prize for a girl who has a taste for caviar. And who knows? Perhaps someday you may discover your loss was a win in disguise."

Lily's eyes traveled to a spindly plant. She stood up and picked a dead leaf out of its pot. She placed the leaf on a side table.

"You must be exhausted," Lily said, before returning to her chair.

"I am, actually," I said. My adrenaline level was still so high it could have been 10:00 a.m. but I just now remembered my deadline, and I couldn't count on Rubenstein to extend it another minute. "And I have a story to write."

Lily walked me to the front door. When she opened it, the purr of the Mercedes greeted us. Kurt held the rear passenger door open. I wondered how long he had been standing there.

"Oh, I almost forgot," Lily said, excitedly. "Wait here." She disappeared and then returned with a large wrapped box. "This is for you."

"I couldn't possibly," I began.

"You could possibly," she said. "My only request is that you open it when you get home because I get embarrassed when people open gifts in front of me."

The look on Lily's face said there was no arguing, so I accepted it.

"Thank you for everything. What an evening," I said.

"You're welcome. Good luck with your story. My father was a luminary in this town, and I would like him to be remembered as such."

By the time I got home it was past midnight, and I had to crank out my article by seven to get it to editorial. My one-bedroom apartment had always seemed humble, but now, after where I had just been, I realized it was downright pathetic. It was smaller than Lily's living room, and the dirt was embedded so deep that not even a few coats of paint could do the trick. Appliances were decades old, the furniture was mine from boyhood, and the ceiling was covered with asbestos rather than ivy.

I was an adult, but my apartment was a college kid's. Bel-Air was too grand for a man like me.

I wrote my article on Joel as quickly as possible and emailed it to the office along with a scanned copy of the photo Lily had given me. I was about to slip into a catnap before work when I remembered the package.

I unwrapped it to find a box from one of Los Angeles's most expensive boutiques. Inside were two perfectly creased shirts and trousers folded in tissue paper. There was no note.

Four

Phil Rubenstein looked as if he had crawled his way out of the pages of a hard-boiled detective novel. He was what you'd call a guy's guy. There was a beefiness about him, and he had a ubiquitous five-o'clock shadow at any time of day. Although I never had the privilege of going to lunch with him, everyone who did came back with bloodred drinker's eyes and speech that sloshed around in their mouths. For Rubenstein the two-martini lunch was a restrained one.

It was Phil Rubenstein who had hired me as a reporter at the *Times* a few years earlier. To say I was at the lowest point of my life back then didn't do the situation justice. I had been unceremoniously fired from the *Wall Street Journal* for an act of plagiarism I didn't intend to commit. That came after my girlfriend of two years had left me—equally as unceremoniously, with barely a phone call. I was broke, jobless and alone in Manhattan.

My job search went poorly. I was told time and time again I was unemployable—not only in the field of journalism, but in any field. After months of futilely applying for jobs, big and small, a college buddy's father called his chum Rubenstein on my behalf. There were favors owed somewhere or another, and Rubenstein had taken a liking to me, so I ended up at the *Los Angeles Times*.

Because of that, I always held a soft spot in my heart for Rubenstein. In fact, whether by exaggeration or not, I considered the man my savior. Never mind the fact that immediately after hiring me he seemed to forget I existed. The newspaper business in Los Angeles was like the film business—it was about who you knew, and that column was blank for me. The well-connected guys got invited to the premieres, club openings and parties, and got all of the scoops that went with them while I had got the smallest local stories.

"Cleary, get in here," Rubenstein shouted across the pit.

Phil Rubenstein never called me into his office, and the other reporters made eye contact in the way grade school students do when they sense one of their peers may be in trouble.

I temporarily abandoned the story I had been researching on the heated council race in District 10 and made my way across the sea of accusatory eyes before arriving at Rubenstein's corner office.

The office was the low-rent generic kind that newspapers with shrinking budgets and insolvent balance sheets tended to have, but Rubenstein had personalized it. Photos of Rubenstein with various studio heads and actors dressed up a stock credenza. Framed movie posters with handwritten notes covered the white walls. He had a plastic statue that looked like a fake Oscar award that said #1 Boss. Rubenstein was a newspaper editor, but judging by his office he seemed to think he ran Twentieth Century Fox. This was not by accident.

"How you feeling this morning, Cleary?"

The truth: I had a headache that threatened to become a full-blown hangover if you blew on it wrong, and I could still taste the stale Grey Goose and lime juice on my tongue.

But it was an extraordinary night that had caused this crappy state to begin with, and the headache made me feel as if the night before was somehow still alive.

"I feel good," I said, opting not to go into detail, satisfied with the fact that my story on Joel Goldman had run on the first page of the Calendar section. There was only one front page of Calendar and it was a daily jostle to get there. The death of one of the most famous titans of the entertainment business was certainly significant in its own right, and I had frosted the story with quotes from David Duplaine, George Bloom and Carole Partridge—three of the industry's hottest commodities.

Rubenstein gazed out his office window. "Your story was good, Cleary. And the quotes were all nice touches. Overkill, but nice. The only time I've seen all those names in one place was at the Oscars."

"Glad you liked it."

"That thing with the *Journal* aside, you're a very good writer. One of our most talented."

"Thanks," I said, wincing at the mention of the *Wall Street Journal* as one might cringe at a chance encounter with an ex-lover on the sidewalk. I felt a bead of sweat race down the back of my neck.

"I need something from you," Rubenstein demanded. "I hear there's going to be a major shake-up at Duplaine's studio. I need you to call Lily Goldman and get the story. I want it to break here, at the *Times*, instead of one of those shitty internet sites or, God forbid, the *Reporter.*"

If Phil Rubenstein had asked for my firstborn, I would have handed him over with a year's supply of diapers. That said, I had no connection with Lily Goldman. Lily had invited me into her circle for a few hours solely for the purpose of putting her father back on the front page, which I'm sure she felt was his right. The shirts and pants were a thank-you gift, significant to me but probably paid for through Lily's petty-cash account.

At the thought of the word *pants* I looked down at my lap. An iron crease cut my thigh in half, lengthwise. I flattened the pants out with my palms as if Lily were peering over my shoulder.

"I don't think we have that kind of connection. Lily and me," I added, when Rubenstein let the silence linger.

"We're getting trumped on everything—all of it," Rubenstein finally said, more to himself than to me. Out the window, a combination of heavy fog and smog was rolling in. The tops of the buildings had disappeared. "Do you know how many Pulitzers the *Times* has won?"

I shook my head.

"I don't know, either, but a lot," Rubenstein said. "Otis is rolling in his grave watching this state of affairs, banging on the cover of his coffin, begging to come out before we go the way of the dinosaur."

His remarks on Otis Chandler, the paterfamilias of the *Los Angeles Times*, might have been an exaggeration, but the dinosaur bit was true. It wasn't just us—it was all printed newspapers.

"You know Lily better than I do," I said. "Why don't you just call her?"

Rubenstein turned around. "She invited you to a dinner party at George Bloom's—within minutes of meeting you."

"Because she wanted quotes for her father's story. She wasn't exactly looking for a new buddy to have beers with."

"I really want this one, Cleary."

I looked at Rubenstein and saw something vulnerable in him. This was the man who had saved me from Milwaukee, where I probably would have been working beside my father in the lumber department at Menards.

"I'll call her," I said.

I cleaned my desk, filed a pile of old documents, scrubbed my spam folder, made my twice-weekly call to my dad a day early and did almost everything except call Lily.

There were myriad reasons for this procrastination, but top on my list was that the night was still untainted. Once I called Lily and she refused to help me out, I would go back to covering freeway expansion plans and a dull life in a modest apartment.

The only way I knew to reach Lily was through her shop,

and once the clock had struck four I knew time was running its course. I had savored the night, and now there was work to do.

Ethan answered the phone on the fourth ring. I imagined him staring at the phone beside him, waiting a moment to pick up because Lily had probably instructed him not to appear too eager. I was told Lily wasn't available. When Ethan inquired if Lily would know the purpose of the call I answered in the affirmative, and then I hung up quickly, before he had time to ask anything else.

Three days passed and Lily didn't call. I couldn't say I was particularly surprised, but I would be a liar if I didn't admit the slightest bit of disappointment. Interestingly, the Duplaine story didn't break—at the *Times* or elsewhere—and all was quiet from Rubenstein's office.

As for the evening, it was like anything else in life; the farther one gets away from it the smaller it appears. What had initially seemed like a life-changing event became less consequential as days passed. The first night, I fell asleep hard on my back, and I dreamed of the leopard cat, tame under Carole's palm and wild in the outdoors. The second day after, which I now remember as a day of waiting for my phone to ring like a schoolgirl waits for a call from a crush, I found myself thirsty for gimlets on ice and I longed to dive into the Blooms' swampy swimming pool and swim with the minnows. By the third day I realized that the night that meant so much to me meant nothing to them. I was a mere reporter.

The upside of the dinner, however, lingered. Based on my Goldman story and the possibility of the Duplaine scoop, Phil Rubenstein had given me a decent assignment on the weekend box office, and I was typing it up when the phone rang.

"Cleary here."

"Thomas, love. It's Lily."

My heart beat a bit faster, and I found myself straightening my spine.

"Lily, what a surprise."

"Oh, I know. I do apologize. I meant to phone you back sooner, but work caught up with me. I had to fly to Aspen unexpectedly to pick out some wallpaper for a house and the jet lag has just about killed me." I was about to remind Lily that Colorado was only one hour ahead of Pacific Standard Time, but then let it pass. "I must say, I absolutely loved your little story on my father. It's been so long since he got press. He adored reading about himself in the papers."

"I'm glad you enjoyed it."

I heard the antique servant bell announce a visitor in the background.

"Oh dear, that's a customer—and a dreadful one at that. Let me cut to the chase. I spoke with David this morning and he mentioned he's making some personnel changes at the studio. I convinced David he should give the exclusive to you instead of that absolutely horrible Blaine Wyatt at the *Reporter*."

Professor Grandy's Journalism Rule Number Three: If a story's handed to you on a silver platter, it's either not worth eating or will cause food poisoning later on.

"I'll be right there, Ethan," Lily called into her store. "David's assistant's name is—" She paused. "Oh, I can't remember now. I'm terrible with assistants. I know you're busy, but take a minute to call David's office and get the information. I think you'll find it worth your while. They're expecting you."

"Thank you," I said, trying to restrain my excitement.

"You're welcome. Oh, and how rude of me. I haven't stopped talking, have I? Did you need something the other day? When you phoned?"

I smiled. "I just phoned to say thank-you for the incredible evening and the overly extravagant gifts."

"Midwestern manners. I should have expected nothing less. You're more than welcome. It was lovely to have you. Now do call David's office and let me know how it goes. Au revoir."

There was a fumbling of the phone, and then the line went dead.

It took a few calls to get to the story, but once I did I was rewarded not just with personnel changes, as Lily had underestimated, but with the untimely firing of the president of the studio, who had been misappropriating corporate funds on private jets, award show after-parties, dresses for his wife and suits for his lover. I got to work, writing well into the night, pausing only to steal a quick cigarette on my balcony.

It was 1:00 a.m. I took a long drag of my cigarette and craned my head toward the hills. That sliver of a view of the mountains was the only reason I had gotten this crappy apartment in Silver Lake in the first place. I couldn't even remember how I'd gotten here anymore, except for the vague fact that around three years ago I headed out to Los Angeles from Manhattan. It was supposed to be a temporary apartment—a stop on the way to greatness, someplace I would eventually point to and say, "Can you believe it? I started out there." It didn't happen that way. I would have left but for the fact I had no place to go.

I looked around me. It wasn't close to being Christmas, but icicle lights hung on my neighbor's balcony, and pot smoke wafted from his apartment day and night. Tall date palms stood high and mighty in the distance, but the foliage in our complex was the indigenous sort that required little water or sun. The U-shaped building was centered on a dilapidated courtyard. There was a sadness to it, because in the 1950s when the building was built someone had tried to make something pretty, but now the courtyard was neglected. Chairs with webbing too thin to sit on were sprinkled haphazardly around a swimming pool. The pool needed a new heater, and the hot tub was drained. Peeling plaster gave the water a cloudy and gray appearance.

I surveyed the surroundings one last time before crushing the remnants of my cigarette into the stone balcony. I had a deadline to meet.

Five

The story, in various incarnations, stayed on the front page for the next four days and then got mileage in Calendar and Business. We had scooped the *Reporter*, ditto for the online sites that were breathing down Rubenstein's back. The story was covered by nearly every national publication—the *New York Times* to the *San Francisco Chronicle*—and I gathered them up and savored the words "The *Los Angeles Times* reported..." because the *Los Angeles Times* meant *me*. I knew the story and the scoop had nothing to do with me. Any community college journalism student who happened to have landed at the right place at the right time could have written the same article, but I was proud nevertheless.

I grew up in Milwaukee, the land of gratitude and manners. So I knew a token thank-you to Lily was in order. Choosing a present that I thought Lily would like was difficult on a reporter's salary, so I did the best I could. I went to the most expensive department store in the city and chose the least expensive item there: a candle.

As I made my way over to the shop I thought of how quickly my prospects had changed. It had been just over a week since I had first met Lily.

The bell announced my arrival. The store was as cluttered as on my first visit, and it took a moment for Lily to emerge from behind the large Asian screen.

"Thomas! How are you, love?"

"Fine. I hope I'm not interrupting."

"You could never be an interruption. What's this?"

I looked around and became conscious of the candle I was carrying. Suddenly it seemed like a totally inappropriate gift. In my weeklong sabbatical I had forgotten how exotic and remote the world of Lily Goldman was.

"Nothing—"

"A candle," Lily said, unwrapping it lustfully. "I absolutely love candles. It's the most exquisite color of vanilla, isn't it, Carole?"

It was only now that I noticed Carole lounging on a sofa, surrounded by pillows in various textiles and prints. She lay on her back, barefoot and beautiful as she had been the night of our first meeting. She looked as if she belonged in Marrakech or Casablanca, not in an antiques shop in Los Angeles.

"Truly a one of a kind" was her response. Her delivery was as polite as the sentiment was sarcastic.

"Carole's here looking for pillows for her aviary," Lily said. "This candle is absolutely spectacular, Thomas. You are so sweet. Isn't he sweet, Carole?"

"Did you find anything?" I addressed both of them. I had no idea why one would need pillows for an aviary, or why one would have an aviary in their home in the first place, but I needed to quickly steer the subject away from the embarrassingly cheap gift.

"My first indication was to use this peacock fabric—" Lily pointed to an ornate fabric with stenciled peacocks, seemingly a perfect fit "—but now I feel it's too predictable. I deplore predictable."

Carole glanced at the peacock fabric with indifference, as if there was nothing about it that compelled her either way, and then she focused on her lap, at a script that lay open to a page somewhere around sixty.

"Your article on the terrible man who worked for David was brilliant," Lily said, addressing me. "You are a fantastic writer, Thomas. Isn't he, Carole?"

"He handled a tricky situation with aplomb," Carole replied, flipping the screenplay's page.

It was true. I hadn't lambasted David as some of our competitors had. Instead I was deliberately gentle, exonerating David of blame while still maintaining my journalistic integrity. It was a strategic move on my part of course. I had to protect my position in their world, and it still felt very precarious.

Lily disappeared into rows of hanging fabrics, and I was left alone with Carole. I opened my mouth to say something, but words failed me. Carole, on the other hand, appeared to almost revel in my discomfort. We sat like this for a minute or so, and then I turned my back, pretending to stoke a newfound interest in Belgian linen.

Lily returned a few seconds later, her face registering the stony silence that hung in the air. "Nothing appropriate. Maybe I'll paint something later."

Carole stood up and slipped on her shoes, throwing the screenplay into a large purse. Then she kissed Lily on the cheek.

"Don't go," Lily begged.

"Are you forgetting I'm cohosting a dinner for seventy tomorrow? I wish I could go off shopping all day, but help requires such micromanagement. And so does David." Carole sighed.

Lily turned to me. "David and Carole are cohosting a little event for the governor at David's. Thomas, I have a glorious idea. Why don't you come?" she said enthusiastically.

I wished Carole would step in and second the invitation, but she didn't. Instead she preoccupied herself with a screen that featured oxen in repose in a meadow, rubbing her fingers over its surface. Her fingernails were painted a shade of olive, and I wondered if the odd, almost grotesque, color was chosen for a horror-movie role or if olive was the new red.

"I couldn't," I said, as transparently as possible.

"Of course you could. Carole, do tell Thomas he should come. Insist he should come. It would be good for you at the paper, Thomas."

"Lily's right. You should come, Thomas. I'll have Adrian add a seventh to our table." Carole said it blandly, and I knew that Carole's word choice was deliberate. Seven not only had an unlucky connotation, as Lily had pointed out, but it also called for a lopsided table arrangement. I could already imagine Adrian, whoever he was, silently cursing me, the nettlesome seventh.

Carole's invitation was disingenuous, and I should have turned it down. Instead I allowed it to hang there. I wanted to jump into their lives again—why, I didn't know.

"Well, it's decided, then," Carole said. "We'll see you tomorrow evening, eight o'clock sharp."

Carole put on a large floppy hat and oversize sunglasses that rested low, almost on the tip of her nose. Outside, a black SUV waited for her, and a driver opened the rear passenger door expeditiously. In ten seconds the car was gone, and a minute later the paparazzi were too late.

Six

I knew I wanted to go to Harvard when I was ten years old.
Harvard was a quixotic dream for someone raised in Milwaukee's gritty public school system, but that dream became my
driving force.

When I was twelve I figured out that it was speed that was
going to get me there. My talent for the five-thousand meter
blossomed suddenly, without warning. Early in the morning,
before the sun came up, I could be found running beside my
father's stopwatch. My dad had barely received his high school
diploma but he would come to share my dream.

This singular intensity propelled me to shatter every state
and Harvard running record. It was that same stubborn determination that made me ignore the small fact that Carole didn't
want me to attend the fund-raiser. I had got a taste of wealth
and power, a mere whetting of the tongue, but I wanted more.

Had I turned down Carole's noninvitation I would have been
at the paper, working on a plum story handed to me by Rubenstein, much to the chagrin of the senior writers. Instead, the
following afternoon when my phone rang I found myself at a
mini-mall in Westwood renting a tuxedo for what promised to
be the fund-raiser event of the season.

"Cleary here."

"Millstone was found dead in his loft in SoHo." It was Rubenstein, and he was referring to a young, up-and-coming A-list actor. "I know you're going to the fund-raiser tonight, but you need to crank out a quick web piece."

"But—"

Rubenstein hung up.

I headed back to the paper, aware that it was nearly impossible for me to get out a story and make the dinner on time. I considered calling Lily and canceling but opted against it.

Five thirty.

I went back to the office to find Rubenstein had lent me an intern to pull together research for the story on Millstone. I paged through his notes. Interns were known to be overzealous: in this case, the guy had pulled quotes from Millstone's eighth-grade teacher in Australia, his tattoo artist in Brooklyn and the sandwich maker at the deli he frequented, but he neglected to get quotes from the costars or producers of his new film.

By six o'clock I had edited most of the research and typed my lead. I had called in a favor to George's office to get an additional quote from the producer of Millstone's new film. In turn, the producer—with the understanding that I was a chum of George's—gave me the private cell phone number of Millstone's publicist, who gave me the first on-the-record quote about the tragedy.

Around six thirty, I finished my story and emailed it to editorial. I was in such a hurry I started shedding my clothing in the hallway, and I finished changing into my tuxedo in the restroom a few seconds later. I glanced at myself in the mirror. Even in the harsh fluorescent light I seemed presentable enough. The governor. A grin broke through my stoicism.

On my way out I looked up at the wall clock in editorial. It was set to precision for deadline's sake, and it was precisely six forty-five.

I descended the concrete steps two at a time and sprinted to my car. Sunset Boulevard was jammed, and when I finally saw the words *Bel-Air* lit up in that eye-blinding shade of ice blue, I exhaled. It was only seven-forty. I had twenty minutes on my side. I drove leisurely through the road between Bel-Air's pillars and mimicked Kurt's serpentine drive to the Blooms' before taking the final hairpin turn that led to David's estate.

I immediately knew something was wrong. There were no signs of a political party—or any party for that matter. There was no security detail, no guards, no music, no catering trucks. The estate was quiet.

I rang the bell on the towering gates protecting the property, but there was dull silence. I heard only the branches of a sycamore tree shimmying in the unseasonably cold fall winds. Lily had definitely said the party was at David's. Kurt had also double-confirmed that the party was this evening. I pulled my phone from my pocket, but I had no cell service.

I had two choices: drive to Sunset Boulevard to call Lily or use the phone at David's estate. I rang the bell again before eyeing a ficus hedge that had to have been five times as tall as me.

Panic started to set in. Lily Goldman was a shiny lucky penny in my pocket, the first talisman in a long time I had managed to pick up and secure in my palm, if only briefly. I imagined her this very second, fielding questions as to my whereabouts from the other five guests while she fingered a ruby ring or ivory necklace. I also thought of Carole, eyes heavy with exasperation, instructing the staff to remove the seventh chair that had been so craftily squeezed into the table for six and exchanging an "I told you so" glance with David, his thick eyebrows coming together in agreement.

Tonight was supposed to be a glittering star of a night. Not only was I going to meet the governor, but I was more determined than ever to make a career comeback. Suddenly, with the Goldman story and the Duplaine piece, I had begun to feel as if the future was once again full of possibility. I had always intended to return to Manhattan in glory, to triumph over what had happened there. Possibly it was a pipe dream—it had only been two big articles after all—but I was hoping the trail of plum stories was leading me east.

"Fuck," I said out loud, still not comprehending where I could have gone wrong.

I backed my car out from David's impenetrable gates and parked it on a patch of gravel on the side of the narrow road. I rolled down my window, and that was when I heard it.

In the distance was the faint, familiar sound of a tennis ball. There was an oddly regular rhythm to it: pong, pong, pong, quick pong, slow pong, pong, pong, pong, quick pong, slow pong.

I got out of the car and walked over to the side of David's property, where I saw a shot of fluorescent white light through the trees. I remembered that during our long drive toward the estate we had passed a gate covered in ivy. Behind it must have been a tennis court.

I crept closer, facing a stone wall that could have fortified a federal penitentiary.

"Hello," I shouted, but the word got caught in the wall. "Is anyone home?"

There was no answer, though there was definitely someone home.

It was then that I noticed an oak tree weeping over David Duplaine's wall, and I glanced at the lowest branch. It would have been a reach for most men, but I was tall and I had had plenty of practice climbing trees during those muggy mosquito-filled summer days of my childhood in Wisconsin. Even in dress shoes, navigating the tree wasn't particularly difficult; I conquered one branch after the next, giving me a feeling of satisfaction I hadn't felt in years.

I scaled half the oak tree and then paused to catch my breath.

My first sight of her was from the back. She stood at the base-

line of a red-clay tennis court surrounded by trellises thickly covered with ivy. Her long limbs were tanned golden-brown; but
they were coltish, as if she didn't quite know how to work them
yet. It could have been my distorted perspective from above, but
she appeared around six feet tall. Her blond ponytail reached
the middle of her back and was tied together with a white satin
ribbon. Indeed, she wasn't dressed for practicing serves at all,
but for a match at Wimbledon. Her white dress had a bunch
of froufrou on it—frills, lace—and it was so short her ruffled
tennis panties peeked out from beneath it. The Nike shoes she
wore looked brand-new, save for the stain of clay near their soles.

Her ritual was exact: first she chose a bright yellow tennis ball
from a hopper, searching carefully for just the right one. Then
she situated her shoe at the corner of the baseline tape and the
center mark. Finally, she bounced the ball three times, tossed it
in the air to the exact one-o'clock position, and served it with
a motion so fluid it was the stuff of physics textbooks and tennis academies.

All this exactitude resulted in a beauty of a serve that rivaled
those on the professional tour and sent a ball with laser precision into one of the orange cones that sat in the corners of the
service box as targets.

This ritual repeated itself eight times until the hopper was
drained of balls.

I had grown up around the sport of tennis, so the sight of a
girl in a tennis dress embarking on service practice was in itself not particularly interesting. But the scene was captivating
in the way that a movie may hold your attention so intensely
your real life vanishes.

I could not avert my eyes.

The girl walked over to a viewing pavilion, a plush mini
Palladian palace. Silver pitchers, a silver ice bucket and crystal
glasses sat on a silver tray on an antique table. She plucked ice
out with silver tongs and placed it in one of the glasses, and then

she poured water from the pitcher into the glass until it reached the glass's equator.

She then took a few sips of the water, surveyed the littered balls and made her way back out onto the chilly court. She picked up the hopper and started collecting the bright yellow tennis balls, but she struggled to line the hopper up to push the balls through its rails. For a girl who could serve a hundred miles an hour, it was odd she moved so slowly on this remedial task.

The girl started toward my side of the net, and I took my opportunity.

"Excuse me," I called down from the oak tree.

The girl stepped backward quickly and looked around, trying to discover where the voice was coming from.

"It's okay. I won't hurt you. I'm up here, in the tree."

She looked up, startled, and for the first time I could see her face. She was a woman, but there was a childlike quality to her. It was difficult to peg her age, but I would have bet she was around twenty. There was something very "heartlike" about her—the wide shape of her face, the cheekbones so high and full they went almost to her eyes and the delicate nose reminiscent of an arrow. It's hard for me to say now if I would have called her classically beautiful, but she was that star in the sky that you can't take your eyes off, even if it's surrounded by brighter ones.

She continued to study me, perplexed. I didn't know what was stranger, a girl dressed for Wimbledon practicing serves alone at night or a guy dressed in a tuxedo sitting in an oak tree.

"Why, what are you doing up there?" she asked.

"This may sound strange, but I thought I was going to a fundraiser this evening at Mr. Duplaine's house," I said. "I'm a friend of Lily Goldman's. I tried phoning the gate, but no one answered. And—" I paused. "And. Well, is anyone here?" I finally asked.

"No, there's no one home," the girl said. Her voice was soft and melodic.

"Is there supposed to be a party here?" I asked.

"It's at the other house—the one on the beach."

"Do you have an address?"

"I've never been there, myself, so no, I have no address. It's in Malibu, I believe, but unfortunately there's no one I can even ask. You must think I'm incredibly unhelpful but I'm not meaning to be."

Malibu was about forty-five minutes away with favorable traffic conditions. So at this point I still had time to climb down the oak tree and call Lily for the address. I could have made it in time to meet the governor, to sip a gimlet while overlooking the gentle, rolling waves of the Pacific. But instead I said:

"You have quite the serve."

"Thank you. My coach says the same thing. One hundred fourteen miles an hour. I got a radar gun for my birthday." She said it with gushing pride and pointed to a black contraption set up in the corner of the court. On the screen, 109 MPH registered in red, digital numbers.

"When's your birthday?" I asked.

"The twentieth of April."

"A Taurus."

"A what?" she asked.

"Astrology. Do you follow it?"

"Not only do I not follow it, I've never even heard of it."

I paused, wondering if the girl was kidding, but I didn't detect a note of sarcasm in her voice.

"I'm from Milwaukee—we don't believe things like that there, either. It's all hocus-pocus if you ask me."

"Milwaukee's in Wisconsin. Wisconsin's capital is Madison. Its state bird is the robin and it's known as the Dairy State because it produces more cheese and milk than any other state," she said, as if reading from a teleprompter. "This thing called astrology—what is it exactly?"

"That's a good question," I said. "It has something to do with the stars. I've never really understood it, either."

"You mean astronomy, then?"

"No, they're two different things—astrology and astronomy."

"So what are you in astrology terms?"

"A Scorpio."

"A scorpion. In other words, you're an eight-legged, venomous creature to be wary of?"

Her tone was deadpan.

"No poison here, just a nice guy from Milwaukee."

She let out a big, jovial laugh.

She was a curious creature, and I was intrigued. Her manner of speech was officious and old-fashioned. She was interested and reserved, insecure and confident, coy and bold. She was unlike anyone I had ever met.

I looked down at her again and realized she was gazing at me with wide-eyed curiosity, too. The tennis court lights made her eyes glitter.

I wanted to see her up close.

"I play tennis—well, used to play tennis. I haven't in years. Do you want to— Maybe, would you like to play sometime?" I said with the insecurity of a fourteen-year-old asking a girl to a Friday-night dance.

She paused.

"Oh, I don't think so," she said sadly, as she traced the *W* on the tennis ball. "Thank you, though, for the offer. It was kind of you."

It's difficult to judge oneself with objectivity, but my whole life I had been told I was a good-looking guy. Sure, I didn't have that well-oiled slickness the other guys at Harvard had. They had Wall Street money, last names with a familiar ring to them and country houses. They were gentlemen who knew what wine to order, gentlemen who winked more than they smiled and gentlemen who could sell you something you didn't even want. Women loved them for all of it.

My appearance was more of the homegrown variety: I had

inherited my father's height, broad chest, strong jaw and blue eyes, and I had my mother's oversize smile and blond hair that looked a touch red when the sun hit it right. I looked like the kind of guy who would run his wife's errands and coach his kids' baseball team, all while hoisting this year's corn crop to the farmer's market. In high school, girls had liked me; in college they had called me "cute," but I wasn't husband material. Marriage for those girls was a game of Monopoly. They wanted the most valuable real estate, and anything less than Central Park West wouldn't do.

But in all of those years, with all of those women, I had never been shot down so directly before.

A story, a date, a friendship, whatever I thought I wanted, whatever she thought she had turned down, it didn't matter. I made the boldest move since I had moved to Los Angeles: I climbed down the oak tree to the stone wall, slid onto the viewing area canopy, then hopped down to the court, with leaves in my hair and a tear in my tux from the canopy spear.

We almost touched. In such close proximity I saw that sun freckles sprinkled her nose and her eyes reminded me of Emma and George's leopard cat's. They were green with black speckles, as if someone had spilled ink on them by mistake. She wore a tennis bracelet with diamonds that I knew enough to guess were two carats each. Plump diamond earrings covered her tiny earlobes. Jewels like this were generally kept between armed guards, not worn for tennis practice.

We stared at each other. I wasn't going to Malibu.

"Why don't we play for a few minutes?" I said. "It would feel good to hit the ball around."

"I'm not so sure that's a good idea," she replied.

As a guy, it was my job to find an open window when a girl closed a door. I found a slight crack here—in her unsure inflection, her avoidance of eye contact, her choice of syntax.

So I climbed through the proverbial window. Five rackets

wrapped in cellophane sat on a bench beside the court. I unwrapped one, took off my shoes and walked to the other side of the net.

I had played tennis in high school and, despite some rustiness, would have considered myself a good player. I rocketed in a pretty decent first serve, but before I had time to admire it she had nailed a backhand return that hit the place where the baseline met the sideline.

"Wow, good shot."

"Thank you," she said.

My next serve was a nasty topspin down the middle, and once again her return skidded off the baseline.

Twenty minutes later the first set was over. I had won a mere five points.

I walked up to the net, and she followed suit. She put out her hand proudly to shake mine.

"I'm now 1–0," she said, glowing.

"1–0?"

"Yes, one win and zero losses. Still undefeated for life."

"You're meaning to tell me this is the first match you've ever played?"

"Correct."

"Your entire life?"

"The whole of it. I only practice," she said, her victory still covering her face.

"How often?"

"Three hours a day." She paused, contemplating what was to come next. "Do you like cookies?" she asked as she headed toward the tennis pavilion.

The tennis pavilion was more elaborate than most houses. Ivy crept up the walls and partially hid glass casement windows. Reclaimed wood covered everything. I had the feeling this wood had been to France and China and back—all before the eighteenth century. A seventy-five-inch television screened a muted Gregory Peck film. An old stone mantel stood six feet high, covering a brightly burning fireplace below, surely crafted before the advent of central heating systems. Silver pitchers of lemonade and water sat beside crystal glasses. Six varieties of cookies were symmetrically lined up on trays, and towels floated in steaming hot water. Every provision was taken care of.

"Lemonade?" the girl asked.

"Sure. Thanks."

She poured me a glass of lemonade to the brim and then put on a short satiny jacket that must have been the companion piece to her dress because the frills matched. Beads of sweat rested in the nape of her neck like seed pearls. She didn't wipe them off.

A bowl of pineapple sat in a crystal bowl. The fruit was diced into equally cubed pieces, small and dimpled like playing dice. The girl plucked out a piece of pineapple with a fork, holding it up so the fruit dazzled under the soft light in the pavilion.

"Can I interest you in a piece of pineapple?" she asked.

"Yes, please. Pineapple's my favorite fruit."

"Mine, too," she exclaimed with great enthusiasm, as if she'd just discovered that we had the same birthday or the same mother.

She slowly placed the fork in my mouth, and I tasted a few drops of its delicious juice before the entire cube of fruit went in. It was sweet, perfectly ripe. I pictured the farmer in Hawaii leaning over fields of pineapples, picking just this one, for just this girl.

She stared at me long after the pineapple had made its way down my throat. I was accustomed to being the observer, but in this case I was clearly the observed. Surprisingly, it felt nice.

The girl sat down and motioned me toward an antique leather chair beside hers. On the wall between us hung a modern painting of a lawn full of sprinklers. It was an image I recognized from art history books as a David Hockney. I assumed the painting was an original.

"I can't believe you beat me 6–0. I didn't give a good first impression," I said. "Do you know what a 6–0 set is called?" I asked.

"No."

"A bagel. Because the zero is round like a bagel."

She smiled grandly, and I noticed she had great teeth. They were a bit crooked, but in a good way.

"I'm Thomas, by the way." I made a long-overdue introduction. "I should have probably said that earlier, right?"

She didn't introduce herself in turn. She took a long sip of lemonade with mint leaves.

"You should really think about playing in some tournaments. I think you'd do really well," I said.

"You do?" she asked, leaning closer.

"Yes. You seem the competitive type."

"Is that a compliment?"

"I like girls with chops, so yes."

"With chops?"

"Yeah, with chops."

"I don't know what that means, but I hope it's a good thing. And I'll think about it—the tournaments, I mean. I don't think I'd be very good at losing. Are you good at losing?"

"No one is," I said, taking a sip of my lemonade. "I'm surprised your coach doesn't encourage you to play matches."

She stared into the distance, where David's grand white house loomed. We could only see its six chimneys—but it was there, in the background, bigger than us.

"My coach would like me to, but it's complicated."

She looked toward her yard, as if a missing puzzle piece lay somewhere in that rolling acreage. But wait, was this even her yard? I was so mesmerized that I hadn't considered this question. Even in a city obsessed with dating young she was too young to be David's lover. And if she were, wouldn't she have been at the political event?

The girl focused her gaze on me—first on my hair, then my forehead, then my nose and then my mouth. She moved lower, studying my body obviously and examining the barrel chest of my torso and the calves that I had spent my boyhood covering up because they were too brawny for the rest of me. She eventually settled on my jaw.

"You have such a nice jaw," she said sweetly. "It's a man's jaw."

I smiled and found myself blushing.

"Thank you. It's my father's jaw. I grew up hating it. It was too big for the rest of me."

"But now you love it I bet."

"I grew into it. Now I tolerate it."

She smiled. She then rubbed the back of her right hand on my reddish-blond stubble—at first tentatively, as if she wasn't sure if it was off-limits, and then tenderly, in a gesture far too intimate for a first meeting.

"It's prickly." She smiled with curiosity. "And coarse."

"By this time of night that's what happens," I said.

I felt the back of her hand down to the tips of my toes. It didn't feel like an experienced touch, one of a woman who knew exactly how to hit the right nerves, at the right time of night. In fact, it was quite the opposite. I pegged her as an amateur at the sport of seduction, but it was refreshing.

She finally dropped her hand to her lap, and she left it there, as if not knowing what to do with it next. It was then that I made my first mistake of the night—well, second, if you count missing a party at David Duplaine's beach house honoring the governor of California. I fleetingly glanced at the wall clock to check if we had time for another set. The girl's eyes followed mine.

"You have to leave," she said. "They'll be back soon. They can't know you've been here."

"Who will be back? The party's going to go late."

"You have to go."

"Can I see you again?" It sounded like begging. I didn't know if it was her naïveté, off-kilter beauty, crooked smile or all three, but I was enchanted. "Can I get your name?" I asked, when she didn't answer the first question.

"I need you to promise me something," she said. "Promise you'll forget you ever met me. Please. Because if you remember, it's likely to get both of us into trouble."

I didn't answer because it was a promise I was unwilling to make.

The girl clenched her fist and then uncurled her fingers quickly, as if they were fireworks or a blooming flower. Then she said:

"Poof. See, you've forgotten me."

"We've gotta work on your magic tricks," I said. "You're still here."

She smiled despite herself, but then she set her eyes on me seriously.

"I don't want you to get involved with me, with all of it. No one can ever, ever know you've been here. And as lovely as our tennis game was, you may never come back."

I could tell that by nature she was a fanciful girl, which made the gravitas of her tone even more foreboding. She had presented me with an opening when she peered up at the tree, but now she had closed the door for good.

I nodded, because there was little else to do but leave her as instructed. I climbed to the top of the canopy, hoisted myself up onto the wall and then swung my way into the oak tree.

I watched from the oak as she eliminated all traces of me. She emptied my glass, clumsily washed and dried it, and put it in the kitchenette cabinet. She fluffed the pillow on my leather chair, slid the racket back in cellophane and swept my side of the court in the awkward manner of someone who was learning a skill for the first time.

Once satisfied that she had effectively made me disappear, the girl abandoned the tennis court, leaving the gate to crash back and forth in the wind because she didn't trouble herself to latch it. She walked up the lawn toward the manor, tightly squeezing her arms around her.

Halfway along the well-lit path to the grand house she turned around and looked up at the oak tree. She extended her right arm as far as it would go and she spread her fingers out in the tree's general direction, as if she were reaching for something on a high shelf, something so fragile it might break into pieces if she grabbed it.

Seven

I drove out of Bel-Air, crossed Sunset Boulevard and ended up in the parking lot of the mini-mall I had been at just hours earlier renting my tuxedo. It was empty, storefronts dimly lit from the interior with single lightbulbs. That was what was interesting about Los Angeles: its great glory and its gritty underbelly were often walking distance apart. I think the city planners created it that way on purpose. Los Angeles is a recycle bin for dreamers, and the dream needs to be always visible but just slightly out of grasp.

I had stopped there to check my voice mails, of which there were many, and then call Lily, but I lit a cigarette instead of doing either. A street lamp above me flickered a few times with a buzzing sound. It made a go of it, but then went black.

It felt like autumn in Cambridge. Or maybe it felt like Milwaukee. I couldn't remember anymore, because those cities felt like lifetimes ago. I wondered sometimes if it was the same Thomas Cleary who had lived there or if it was a different man, one I had met in a bar and who had told me his story over a couple of pale ales.

And as for Manhattan, well, that definitely couldn't have been this lifetime.

I stopped and realized it had been two hours since I had

thought of Willa. I hadn't thought of her once on that tennis court. Relief—or was it sadness?—crept into my heart.

Sure, I had been on dates after Willa, but inevitably, some-time around the appetizer, the comparisons would creep in, and the date would end in a promise never kept.

Willa.

I had lived with an imaginary lover for so long, and it was becoming almost impossible to believe that at this very minute she still existed, in a place so different and far from mine. In the first days without her she was as vivid and clear as a pho-tograph, and I knew where she would be at any moment, or I could have guessed.

In those first weeks without her it was the nights that were the worst. I lay in bed begging for sleep; and if not sleep, the morning, because at least the morning brought the sun. In those black nights I would feel her forgetting me, and somehow that was the worst part.

I began to forget her eventually, too, and it was both my bless-ing and punishment. After two years her face finally started to blur, and soon after, the fruity smell of her shampoo and the scent of the jasmine behind her ears stopped haunting me. Her eyes became a vacant place, a blackness from which someone had once looked at me lovingly a long time ago. The same went for her arms and her toes, the lips I kissed past midnight, the slen-der long neck I whispered into in Central Park.

I was lost in thought when my phone rang. The number was private.

"Hello," I said, tossing the stub of my cigarette to the ground.

Lily skipped salutations. "My goodness, Thomas. We were worried sick about you. You never showed up to the fund-raiser."

"I went to the wrong house. I went to David's house in Bel-Air by accident."

"Kurt did give you the address, didn't he?" Lily asked. In fact, Kurt hadn't specified an address. I barely knew Kurt, but I already didn't much care for him. He always lurked around, like a prison warden searching for an excuse to use his club. And then there was that handshake. Never trust a man whose grip is too sure, my father had always preached.

Could Lily have manipulated events to send me to the wrong house?

I paused before answering. I could lie to Lily and tell her Kurt gave me the address, or betray Kurt and tell Lily he had called me to confirm but hadn't told me that the party was in Malibu. I was under the early impression lies were passed around this group like hors d'oeuvres at a cocktail party. But I suspected loyalty was deemed a valiant trait.

"He did, but I forget to check my messages and only received it a minute ago. I apologize. It was a stupid oversight. How was the party?"

"I hate political parties—they're terribly boring. You didn't miss a thing. Even the filet was tough." Lily paused then asked offhandedly, "Was anyone at David's?"

I didn't answer right away. The girl had made me promise to keep our meeting a surreptitious one. And, besides, it was such an enchanting evening that sharing it would feel like marring its perfection.

"No. There was no one home."

"What a terrible coincidence," Lily said, sounding genuinely disappointed. "David has more security than royalty. They must have all been at the governor's party. This had to have been the only night of the year the house was vacant. Otherwise, some-one could have driven you to Malibu or at least pointed you in the right direction."

"I'm sorry I missed the fund-raiser."

"I knew it had to be a mix-up, because Midwestern boys are *so* typically reliable. David said it would be possible to arrange a short interview for you tomorrow with the governor."

I skipped forward and imagined what Rubenstein would say

when I told him I'd landed an interview with the governor. He had been my salvation after my fall from grace, and I still wanted to make him proud.

"Would you like that?" Lily asked, when I didn't answer.

It was another one of Lily's rhetorical questions. I accepted and then hung up. I lit another cigarette, and the world seemed to light up, too. The governor. The world of Lily Goldman was full of presents, and I couldn't help but wonder if there were strings attached to every last one of them.

Eight

The next morning the rain started.

It began with a few stray drops, gentle and unassuming. But by afternoon, as I sat down with the governor in the library of a private club in downtown Los Angeles, the clouds had opened. Water puddles had turned to flash floods and roads across the city were closed.

It rained for the next four days, and the young woman on the tennis court handcuffed my thoughts. When I think back on those days after our first meeting I only recall staring at the rain and thinking of her. Everyday tasks—work, errands and sleep—sparkled somehow, as if her enchanting spell hung over even the most mundane things. She was ubiquitous; no corner of the world could hide her. I thought of her bare shoulders, the way her long ponytail brushed against her dress when she ran for the ball, how her diamond bracelet got caught in her hair each time she put her hand through its blond tendrils. All other food tasted dull compared with the pineapple she had placed on my tongue, and no air tingled my skin like the cool air of that night on the tennis court, and no touch felt as electric as her fingers on my skin.

Had the situation been different—if she was the friend-of-a-friend, a girl I met at a bar—I could have just asked about her.

But that was not an option. Asking Lily would have been retracting my previous story, and I got the distinct sense from the girl that she didn't want anyone to know about our secret tennis game.

So, instead, I tried to learn more about her. The evening had left a bread-crumb trail of clues behind. The food and drink seemed tailored to the girl's taste, and she had a ball-speed radar device, which wasn't the sort of thing one would bring along for a visit to someone else's house. I thought then of the evening of the Blooms' dinner party, the single upper-floor light that had gone dark when we dropped David off at his estate. I supposed it could have been the staff, but I doubted a housekeeper would be upstairs at that hour. It had to have been her.

While at work, I crawled through David's life virtually on hands and knees, searching for a pinhead of a clue. I scanned microfiche, birth certificates, city hall records and school attendance lists at all the top private schools, but every search was coming up empty. As I had suspected, David had no children. His romantic life was nonexistent. He hadn't been photographed beside a lover in years, and there hadn't been any mention of anyone in the ample press he received.

On nothing more than a whim, I then did the same searching for Lily. I found pictures as far back as her childhood. There was Lily at five years old, flanked by her parents at the premiere of one of her father's movies. Then Lily winning her science fair with the invention of the lightbulb at John Thomas Dye. Then there was a thirteen-year-old Lily, in jodhpurs and a crisp white shirt, racing a beauty of a Thoroughbred in Hidden Hills at what must have been the Goldmans' equestrian estate—a stone mansion draped in ivy with shutters.

After eighteen, Lily disappeared from Los Angeles. I had learned in bits and pieces through our dinner-party conversation that Lily had eventually "escaped to the Rhode Island School of Design," and then she had gone even farther away to work for an editor at *Paris Vogue*, to "learn French and sleep with the French"—a quote Lily had tossed out over a dessert wine. In her midtwenties Lily made an abrupt U-turn and returned to the city of her birth and good breeding and started her antiques shop as a hobby. Years later she had created a quiet empire of furniture, fabrics and real estate holdings.

I was ready to put my search to rest when I stumbled upon a photo in the *Los Angeles Times*, which I would have missed if the shuffling microfiche hadn't decided to stop on that specific page. I enlarged the page tenfold, trading crisp for fuzzy.

The caption read, "Movie mogul Joel Goldman, his daughter, Lily, and friends play tennis at Mr. Goldman's vacation house." I looked closer, shocked to discover that one of the friends was none other than a very young Carole Partridge.

The four stood on a clay tennis court. Joel commandeered the photo—as he always seemed to—holding a racket in his left hand, a drink in his right, and wearing a wide victorious grin on his face. Lily seemed to be in her midthirties at the time, and she wore a demure dress and a ponytail and carried a bottle of Orangina. Behind her, almost off camera, was another man of indeterminate age. I tried to focus the microfiche on him, but he turned grainier rather than clearer. What I could tell was this: he was tall, broad and focused on Lily.

Carole was the youngest of the group, and she stood in front. My guess was she was about seventeen compared to Joel's sixty, and he rested his drink on her shoulder in a protective manner. She donned a barely there white tennis dress and posed with her hand on her hip, as if she were emulating an older, more experienced woman she had seen strike the same pose. She was all legs, and her breasts seemed too big for her, as if they were things that needed to be grown into. Her hair was pinned up in a beehive—an odd hairstyle for tennis—and her charcoal-lined eyes teased the camera.

My gut told me that the photo meant something, something

more than the rest of my research combined. I looked at it again, focusing on that mysterious man in the background. Lily had never married—unusual for a woman of her social standing—and judging by the photos and news clippings there hadn't been a significant other throughout the years. It was possible this guy was a lover. If so, that begged the further question of what had happened.

There was something about the photo that seared through me.

I couldn't figure it out. I printed the photo, and I pressed it between the pages of my notebook like a rose from a long-lost love. A reminder of something important—something not to be forgotten.

Ironically, it was in this period of distractedness that my star was finally rising at the *Times*. I learned quickly that once Los Angeles decides to sprinkle you with its stardust, it shakes so generously you glitter.

I say this because after those first few stories my sky twinkled brightly. There was the story on Joel, followed by the David Duplaine shake-up, the Millstone coverage and then the interview with the governor. I would never know how I had won Phil Rubenstein's favor after what had happened at the *Journal*, but what I came to understand was that Los Angeles, above anything else, was a city of forgiveness and second chances.

Scarcely three weeks after my first meeting with Lily Goldman, life moved from slow motion to the speed at which a race-car driver accelerates at the drop of the green flag. The invitations poured in—not to the second-rate parties that had always been my lot, but to first-rate premieres and galas. I attended a few, met new people and was invited to more. Studio publicists lunched me and Rubenstein slipped me the choicest articles.

I was working at the paper early one morning—no later than 7:00 a.m.—when my phone rang from a private number. It was Lily.

72

I barely had a chance to say hello.

"Thomas, darling, I only have a moment, but I'm calling to insist you join me this evening at Carole's. She and Charles are having a small dinner, and I haven't seen you in months."

This was a slight exaggeration. "I'd love to come," I said stoically, for I believed that emotion was a badge of weakness in this group. "Please extend a thank-you to Carole. Is there something she'd like me to bring?"

"Absolutely not. The last I heard you are not a member of Carole's staff," Lily said. "Kurt will pick you up at six thirty."

As promised, Kurt picked me up at six thirty. This time we fetched Lily on our way to our destination, and after Lily's house we drove a few blocks before reaching a pair of stone columns, each crowned with a vintage gas lamp. A tall wooden gate stared at us, and a personal security car waited beside one of the columns.

Lily waved in the general direction of the security guard in a familiar manner and the gates opened.

We wound our way up a steep driveway that must have been a quarter of a mile long. Once we arrived we were rewarded with an incredible view of Los Angeles. It was a view that shouldn't have been available for private purchase. Below us, sprinklers watered the fairways of the Bel-Air Country Club with perfectly arched trajectories, and uniformly dressed groundskeepers raked the country club's sand traps. Beyond, Los Angeles was just beginning to wake up and glitter for the night as the sun was setting over a sliver of ocean that sparkled like a mirror.

I wished I could bottle that view. I looked over to Lily. She seemed indifferent to the blanket of lights that lay before us. She straightened out my new shirt and pants.

"The city feels so small from up here," I said.

"It's trickery," Lily said. "It makes us feel like we're the powerful ones, even though nothing could be further from the truth."

I glanced at her incredulously.

"It's true. We're all just renters, Thomas. Someday our leases will be up. Carole's, mine, yours… Look, my father's just ended. An eighty-one-year lease on life—that was all he got."

The city buzzed dully in the distance. Lily squinted at an imaginary point, and I wondered what she was thinking about. It was strange; her father had passed away around a month ago, but Lily hadn't seemed deeply affected by it. I wondered if it was a veneer as fastidiously crafted as her shop and her house.

I turned around to give Lily a moment, and for the first time I noticed the house. The white brick mansion was perched adjacent to the egg-shaped cobblestone motor court. It was a wedding cake of a house—with a second story slightly smaller than the first, and a few curlicue frills for decoration. It was a grander, whiter, more sprawling version of the traditional house surrounded by the picket fence that suburban girls dream of. I imagined it was built in the late 1930s or early '40s, post-Depression for a manufacturing or real estate tycoon. The mansion appeared purposely situated to get the maximum vistas, but it was plotted in such a way that you might almost miss it when you drove up—the real estate equivalent of Lily Goldman's false modesty.

There was no need for doorbells at houses like these. Instead, a butler in a black coat and white gloves held the door open for us and led us into the foyer. He greeted Lily by name and Lily introduced me as "Thomas Cleary, the finest reporter in Los Angeles."

A large antique iron birdcage hung from the entry's ceiling in lieu of a chandelier. It had a whimsical effect, as if the house's owners were trying not to take themselves too seriously. A sweeping stairway made for brides or goodbyes crawled up the wall, and sconces cast a soft glow over us.

The butler escorted us toward the stairway, under which a secret door led us into a formal dining room wrapped in hand-painted wallpaper depicting an ancient Asian landscape complete with geishas, canoes, swans, hummingbirds, pergolas and flowers. The Asian chandelier overhead seemed plucked from the wallpaper into real life.

The group was sipping before-dinner cocktails. I decided that there must have been a tribal theme to the evening: Emma wore a feathered headdress, Carole donned heavy silver-and-turquoise jewelry that contrasted with her red-apple lips, and the menus that rested on our plates indicated we were to be served buffalo as our main course.

Charles approached us eagerly. He kissed Lily's cheek and shook my hand.

"Thomas, thank you so much for joining us. I've been reading your bylines. You sure have a knack for the written word."

"Thank you," I said, because Charles was the type of man who would say something like that and genuinely mean it. "How's the screenplay coming?"

"Fantastic, chap." Charles swept David into conversation with his right arm. "David, you remember Thomas?" He always seemed to veer the subject away from himself, as if he wasn't worthy of discussion.

"Of course." David's expression was even. "We missed you at the governor's party, but I trust your reason for absence was a good-looking one."

My stomach dropped. I glanced to my left, to where Lily had just been, but she was no longer there. Instead, she stood alone on the other side of the room, adjusting a painting that had tipped slightly off its proper axis.

The girl had made it clear that no one could find out about our tennis game. I wondered if David had known I was there. The estate was peppered with video security. I had seen the cameras outside when I was waiting at the gate for someone to answer the buzzer, but surprisingly I didn't see cameras around the tennis court.

Just then, Charles squeezed my arm and presented me with a gimlet stuffed with ice.

"We have a gimlet prepared, just the way you like it."

I took a deep well-needed sip. Charles and I stood at the doors, looking outside at a carpet of green.

"How are your birds?" I asked. "I heard something about homing pigeons."

"Yes. Interesting sport, if you can call it that. I picked it up in my youth." Charles smiled to himself, and there was something sad and longing about it. "We lived in Manhattan during the week and Tuxedo Park on the weekends. The pigeons would follow us between the two."

"How did they find you?"

"Scientists don't know for sure. It's one of life's mysteries."

Just then a gray pigeon, all barrel chest and beak, waddled toward us. His leg was tagged.

"Not to bring up a sore subject, but did you ever find the one you lost?" I said.

"No. That's the only one, believe it or not. Even as a kid, I never lost a single bird."

"I'm sorry. You don't know what happened?" I pressed.

Charles looked wistful. The pigeon in the yard waddled away.

"Thanks for coming tonight, chap." Charles changed the subject. "Next time, let's go to the Malibu house. The aviary there is unbelievable—and so is the bourbon."

"Dinner is served," a staff member said quietly, a welcome interruption in conversation.

We sat down at the long dining table. The centerpieces overflowed with roses the size of cabbages that still sparkled with dew, and the glasses were made of honed French crystal.

Unlike the last dinner party, where the group had quickly divided into factions, this time the six remained cohesive, focused on a heated conversation about technology's influence on the music industry. Ever the reporter, always the observer, I stayed on the sidelines of conversation, which was just fine by me.

I hadn't noticed it at the previous dinner, but this evening Charles attended to his wife's every comfort, more like a personal valet than a husband. He asked Carole twice if she wanted more Brussels sprouts and checked her wineglass carefully to be sure it never dipped below half-full. If and when it did, a server was immediately summoned to top off the glass. At one point Carole's heavy clip-on earring slipped low on her left earlobe and was in danger of falling off into her soup when she leaned into conversation. Charles reached out to pinch it between his thumb and index finger, positioning it back into place. Carole did not acknowledge the intimate gesture. In fact she seemed to stiffen under his touch.

When the group left the dining room for dessert wine in the conservatory, I excused myself to the bathroom. I washed my hands and stared at myself in the mirror. I needed a cigarette.

I opened the door to find Carole standing in the hallway. Her porcelain face was flawless.

"I thought perhaps you'd gone for a cigarette," Carole said, and I was flattered that she had remembered my vice.

"I've been trying to quit," I lied.

"I never quit anything I enjoy," she said matter-of-factly. "Charles insisted I show you the aviary. Follow me."

I followed Carole down the hallway and then through a tall French door outside. I heard the sound of paws on grass, wet and saturated with weeks of rain, and then a German shepherd as big as a wolf appeared.

"Malcolm, this is Thomas. Thomas, Malcolm," Carole said.

Carole leaned over and stroked Malcolm's neck. He was a beast of a dog, with streaks of pecan brown and white through his fur. Carole tucked a pin curl behind her own ear and then adjusted Malcolm's collar so his tag was in its proper spot tucked beneath his chin. There was no chance of Malcolm leaving this fortress, so I wondered why he had a tag at all.

In front of us lay a lawn so vast I expected to find polo ponies roaming about or men in white playing cricket. On either side of the expanse, box hedges and plants were sheared to tight, geometric lines. There was not a single errant leaf.

Carole and Malcolm led the way. There were paths, but they opted to walk on the middle of the grass instead. I walked two steps behind.

We passed a swimming pool—refined and rectangular, in contrast to Emma's fishy swamp—and then a tennis court with a small viewing area. Not every tennis court should have reminded me of her, but this one did. I must have slowed a step or two, not realizing it, because Carole turned around.

"Do you play?" Carole asked, glancing at the court with her sleepy eyes. I got the first glimpse of a glass structure in the distance. It must have been the aviary.

"I did—in high school. You?"

"You'll be surprised to learn I was a good player in my youth."

"That's not surprising," I said, thinking of the photograph and attempting not to look obviously at Carole's body, but my eyes traveled there nevertheless.

Carole must have been accustomed to it. She slowed her pace so we were closer to each other.

"Next time you visit we should play," Carole said in a tone I took to mean that if we played she would not only win, but crush me. Judging by the Academy Awards and Tony I had spotted earlier in the evening in the library, Carole Partridge didn't like to lose.

"That would be wonderful. I better hone my skills."

"You better," she said mischievously.

As we reached the glass-enclosed aviary my mood was buoyant. I was starting to feel like a part of the group, not realizing it was their collective charms that created the mirage. I found myself fast-forwarding, in a delusional manner, to a day when I would be exchanging cross-court backhands with Carole on her court while the staff provided us with cool towels and lemonade.

Carole, Malcolm and I stood in front of the aviary. It was hexagonal in shape and lit softly from the inside. Tucked away between formal gardens and fountains, the structure looked like something out of Grimm.

Carole opened the metal door with an old-fashioned key. I followed her in and Malcolm sat at the door obediently.

Once inside, I was surrounded by a burst of activity so vari-colored and fanciful it made me forget I was in the refined, staid hills of Bel-Air. I had always thought greenhouses to be extra-ordinary places in their own rights: the condensed microcosm of flora and fauna all thriving in a glass environment. In this case, it was a greenhouse as large as most people's homes, potted with the world's most exotic plants, flowers, cacti and trees—mostly of species I had never seen before. There were dozens of birds nesting in those trees or flitting about, exploding in song.

"It's quite boring, actually—the aviary." Carole's eyes were trained on Malcolm, who sat regally. "The only reason every-one's so fascinated by it is because no one else has one."

"It's amazing. I've never seen anything like it."

"Nor will you. An incredible waste of time," Carole said. "Charles spends hours a day here with his birds."

"What does he do?" I asked. It was a rude question, but cu-riosity trumped manners.

"He comes from the East Coast," Carole said, as if those who did weren't required to hold employment. "Have you ever been in love, Thomas?"

It came out of the sky, as if the question was flitting about with the rest of the birds in the aviary.

"Yes."

"Are you still?"

"That's a bit of a trick question," I said.

"It seems to me it's a yes-or-no question."

"Does it?" I asked. "I guess you're not one for gray areas."

"Not when it pertains to love. You're either in it or you're not," Carole said. "I'm guessing your love is the unrequited type."

"How did you know?"

"Because those are the types that fade into gray. The other person has already killed it, but you hang on because you think the longer you keep it in your heart the longer it still breathes. Who is she?"

"A girl from college." It felt good to say it. Talking about Willa brought her to life again, and part of me wanted to hold that crisp memory of her forever. "She was supposed to be the one."

"'Supposed to' is a terrible phrase because it's always followed by something nice that didn't happen," Carole said. "Were you good to her?"

"Too good. It screwed up my life."

"Your life is too young to have screwed it up," Carole said. "My mother always told me you were supposed to marry someone good to you. But you know what? That's a lie. 'Good to you' never inspired me to be good in return."

Willa had left me easily it seemed, as easily as leaving a party that had run out of alcohol and grown dull, and for the first time I wondered if the problems between us had been as simple as I had thought.

"I'm not one to give advice," she began, but in fact, she was. "Be careful. I know this—" Carole meant the aviary, the estate, the group of people sipping dessert drinks in the conservatory "—can be very intoxicating, but everything has its price, Thomas. You'll get charged without knowing it, and you won't know the price until the bill comes in the mail."

"Are you saying I can't afford it?"

"I make twenty million a picture and I can't afford it."

The conversation had turned dark all of a sudden. A canary flew into Carole's pale palm. She touched its matted yellow back, and then the canary flew away, toward a feathery green plant.

"So what are you suggesting I do?" I asked. "Walk away?"

"I'm saying be careful. I wish someone had warned me when I was younger. But no one did."

She stared at herself in the glass for a moment, and then she turned out the lights and the aviary went dark.

"Come, Malcolm, you sweet dog." Malcolm did as Carole ordered, and the three of us walked toward the mansion.

Through the leaded glass I saw David, Lily and Emma hovering near the bar laughing, huddled together like schoolgirls sharing a secret. George was off to the side typing into his phone, and by the clip at which his fingers were moving I suspected he was tending to a work crisis. Only Charles looked toward the windows.

The butler helped Lily into a black shrug.

"Goodbye, dear," Carole said to Lily. "Let me know if you find anything for the aviary. The lack of pillows is driving Charles to drink." Carole then focused on me. "Good night, Thomas. I enjoyed our conversation."

"I did, too," I said, walking into the brisk night, where two drivers waited in the motor court and George's car purred.

Once inside the car, Lily turned to me. "What did you and Carole speak about?"

"A press junket she's doing for her next movie," I lied, because I wasn't a guy who betrayed confidences, and I was under the distinct impression my conversation with Carole was the off-the-record sort.

"I should have figured as much. She's very self-absorbed, you know. Actresses always are. And she can't be trusted. She spends so much time acting she can't differentiate truth from reality anymore."

"Can you blame her? Being someone else for ten hours a day may muddle things a bit."

"That's no excuse," Lily said. She fingered her bracelet, a series of ivory pyramids bound together by gold. I had noticed Lily had a habit of touching her jewels, stroking them like talismans. "Don't spend another second thinking of Carole. What is it the psychiatrists call it? Narcissistic extension. The more you think about her, the more she'll think of herself."

In fact Lily might have been thinking of Carole, but I wasn't—not per se. Instead I was thinking of our haunting conversation. My guard was up, but what could they want from me? I was a waiter standing in front of them with an empty tray. I could offer them nothing.

"By the way," Lily said, as she intently stared down at her wrist and twisted her pyramids into symmetry, "George is going to be phoning you. Look out for his call."

"Thanks." I could only assume that George's call would bring something good—a story, a scoop, a party invitation.

We dropped Lily off. Kurt drove me out through the pillars of Bel-Air, and we then passed by the mansions on Sunset Boulevard in Beverly Hills. Eventually, we made our way to the other side of town—the part where I lived.

I thought again of Carole's forecast, and I wondered if it had come too late.

Nine

George called me two days later, asking if I would cover an album launch. The artist happened to be one of the most famous pop stars in the world, and the album was a surefire catapult to number one. The story included an exclusive interview worthy of a *Rolling Stone* cover. At the end of the conversation George happened to mention that the gang was leaving on separate holidays that afternoon. Emma and George were heading to Wyoming for some rest and relaxation on their horse ranch. David was flying to London on his plane for a series of meetings, and the others were "hitching a ride"—George's term, not mine—as if David's plane was no different from climbing into the backseat of a buddy's convertible on the way to a party.

It sounded like a case of meticulous planning. David would first drop Carole and Charles off in New York where they kept a pied-à-terre—more specifically, a five-thousand-square-foot prewar brownstone on Fifth and Eighty-Second. David would then stop in Martha's Vineyard, where Lily was embarking on an off-season remodel of her summer home. Finally, David would fly across the pond to London, and the same exacting flight plan would occur in reverse ten days later.

Within minutes of hanging up, I received a phone call from a private number.

"Thomas, love, it's Lily."

"Hello, Lily," I said. "Shouldn't you be at the airport?"

"How did you know?" she asked with a hint of paranoia.

"George phoned me and mentioned you were leaving today."

"Oh, good," she declared with a sigh of relief. "I'm glad you're communicating with George. He adores you. It's good for you at the paper. And, yes, to answer your question, I absolutely should be at the airport. David's going to have my head. He hates it when his schedule is disrupted, particularly with that god-awful stop at Teterboro. I do love Carole, but she's so selfish sometimes. If she weren't so cheap she would stop glomming off David and buy her own plane already."

I didn't know Carole well, but judging by her roughly hundred million dollars in residential real estate holdings and her affinity for off-the-runway fashion, I wouldn't have pegged her as cheap.

"The reason I'm phoning—and I do realize this is very last-minute—is that Kurt's mother in Taiwan is very ill, so he has to leave for Asia unexpectedly. I was hoping you might consider house-sitting for me."

I immediately fast-forwarded to the near future: I was lounging in Lily's grand living room, sipping tea while writing.

"I'm in such a bind," Lily added. "It's terribly dangerous to leave a house in LA vacant for ten days. I know something dreadful will happen, Thomas."

"Of course. I think I can make that work," I said, I hoped not too eagerly.

"Delightful. I owe you a huge favor in return. Pick whatever you'd like, but you don't have to answer now," Lily said, ironically, since my life had been replete with favors from Lily Goldman. "Kurt will deliver the gate opener and key to your office, and if you need anything while I'm away, don't hesitate to go to David's. His staff is incredibly attentive."

I again fast-forwarded: I was already imagining excuses—however flimsy—to visit David's estate in hopes I'd see the girl again.

"That's all you need to know," Lily declared. "You went to Harvard—you can figure out the rest. Now I must go or I'll be flying commercial to the Vineyard, which would be an absolute nightmare or may be impossible for all I know. Au revoir."

Less than fifteen minutes after Lily's phone call, I received a summons from the front desk informing me that I had a delivery. A square and oversize linen envelope was waiting for me, my full name written on the front in a prim and feminine penmanship. It was the type of envelope that should have been sliced with a silver letter cutter, but I tore it open.

There was a clicker and a single key and no accompanying note.

I left my apartment in Silver Lake and drove through the now-familiar white pillars of Bel-Air.

When I arrived at Lily's, I pointed the clicker at the gate—covered in so many wildflowers it had nearly disappeared—and I drove up the steep driveway, past Lily's own smaller version of David's oak tree.

I walked through the twelve-foot French doors into the foyer. The house was cold and dark. Unlike my previous visit, there was no fire crackling in the fireplace and no gentle opera music filling the air.

The guest bedroom had been set up with a silver pitcher on one side of the bed and a glass bottle of Evian and crystal glass beside it. The towels were not only laundered but appeared to be brand-new. A jasmine candle sat on a writing desk.

I took a hot shower before lying in bed. The leaded glass windows overlooked giant specimen trees lit by the moon, and the breeze cast odd, ever-changing shadows over the grounds. Lying there, staring at those trees, I thought once again that I had walked into a fairy tale, and I was a hero on someone else's pages.

Two days into my house-sitting assignment, I was already growing restless. That evening, as Bel-Air's soft sunlight was fading, I transcribed my interview with George's artist in anticipation of the album that was dropping on Tuesday.

Despite being a journalist, I had prided myself on never being the snoopy sort. The private corners of others' lives were strictly off-limits.

I don't know if it was the eerie quiet that made me do it, or the feeling, however oblique, that I was so close to a story that I could feel its breath on my neck. Whatever the case, I walked down the hall to Lily's bedroom and tried the hefty antique latch, almost hoping it was locked.

It wasn't.

I first looked for video cameras, but there were none. Lily's writing desk was spare: three perfectly sharp writing pencils rested in a hollowed-out tusk, monogrammed paper sat lonely in a drawer. The only other object was a silver-framed photo of a thirtysomething Lily and her father eating lunch at an outdoor café in Europe. Lily wore an oversize scarf in her hair and stared up at her father, as if he could solve any problem the world threw her way. Joel, on the other hand, leaned into the photographer aggressively, staking his claim on the photo the way powerful men put their mark on everything.

I moved away from the desk to two bedside tables. One held a silver pitcher and a crystal glass. The drawers were empty.

A wall of wood-paneled doors served as Lily's closet. Inside were dresses so delicate I was afraid my fingers would disintegrate the fabric if I touched them. Their labels read Chanel, Valentino and Yves Saint Laurent. Handbags in Hermès boxes were piled high, and shoes were arranged according to color. The closet smelled of fine leather and lilacs.

I was ready to close the doors and retreat to my bedroom when a man's suit caught my eye. I pulled the suit off the hanger. The inside pocket was monogrammed with the initials *JG*. It had belonged to Lily's father.

I felt the urge to try it on. I slipped on the coat and glanced at myself in Lily's full-length mirror, feeling vaguely empowered by wearing a jacket that belonged to the most powerful man in the history of the movie business.

When I pulled the jacket off, I felt something in the interior pocket. I reached in and pulled out a key and a letter. The key was a single one, dangling from a key chain with a handwritten tab that said "Honolulu" in a man's quick hand. As for the letter, it was written on the powder-blue lightweight airmail stationary of its day and postmarked Cap d'Antibes, France. There was no date. It said:

Dear Daddy,

I am sending this to the studio in hopes Mommy doesn't read it, as God knows she has had enough to deal with in recent months.

You have left a mess of things in France, a much bigger mess than you realize. I need to return to the States for my wedding and to a fiancé who is waiting for the same, but I cannot do so before you come back here. This isn't one of your movies, Father, this is real life. There are not a bevy of directors, writers, actors, designers and editors to set this film. It is yours alone.

Please telegraph me when you have received this along with a definite arrival date, at which point I will pick you up at the station.

Despite all of it, with much love still,

Lily

Deception begets deception.

Four days after I discovered the letter, I found myself in Lily's grand living room, staring at a lonely Saturday. It was one of those days distractions had no appeal, but the alternative, sitting home alone waiting for dusk to descend, had even less. Stories were in, deadlines struck. I sat in a stiff-backed armchair sipping a tea and reading the morning paper—more specifically, my article on George's pop star. It was a gold mine of a story because the star was typically elusive and press-shy but in this case he had opened himself up to me like a book.

I finished reading the story and looked outside. It had ceased raining for a transitory moment, and I could see a sliver of brightness between the clouds.

The iridescent sky was enticing. I grabbed a bath towel and walked outside up wooden steps to the grassy pad that held Lily's swimming pool. The air was wet but warm.

The pool resembled that of the Blooms'. Long strands of thin grass drooped into the pool's muddy walls, and the water's tint was green rather than the vivid sky blue one expects from a swimming pool. Everything around the pool was wet. Fabric chairs had soupy middles to them, and concrete and wood were soaked. A large damp wooden structure sat beside the pool, and it covered a fireplace, a few half-burned logs in its center.

A heart-shaped cocoon of a hornet's nest rested in the trees, and wasps were everywhere. The nest might have arrived by accident, but I suspected it was now here on purpose. I could imagine Lily's staff informing her of the hornets, and Lily trudging up the hill, examining it closely—because she seemed scared of nothing—and then, in appreciation for its natural beauty, a beauty even she couldn't manufacture at her shop, instructing the staff to leave it.

I jumped in the pool without as much as dipping my toe because, despite days of cold rain and a strong chance this pool had never been swum in, I had no doubt that Lily insisted the water be kept warm.

The water felt good.

My strength as a journalist was reading and interpreting other people, so I was befuddled why I hadn't been able to piece together this mosaic of clues to create a clear picture.

I thought about the letter that had gnawed at me for days, and then there was the photograph still sitting in between the pages of my notebook. I thought about Lily—who lived alone in this big house with dead ivy crawling up its walls, about a wedding that was supposed to happen but never had.

As I toweled off, I remembered the strange encounter I'd had with Carole the night of the dinner party. There was something about those birds in the glass aviary that was foreboding and sad. They could fly, but they had no sky. The one who had escaped— the homing pigeon—was mourned, but shouldn't he have been celebrated? He had freedom; he had escaped his predictable route between Malibu and Bel-Air and was now flying in bigger and brighter skies, with a flight plan that was spontaneous and new.

And then there was the girl: I had forced myself to forget her but was only successful for an hour or two, and then she would creep back in, the way a spider returns to a musty corner of a room to spin her web.

My love for Willa remained long after she had gone, as water continues to ripple in the wake of a disturbance. I thought of Willa constantly, but I never called her after she had left me. The timing never seemed perfect, the event not glamorous enough to invite her to, and there was always tomorrow.

Likewise, it had been three weeks since I had seen the girl on the tennis court, and life was again leading to that dangerous and nebulous place of gray. The girl captivated my thoughts, yet I hadn't made any attempt to see her again. I was beginning to realize something about myself: I preferred to live in hope than take a risk—a risk that may have quashed it.

I needed to change that.

I walked inside, tossed the towel into the washing machine and decided I would take a gamble. It was a quick toss of the dice, a snap decision. Sometimes the impetuous bets can be the best ones. Throw a few bucks on a derby long shot, and you may defy those odds and emerge a winner. I wasn't sure if this was the case here, but I was ready to step up to the proverbial table and test my luck.

I put on a dress shirt and pants and prepared to take the few blocks' drive to the house that belonged to David Duplaine.

Ten

It had just got dark, and raindrops dripped off the hedges. I drove up to the gates of David's estate and rang the buzzer, suddenly self-conscious of my old jalopy of a car.

"Yes?" A man's voice that sounded slightly British traveled through the intercom.

"It's Thomas Cleary. I'm house-sitting for Lily Goldman, and she suggested I come by if I need anything."

The gates opened in a slow "come in if you dare" manner. As I drove through the gates up the serpentine gravel driveway, I thought about the fact that I was betraying David Duplaine, which in Los Angeles was the equivalent of double-crossing a mobster. Eventually you were going to die; it was just a matter of when and how.

I passed the sunken tennis court. The lights were off, and the gates around it were so ivy-drenched the common observer wouldn't have known it was there. There was something furtive about the estate. At Emma and George's you got the sense there was always a breeze of people rolling through—musicians and executives, actors and general wannabes—day after night, carousing with expensive liquor in hand and the latest in designer substances under tongue. David's estate, on the other hand, was still and quiet. It felt like an architectural trophy created for one.

The valet approached as I pulled into the motor court. He opened my car door.

"Good evening, sir," he said.

"Good evening."

David's butler stood in the entryway. The valet didn't close the car door behind me as I walked to the front door.

"May I help you?" the butler asked, and now, on second hearing, the accent sounded foreign, but not British—maybe South African. I wasn't good at estimating age, but I guessed he was on the unfortunate side of seventy.

"I hope so. My name is Thomas Cleary. I'm a friend of Lily Goldman's. As I mentioned, I'm house-sitting for her, just down the street. I think I left her front-door key at my office," I said. Here I was lying again. "I thought you might have a spare. My guess is a locksmith would completely ruin the eighteenth-century hardware—and you know Lily."

"Miss Goldman did inform me you would be caring for the house, which is very kind of you, indeed. You're fortunate—we do have a spare. I'll go fetch it. Please wait here. Outside." The butler looked upward, toward something that I assumed was a video camera. I wondered if it was a warning.

He left the door ajar just enough for me to peek in. I wanted to push my way inside and race through the estate to find the girl. But instead, I stayed put.

A few seconds later, the butler returned with an oversize vintage key in hand.

"This should work," he said, noting I hadn't stepped over the threshold. I felt like Malcolm, Carole's dog, obediently waiting on the outside, looking in.

"Thank you," I said, wanting to steal a moment at the estate. "You know Lily," I repeated. "I can't imagine her arriving home to find a brand-new shiny lock on her front door."

"You're right—that would not be good. You're welcome, Mr. Cleary. Now, good night."

He closed the door gently, but just before he did I saw a flash of blond hair dart behind a modern sculpture in the foyer.

She was here. So she hadn't traveled to Europe with David. I didn't know what this meant, but I noted it. My heart fluttered and I ambled to my car, hoping she would call my name and stop me from leaving. Instead, the valet ushered me into my car and closed the door behind me, a little sharply.

I made my way around the bend. The house disappeared behind me, and I was worried it would fade into my past for good this time. The girl had come to life again. I didn't want to leave.

I was so lost in the thought of her that I almost saw the real her too late. I veered to the right and screeched my car to a stop, narrowly missing a tree.

I lowered my window and realized that my memories of her had been a lie; she was more beautiful than all of them put together.

"It's dark out," I said. "You jumped in front of a car going twenty miles an hour. You could have been hurt."

"At twenty miles per hour? You're grossly underestimating me. It's the car that would have sustained the damage," she said with a sly smile. "Now park in the street and use this key to get in the side door."

I did as she instructed, pulling into the edge of the bushes and opening a hidden ivy-covered gate. I found myself in a little patch of a garden with a small trickling fountain. She stood against one of the walls, with one foot propped perpendicular on it. She was wearing a long white Juliet-style nightgown. I was not exactly a ladies' man, but I had been with enough women to know that these weren't garments women wore to bed anymore.

"You took a long time to come back," she said. "Twenty-two days, in fact."

"I came back way before you told me to."

"You mean never?"

"Exactly."

She smiled shyly.

"From what I understand, rejection can be very enticing for a man," she said.

"Where did you learn that?" I asked.

"The movies, Davis and Garbo. They were always four steps ahead of the men who loved them."

"So was the whole thing a ploy?"

"No, not a ploy at all. I was honest. Being here is going to cause you grief later," she warned. "What are you trying to find out?"

"Nothing," I said candidly.

"Are you trying to discover something about me?"

She had Lily's ability to put people on the defensive.

"Believe it or not I wasn't trying to *find out* anything. I went to your house for a fund-raiser—the wrong house, it would turn out—and I saw you playing tennis."

"And now? Why are you back?"

"I wanted to see you again."

"I wanted to see you again, too."

The succulents dripped rain, and for some reason I suddenly felt as if I was setting myself a table of heartbreak. I pulled out a cigarette. It was a nervous habit. I never intended to light it.

"I don't think people are allowed to smoke here," she said.

"Got it," I said, dropping the cigarette on the wet sand of the garden floor and stomping it out as if I had actually got around to lighting it.

She leaned over, picked the cigarette out of the sand and examined it. The full moon reflected on the crown of her head. Her blond hair was uncombed and parted in a messy zigzag pattern. She was breathtaking.

"What's smoking like?" she asked.

"Do you want one?" I said, plucking the last one from the pack.

"I just said there's no smoking on the estate."

"Rules are meant to be broken," I said lightly.

"I never break rules," she said, though she had just sneaked me in.

Despite myself I smiled, as a reel of my past—what had happened at the *Journal*, going through Joel's coat and now this latest indiscretion—flipped through my head. "I didn't break rules for a long time, but once you start it's a slippery slope."

"Slippery slope? What's that?"

I paused, again wondering if she was kidding. The girl seemed astutely intelligent, yet she didn't understand basic terms like *slippery slope* and *astrology*. It seemed odd.

She waited, wide-eyed, for the definition.

"*Slippery slope* means a relatively small action can lead to a chain of related events culminating in some significant effect, much like a ball given a small push over the edge of a hill will roll all the way to the bottom, gaining velocity."

"That's a nice phrase," she said. "Slippery slope," she repeated.

Strategically placed spotlights illuminated the garden, and when she moved in front of one I could see the outline of her body through her filmy nightgown. She was curvy and woman-like, but her aura exuded innocence.

In the past twenty-two days I had convinced myself that I was wrong, that it was curiosity or my quest for a story that fanned those sparks that had been dead in me for so long. But now, here, I knew it was a primal attraction I hadn't felt since Willa—the sleepless nights with her, the sleepless nights without her.

She didn't appear to notice. Instead, she sat down on a moss-covered bench. I sat beside her, one inch away, and she scooched closer, so the sides of our thighs touched.

A car drove past, and the sounds of "Boots of Spanish Leather"—a melancholic Dylan tune about a guy whose girl leaves him to sail around Spain—floated in from its stereo.

"Bob Dylan," she said, smiling sorrowfully. "I feel when I listen to his songs that he knows me. Do you like music?" She looked at me with doelike eyes, and it felt as though my answer was the only one in the world that mattered.

"Yes. Do you?"

"Music's saved my life a million times," she said. "And there's not much else to do here. I'm bored a lot."

"I'm bored, too. At twenty-six I shouldn't be, right? That's supposed to happen later."

"Tell me," she said. "What could you possibly be bored of? If things out there are boring, too, that's not very encouraging."

I almost asked what she meant by "out there," but then didn't. I avoided answering the question. I studied the garden. It was covered in moss, but that didn't seem accidental. In fact, I imagined gardeners cultivating green moss to exact specifications in a greenhouse on the perimeter of the grounds, and then transporting it here and applying it carefully.

"Thomas? What's boring about the world?"

"I don't know," I said honestly. "It's not the world's fault. It's mine. I feel stagnant."

"Stagnancy and boredom are two different things. I would know, because at twenty I've experienced my fair share of both."

"So why are you bored?" I said, thinking of wealth, something that I had always assumed bought the ultimate freedom and the most exotic adventures.

There was a long silence then, heavy as the air that was soaked from days of rain.

"Maybe this was a mistake," the girl eventually said, but it was the same way she had rebuked me at the tennis court—with uncertainty. "I should have let you leave."

"It wasn't a mistake." The winds shifted and I begged. "The night on the tennis court—there was something between us. I haven't been able to stop thinking of you. Was I imagining it?"

"I have to go. Hector will wonder where I am."

"Who's Hector?" I asked, suddenly afraid she had a boyfriend waiting for her inside.

"Our butler."

"I want to see you again," I said. "Even if you say no I'll come back. I'll keep coming back."

She paused, and what came next was the exact definition of a slippery slope.

"I overheard Hector say there's an award ceremony next Friday. How about seven o'clock?" she asked.

"Yes. Seven. Seven's great. Can you tell me your name?" I asked. "So I know it for next Friday at seven?"

"Matilda," she said, as she unlocked the garden door. "But that's off-the-record."

I stepped into the street, hesitating because I wanted one last second of her. And then, a moment later, just as quickly as she had appeared in front of my headlights, Matilda closed the door behind her and was gone.

Eleven

Lily returned.

We stood in the foyer, and I handed her the keys to the estate as she told me about her trip. The Vineyard house was coming along "extraordinarily well" and would be ready in time for summer. Her step seemed lighter. She had found the perfect fabric for the dining room chairs and scoured the world to locate an antique fireplace in France that was being loaded on a cargo ship as we spoke.

I was almost out the door, dreading my drive back to my decrepit apartment, when Lily said:

"I am so terribly rude. All I've done is talk about my silly little summer house, which is so insignificant in the grander scheme of things—or any scheme of things for that matter. Did you have a nice week, heart?"

"I did. As you can tell, your winter house is very much in one piece."

"Oh, I knew it would be. You seem like the type to take care of things," Lily said. "I hope there was a little respite from that god-awful rain. Did you get a lot of writing done—for the paper?"

"Yes," I said honestly, thinking of the article on George's pop star, an article that had been very well-received. "And I took a dip in your pool."

"Oh dear. I'm terribly embarrassed. It's so neglected. Was it in a terrible state? I can't bear to get rid of that jewel of a hornet's nest, but it's made for a dangerous mess up there I'm afraid."

"It was lovely," I said, stealing a word from Lily's vocabulary. "All of it."

I paused then, because on the proverbial tip of my tongue was the question I had been wanting to ask for weeks now: Who was the girl on David's estate?

But then I thought of the clandestine nature of things, of the meeting in the purgatory garden. She seemed a secret I was meant to keep.

"Good night, Lily," I finally said, awkwardly. "Thank you again for the nice stay."

I got into my car and before driving down the long cobblestone driveway, I looked up at the guest bedroom window. Through the leaded glass I saw the flame of the jasmine candle I had left burning on the writing desk. A second later the flame fluttered, as if someone had blown it. Then it went dark.

The following Friday evening, I drove down Sunset and parked a few blocks away from David's estate. I left my car and walked toward the Blooms' property, choosing a spot to wait just outside the sweep of the security cameras.

I couldn't see much of the Blooms' house from here, but I caught a glimpse of the red-clay tile roof, the turreted breakfast room, the highest reaches of the old trees on its perimeter. It was October, and Emma had illuminated the wild foliage and tall hedges with orange lights. Eight elaborately carved jack-o'-lanterns guarded the front gates.

Six thirty, six fifty, seven o'clock sharp. Just when I thought David was going to be late for the event, I heard the slow creak of the gate and saw a sedan drive through. Once the car had safely disappeared around one corner and then another, I walked to the garden door, savoring the anticipation.

When I entered, Matilda was sitting on the stone bench. Her attire was not appropriate for the plans I had made—dinner at a somewhat-nice restaurant and a movie—and I found myself briefly panicked and recalculating. She wore a pink and demure dress that was blousy to cover her curves and cinched narrowly at the waist. Her patent leather high heels elevated her to well over six feet tall. Teardrop diamond earrings weighted her tiny earlobes, and her hair was set in tight curls. Her dewy makeup appeared professionally applied.

The effect was breathtaking, particularly in the glowing light of the garden, but she appeared dressed for a coronation or cotillion, not for a first date.

Was this a date? She was an impossible read, but for the first time, I thought maybe she really liked me.

"Hi," I finally said, all breath. "You look pretty."

"Thank you," she responded formally, tilting her head down to the left and blushing. "I got this dress a year ago and I've been dying for an occasion to wear it. I decided this was as good as any. Does it look okay?"

"*Okay* is one way of putting it."

We both smiled coyly.

"Well, should we go?" I asked.

"Go?"

"I made a reservation. I hope you like Italian."

"I love Italian. It's my favorite. The chef makes an incredible lasagna—with extra cheese and Italian sausage sent from Italy," Matilda said. "But as for restaurants, you see, my life isn't like that. I was thinking we could do something here—at the house. If that's okay?" She added the last part with insecurity.

I had planned the evening fastidiously. I had chosen an Italian restaurant so hot I had to call in a favor to get the coveted seven-thirty reservation, and then I had procured prerelease tickets to a movie recommended by the *Times* film reviewer—a movie that wasn't even in theaters yet, so our viewing was on a studio lot. I'd been looking forward to the date all week.

Matilda sensed my hesitation.

"That's okay for you, right?" Matilda asked. "That we do something here?"

I got the sense there was no changing her mind, that there was no alternative.

"Sure, why not?"

"Phew. Good. Travel along the outskirts of the grounds," she said quietly but quickly, so I wouldn't change my mind. "You'll see a basement door in the back of the house. It will lead you to a tunnel. Wait inside until I tell you to come out. Go quickly and look down so the cameras don't see you. I'm going to distract Hector."

She then left the garden swiftly, and I wondered, for the thousandth time, what this girl was hiding or, conversely, what was she hiding from. I had known she wanted our relationship to remain a secret, but until that moment I hadn't realized exactly how secretive she wanted it to be.

She wobbled up the lawn in her high heels. She got stuck in the grass several times and eventually took her shoes off and walked barefoot. I watched her until she was as tiny as an ant.

Satisfied that enough time had elapsed, I followed her path up the lawn and around the back.

There were two subterranean bronze doors. Matilda had forgotten to tell me which one I was to open—north or south. I tried the northern one first, but it was securely locked. The second door opened with a strong tug, and below me was a narrow stairway.

I made my way down the stairs and found myself in a tight crawl space, which must have been the tunnel to which Matilda was referring. I thought of our initial plan for the evening and I wondered how I had ended up here, on my hands and knees.

Nevertheless, I crawled onward until I reached the back side of what appeared to be an arrangement of bowling pins. Crouched down, I waited there as instructed.

I heard the door open and close and two sets of footsteps.

"Hector, can you please prepare the bowling alley?" I heard Matilda say.

"Of course, Miss Duplaine."

Miss Duplaine. By this point I certainly had figured out she lived here, but hearing her last name confirmed that she was David's daughter—or at least a relative. It was a solid clue, except for the fact that as far as my research was concerned, such a girl didn't exist.

Hector came dangerously close to me when he realized one of the pins was positioned a bit to the left of its proper spot. I hugged my knees closer, shrinking myself. Once the pins were set with exactitude, he called to Matilda.

"The pins are ready," he said.

"Thank you," Matilda replied with trained politeness.

"Would you like me to keep score?" Hector asked.

"No, thank you. I'm going to spend some time by myself this evening."

"Very well. Would you like some music?" Hector hesitated.

"Yes." There was a pause. "I think Air Supply would be nice. Do you?"

"I think that's an excellent choice," Hector said reassuringly.

I heard the beginnings of "Making Love Out of Nothing At All."

"Are you going to bowl in that fine attire?" I heard Hector ask. My heart sank. He sounded suspicious.

"Yes," Matilda said. "It's getting late, and I'm far too lazy to change."

"If that's what you prefer," Hector said, and then a door closed, heavy like a vault.

There was a moment of silence. I wondered if she was as nervous as I was.

"Thomas?" Matilda asked. "Are you in there?"

I clumsily crawled down the alley, slipping on the wax. Matilda laughed her bold and idiosyncratic laugh, and I would always remember it as the first time I ever saw her really happy.

I would grow to love the musty wooden smell of the bowling alley, the clankety-clank of the balls as they crashed against pins, the four seconds of suspense as a well-thrown ball awaited its destiny. For now, though, I was struck by its quietness.

"I don't have any bowling shoes for you," Matilda said, as she put on hers.

"No worries. I can bowl in my socks."

"Good. I hope you like bowling."

"Love it," I said, which was a stretch of the truth.

While Matilda tied her shoelaces, I looked around. A single bowling ball sat by itself on a long rack and the scorecard for this evening's game had the penciled initials *MD*. A large refrigerator with a glass door held tin cans of Dole pineapple juice and single-serving bottles of Arrowhead water.

"I hope you can fit your fingers in the ball," Matilda said, passing it to me. It was bright and shiny as if it had been waxed that afternoon. "It was custom-made for me."

Matilda placed her hand and mine palm to palm, so the tips of our fingers touched.

"Oh no, it's quite possible your fingers won't fit." She handed me the ball carefully. "Try it."

My fingers didn't fit—but I could jam my fingertips in enough to hold it.

"A little tight, but definitely workable," I said.

"Are you sure?" Matilda asked.

"Yes," I said. "Positive."

"Okay, then. How about the temperature in here? Is it okay for you? I have it at seventy-two."

"It's all perfect."

Matilda picked up a stubby yellow pencil, the type golfers keep in their carts. A chalkboard on the wall featured the top-scoring games: Miss Duplaine 231, Miss Duplaine 229, Miss Duplaine 214.

"I think you're going to beat me. The last time I bowled was when I was sixteen and I bowled about an eighty," I said.

Matilda laughed. "What are your initials, so I can add you to the game?"

"*TC,*" I said.

"What's your last name?"

"Cleary."

"That's a good last name," Matilda said. "It means you can see things exactly as they are. Go first."

"Are you sure? Maybe you should bowl a warm-up game? I'll watch."

"No, you're my guest—my first guest ever, in fact—so you go first. I insist—absolutely and completely insist. I can bowl anytime I want."

I lined up and tossed the ball down the right side, thinking it was odd I was her first guest ever. If I had an alley like this I would have had friends over all the time. The ball skimmed the gutter before hooking left at the last second, leaving only one pin. It was a beginner's-luck shot.

"That's excellent! You're well positioned for a spare." Matilda wrote the number 9 beside my initials on the scorecard.

"I wouldn't consider 'well positioned' to be the correct term," I said as, sure enough, I tossed the ball into the gutter.

"Oh no," she said in a deflated manner. "I know you'll get it next time."

"Your turn," I said.

Matilda rotated her dress slightly, so the waist was properly set. She placed a curl behind her ear, and she took a deep breath. And then, with one deft and uninterrupted movement, she tossed a hook that swayed theatrically before knocking down all the pins.

Matilda returned to her seat and wrote an X in the box beside the initials *MD*. "That was pure luck," she said modestly.

We bowled three games, and on the third I managed to break a hundred. Meanwhile, Matilda hooked and sliced her way into the two-hundred range.

After the third game, Matilda and I sat down and ate pretzels and drank pineapple juice. I had been disappointed to abandon the more glamorous evening I had planned, but now I didn't want to be anywhere but trapped in that turn-of-the-century basement. The rest of the world suddenly seemed ordinary compared with the extraordinary world that was Matilda Duplaine's. She was unlike any girl I had ever met.

"Thomas?" Matilda asked. Pretzel bits were stuck to her glossy lips, but she didn't pick them off. Maybe she didn't know or didn't realize that it was something to be self-conscious of. "What are real bowling alleys like?"

"You've never been to one?" I asked, surprised.

Matilda shook her head.

"They're automated. Computers score for you so there's no cheating, and there are big monitors that show funny animated cartoons when you get a strike or spare or gutter ball. They're noisy and crowded. Sometimes you have to wait an hour just to get a lane. They're different than this, but not necessarily better. We can go whenever you want."

It was that time in a relationship when all you wanted was the next time. You wanted the event to come in a hurry, and you imagined it would be so dazzling it would glow in the dark. The world was full of possibility.

I looked over at Matilda. I wondered if she was imagining bowling alleys bustling with leagues and birthday parties, where scorecards were covered with initials and where there were many high scorers, not just her.

"Why are you keeping me a secret?" I whispered so Matilda would have to come closer. When she didn't answer, I continued, "Am I not supposed to be here?"

"I don't know," she said.

"Would you get in trouble if they knew?"

"Probably, but so would you, I suspect."

My stomach felt hard as lead.

"What's the worst that could happen? They'd ground you?" I asked sarcastically, not wanting to think of what could happen to me.

"I think I've been grounded for a while," she said enigmatically.

"What I'm asking is 'Can we do this again?'"

"I would do it all over again tonight if I could."

I think it was the nicest thing anyone had ever said to me.

"Me, too," I said. "Do you have plans for the weekend? Should I call you tomorrow?"

"I don't use the phone."

"You're kidding. What do you mean you don't use the phone?"

"I have no friends," she said candidly. "Except for you. And, well, my tennis coach and Hector—if you could call them my friends but they're much older than I."

It was an odd admission. This girl was a maze; she grew more complicated the more I tried to navigate her.

"I overheard Hector say that everyone's going to be away next Friday. Can we get together then? Let's say eight o'clock?" Matilda said.

"Next Friday seems awfully far away."

"Oh, I know. Too far. What will you do in between Fridays?" Matilda asked.

"Work, I guess," I said, already envisioning how I would stuff the hours full so they would go quickly. "How about you?"

"Tennis, bowling, school and perhaps play a few rounds of golf."

Golf was the first pastime Matilda had mentioned that required her to be off the estate. I perked up.

"Where do you play golf?" I asked.

"Why, here of course."

Just then the door to the basement opened and Hector shouted down the stairs, "Miss Duplaine?"

Matilda put her index finger over my lips, to quiet us. It was surprisingly sensual.

"Yes, Hector?"

"I think you should prepare for bed."

"I'll be right there," Matilda called to him.

The door closed. Matilda waited a moment until she seemed certain that Hector was out of earshot.

"So," she said then.

"So."

"I guess this is the end." She looked at me with eyes that said she hoped it wasn't.

It was that pause at the end of the evening when you savor every morsel of time, every crumb of it. I didn't want to leave, so I made a bold move. I leaned closer to Matilda, touching my lips gently in that place where her face met her ear. Her shoulder blades tightened together and the wisps of blond hair on her arms stood straight up. It wasn't necessarily a kiss, but I would remember it as our first. When leaving became inevitable, I escaped through the tunnel from where I had entered and ran through the night, the only tangible memory of the evening the scorecard in my hand.

Twelve

Days between seeing Matilda stretched out like taffy at a fair, and the next Friday seemed to arrive months later.

During my week without Matilda I occupied myself with work, which had been exploding as though my career was a bright, bursting fireworks show, with the grand finale still to come. I was beginning to learn how Los Angeles worked. There were only a small handful of movie studios, record labels and A-list talent worthy of the written word. As a reporter, once you were accepted into that small clique, you had exclusive access to anything and anyone worth writing about.

Matilda was vivid in my mind during our days apart, and I would wonder what she was doing at any given moment. At this point I was getting the strong impression she didn't leave her house a lot, which led to further questions. For example, why wasn't she in college? Why would such a sweet and affable girl have no friends? To that same point, who doesn't use the phone? Matilda wanted to keep me a secret, but why would David care if Matilda had a friend visiting her? Then there were the odd social skills. The fancy dress for bowling, the uncomfortable silences, the awkward word choices all seemed incongruous for a girl who had grown up the daughter of one of the most sophisticated men in the city. And, of paramount importance, there was the fact that according to birth records Matilda Duplaine didn't exist at all.

There were always more questions than answers.

I was at work, ready to head out to see Matilda, when my name was called twice across the pit, from two different angles. I opted for the front desk first.

A cardboard box sat beside the receptionist, and my first instinct was to look around to see if there were other boxes piled up. There weren't. The box wasn't particularly big, but it was so weighty it must have been filled with rocks. It was labeled with my name in calligraphy, and its return address was the Los Angeles County Museum of Art.

I opened the box to find what, oddly, appeared to be a miniature marble bench engraved with the words: Use What Is Dominant in a Culture to Change It Quickly.

It took me a moment to realize that this marble bench was actually an invitation in its most decadent form: it requested my attendance at a costume ball in honor of a new wing of the museum donated by David Duplaine. As I shuffled through parking instructions, maps and the invitation—all separated by vellum—I found a handwritten note that said: "Thomas, I do hope you can come. Lily."

I glanced around the office, double-checking to see if I was the only one who got the invitation. It appeared so, as a couple of other reporters were hunchbacked over their computers, tossing side glances my way to see what the commotion was about. I quickly shoved the invitation under the desk.

I then walked over to Rubenstein's office, where he spent ten minutes wrapping up a phone call. There was a general cast of smoke to the room, the lingering effect of a few cigars most likely smoked earlier in the day.

"I have good news and good news for you, Cleary," Rubenstein said, after he had hung up. He leaned back deep into his chair.

"Well, that's good news." I fidgeted a bit, now concerned I'd get to Matilda's a few minutes behind schedule. I had a feeling she didn't understand the concept of being late. And there was the no-phone thing, which made contacting her impossible.

"Which do you want first?" Rubenstein asked.

"How about the good news?"

"You're being made associate editor of the *Los Angeles Times*." I was so stunned I was initially rendered speechless.

"Wow, I don't know what to say," I eventually said when my vocabulary returned. As Rubenstein outlined a slight raise in my pay package and mentioned a new office was in the works, it registered: I had redeemed myself, finally, in Los Angeles.

"And the good news..." Rubenstein introduced the second good news with such theatrics I was expecting a drumroll. "I'm sending you to New York to cover the art auctions. It's a trip I usually take—my favorite of the year—but you've been working hard and they're auctioning off the art from Joel Goldman's estate. Lily called and suggested you were the ideal person to cover it, and I agree."

In fact, that last bit was not good news at all. First, it meant not seeing Matilda for an indeterminate amount of time. And second, such a high-profile art auction was bound to attract reporters from the *Journal*, and it was the ideal spot for Willa's social frolicking.

I forced a smile because I understood the size of the gift I was being given.

"Thank you," I said with as much earnestness as possible and a warm handshake to seal the deal. "I'm sure it'll be a fantastic trip."

"You're welcome." Rubenstein was already shifting his focus to his cell phone, moving on to his next story.

I lingered for a second longer.

"How well do you know Lily Goldman?" I asked with forced casualness, as if it was an afterthought.

"I've known Lily for almost thirty years," Rubenstein answered. "She was always a bit of a strange one. But I gave her a pass. Growing up as the daughter of Joel Goldman couldn't have been easy. That money didn't make up for it. Well, maybe it did."

Rubenstein laughed, because in this world money made up for almost anything.

"I'm sure not," I said, trying to continue the conversation, hoping it might yield something interesting. "Joel seemed like an interesting guy."

"Yeah, Joel and Lily had an odd relationship."

"It was contentious, you mean?"

"At times."

"And Lily's mother—what was she like?"

"Different than the other wives of prominent people in this town. She was prettier than a movie star—a prim Southern girl from Tennessee or Georgia, someplace like that," Rubenstein said dismissively, as if the places were all the same. "Cressida fell in love with Joel when he had nothing and everyone always believed it was out of rebelliousness. She was a wealthy debutante and he was a scrappy Jewish kid. Once Joel succeeded it was almost like she lost interest." Rubenstein chuckled. "The opposite of every other woman in this town who waits for that exact thing to happen."

"Lily never married?"

"Nope."

I was bolder than I had been just a few months earlier. Power did that, I had learned.

"Why? What happened?"

"Are you interviewing me, Thomas Cleary?"

"Off-the-record. Yes."

Rubenstein paused, as if filtering exactly what he should or shouldn't say.

"Lily was a carbon copy of Cressida. She could have had any man in the city and she chose their family's stable hand. He was a good-looking guy—about a decade younger than her and as different from her dad as a cat from a dog. They were supposed to get married, but it didn't happen. He ran off to someplace far away—Hawaii, I think it was—and never came back."

As eccentric and unusual as Lily was, this news had surprised me most of all. Refined Lily—Lily of the jewels, of the mansion, of the sedans with new leather—set to marry the guy who took care of her horses.

"You seem surprised," Rubenstein said, reading my mind. "Has LA jaded you so quickly that you think marriage for love is impossible?"

"I've always believed marriage for love is possible—it's generally others that don't share that opinion." I thought of Willa. "Who was he?" I asked. Suddenly this answer seemed integral to the mystery that had been puzzling me for weeks.

"I told you—a stable hand."

"Do you know his name?"

Rubenstein clucked his tongue. Maybe it was my imagination, but he had chilled suddenly and without explanation.

"It's Friday night. You must have somewhere to go," Rubenstein said.

I did have someplace to go—someplace important. Behind Rubenstein, through the glass, Los Angeles was lit for the night, and as Rubenstein allowed his attention to roam to his computer I was once again swept back to that foggy hungover morning after the Blooms' dinner party when I was last called into this very office.

How life had changed, I thought. There was nothing in front of me but hope.

Thirteen

That Friday evening the Santa Ana winds rolled in, and they remained for the rest of autumn. The devil winds, the hot Santa Anas were called, because they often left fires and earthquakes in their wake. The heat lingered so intensely it seemed to have a voice of its own.

Traffic was light, and I managed to arrive ten or so minutes ahead of schedule. I opened the unlocked door to the garden anyway, thinking it was possible Matilda would arrive early. She wasn't there. I considered turning around, but then decided to wait.

The garden was almost too quiet. The only sound was the trickle of water in the fountain and the occasional chirp of a bird. The roses were so pungent the smell had almost put me to sleep, when I saw someone coming toward me.

My heart sank when I realized that it wasn't Matilda, but Hector, her butler.

"You're early, aren't you? By eight or nine minutes? But who's counting?"

The entire rest of my life flashed before me in an instant. I imagined David Duplaine standing beside a large chalkboard, erasing my life as I had known it. My job was gone, I was blacklisted in Los Angeles, and worse, I had no Matilda.

I took a moment to wonder if it had been worth it, and then thought of that evening in the bowling alley.

It had been.

"You shouldn't build castles in sandboxes that don't belong to you, Mr. Cleary."

"Believe me, it wasn't intentional," I said, which was the truth. If I was going to fall in love again, this was certainly not the manner in which I wanted to do it. "It wasn't as if I was snooping around trying to find...this." I didn't even know what *this* was. "It started as an accident. Lily invited me to a party for the governor and I didn't realize it was at the Malibu house. I showed up here and—"

"And at some point you must have realized that you had the wrong place?"

"I rang the gate buzzer and no one answered. I was going to call Lily but I had no cell phone reception. I just wanted to use the phone."

The memory came rushing back: the beads of sweat, the lemonade, the smell of her.

"Which then led to you climbing up an oak tree and trespassing on private grounds?"

"What did Matilda tell you?"

"Nothing at first. I sensed her behavior was odd—she was giddy, distracted in her courses, which isn't like her. And then there was the dress she wore for bowling. I knew something was going on. I threatened to tell Mr. Duplaine, and that's when she confessed." Hector paused. "I've worked for this family a very long time—much longer than you've been alive, Mr. Cleary. And I'm putting my livelihood in jeopardy for this."

He paused. "We have rules here—very strict ones. And I'm breaking them because I want what's best for Miss Duplaine. But you must play by the rules. If you don't the consequences will be catastrophic for all of us—you, me and Miss Duplaine. Do you understand?"

I nodded.

"You may never—under any circumstances — tell anyone about her. You're only allowed on the estate when you're specifically invited by Miss Duplaine via me. You'll use this door—and this one only. No gate, no buzzer and certainly no oak tree—unless you're informed ahead of time that that's how you'll be entering."

It was the first time I recognized the gravitas of the situation, that we were doing something very surreptitious with potentially life-changing consequences.

"Thank you. I know this is a risk for you." It was an understatement.

"That's putting it gently."

"Does Matilda know?"

"Yes, I've already had this discussion with her and she understands."

A sense of relief rolled over me.

"Oh, and one more thing—Miss Duplaine is never permitted to leave here. Ever. Should I hear that you are considering taking Miss Duplaine off the property, you will be banned and you will never see her again. Do I make myself clear?"

I answered in the affirmative. Soon after, though, I realized the great oddity of what I had agreed to. My future with Matilda would be devoid of shared experiences outside these six acres. Was it even possible to date someone without taking her on a date? And why was Matilda never permitted to leave? Hector made it seem as if she was being held captive, and I wondered if I was signing myself up for the same fate.

Hector paused again, plucking a dead leaf of ivy off the wall. The gesture reminded me of something Lily would have done.

"Matilda has requested that I prepare the horseshoe pit. Come, follow me. She's waiting for you on the croquet lawn."

Matilda had dressed down this time. She wore a flowing dress, flat sandals and almost no makeup. Her long blond hair swirled in the strong Santa Ana winds, and she struggled to tame it. I longed to put it behind her ear and brush my hand against her cheekbone.

In Los Angeles it's extremely rare to own a piece of land where a walk is possible. David's six-acre property was one of the biggest in the city. It felt more like a park than a residence and featured walking paths that wove through the entire estate. Matilda pointed to specific activities as we passed each one.

"This is the horseshoe pit," she said, but not in a boastful manner. I thought of my apartment, how I could never show it to her. The horseshoes were polished brightly and shone as if they belonged in a window at Tiffany's. "Do you play horseshoes?"

"No, I don't think so."

"I'll teach you. It's a remarkably simple game to learn," Matilda said. "The pit's prepared so we can play later. Night horseshoes is magnificent."

Matilda pointed at a distant place to the northwest. "Now follow me, this way."

We continued onward, through walking paths filled with pea gravel. We passed a sculpture garden that featured the real-life version of the marble bench I had received with the invitation—it was a Jenny Holzer, Matilda explained, with slight officiousness—and then a small stream Matilda said she used for fishing. I wondered if David flew in salmon or tuna and dumped them in the stream late at night when Matilda had gone to bed.

"This is the golf course," Matilda said, pointing to her left at a single golf hole complete with a mini fairway, water hazard—even with turtles submerged for the night—sand trap and a flag that said Hole 1.

I started to correct her and point out that a golf course and golf hole were two very different things, but then I caught myself. By this point it was clear to me that Matilda's version of the world and mine were very different.

Our hands brushed together accidentally as we walked. I allowed it to happen, accidentally, again.

We walked past the pristine tennis court, and I was whisked back to that night we first met, in all its splendor. The oak tree canopied above it, as if protecting it from something.

"And this, of course, is the glorious spot where we met. Did you like me when you met me? That first minute?" she asked.

"Yes," I responded with candor.

"How about the first thirty seconds?" Matilda asked.

"Two seconds. Flat."

Matilda threw her head back and giggled. "Not one?"

"Don't press it." I paused, because in recent years I had been afraid of asking questions I didn't want the answers to. "What about you?" I asked. "Did you like me, too?"

"I didn't realize it at the time, as this was the first time something like this has happened to me, but I did—like you, that is." Matilda bit her lip in contemplation. "When you like someone, does it mean you think of them long after they've gone? Like they've left a bit of themselves behind that stays with you even though they're not there anymore?"

"Yes," I said, thinking of how Matilda never strayed far from my thoughts, even in all those days we were forced to spend apart.

We ended our tour at the outskirts of the property, a densely forested part where ficus and oaks sheltered a large octagonal swimming pool with two diving boards at different heights. The bright moon reflected on the pool, making it look like ice.

Matilda looked at me seriously, in the eyes. "The evening we first met—I felt you near me even though you were gone. I could smell you, hear you breathing. I found every distraction not to sleep because not sleeping meant that I could think of you."

I wasn't sure when I fell in love with her. I would like to say that it was the moment we met, but I knew for sure, at this moment, that I loved her.

"I thought we'd take a swim before tossing horseshoes," Matilda said, bringing me back to the present. "If that's okay with you, then I'll be right back. I need to change into my bathing suit."

Before I could explain I hadn't brought swim trunks, Matilda had disappeared into a pool house. It was a smaller version of the main house, a neoclassical structure with sturdy columns.

Matilda emerged a few minutes later in a silver one-piece swimming suit with rosettes at the top. She looked like a pinup girl who had stepped out of a '50s *Vogue* magazine. It was the most of her I had seen, and I suddenly felt as if I had to look away, to somewhere less dangerous.

"Do you like my new bathing suit?" she asked. "I got it when the winds changed."

"It's gorgeous," I said. "Very fashiony."

"Fashiony? Is that a word I should know?" Matilda asked curiously.

"Technically it's not a word."

"Oh, then I need not memorize it. What is it like being a journalist?" Matilda asked.

"It involves living in everyone else's life but your own," I said. "Which isn't always a bad thing," I added.

"Not at all. I would love to step into someone else's life." Matilda paused, in contemplation. "Like Audrey Hepburn in *Sabrina*—when she goes to France to cooking school and comes back not only knowing how to cook but a totally new person. I wish I could reinvent myself sometimes. Did you always want to be a journalist?" she asked.

"I did. What do you want to do when you grow up?" I asked. "'Grow up' sounds silly, right? We're grown-up now."

"Learn Italian, maybe. It's such a pretty language. I just saw Fellini's *8 ½* yesterday evening," Matilda said. "'Could you walk out on everything and start all over again? Could you choose one single thing and be faithful to it? Could you make it the one thing that gives your life meaning…just because you believe in it? Could you do that?' That was from the movie. It's beautiful in English, but it shines like gold in Italian."

Matilda paused and caught her breath. "I left a pair of Daddy's bathing trunks for you in the pool house."

I walked over to the pool pavilion, where David's brightly flowered bathing trunks rested on a chair upholstered in green-and-white-striped linen. I had sneaked onto David's estate, stumbled upon his biggest secret and now was falling heavily in love with his daughter. But somehow wearing his bathing trunks seemed more wrong than all of it. I reached over to pick them up, but didn't.

"Come on," Matilda shouted from the pool area. "The water's eighty-seven degrees. My perfect temperature."

A strange thought drifted into my mind. Keeping that huge pool at eighty-seven degrees probably cost more than all of my monthly expenses. I grew up in a paycheck-to-paycheck family, and I appreciated what little we had because I knew it didn't come easily. So the world of Matilda Duplaine was a foreign one to me. I would never have the means to support her lavish lifestyle. In fact, no one would. I imagined a time in the future when Matilda and I would live in that pool house with our children because we couldn't afford to live anywhere else she'd be happy with. It scared me.

I glanced at David's trunks for another second before abandoning the idea of them completely.

I walked out to the pool area, fully dressed. Matilda stood on the high dive, peering down at me.

"Dive in," I called out.

She did as told, as if she was waiting for my "ready, set, go." Her highly arched swan dive left a tiny ripple of a splash in its wake. She disappeared for what seemed like minutes, and when she resurfaced her face was dewy and shiny.

"The water's wonderful, Thomas. Get changed, come in."

I stripped down to my navy blue boxers. My dive off the low board was much less eloquent than Matilda's high dive.

I surfaced and swam in Matilda's direction. She giggled, and her eyes were wet, creating the illusion of tears. I moved closer to her so my right leg brushed her left.

She pulled her leg back, as if she was trying to figure out what to do with it. Soon I felt her knee on mine again, as if she had decided touching knees was all right.

"Isn't the water perfect?" she asked, smiling. "It's ozone, so it doesn't have that terrible chemical chlorine in it."

"More than perfect," I said, grinning at her quirkiness.

I looked around at the vast estate. I understood that Matilda's life wasn't normal. But before diving into her strange life headfirst, I needed to know why she spent so much time here, why she appeared to be hidden from the world, why she had been hiding me.

"Matilda," I began. "I don't understand it. No one knows about you. No one's ever seen you. Your father's one of the most photographed men in the city, but you've never been in a single photo with him. According to the world, you don't exist. I need to know what's going on."

She didn't say anything for a minute. I followed her eyes downward, toward an old mosaic on the pool's floor. It was a star, but the water's ripples distorted it.

Finally, she said, "You're putting me in a bad position. I have two choices. Lie or tell the truth to a reporter."

"I wouldn't betray you, you know that."

Matilda swam to the edge of the pool, leaning back on the blue and pink tiles that were most likely imported from an eighteenth-century bathhouse in Europe or something of the sort. She drew figure eights with her index finger. Its pink-colored nail matched the tiles and I wondered if she had coordinated it. I wouldn't have been surprised if she had.

"I've never left the estate," she said.

I had probably known—of course, I had known. But when she said it I still couldn't believe it. It didn't sink in then; it never really would.

"Well, actually, my dad tells me I've always been here, but it can't be true. I can't remember much about when I was younger, but occasionally I will dream of a place so specific, so exact, that it must exist in the real world and I must have been there. I dream of the ocean, wide and gray during a storm. And I dream of salty air, of a woman—a woman who must have been my mother. But now she's as filmy as a ghost. I can't remember her hair, her eyes, her laugh, a single feature about her."

"Do you know who she is?" I asked.

"No. Eventually I stopped asking my dad. My father says that if someone doesn't want you, you shouldn't want them." She looked at the water sadly. "I don't want you to think less of me, Thomas. And I definitely don't want you to think less of my father. You see, it was a terrible thing that grew bigger than it was meant to be." She paused, to catch her breath. "At first my dad just kept me at home because my mother wanted me to be a secret. She hadn't thought of the ramifications of it—of all that it would entail. When I was little I would beg to leave. But then by the time I was ten or eleven I decided I didn't want to leave anymore, either. It became too scary, too unknown."

"So your father keeps you here? Captive?"

"You mustn't think that. It's not his fault at all and, well, I don't press it because I'm afraid the real world holds no appeal for me."

"You're happy here? Not experiencing any part of the world?"

"I have everything I need here. The best teachers, a movie theater, a tennis court and a yard bigger than most parks. The only part of the world I haven't experienced is love, but now I've met you."

The future suddenly turned eerie, too dark to really contemplate. In the short time I had known her I had fallen in love with

Matilda Duplaine, and I would have sacrificed almost anything for her. But there was no possibility of a future without freedom.

"Matilda, you have to leave. You know that. Even if your father prohibits it, he has no right to keep you here, in captivity, as a prisoner."

"It's easy for you to say, because you've had twenty-six years of learning that I haven't had. I've never met a single person who doesn't work for my father except for you."

It was a glorious night; the wind blew strong and warm, and it was beautiful here. David had made certain Matilda had every creature comfort. But as majestic as it was, it paled in comparison to the real world.

"I want to take you away," I said before realizing what that really meant. I recalled the haunting conversation I'd had with Hector earlier that night.

"I don't know if I want to go anymore."

"You would love the world, Matilda," I said quietly. "You'd love the taste of snow on your tongue, what it feels like to get pushed underwater by a wave and for a split second feel like you may drown. There are so many different types of people, but no two look alike. Some will scare the heck out of you. Some will be so awe inspiring they'll make you believe in God. There are museums where you can see whole dinosaurs and prehistoric animals, and chapels in Italy where famous artists painted entire scenes on the ceilings." I paused, thinking of the enormity of it, what I took for granted. "I'm so jealous you're going to get to experience the world for the first time—to see everything new. I'll never remember what my first snowflake tasted like because I was too young. I can't remember what it was like to first lift off the ground in an airplane and fly through the clouds. But you have this all ahead of you."

"Maybe I'll never see those things."

"You will. I promise. Even if I have to kidnap you and take you away with me, you will."

The only sound then was of our breathing, which had synchronized. We swam for a few more minutes before retreating to the pool house and wrapping ourselves in fluffy, oversize towels that were warm, as if they'd just come out of the dryer.

I had stumbled upon a secret that was far bigger than just one girl; I was now suspecting it was a story vast and far-reaching, one that was created by some of the most powerful people in the world. Being here was a risk, and I couldn't afford another misstep. I didn't know how Lily was involved, but I was most certainly sneaking behind her back by visiting her best friend's house surreptitiously. She had reignited my career. I had been on life support before her, and she and David had the power to pull the proverbial plug.

I looked at Matilda—the girl I was gambling my life for. A fire burned in the fireplace of the pool house, and as embers grew into flames that disintegrated into ash, we made small talk and sometimes sat in silence listening to the crackle of the fire. All the while, though, I couldn't help but sneak glances at David's floral bathing suit, still folded on the chair.

Fourteen

It was Hector who had called me on an otherwise dull Wednesday to inform me that he would be by that evening to pick me up, and that I should prepare a suitcase with enough provisions for a week.

Fortuitously, the Bel-Air group had disappeared, to Hawaii or Aspen, or Australia or Chicago. It might have been none of those places or all of them, for I cared about nothing but Matilda in that time. The world could have tipped on its axis or, for that matter, come to an end and I wouldn't have noticed.

As Hector drove through Bel-Air's grand pillars, I thought about the first time I had traveled that same journey. Like Lily's car, David's still smelled of the factory. I tried to garner clues through it, but there were none. There were no newspapers left on the seat, the radio was off and the seat compartment was vacant of things like sunglasses and quarters. Had I taken a microscope to the vehicle I would likely have found no DNA. Like his house, and his eyes, and his expressions, David's car was sterile. I had learned that was how things worked in their world. They gave away nothing for free.

I am not a delusional man—in fact, quite the opposite, as I am practical and tied firmly to earth, to a fault—but as we traveled through flower-lined streets, my mind played a trick and I was fooled, for just a moment, into believing that I was going home.

We drove past Emma and George's property. Halloween had come and gone. The jack-o'-lanterns weren't around anymore, the gates went unguarded by ghouls and now only video cameras kept vigilance. The orange lights in the trees had been replaced with yellow lights, but only at the highest branches. The lower branches were bare of leaves and color.

One turn and a few seconds later, we drove through the gates of David's estate.

Matilda stood at the front door, waving. It had only been a few days since we had last seen each other, but it had felt like a lifetime.

"Thomas," she said with bright enthusiasm. "You're here!"

She hugged me, then looked over to Hector, as if asking permission for a fait accompli. Hector nodded discreetly.

"Most of the staff is away this week on vacation, so we'll have a lot of time together, alone. We've prepared the reading room, so we could do work together," Matilda said. "If that's okay, of course. I have an amphibian biology exam in the morning and I am utterly confused between the larynx of the throat of the eastern newt and that of the salamander."

"And I can't imagine you'll be able to exist in the world without that knowledge," I said.

"I'll fumble through life—for the whole rest of it—if I don't figure it out. So, come, I'm hoping you like chocolate-chip cookies. They're warm, just out of the oven. I was persnickety on the timing of it all, and I asked them to include pecans in the recipe. I want to have everything—absolutely everything— exactly right for you."

Besides my evening in the bowling alley, it was the first time I was privy to the inside of the estate. The house smelled of dark chocolate, exotic spices and nuts. We passed the foyer, then walked through an intimate parlor, a waiting room. My knowledge of art was limited, but I knew enough to know who Jasper Johns was. Two of his paintings hung in the parlor.

When one thinks of the word *mansion*, particularly in Los Angeles, one imagines double staircases, marble and gold. In fact, the estate's decor was a study in richness. The luxury of the house was in the materials—the stain of the woods, the thread count of the fabrics, the softness of the lighting, the veiny leaves of the plants. And, of course, the art. I felt as if I had crawled into the pages of a book on seminal twentieth-century art, and I was granted permission to sleep in its pages and touch whatever I wanted, leaving fingerprints behind—fingerprints that would be gently dusted off by someone other than me.

The reading room was cozy, with paneled walls and a gentle fire beneath its mantel. The flames snapped like fingers, and I kept thinking they were trying to tell me something or jolt me back to reality, though I wasn't certain what reality was anymore.

There were three wooden tables, each with lamps to illuminate them, and Matilda had situated herself at one. A bottle of water, some sharpened pencils and two chocolate-chip cookies meant for me sat on another. I looked over at Matilda's table, where a few remnants of some coconut cookies sat on a plate. Matilda, who was consummately polite, mustn't have learned the etiquette of waiting for others to eat yet, since there hadn't been any "others" in her life until now.

She leaned over on my desk and cupped her chin in her long fingers. Matilda's cherubic face made her seem youthful and soft.

"I'm so very happy you're here," Matilda declared. "It's going to be a wonderful week."

It was not only a wonderful week, as Matilda had predicted, it was blissful. Everything was taken care of for us: an entire suite on the servants' wing of the house was made up for me, and I went the whole time without going to my own apartment. My nine iron was buffed daily, my tennis rackets restrung and a bowling ball had been provided for me. There were tennis, golf, tea and scones in the morning, movies and horseshoes until late in the night and midnight swims.

It was during those days that I began to piece Matilda together, little by little. Her life was very different from that of other girls. Matilda's contact with the outside world was limited. Had she had a phone, the address book would have been devoid of contacts. Matilda had no friends, which made her impervious to things like peer pressure, social standing and even knowing her place in the world. Matilda spent hours reading through fashion magazines, but she had never been to a boutique. Instead, she would put Post-it notes on the clothes she wanted, and they would be sent to her. What Matilda wanted, Matilda got—be it tennis rackets, golf clubs, custom ribbons for her hair, or the latest in shoes, handbags and eye shadows.

Matilda's schedule was rote and simple. Every morning, she would traipse across the lawn to the large auditorium-like classroom on the back of the property. Courses were taught by former Ivy League professors who were handsomely remunerated and tied to strict confidentiality agreements. Whether it was due to her extra time, DNA or brilliant professors, Matilda was the most book-smart person I would ever meet. She had already mastered fluency in French, Spanish and German and was now studying Mandarin; she was enrolled in abstract mathematical theory because she had already conquered concrete math. She had read Chaucer, Faulkner and Dostoevsky years earlier.

After school Matilda partook in her limited scope of activities. She played tennis for three hours a day with her tennis coach, who had taught her how to play at the age of four and whom Matilda spoke about adoringly. Besides Hector, Matilda's tennis instructor was her only friend. After lessons they would sip lemonade and eat pineapple and talk in the tennis pavilion, sometimes for hours at a time, about "everything—absolutely everything" according to Matilda. In the rare times her coach couldn't teach due to travel or another work commitment,

Matilda would practice serves on the court alone, hit with a ball machine and precisely follow a charted map for her practice. While Matilda preferred tennis, she also played golf, bowled, fished and tossed horseshoes in the pit. She played croquet on the vast lawn and violin in the conservatory.

Matilda was seasoned—a pro, in fact—at the estate's limited activities, but her social skills seemed stunted. She was brilliant, but when it came to common sense she was sometimes lacking. The same for niceties. I could say, "That dress brings out the green in your eyes," for example, and she would respond with a comment like "Thank you. Why are your sunglasses always full of dust?" Colloquialisms befuddled her, and in cases where a harmless lie was in order, she would choose the honest insult instead. It was as if her father had forgotten to hire her a tutor for social behavior.

In the evenings, when David was in town, he and Matilda would dine together in their formal dining room, at a table that could seat twenty. I had never seen them together, so I couldn't imagine what they spoke about. After all, David entertained tens of millions of people a year, and Matilda entertained only herself. After dinner, David would retreat to his library to work, and Matilda would be left alone. Matilda used television and the internet sparingly because, as she later told me, she didn't want to know what she was missing out on. So she spent her evenings watching old movies in a screening room. I was discovering that Matilda had adopted her unusual syntax and mannerisms from figures like Bette Davis and Audrey Hepburn—appropriate for yesteryear, but not for current times.

Around eight o'clock, Matilda would retreat to her bedroom suite. I wasn't allowed to visit Matilda's bedroom, but I imagined it as a dreary and sad place, because that was how Matilda described it. She would take a bath with extra bubbles in a claw-foot bathtub made of porcelain so it wouldn't chill. Next Matilda would close the door to her bedroom, turn off the lights and

turn on her music. Matilda's knowledge of music was encyclo-
pedic. She said that music had saved her life on multiple occasions, and the more I got to know Matilda the more I realized
this might not have been an exaggeration. She confessed to me
that in those late nights alone she would listen to music and
dream about the world. She had a finely tuned imagination, so
she was able to dream of the real world so vividly that for a moment or an hour she escaped the estate. Her fantasy life would
often replace her real one. She dreamed of gossiping in dorm
rooms with friends, of a first kiss. Other times she imagined
winning the French Open, hoisting a trophy over her head and
squinting at the flashbulbs of the international press. She imagined shoe shopping in a fancy boutique with her tennis coach,
playing eighteen holes of golf instead of one.

But more and more often, Matilda said, she dreamed of me.

Our last evening scurried in too quickly. David was due to
return the next morning, and my belongings had already been
packed, all evidence of our joyful week carefully removed by
Hector, who, I knew, was risking his job and his welfare allowing me there. My tennis racket had been messengered back to
Silver Lake, my footprints fastidiously swept from the court. In
the bowling alley, my ball was nowhere to be found. Matilda's
once again sat alone on the rack.

The Santa Ana winds had carried the stars in from the desert,
and Matilda and I lay on our backs on a plaid cashmere blanket in
the sculpture garden, where just days earlier she had introduced
me to artists like Richard Serra and John McCracken. Her cotton skirt fluttered gently in the languid breeze. It felt as if time
was moving in slow motion, as if it knew it was running out.

Matilda rolled over and moved closer to me. My shirt had
crept up a bit, exposing the row of chestnut hair that led down
from my belly button.

She looked at the hair curiously and then reached out to touch it, before reconsidering and placing the back of her head on it instead. Throughout the span of the week, she had touched nearly every part of me, in a nonsexual and exploratory way, the way one might examine a diagram in biology class. None of these gestures ever seemed to lead further, but I respected her pace lest I scare her away.

"Look," Matilda said, when she had turned her gaze to the sky. "That's Orion's Belt."

I followed her stare upward. Most of Orion was covered in the depth of the black night, but I could see the three stars that would have covered the tops of his pants, if a mythological god really did wear trousers.

"That's my favorite constellation," Matilda said. "Someday, when I die, and you're looking for me, you'll be able to see me in the middle star. The buckle. That's where I'll be hanging out."

"Don't say that. That's sad."

"It's the plain old truth. And someday, in the way distant future, if I die before you, you'll be happy I said it, because you'll know exactly where to find me. I'll be twinkling for you."

"I'll die before you anyways, because I'm older," I said.

"That's a broad assumption based upon the fact that we will both die of old age when, in fact, one of us may be struck with a terrible disease or a tragic event," Matilda said.

"I can't think of you gone, relegated to a star so far away we'd be hundreds of years apart," I said.

"Because I am very much here, lying on your stomach, on that patch of hair that leads to someplace I have never been."

I smiled. I wanted her to visit that place, but I knew it wasn't going to happen—not tonight, not in the near future. We had never even kissed because I hadn't known if it was appropriate.

I looked at the oak tree as a distraction. The top branches were covered in glittering yellow lights. Then I understood: Emma had decorated her trees to blend in with the star-covered sky.

"Thomas," Matilda said, "would you consider me pretty?"

"Of course. Haven't you noticed the way I look at you?"

"Hector says people are attracted to each other because they like each other's smell."

"Hector's simplifying things a bit," I said, thinking that it would all be so easy if love was only the result of one sense.

"What am I like, Thomas?" she asked. "I have no one to compare myself to. Am I shy or loud?"

In fact, that was a difficult question to answer. Sometimes Matilda seemed coy and demure, but other times bubbly and vivacious.

"Someplace in the middle I think," I replied. "But I'm not sure yet."

"Smart or dumb?"

"That one's easy," I said, smiling. "Brilliant, like your father."

"Tall or short?"

"Another easy one. I'd say about six inches taller than the norm," I said, glancing down, obviously, at Matilda's beautiful, coltish legs that were so long they stretched beyond the bottom edge of the blanket.

She giggled when she saw me looking at her.

"Compassionate or selfish?"

I didn't answer right away because I didn't know.

"Thomas?" she prodded, stroking my arm. "Which am I?"

"I haven't seen you around enough people to know. But my guess is compassionate. You've always been that way with me."

"And what about this boy I've fallen for? What is he like?" Matilda asked flirtatiously, but also curiously.

I looked toward the sky, finding my cheeks redden with embarrassment.

"I don't know," I said, focusing my gaze on a star. "Boring, I guess."

"Are you telling me I've fallen for a boring boy? I don't believe it. My taste is far better than that."

She wasn't letting me get off easily. She looked at me with anticipation.

"Well, like you, I'm taller than the norm. Is that enough?" I asked jokingly.

"Are you intense or laid-back?" Matilda asked.

"Intense—definitely intense."

"Are you an open book or a closed one?"

"Both. Sometimes I'm as easy to check out as a library book, other times I'm out of print."

Matilda laughed. "Athletic or clutzy?"

"Adonis." I thrust out my chest and smiled.

"I thought so. Persistent? Or do you give up easily?"

"Persistent—ridiculously persistent." I thought of my days at Harvard, of that almost maniacal ambition that had allowed me to escape my humble beginnings. "I grew up—well, I grew up different than you, and that's putting it mildly, but I was also a guy who always believed that where I *grew* up had nothing to do with where I would *end* up. And because of that I go into things with passion—maybe too much, but I think that's my biggest strength. And maybe my biggest weakness, too."

"Being passionate is never a weakness," Matilda declared. "The best things in the world come from passion."

"It can be a weakness too, though—passion." I thought of the many nights I burned for Willa, long after I was even a memory to her.

"I don't believe that." Matilda leaned closer to me, and she whispered into my ear, "This week was flawless. Thank you. Thank you for every minute of it. And I can't wait until Friday. I hear that Dad's having a costume party at the museum. Shall we arrange for a game of croquet and take-in? You can come at six because Dad's going to be leaving early."

"I'm sorry." I played with a wisp of Matilda's blond hair. "I have to go to the party. It's a work thing. I would much rather be here, with you."

Matilda's expression deflated.

"Are you taking a girl?" she asked.

"Of course not."

I thought of Matilda's bowling ball, by itself on the rack.

"Why? Has there ever been another guy? Is there someone who gets Thursdays?" I said to make light of a situation that had suddenly turned heavy.

It was quiet for a long moment.

"This isn't going to make any sense to you probably, and you're going to think I'm weird," Matilda began. "But sometimes, when I look down at the swimming pool at night from an upstairs window, I see a blonde girl treading water. She's alone, under a sky that looks way too big for her. She has no friends. I know something that she doesn't—I know that she'll be treading water in that same spot the next night, and the next after that. I look down at this girl, through old leaded glass that distorts her a little bit and cuts her off at the panes, and I think 'Who is that poor girl?' And then it all comes into focus, and I have the terrible realization that the girl is me."

Matilda rolled over, and she put her face so close to mine our noses touched. Her hands were crossed on my chest.

"There hasn't been anyone else," she said. "And because of you this is the first time that I've looked out my window at a girl who I wanted to be—a girl I didn't feel sorry for."

I thought of that bleak time in Manhattan, when I was a guy I felt sorry for, too. Just like Matilda, I had transcended that. We were more alike than either of us realized.

"I'm sorry about the party," I said, meaning it. "Why don't you pick a costume and I'll sneak out after—to see you?"

"Really?" Matilda's face was aglow with the stars and our newfound plan.

"Yes, we'll have our own costume party—here. Who needs the museum?"

"You're exactly right. Who needs the museum? We have all

this important art here. That's a wonderful idea. We can do it here—our own costume party. Oh, Thomas. You're absolutely perfect. I'll spend the whole week working with Hector to co-ordinate a costume—one that will take your breath away when you step in the door and see me in the garden."

I put my hand over Matilda's, caressing the little blue veins that swam just below the skin and squeezing the chunky black pearl-and-diamond ring that adorned her middle finger. Happiness washed over me. We were in a magical place between warm sky and cool grass, between a soft cashmere blanket and a glittering sky. There were so many stars they seemed to rain like confetti at a celebration, and I felt as if Matilda and I were its guests of honor.

Fifteen

Whether by serendipity or fate, I was publicly named associate editor of the *Los Angeles Times* the day David Duplaine's wing opened at the Los Angeles County Museum of Art.

I was both modest and self-aware enough to know that the announcement wasn't a big one, but it was still released to the Associated Press. David Duplaine and George Bloom were both quoted, and I couldn't help but think that Lily Goldman had been the one to call in the favors.

The Los Angeles County Museum of Art is a nondescript building at a busy intersection. But the new wing was an architectural wonder—all glass and modern. When I drove up I was conscious of my old car; it seemed like a tin can among the sea of gold. And when I walked through the pathway lit with lanterns, I was glad I was in costume, dressed as someone else. Despite the invitation, I felt like a party crasher.

Cocktails were first, and the hundreds of costumed guests milled about in the atrium with the art. I didn't know anyone—or at least anyone I recognized in costume—so I walked through the crowds alone, feigning interest in a painting or a sculpture, pretending it was the most fascinating piece in the world. There were two pieces of art I recalled seeing on the estate, and as I looked around I realized that, due to the odd circumstances, I was one of the only people who had ever been to David's house, one of the few who had seen his private collection.

They announced they were ready for us, and curtains opened and we were escorted into a spectacularly staged room. Every inch of it had been covered in flowers, crystal, china and expensive linen. And not only that, dozens of twelve-foot olive trees had been imported for the occasion, and lighted crystal globes hung from their branches. I felt as if I had been transported to the rolling vineyards of Tuscany.

Calligraphy numbers written on fine stock waited for us, and I picked up the one with my name. While others scurried about, referencing the numbers in their palms, hoping for prime placement, I went directly to the front of the room, to Table 1.

Our round eight-person table was set for seven, and I was the first there. I leaned against the back of a chair with both hands, marveling again at how expeditiously I had been swept into this glamorous world of privilege.

"Thomas, so glad you could make it," a voice said.

I turned around and found David standing behind me. He was dressed in an ancient Florentine costume.

"Leonardo da Vinci," he said, outstretching his hand.

"Emperor Nero," I responded, as I shook it.

I rubbed up against David's life all the time now, but I hadn't seen him since the dinner party at Carole's. He was shorter than me and skinnier, but he loomed taller and broader because his aura took up space.

"Gimlet?" he asked, and on cue a waiter showed up.

"Good memory."

"Always remember a man's drink."

"In Milwaukee we said you should always remember a wife's name."

"In my experience men are more faithful to drinks than to wives," David said.

I looked at David's drink. He sipped what looked like an Old-Fashioned. Reddish-bronze liquid coated a single cube of ice.

I was certain David didn't know I was seeing his daughter, but his presence scared me nevertheless. As I pushed my hands farther into the back of the chair, I felt the beginnings of sweat on my back. My costume must have weighed twenty pounds. I looked at the table, where an eighth person should have been. I longed for Matilda to be there. I imagined her dressing for the costume party—a party for only two.

"Congratulations on a well-deserved promotion," David said.

"Thank you, and thank you for the nice quote in the press release. Sorry, I should've said that earlier."

"My pleasure." David inhaled deeply and scanned the room, like a lion who had just fed.

Silence seemed conversational in its own right, and while David stood there quietly, passing a wave to a partygoer here and there, I studied him. His eyes were brown. His hair, what little of it he had, was very dark. His mannerisms were deliberate and in no way fanciful. Matilda must have resembled her mother. I wondered if David had loved her.

"Thomas, darling, you're here!"

I turned to find Lily dressed as Florence Nightingale. She kissed me warmly before straightening out my spine in my costume.

"I'm so happy you could come. Associate editor of the *Los Angeles Times*—how proud you must be." Lily's enthusiasm wasn't commensurate with the situation, particularly since I was standing beside a man who had just donated an art wing. She then turned her attention to David, placidly, and he responded with his slightly impish smile. I hadn't noticed it before, but Lily and David turned almost childish beside each other. "I'm so immensely proud of you, too," Lily said, rubbing David's impressive biceps. "I just wish that Dad could be here to see this. I guess our timing was off."

"I guess so," David responded, as if death was something that could be timed. My eyes followed David's hands as they rotated the clasp of Lily's diamond necklace ever so slightly so it rested exactly at the base of her neck. The diamonds refracted the light, tossing white sparkles on partygoers around us.

"What time are we leaving tomorrow, doll?" Lily asked David.

"Ten, give or take."

"Thomas, dear, Phil tells me that you're going to New York, as well?"

"Yes." I looked down, though I didn't know why. I needed to learn to be more like my counterparts and wear my successes with pride.

"Why, I hope you're not planning on traveling commercial. David, do tell Thomas there's room on the plane. Plenty of it, in fact."

"There's room on the plane, Thomas. Plenty of it, in fact," David said.

"That's okay. I already have a ticket I should use—"

"Knowing the *Times* you'll be in cargo or, best-case scenario, 26C," Lily interrupted. "It's decided, Thomas. You heard David. You'll be traveling to New York with us tomorrow on the plane."

Just then Emma and George approached—with flair. Emma was dressed as Holly Golightly, and to the common observer George appeared dressed as himself. Emma carried a long cigarette holder with a joint at its tip and she wore a black dress adorned with strands and strands of pearls. I heard a slight hiss and I noticed that the fur that draped on Emma's arm wasn't fur at all, but the leopard cat, apparently dressed as Holly's Cat. He looked bored, as if he'd rather be at home.

"Emma, doll, you look divine," said Lily. "And, George, I knew Truman well, and you are far better looking."

"Well I didn't know Nurse Nightingale, but I'm certain her beauty paled in comparison to yours," George said. "And, as for Capote, it was an easy costume. All I needed was a drink in hand."

Carole and Charles arrived next. Charles, dressed as a pretty true rendition of Sinatra, was overshadowed by his glamorous wife, who was dressed as a Vegas showgirl—all sequins, breasts and legs as long as a June day. The outfit in its blatant sexuality was out of character. Carole scanned the group and seemed most interested in the leopard cat, burying her hand in his neck folds. The animal purred under her touch.

Lily leaned in and kissed Carole on the side of her cheek, leaving a slight red lipstick mark. Lily looked twice, as if debating whether to rub it off, and then decided to leave it.

Emma looked over at Carole affectionately. "Hi, darling. Who knew you had it in you? If your day job doesn't work out there's always the Bellagio. Or strip clubs."

"I'll take that as a compliment," Carole said, smiling that same off-center grin that had graced the cover of the July *Vogue*.

"Good, because it was meant that way," Emma said. "Seduction is a woman's greatest power. Feminism had it all wrong. No man ever got off on a woman because she was a hard worker."

Emma laughed at her own joke, and then she spotted a flamboyant fashion designer in the distance and darted off in his direction. My eyes absently followed her as she was absorbed into conversation, and I thought of strategic socialization. The world of the Los Angeles rich was its own version of high school—a popularity contest with stakes like private planes and studio jobs.

By the time I looked back at the table, the group had dispersed to their own cocktail cliquery and I was left alone with David and Carole. I pretended to occupy myself with a gimlet that had arrived not a second too soon.

Out of the corner of my eye I noticed David looking at Carole. She looked straight ahead, but she glowed, like women do when they know they've caught a man's eye.

"The boys at the strip club only pay five dollars a picture,"

David joked under his breath. "Not the twenty million you're used to."

"The boys there are much less work, though," Carole said, still looking ahead, as if she was talking to an imaginary man in front of her. "Much easier to get off than studio heads."

"You'll have to do your own stunts," David responded with a glint in his eye.

"I'm surprisingly good at those," Carole said.

"Nothing surprising about that," David whispered under his breath.

Carole didn't respond; she just pursed her pillowy lips together and adjusted a bobby pin in her hair so a pin curl loosened around her full face.

I suddenly felt like an intruder in a private conversation I wasn't supposed to hear. I glanced around to see if anyone else had returned. No one had. Lily spoke with a talent agent; Emma had disappeared; George schmoozed with a country music star; and Charles, the man who had the greatest stake in the conversation, was across the room at the bar.

"You have lipstick on your cheek," David said, as his eyes followed the pin curl that now rested on Carole's sculpted cheekbone.

"Dear Lily, always trying to leave her mark." Carole presented her flawless cheek in David's direction. "Would you mind rubbing it off?"

David wet his right index finger with his tongue and then moved his finger to Carole's face, erasing the lipstick slowly, exactly. He cupped Carole's face with his left hand, letting it linger under her square jaw a moment too long.

They were having an affair. It was as clear as a winter night in the mountains.

I studied my drink, feeling the driving need to walk away. I scanned the crowd for a recognizable face, but there was none. I already had my drink, so a trip to the bar was unnecessary. I decided a cigarette was in order. I glanced around, choosing an escape route through a cluster of olive trees. As I walked past Lily, I heard:

"Thomas, dear, where are you going? I don't want you to miss the first course. You must be famished."

"Excuse me for a second. I think I see Arthur Shields over there." I pointed in the general direction of the bar and referred to the publisher of the *Times*, a man I didn't even know. "Work thing."

In fact, I walked outside to the garden. Abstract sculptures peppered the grass—the vague outline of a man, a few sticks I couldn't recognize as anything, blobs I think were a man and a woman lounging, a simple circle, a star and a bench with the etching Use What's in a Culture to Dominate It Quickly.

I sat on the bench and the cold marble sent a chill through my Nero costume. I lit a cigarette, which I was sure wasn't allowed in a public park in this city of good health, and then I leaned my elbows on my thighs and looked up. On the wall of the building I saw a piece of projection art two stories in height.

I Lie was all it said, in golden lights so bright and bold I was sure you could see it in New York.

The rest of the dinner progressed uneventfully, if you can call such a spectacle uneventful. Two major pop stars performed, and David gave a speech chronicling his passion for art, a passion that had begun in his early twenties, when he had combed flea markets for pieces of interest. Publicly, he only thanked two people: Lily Goldman and her father. But I knew there was another family member David should have mentioned: his daughter. I wondered if he thought of her when he was onstage.

I trudged through four courses methodically, fielding the very occasional question, but generally just observing the greatness around me and counting the minutes until I could slip out to see Matilda. Lily was in a better than usual mood, as she always seemed to revel in her friends' accomplishments. Charles remained quiet throughout the evening, even going so far as to sit on his hands through most of it, George tossed his wide game-show-host grin to partygoers, and Emma missed multiple courses to hobnob with a table of fashion designers.

As for David and Carole, I scolded myself for not seeing signs of their affair sooner. Tonight alone there were a multitude of clues: Carole's pupils lived in their lower corners, looking to David. To the outsider, David spent the evening basking in congratulations, but it was Carole's long fingers that captured his attention. He didn't touch them, but she kept them splayed on the table deliberately. I thought back to Emma's garden, to the shadows I now realized were inappropriately close. And I recalled the evening Charles adjusted Carole's earring and she had recoiled at his touch.

Los Angeles is, ironically, an early-to-bed city, and by ten o'clock the party began to disperse. Lily invited me to go with the group to a film director's house in Beverly Hills for an après-opening drink. I lied, insisting I needed to prepare for the trip to New York.

I went outside alone and gave the valet my ticket. My old, dirty car was parked in front, just between Lily's and David's sedans, which gleamed as if they had been washed for the occasion. Table 1 must have come with premier parking.

It had been the social event of the year—a million-dollar party. Sure, the invitation had been a kind one and, whether an illusion or reality, as I drove away it was nice to feel that I was starting to belong among some of the most celebrated people in the world. But while I traveled down Wilshire Boulevard, sad storefronts asleep for the night and empty intersections' stop-lights blinking red, I thought again that the imported olive trees, elaborate costumes, pop-star performances and world-class art all paled in comparison to Matilda. I wondered who she would be dressed as, for hers was the only costume that mattered.

★ ★ ★

I arrived at the garden door, and it was locked.

The circumstances were strange. Matilda and I definitely had a plan to meet in the garden in costume, and since her social life wasn't exactly bustling, she wouldn't have forgotten. I played back my last conversation with Matilda, wondering if I had done something wrong to be relegated to the street.

I had been specifically instructed by Hector never to enter through the main gate. But there had to be something wrong. I debated. I knew David wouldn't be home for hours, so I buzzed the gate. It opened.

The house was uncharacteristically dark. The only light came from a first-floor room with walls of glass.

Before I could get out of my car, Hector opened the front door. He exchanged glances with the valet. His look indicated that my car was not to be parked, but left to idle.

"We had an explicit agreement, Mr. Cleary. No front gate."

"I understand, but Matilda and I had a definitive plan to see each other tonight. I leave for New York tomorrow."

"I think Matilda would rather be alone this evening," Hector said. "It's best you leave, Mr. Cleary." He subtly glanced at the video cameras. Matilda had told me he turned them off when we were together, but he probably hadn't realized I would come barging in when the garden door was locked, so the cameras must have been on.

Hector was my only ally, so I was gambling on a losing bet by ignoring him. Nevertheless, I brushed past him and walked through the parlor, where the two Jasper Johns hung. One was a map of the United States, which was ironic since the woman of the house had only been to a pinprick of our vast country.

I walked down the hall, toward the lit glass room, and heard the sound of Debussy on a lone violin, which I assumed was Matilda. I had never heard her play before, and I was astonished at just how good she was. In fact, she would have been considered concert-level had she opted to perform for anyone besides Hector and her father.

I inched the door open. Matilda was sitting on an uncomfortable-looking wooden chair in the middle of an octagonal room. She held a violin delicately tucked in between her soft neck and athletic shoulder, and she was dressed in a white goddess-like gown that pooled on the floor. Wide gold cuffs covered her wrists, dangly earrings hung from her ears and an ornate headband haloed her sharply bobbed black wig. Her eyes were outlined in a smoldering, liquid black, and her lips were the color of blood.

She was dressed as Cleopatra.

Is there a moment in every relationship when it becomes life-threateningly dangerous? When you realize that your heart is so comfortably resting in someone else's hands that should they decide to drop it you would never fully recover? In the case of my relationship with Matilda Duplaine it was at this very moment.

I stood watching her, and then she became aware of my presence. She rested her bow on a stand.

"Why was the door locked?" I asked.

"You mustn't be here," Matilda said. "The cameras are on."

"I don't care about the cameras. I'm tired of sneaking around. Why were you keeping me out?" I repeated.

"Because I would prefer to be alone tonight. Didn't Hector tell you? I told him to turn you away."

I walked up and brushed Matilda's face with my fingertips and touched her red-stained lips, tracing their slightly imperfect shape. Her eyes were bloodshot and her makeup ran.

"Have you been crying?"

She didn't answer. I licked the top of my index finger, and I wiped away the teardrop-shaped spots of salt that had calcified on her cheeks.

"Matilda, what's the matter?"

Matilda turned and walked away, toward floor-to-ceiling

doors that opened to the vast grounds. The rolling hills were speckled with priceless sculptures illuminated by spotlights. The doors were open, and the air filtered through Matilda's long dress.

"I've spent all this time, all these hours, learning about the world. And I've fooled myself into thinking that it was enough, that there was no difference between being out there and reading about it in books. And for a while I was content with it. I made myself believe it was all the same. But when I met you, the world shifted on its axis—at first only a little bit, but now it's seismic. And I've been plagued by the fact that I don't know where you are when you aren't with me. It sounds silly or selfish or jealous, but tonight I was upset with you because you weren't here."

"It was a work thing, Matilda—" I began defensively.

"I try to imagine what your newsroom looks like or what restaurant you're in. If you're at a party I try to think of it vividly—the food they serve, the drinks at their bar, what the view is like. Is it a city view or a view of the ocean?" Matilda paused. "And tomorrow—tomorrow you'll go to New York, and when you're gone I'll watch *Annie Hall* alone in the screening room, or *Manhattan*, and I'll think that's where you are, in that movie. But it's not real, Thomas. And just this evening, when you were at a party with my father and I was dressed for it but not there, I realized there's a gap between us. It's small now. But I'm worried it will keep growing, keep getting bigger until it becomes a schism too big to cross."

I didn't respond, because her story was one I couldn't dispute. I had thought of it, too, and I was beginning to wonder how to sustain this odd relationship long-term. Matilda walked toward me and took my hands.

"I'm sorry I kept you away, that I locked the door. It wasn't right. But for the first time I'm worried—about us."

"Matilda—"

"We mustn't talk about it. Not now, not before your trip. How was the party?"

"Dull, without you there."

"You look like a king or an emperor," Matilda said.

"Nero. Emperor Nero."

"Ah, Nero. He was a corrupt man who fiddled while Rome went aflame. He was known for having captured Christians to burn them in his garden at night for a source of light," Matilda said. "He was so devastated over the death of his wife that he didn't cremate her. Instead he stuffed her body with spices so she would be embalmed. I hope someone loves me that much someday, that they will fill me with spices when I die because they can't bear to say farewell. I'm not worthy of anyone's love. Not like this. Not here."

"I love you here, and I would love you everywhere," I said. "Every corner of the globe—the top of the pyramids in Egypt, the oil fields in Saudi Arabia, the bistros in Paris, the snowy Himalayas, the fjords of Norway. There is nowhere I wouldn't love you."

"Imagine loving someone so much you love every strand of their hair. That's how much I love you," Matilda said.

There is nothing quite like having a girl tell you she loves you, and I was still reveling in the sweetness of it when Matilda put her hand beneath my jaw, tilting my face slightly. The movement was wobbly, unsure.

I had imagined this moment, every scenario. Would she lean to the left or the right? Would she close her eyes or leave them open? Would she put her hands on my face or wring them on her lap?

But what happened wasn't what I had imagined at all.

She was the one to kiss me, nervously, because it was something she had never done before—with me or with anyone else. At first she just brushed her lips on mine, and she was on the precipice of doing something more, but she didn't quite know what to do. I took over then, leaning into her and kissing her. She tasted of tears and toothpaste, salt and sweet.

So often in life you imagine a moment and it lets you down, but the first time I kissed Matilda Duplaine was bigger than all of my daydreams put together. It was a kiss that turned me inside out. I never wanted to let go of her.

"Did I do okay?" Matilda asked.

"Perfectly." I stroked Matilda's fake Cleopatra eyelashes and the sun freckles on her chest.

"That was wonderful." Matilda looked down and then up at me. "It felt so nice I don't know how I went without it for so long, and I want to do it again and again."

I leaned in and kissed her again, more passionately this time.

"Come away with me," I said, when I forced myself to pull away from her.

"I can't," Matilda said, as she put her fingertips on the side of my face. "There's so much to learn."

"I'll teach you. We'll go someplace just the two of us. Someplace far away."

"You'll get bored with me."

"Never. I want you to see everything that I see, to hear everything that I hear. And I want you to love me everywhere— not just here. I want to know that if you walked into the world and you met a million men you'd still come back to me."

I wanted to take her away right then, but it wasn't to be. So instead, we walked outside together, hand in hand, and looked at the rolling hills of sculptures. I thought again of the party, of the dual lives I suddenly and inexplicably found myself living, and I wondered if either of them were even real.

When the end of the night rolled in, Matilda and I kissed again, in the warm breeze of the sculpture garden. We held on as long as we could, knowing our minutes together were numbered.

The clock struck midnight, and I escaped out the garden

door. We had cut it close this time, for David was the type to skip out of parties early, not late. Sure enough, when I drove through Bel-Air's white pillars, David's sedan passed me on the narrow street.

The car was going too fast for those tight roads, as if there were a destination that needed to be reached expeditiously. The rear window was rolled down halfway, a set of eyes and bushy eyebrows peering over its glass. David Duplaine had his fingers on the pulse of all of Hollywood, and I wondered, not for the first time, if he had his fingers on mine, too.

Sixteen

Set deep in the San Fernando Valley, Van Nuys is a middle-class neighborhood of modest homes, hundred-degree temperatures in the summer and what appears to be an extraordinary amount of dust. For the upper class, the only reason to visit this part of town is the private airport.

I am a chronically early guy—a vice, I joke, because I've spent more time waiting in the car than working—and I arrived at Van Nuys Airport a half hour before "ten-ish," our scheduled departure time. The gleaming airplanes were lined up in their hangars, perpetually on call to the whim of their wealthy proprietors. I couldn't help but be a little bit giddy. I told myself again that none of this was mine—quite the opposite, in fact, because I was deceiving the very man who was sharing it with me.

I drove to the front gate and gave my name to a young man carrying a clipboard. He rolled his pen down the list twice, then again.

"I'm sorry," he said. "I'm not seeing your name on our admittance list."

"There must be a mistake," I said. "I'm supposed to be traveling with David Duplaine. To New York. At ten."

The guy shot an odd glance in my direction, but I chalked it up to my decidedly middle-class car and general appearance, which were both incongruous with the types who generally populated the admittance list.

"I appreciate that, but your name is not on the manifest," he said a bit more aggressively this time. "Perhaps you can call Mr. Duplaine and he can speak to the front desk."

"I'll do that."

I didn't have David's cell phone number, so I dialed Lily. It went directly to voice mail, and I was confronted with her greeting:

"If it's good news, leave a message; if not, hang up."

I hung up and leaned out my window. "I've left a message for him. I'll just pull over and wait for him over there," I said, imagining David's and Lily's wrath when they would arrive to find me waiting in my car beside the front gate because David's third or fourth assistant had forgotten to add my name to the list. I was certain someone would be fired over this.

I pulled to the side and parked, glancing a few times in my sideview mirror, waiting for a car carrying Lily and David to arrive, at which point they would wave me in and curse at the man at the gate for his error.

It didn't happen, though.

I waited for fifteen minutes and then a half hour. Our rough departure time came and went. I tried Lily again, but it went directly to voice mail. This wasn't highly unusual since Lily was the type to dial out, but never receive. If she needed someone she did it on her time.

Finally, I took a gamble. Panic was setting in. I had missed my commercial flight, and suddenly 26C and a half-sized bag of peanuts were enormously appealing. I needed to get to New York to cover the auction of Joel Goldman's art.

I dialed David Duplaine's house to speak to Hector.

"Duplaine residence."

It was an unfamiliar voice. Hector was the only one allowed to answer the phone, and he hadn't had a day off in decades.

"Duplaine residence. May I help you?"

"Is Hector available?" I asked.

"Hector is no longer employed here. May I help you in his stead?"

I was stunned. I thought of the evening before, of my brazenness, of ringing the buzzer, driving up the front gate, brushing past Hector with video cameras blinking red warnings and then kissing Matilda in the conservatory—probably under the spotlight of a multitude of cameras.

Suddenly the situation in which I found myself made sense. In their world of lawns shaped with tweezers, butlers with dry-cleaned white gloves and birds of good breeding, there were no oversights. Assistants—even third or fourth ones—didn't make mistakes like leaving their boss's guest on the tarmac.

David Duplaine had discovered I had been there last night. My heart sank.

I got out of my car and walked up to the man carrying the clipboard. He looked at me warily.

"I need a favor from you—working-class guy to working-class guy," I said. "I'm supposed to be traveling to New York for work, and I was going to be flying with David Duplaine. I know he keeps his jet here, and my guess is he already left without me. If he did I have to know, so I can go to the other airport— the one where guys like me fly out of—and go commercial."

The man hesitated for a moment, and that hesitation told me all I needed to know.

"Thanks," I said.

Once in my car, I sat there for a moment—a moment I didn't really have. In front of me a shiny white airplane awaited its turn to leave. It was unadorned but for a single magenta stripe and tail number. There is not a lot of waiting at Van Nuys Airport, so it was a mere minute or two before the plane took off. It took off to the east, over the rows of carbon-copy houses, and I wondered if it was taking the same flight plan David had taken, if it was going to New York. I watched the plane until all that was left was a thin trail of exhaust in its wake. It reminded me of when I was a little kid and I watched my father drive off to work, and I would worry he was gone forever, that he would never come home.

My last-minute flight to New York was over one thousand dollars, money I didn't have. I had missed my earlier flight, and my ticket wasn't the changeable sort.

I sat in one of the last rows—as Lily had predicted—and I ordered a beer. As soon as I did, I found myself counting the dollars for it in my head.

Love blinds, they say, but in my case love tended to have much more dire and far-reaching consequences. My loves were always the high-risk kind with stakes too rich for my blood. It was as if I was playing in the high-roller room with a couple of bucks in my pocket.

As I drank my beer I was finally clearheaded enough to objectively sort through the facts. If David had discovered my relationship with Matilda—which, after being left on the tarmac, I was pretty sure he had—the consequences would be catastrophic. I had learned over the past few months that Los Angeles was the smallest big town in the world, and David had every one of its most powerful men in his contact list. David was known to be dangerously vengeful, and he would smear my name across town like wet newsprint. I had been fortunate to get this second shot at life, but there were no more second chances for me. If I failed gloriously and publicly in the two most important news cities in the States, that was it. I was done. I had already been through a public undressing once at the *Journal*, and I couldn't go back to those sleepless nights and days of shame.

On that thought, I ordered another beer, and my mind went to Matilda.

Matilda: put simply, I couldn't imagine life without her. In our string of days apart I was beginning to miss her terribly; a gray film had descended over the days I couldn't see her. I needed to get to her, but there would be no way. Security guards had turned their backs to me when Hector had informed them to, but now they knew better; none would succumb to the same fate as Hector. And, certainly, Matilda would be in trouble, too. But what could David do to her? After all, as Matilda had pointed out that first evening in the bowling alley, she had been grounded for a very long time now. She had simply fallen in love. Even David couldn't possibly view that as a foible.

And then there were Hector and Lily—both of whom I had betrayed, despite everything they had done for me.

Five long hours into the flight, after much reflection, I pulled the shade up and gazed out the window. We were below eight thousand feet, then seven, then six. There were low willowy clouds hanging over the city. I could feel Manhattan's energy even six thousand feet in the air.

I had thought it would be an emotionless thing—an uneventful return to a city that had left me brokenhearted the first time around.

But, in light of recent events, I was wrong. As I finished my fourth beer, I prepared myself—no, braced myself—to see Lily. I was to meet her at a brownstone on the Upper East Side, but I was beginning to suspect there was a strong possibility I would have to find other accommodations—far less glamorous ones.

I directed the cab driver to Carole and Charles's brownstone, where Lily had insisted I stay. David had opted to stay at a hotel nearby on Central Park. The decision was a fortuitous one in the sense that I would temporarily avoid David, but there was still Lily to contend with.

Forty-five minutes after landing, the cab pulled over in front of a narrow town house a half block off Central Park in the East Eighties. The wind had picked up, and when the car door was opened for me I was greeted by a brisk autumn. It was not the pretend autumn Bel-Air had to offer—a stray red leaf, temperatures that swayed from fifty degrees to eighty-five, jack-o'-lanterns but no trick-or-treaters. Here, in New York, autumn was a real season.

The five-storied brownstones on the tony block stood shoulder to shoulder. The street's skinny maples were mostly leafless, and their dead leaves whirled on the pavement, crackling like fire. Dim streetlights barely illuminated the block. The chimneys puffed smoke, and the air smelled of burning wood.

I stood at the door of Carole's brownstone for one last minute, garnering up the courage to see Lily. Finally, I knocked, awash with fear.

The door opened, and Lily was there, bundled up in fur and scarves, despite the eighty-degree air that blew out at me. She leaned in to kiss me on the cheek, but I got a mouthful of angora instead.

"Thomas, you made it," Lily said with typical enthusiasm.

I waited for something else, some other reaction. But it didn't come. I tried to detect a chill in those green eyes, but they were warm.

"I did," I said, unease still in my voice. "Better late than never, they say?"

"I say better never than late. But I know you're typically on time, so we'll excuse you just this once," Lily said, leading me through two doorways to a small lounge area. Its fireplace burned so brightly I was surprised the fire department wasn't on high alert.

I set my carry-on down and took a quick glance around me. The decor had Lily's stamp on it, but it was more modern than Carole's home in Bel-Air—it was glass, bronze and sleek. Furniture was low to the ground and upholstered in exotic skins—like Emma's outfits. Much of it seemed to hail from the midcentury, and there was a streamlined look to it, all glamour and seduction.

I thought back to Carole and Charles's Bel-Air manor. If that was a wedding cake, then this was the affair that came after the honeymoon bliss had ended. It had an overt sexiness about it, as if it was the type of place most appreciated in various states of undress.

Lily took a quick sweep of her geography. "If you'd like to be chivalrous, you can reach up there and adjust the cork on that bottle for me. I've been staring at it all evening. It's an abomination."

There was a mirrored bar, and among its thirty or so bottles Lily had somehow spotted one with its cork slightly askew.

"Of course."

I reached up and, I thought, properly plugged it. Lily beckoned me to give it to her, though, and then she plugged it all over again, as if my job had been haphazard. Now it was ready to go back.

"I'm sorry you didn't join us on the plane this morning," Lily said, as I returned the bottle to its position, making sure it was straight. "I couldn't believe it when David said you had opted to fly commercial. For the first time I questioned your decision making."

It confirmed what I had already known—David had deliberately left without me. I tried to read Lily for the tiniest of clues that she was aware of recent happenings, but there were none.

"Thomas, is everything okay?" Lily asked.

"Yes, I think I'm just tired."

"Twenty-six C will do that to you. I'm going to take a hot bath. You look like you could use a drink," she said, pointing at the bar with her eyes. "I'm not a scotch drinker, but Charles tells me there's a phenomenal bottle of twenty-one-year somewhere or another—no reason for it to go to waste or become twenty-two-year."

Lily wrapped herself more tightly in her layers of fur and ex-

154

pensive cashmere, and she walked to the elevator, putting a single crease in an accent pillow on the way.

"Good night, dear. We have a very busy day tomorrow, so sleep tightly."

She disappeared into a century-old elevator that creaked its way up to the fourth floor.

I took Lily's advice and opened the bottle of scotch. I had two drinks then went to my bedroom, which was as plush as the finest hotel rooms in New York. I wondered if my time in luxury was limited. I couldn't help thinking of everything that way now—perhaps it would be my last sip of expensive scotch, my last conversation with Lily, the last night I would spend in a house on one of the most rarified blocks in the world.

It had been a traumatic day, and despite the posh accommodations, my nerves were so frayed I couldn't sleep. I tossed and turned mercilessly, until finally at 2:00 a.m. I decided to go outside to have a cigarette, hoping it would calm me down.

The air was chillingly cold, but it made me feel alive. I walked down the block, toward the Park. I wrapped my jacket closer to me and strolled down Fifth Avenue, glancing at the few windows that were still lit, wondering what was happening behind their closed curtains.

I was reminded of a time when I went to visit Willa's family. It was Thanksgiving break, and Willa had invited me to spend the four-day weekend at her parents' apartment overlooking the Park. In fact, it could have been one of the buildings I was looking up at now. It was senior year, and I should have known then, after that weekend, that our relationship would eventually come apart at its seams. Willa's parents hadn't included me in conversation and, worse, they had constantly referenced this-guy-and-that-guy, all who sounded more pedigreed than I. After dinner I had thought of ending things, but Willa and I took a walk that night—this same walk down Fifth Avenue—

and she assured me we could make it through, that we could come out the other side.

We didn't.

I was cold and nostalgic when I finally returned to Carole's street. I saw a light on inside the first floor of one of the brownstones, and it took me a moment to realize it was our own. I stepped closer and peered in the window.

Lily sat on the sleek ostrich lounge chair by the fire, drink beside her, lovingly holding a picture frame. I had known Lily for over two months now, but I had never seen her look at anyone or anything in the manner she looked at that photograph. I thought back to those years after Willa had left me. Lily looked at the picture with the same sense of longing.

I was stuck. I waited for ten minutes, then fifteen. There was only one entrance into the house, so skirting Lily was impossible. But it was thirty degrees out and I had been dressed for a walk around the block, not for hours outside.

Finally I opened the door.

Lily must have heard the front and inside doors open and close, but she didn't look up.

"Lily? Is everything okay?" I asked, repeating a question she had asked of me only hours earlier.

"No," Lily said, as she gazed at the picture. "But there's nothing that can be done about it now."

I scanned the bar and noticed an empty space where one of the bottles should have been. Lily had always been one for self-control, so this indiscretion was out of character.

"Do you have a girlfriend, Thomas?"

She said it in an omniscient way, and I wondered if she already knew the answer.

I paused. "Yes, I think so."

Lily squinted her eyes suspiciously. "You think so? What does that mean?"

"It's a bit of an unusual situation," I said, putting it mildly.

"Is she beautiful?" she asked.

"She looks like a movie star," I declared, thinking of Matilda in the bowling alley and in her rosette bathing suit at the swimming pool.

"That's the gold standard in Los Angeles, isn't it? Elsewhere it's about so much more, but every man in Los Angeles wants to marry a girl with stardust on her."

"I didn't fall in love with her because she's pretty," I said.

"You're defending yourself against something I didn't accuse you of."

It was silent for a moment. Outside a gust of wind rolled down the street.

"Why did you fall in love with her, then," Lily asked, "if it wasn't, as you say, because she's pretty?"

"I don't know," I said honestly. "I think in hindsight I fell in love with her the first time I met her. She's different than other girls," I said in a dramatic understatement.

"Different isn't always good," Lily said. "It can be complicated. And in my experience men don't like 'complicated.'"

"You're right, and different isn't always good with her, either. But I like her." I found myself thinking of her so vividly she could have been beside me. Sadness rolled over me. I wondered if I would ever see her again. "And I'm not saying it's a bad thing she's pretty." I smiled, to disarm Lily for what was coming next. "And you—why did you never marry?"

I asked it because Lily appeared vulnerable, and as a journalist it was my job to prey on weak moments like these.

"I was supposed to—once," Lily said, looking down at the black-and-white photo. "But then he decided he didn't want me anymore. And it broke my heart for the rest of my life."

"And why did you love him? Was he beautiful? Did he have stardust on him?"

"I loved the way he looked at a horse," she said simply, after a pause as brief as a blink.

That was all I was going to get. A tiny explanation for a life derailed. There must have been other men who looked at horses like that but that wasn't the point, was it?

I was going to press further, but I didn't. Instead, I said goodnight, again, for the second time that night.

Lily tore her eyes away from the photo. "Sleep tight, love."

I took the elevator up to my bedroom. I had left my bed a tangled mess of blankets, but someone had remade the bed and the sheets were opened for me in the shape of a half V, like an envelope waiting for a letter. A new pair of slippers sat on the floor next to my side of the bed, a fresh glass of water waited on the night table and the lights had been dimmed one click away from dark. I turned them off and, within seconds, fell asleep.

Seventeen

I had first learned about bon vivants and their playgrounds while at Harvard. Their choices in sandboxes varied soul to soul, taste to taste, but generally the playbook went something like this: the Hamptons in July, Saint-Tropez in August, Aspen and Gstaad for ski, the Sundance Film Festival for hobnobbing with young starlets, St. Bart's at some point during the winter months for a suntan, the Kentucky Derby for bourbon and a gamble, a sporting event or two, maybe a Fashion Week somewhere, and then, the following year, the same or some variation of it.

For those who liked art, there was only one place to be during the second week of November, and that was New York, at the Impressionist and Modern art auctions. This year, Sotheby's was auctioning the art of Joel Goldman, which made for a frenetic occasion for Lily and David.

Lily and I walked in early, before the auctions began. It was quiet in those hours, the exact definition of the "calm before the storm," and Lily and I were surrounded on all sides by fluorescence and priceless works of contemporary art. Lily paid attention to each painting in her father's collection and discussed with me their history, when her father had acquired it and in some cases exactly where it had hung—in which estate, in which room. Much to the chagrin of the security guards, Lily tilted

ALEX BRUNKHORST

the paintings one or two degrees if she felt they were off their axes. Oddly, Lily hadn't previously seemed affected by her father's death, but this evening in New York, she seemed deeply melancholic. She needed to be torn away from each painting, and she had a wistfulness about the art that she didn't seem to have about the man who had owned it.

I took notes quickly and furiously, aware I was here for a purpose. I kept a careful leash on my eyes, lest they roam too far and find David.

My head was buried in my notebook when I heard Lily exclaim:

"David! You're here. Where on earth have you been?"

David didn't answer. Instead, I felt his eyes on me. I scribbled nonsense so feverishly in my notebook my pen punctured the page.

"Is everything okay, love?" Lily asked with genuine concern.

I was forced to turn around at that point, and I courageously met David's gaze. We were like soldiers on opposite sides of a battlefield.

"Why were you so late?" Lily pressed. "It's not like you."

"We have a little pest problem," David said evenly. "At the house."

"Oh dear, what kind? I hope not fruit flies. They can be the worst to cure."

"No, nothing of the sort. Something bigger and peskier than that. But we'll take care of it—we always do."

I felt David's eyes on me again. And then, as if he was bored with me, he shifted his attention toward a sculpture. It was a Joel Shapiro, Lily had told me minutes earlier, but to my untrained eye, a million-dollar stick figure. It looked like a man running awkwardly, and I couldn't help but think that soon that man could be me.

They announced the auction was about to begin, and David, Lily and I sat in the front row—in that order. David's hands

160

cradled his phone on his lap, and I wondered if the subject of any of his communication was related to Matilda. I longed to extract the phone from his hands. Lily leaned in to say something to me, the art auctioneer rattled through numbers, a paddle went up, another went down. It was all jumbled, and the auction ended too quickly and yet not quickly enough. Just like that, Joel Goldman's art—the priceless pieces he spent a lifetime acquiring—were dispersed for collectors across the globe. It seemed sad and significant.

I glanced over at Lily to read her expression, to see if she was thinking the same thing. Instead, she seemed detached. She was animatedly speaking to David about a sculpture that had sold to a friend of theirs. And it was then that I felt her. Willa's stare was on my upper back, and it burned the way her forgetting me once had.

I turned around to find her eyes set squarely on mine, as if it was the first time we had met, during that autumn day at Harvard.

Had I avoided her it would have made her think I still loved her, that there was something about her worth skirting. I would never give her that satisfaction. It was a few minutes before David, Lily and I left our seats, and when we did she intercepted my path, making it impossible to move around her.

"Hello, Thomas," she said.

Apart from nascent wrinkles around her eyes, she was still attractive in the way well-bred girls who take care of themselves are. Her long brown hair was feathered in a bygone way but it must have been in vogue again, for Willa was always in vogue. Her red lipstick was a shade too bright for my taste, her eyes heavily made up, and her fingers were covered in gold rings, as if she hadn't been able to choose which one to wear. I could tell she was nervous.

"Hey, Willa," I said with a deliberate aloofness, meant to convey I had other places to be. She leaned in, expecting something—a kiss, maybe, or a hug—but I stood firmly outside her radius and offered neither.

"You're here with David Duplaine?" she asked with forced casualness.

I nodded, even though it was, in a sense, a lie.

"And another friend." I tossed my head in the general direction of the front row, which was now empty. "And you? Are you buying?" I asked, even though I knew she wasn't.

She chuckled conspiratorially, as if we were in on the same joke. "No. Just observing I guess." There was a pause then. "I hear you're doing well. In LA."

I didn't know how she would have heard that, but I nodded. "I'm doing okay."

"You're being modest, Thomas. Your parents did you a terrible disservice with all that," she said. I briefly thought of mentioning that my mother was dead now, but I didn't bother. "I heard you're a superstar at the *Times*—or at least that's what Jacob says," she declared, referring to my friend whose father had introduced me to Rubenstein.

In light of her modesty comment, I didn't deny it. "And you? How are you?" I asked instead.

"Oh, good, I guess. The same." She said it in a sad way, as if I was the one who had ended things, and she had been home nursing that sick heart of hers ever since. "How long are you here for?"

"A few days, I guess."

"Thomas, I need to tell you. I've felt awful about everything."

I opened my mouth to disagree and she put her finger on my lip, the way she used to before we fell asleep.

"I know you don't believe me, and I may be many terrible things and not as good a person as you, but one thing I'm not is a liar. I've thought of you so many times, more than you could ever believe."

"Then why didn't you call?" I asked, thinking of the years

of nights I fell asleep with the phone under my pillow, waiting for a ring that never came.

"I don't know." She shook her head. "That's the honest answer. There's so much we need to talk about. If you're here tomorrow, can we...could we have dinner? Please?"

Men of greater willpower would have said no. I wanted to, but I couldn't. I couldn't because I had spent years missing her. I couldn't because I was now in danger of never seeing Matilda again. I couldn't because David Duplaine was about to flick my life away, like the ash from the tip of a cigarette.

So I agreed.

"Tomorrow, then," she said, as she turned around to leave.

Just before she did, I touched her wool coat lightly, somewhere around her hip and with such gentleness she might not have even known. I touched it because there had been all those years between then and now, years when she was imaginary. In those years I would have given anything to see her smile, to hear her laugh, to touch the wool of her coat, to smell the scent of grapefruit on the nape of her neck. My greatest fear all those nights, the fear that had blackened my soul at three o'clock in the morning, was that she was forgetting me, and here she was, once again, remembering.

I returned to the brownstone late. I had told Lily after the auction that I needed to meet some friends from Harvard, but in actuality I had gone to one of my favorite bars and had a few drinks alone.

The brownstone was quiet. A single lamp illuminated the living room.

I was ready to retreat to my bedroom when I remembered the picture.

The wall was covered in black-and-white photos. I scanned the photos one by one. Most were of Carole. There was one picture of her shaking hands with the president at an orphanage fund-raiser, another with her smiling demurely and hugging an Academy Award against her chest, and one of her walking down a rainy Manhattan street with a newspaper over her head beside an unfamiliar man. Charles was in exactly three of the photos, and in each case he was in the background, out of focus even. I reflected, for not the first time, on their odd marriage. It seemed loveless—almost a marriage of convenience. Yet Carole Partridge hardly seemed like the type to have to do anything for convenience. I suspected quite the opposite in fact: she paid others around her to make her life effortless.

I continued through the trove of photos, eventually homing in on one with a familiar man on a movie set. It took me a moment to figure out how I recognized the face. It was Joel Goldman—Lily's father—on the set of one of his movies. It was a grand scene from an epic film, with actresses in heavy makeup, set designers carrying elaborate art, people scurrying about. I smiled nostalgically, because it was a scene from the motion-picture business of yesteryear—before computers did the heavy lifting. Movies in those days were productions, and men like Joel Goldman true producers.

I studied the photo one more time, wondering what about it compelled me so, and then continued onward.

Finally, in the upper right corner of the photo collage, I found what I was looking for.

Lily had returned it to its place, but I knew it was the one as soon as I saw it. It was a photo of a handsome guy around eighteen years old with his hand resting on a beauty of a Thoroughbred. He stood in front of the stone manor I had seen in the background of Lily's dressage photos—her family's equestrian estate, I presumed—and he was dressed in jeans and a plaid shirt. A wickedly mischievous smile covered his face, as if he had just done something wrong, or was about to. He was a guy from another era—the type of man to lasso cattle, to promise loyalty and mean it.

He wasn't alone. Beside him stood Carole Partridge. She was around eight and wore jodhpurs and boots that covered her knees. She looked up at him adoringly, laughingly. Their resemblance was uncanny; I could see it in their heavy eyelids and off-kilter smiles. It was remarkably clear:

The person who had broken Lily Goldman's heart was Carole Partridge's older brother.

Eighteen

When I woke up the next morning, Lily was already gone. She had left a note requesting I meet her for drinks at the Four Seasons that evening around ten. I considered phoning her to ask what this mysterious late-drinks meeting was about, but then remembered her habit of not accepting calls, so I figured it was futile.

I spent the day in work meetings. I went to the art auction houses to do some research, and while I was in town Rubenstein had arranged for me to interview a film actress who had just wrapped up a stint on Broadway.

I went back to the town house and showered before hailing a cab to take me downtown. I waited outside and in my periphery I thought I caught a man in a nondescript car watching me. When I looked his way he drove away, and I realized I was turning paranoid. David knew I was sneaking onto his estate, but there was a leap between knowing I was visiting his daughter and having me followed in New York. Besides, I told myself, I was only having dinner with an old friend. There was certainly no harm in that.

Nevertheless, as the taxi drove through streets stuffed with rush-hour traffic, I found myself glancing over my shoulder.

Willa had picked a restaurant in Tribeca, a glass, steel and brick eatery that served Italian food in low light, bad acoustics and small portions. We agreed to meet there at seven, but in typical fashion I had arrived early, so I sat at a bar with a mirror that ran all the way to the ceiling. The gimlet was Willa's drink, so ordering that was not an option. I needed something that felt grown-up and masculine, as if I had graduated from her.

"An Old-Fashioned," I said to the bartender, usurping David's drink of choice.

I discreetly examined my reflection in the mirror between liquor bottles. I had aged better than Willa—the advantage of being a man and, I supposed, of having a wide frame and formidable jaw. While at Harvard I had a round, boyish face, but now my jaw seemed more squarely cut and my cheeks more angular. Gone was the messy shag, reminiscent of a Milwaukee kid on a baseball diamond—or track, as the case may be. My reddish-blond hair was cut closer to the scalp, and I still had a full head of it. I wore the checked shirt and gray wool pants Lily had brought me from Boston as a present for house-sitting.

I had met Willa during our junior year at Harvard. It was fall, and I had chosen to go to the banks of the Charles to study for a midterm. It was a postcard of an afternoon. The fog hadn't lifted, and the air smelled of wet leaves and heavy smoke. It screamed so intensely of fall that for years that afternoon defined autumn for me.

I lay on my side on a blanket, damp from the grass. I was working on a term paper on Faulkner, scribbling commentary on *As I Lay Dying* in a notebook.

"Is that a *notebook* you're writing in?" Willa had asked, bundling her plaid scarf closer to her neck and blowing at a wisp of hair that crept into her eye. She had appeared from nowhere, as if she had been conjured up just for me.

"It's a wonderful invention—the notebook," I declared, mesmerized by her the way I would be years later by Matilda. She was different than the girls in Milwaukee—a higher level of sophistication, a more angular bone structure, a greater aloofness. "It's going to overtake that thing called a computer. Just you wait and see."

Willa sat down beside me on the blanket. She chose a spot close to me, as if we had known each other for years rather than minutes. She wore a big diamond on her right hand, and it was the first time I had been approached by a girl rich enough to wear a diamond that hadn't been given to her by her husband.

"When it does—overtake the computer—I'll remember that the boy who first introduced me to this thing called 'the notebook' was…"

"Thomas. Thomas Cleary. And who am I enlightening?"

She giggled then, like a schoolgirl who just returned to her friends after a dance with a crush. "Willa Asher." She gave me her last name with a flourish, with the implication that it was a gift of a last name. She crept closer then, so close I smelled her grapefruit scent, and she peeked at my pages. "You have exquisite handwriting, Thomas Cleary. So straight—the handwriting of an architect."

That was how it began. We sat beside each other for hours, discussing everything from Faulkner to the Revolutionary War. We took in coffee later in the afternoon at a Cambridge café and rendezvoused for a cocktail the following evening. She had been at the Charles looking for someone, or so she later said, but we had never revisited that moment so I could ask if she had ever found who she was looking for. If she had, my whole life would have been different.

Had we met at a Harvard event we surely wouldn't have fallen in love. I would have looked at her like the shirts and pants I was now wearing, as something nice but unaffordable, and she wouldn't have noticed me at all. Instead, that patchwork of fog was our candlelight—in its glow we saw each other as flawless.

Our love lasted longer than it probably should have; it endured through semester after semester, much of the time seeming to run on the fumes of an incredible chemistry. Our friends—her high-society ones and mine, who work-studied and borrowed their way through Harvard—watched from the sidelines the way people watch a house of cards knowing someday the winds would change and the streets would be littered with queens of spades and jacks of hearts.

The winds did change. We moved to Manhattan—she to work for a fashion magazine, I to work at my dream job covering tech finance at the *Wall Street Journal*. She wanted to move in together, but I insisted I make it on my own before we took such a big step. So I lived the humble life of a reporter in a walk-up on York Avenue, while Willa moved into a loft downtown, in a building that was owned by her father. She played the Manhattan social-climbing game—a ladder to nowhere in my opinion—and I worked a grueling schedule that involved short deadlines and trips cross-country to Silicon Valley. It fell apart quickly and irreparably. Willa left me in September. I always suspected she had left me for someone else—she was never one to leave something without a backup—but the official reason was "too many differences between us." I was left devastated and broken.

"Don't you look pensive, Thomas Cleary."

I saw her reflection in the mirror and turned around. She had a terrible habit of being late, a habit I had excused repeatedly because she had trained me to believe that due to upbringing and social standing her time was of greater value than mine. Tonight she was on time, to the minute.

The first thing I noticed about her was that she wore the emerald earrings I had given her as a gift for her twenty-first birthday. Even in her dainty earlobes they were undersized, the size of earrings for a child.

I had saved for months to buy those earrings. I had chosen them because there was something about emeralds that sounded rich, like Willa.

"I don't deserve these," she had said that night, glancing at the earrings for only a second before stuffing them back into the crumpled-up paper in which I had so carefully wrapped them. It was a terrible phrase that really meant "You don't deserve me."

But she had kept them, all these years.

"Hi," I said, standing up because that was what David did when Lily joined him at a table. "Can I get you a drink?"

She studied me obviously—first my hair, then the checked shirt, the wool pants, the shoes and finally the Old-Fashioned. She seemed impressed and there was a smugness to her, as if she was taking credit for some of it.

"A gimlet, please. Rocks," she said to the bartender.

Now it was my turn. It was neither arrogant nor presumptive to say that Willa had dressed specifically for me. Gone was the gothic black eyeliner, the clunky rings and the lipstick the color of fire. Here was the girl next door: a touch of mascara, clear lip gloss, bare fingers punctuated with clear nails, a prim coat cinched at the waist with a belt and slightly red cheeks, which made her look as if she had just come in from a cold day of sledding.

"What are you drinking?" she asked to make conversation. Before I had been the one to fill uncomfortable silences, but now Willa was the eager one. She leaned in and studied my drink.

"An Old-Fashioned. Do you want to go to our table?"

"Couldn't we both use a drink first?"

She tapped my glass with hers, making direct eye contact with me as she did.

There was a rowdy group of Wall Street guys beside us who dropped the names of commodities and stock tickers. They shouted to each other about the nets of their trades—thirty grand here, forty there—and it was hard to hear my own thoughts.

Willa leaned in close. "I'm sorry about everything, Thomas." Maybe she thought I hadn't heard her apology the evening before.

"Yeah, I got that. All's good."

"No, really, I feel like I have to get that out of the way and make you understand," she implored.

I nodded, not knowing what else to say. We both went back to our drinks. The bourbon tasted medicinal, and my mouth watered for Willa's lime.

Once at our table, there were three drinks, or maybe four. Then three plates of appetizers and another round of drinks.

She sat beside me rather than across. Every drink seemed to give Willa the courage to inch closer to me, so that eventually our thighs were touching.

Conversation started off as small talk between old friends who happened to bump into each other. Willa had changed jobs from one fashion magazine to another and now was working for a fashion website. She had upgraded her loft for one with more closets in the same building, and she had just returned home from Italy, where she had gone for a friend's wedding.

As for me, I told her generally about the *Times*, making it seem more of a gradual rise than the meteoric one it had been. When pressed for my accommodations I mentioned that I was staying at Carole Partridge's brownstone.

"Carole Partridge? The movie star Carole Partridge? You're staying in her brownstone? Thomas, your life seems so glamorous." She dragged out the last word in an alcohol-induced slur that sounded ugly or sarcastic, I wasn't sure which, but certainly not glamorous.

Willa leaned closer now and put her hand in my hair.

I felt for the first time that night that I was doing something wrong, and I wanted to leave.

I motioned for the check, and Willa noticed.

"Everyone from LA wants to go to bed so early," she said. The comment initially seemed innocuous, but then Willa rubbed the back of her hand on my cheek. It was a gesture from nights past—our precursor to more.

I thought again how I had wanted this for so long. But something in me had changed, because now it felt like nothing.

"Yeah, well, I don't know what time I'm leaving tomorrow," I said. "So I should get home and get it all worked out."

"I do wish you'd stay in New York a few days longer." Willa's tone was overtly coquettish. "Can't you do what it is you do from New York?"

"Unfortunately not."

Willa tried another tactic now: she sipped her drink more slowly, petulantly, as if to say that we couldn't possibly leave until there was nothing left of it.

"Thomas," Willa breathed into my ear. "What happened that winter? With the *Journal*?"

My heart quickened and I found myself embarrassed for the Thomas of old, that poor chap.

"Let's not go into that. Let's pretend it didn't happen."

"But it did," she pled childishly. "I want to know what happened."

"It was a long time ago, Willa."

"Everyone was talking about it..." Willa paused, looking at her drink sadly. "I feel like I should know."

The check came in a highball glass. I reached for it, but Willa grabbed it first, putting it someplace on the other side of her. It was another act of petulance. I could leave before she drained her drink, but she knew I wouldn't walk out on a check.

The Wall Street crew was drunker now, and I heard them from four tables away talking about a girl they had met in the Hamptons whom at least a few of them had slept with.

"Thomas—" Willa egged me on, as if begging for an encore. She played with one of her emerald earrings. It was so small I feared it would disappear into its hole.

"It was a mistake, an honest mistake. I was lost when we ended things, and I could barely function at work. I had to write a story on a software launch—too complex to go into now and it doesn't matter anyways—and I was supposed to go to Palo Alto to interview the company's founder. I missed my flight. I overslept." I paused. "Anyways, I called him for the interview—it turned out I didn't even need to be there for it—and I wrote the story and it came out. Initially uneventfully."

Willa's expression was rapt.

"Two days passed, and I was in Palo Alto for real this time when I heard. I'll never forget. I was eating a falafel pita in this little hummus joint on University called Oren's, where all the software guys go, when my phone started to blow up with emails about how I plagiarized a story. I honestly had no idea what everyone was talking about."

Much to my surprise, I felt shame rising to my cheeks all over again.

"Apparently, three sentences from my story had also been used in the *Chronicle* two years earlier about the same company. I didn't copy it—I swear on my father's life I didn't. I would never do that for a thousand different reasons—but somewhere in the recesses of my mind I must have read it and retained it. So I was fired, and I spent the next three months getting rejected by every newspaper in the country. The *LA Times* was my last hope."

I glanced at Willa's drink, hoping she was finished so I could pay the bill. It was still half-full, and I felt her gaze on me intensely.

"That doesn't seem enough to get fired," Willa said. "Are you sure that was all?"

"Am I sure? No, I'm forgetting a part of it," I said sarcastically, feeling a strong anger coming on. "Tens of thousands of reporters line up to work at the *Journal* every day. The paper doesn't have to keep one they think plagiarized a story."

I had blamed the *Journal* for throwing down too harsh a punishment, but in speaking it aloud it made sense.

Willa rattled the ice in her drink, a habit of hers I had forgotten.

"I'm sorry, Thomas," she said disingenuously. "I'm sure it was that photographic memory of yours. It was always crazy, that memory."

Crazy didn't sit well with me. Neither did the insincerity, nor the fact that she was hiding the check from me.

"Do you have a girlfriend? Are you dating anyone?" she asked, changing a subject that shouldn't have been changed so quickly.

I knew it didn't matter how I answered her questions. At this point it was clear I could have taken Willa home and had sex with her and never called her again. Instead, I simply said, "Yes."

Her face fell obviously.

"Is she an LA girl?" she asked with repugnancy.

I nodded. "Yes."

"What does she do?"

"She's in school," I said to keep matters murky.

"What is she studying?"

"A lot of different things."

"A lot of different things," Willa repeated. Her speech was slurred. "That sounds dangerous, or nebulous, or lazy. I don't know which. Probably the latter."

I put down two one-hundred-dollar bills and turned to leave.

Willa, with a slight wobble to her step, followed me. Outside she caught up with me quickly. She grabbed my arm with undue strength and forced me to turn around to look at her.

"Who is this girl who studies a lot of different things? And who are you that you carry all hundreds now?"

I turned away quickly, shaking her arm off me. I had had too much to drink, too, and I hated the fact that one of us or both had dragged innocent Matilda into this. It was early evening Los Angeles time, and she was probably bowling a few frames in her lonely basement, eating pretzels and drinking Arrowhead water. She didn't deserve this.

"Where are you going?" Willa shouted when I had walked a half block ahead of her.

"Did you expect me to remain faithful to you? Huh?" I raised my voice, which I never had—not to my parents, not to a teacher, not to a boss and certainly not to a girlfriend. "You were a dead thing to me. A corpse. That was how I got through it all. I told myself you were lying in a cemetery in New Jersey, somewhere in between your dead grandparents."

She was crying now. It empowered me, the way those Wall Street guys were empowered by their trades, their money and fucking that girl.

"You never cared about that winter, Willa. I wasn't even worth a phone call. I wasn't even worth a 'How are you? How you holding up, Thomas?'" I paused, needing to inhale. "For me that winter nearly ruined my life. For you it was merely a season when you had to field a few questions."

She had caught up with me and was crying so hard she couldn't catch her breath.

"I'm sorry," she sobbed. "It wasn't like that."

"It was like that. It was exactly like that," I said. I hadn't realized it, but I had been squeezing Willa's left wrist with my right hand so tight I was sure it would leave a red ring the next day. She was wearing gold bracelets in the shape of serpents and they dug into my palm. "It was like that, and I wish you had stayed dead for me."

I loosened my grip, and her arm dropped to her side like a doll's. I looked at her one last time. The street lamps cast their light on her little emerald earrings. Willa had been right the first time. She had never deserved them.

Nineteen

I arrived at the Four Seasons Hotel at a quarter of ten. I half-heartedly expected to see David waiting for me instead of Lily, telling me that I was banned from his life and Matilda's, and that I best be staying in Manhattan, because there was nothing in Los Angeles for me to go back to.

Instead, in the corner of the dining room, among the spot-lighted trees and leaded glass casement windows, I saw Lily. She had chosen the darkest table there, as if she was waiting for something illicit to happen. In front of her was a clear drink; in front of my seat was a gimlet.

"Thomas, my love. How was your evening?" Lily asked when I sat down. I must've looked worse for the wear, but in atypical fashion Lily refrained from commenting.

"Not good," I said, sipping—more like gulping—the drink. The Four Seasons was one of the most venerable hotels in New York, and even its gimlets tasted of better stock.

"Oh dear, I'm sorry to hear that," Lily said, but she seemed unflustered by it.

"Yours?"

"David and I went to the auction and then had dinner," Lily said. "Which was when he told me the unfortunate news."

"What did he tell you?" I asked, already knowing the answer.

It was clear by this point all secrets that were David's were Lily's, too. They were as close as siblings.

"That you've been sneaking on his house and seeing Matilda."

"I didn't mean to betray David," I said. "But more important, I would never go behind your back. You know that. I know you've been ridiculously generous with me."

"I *have* been ridiculously generous with you. And you did go behind my back," Lily responded with an expression difficult to read, but she didn't seem particularly angry.

"Not initially, though. I met her the evening of the governor's party—when I went to the wrong house. And I know you blatantly asked me if someone was at David's house."

"And you blatantly lied."

"I didn't tell you because she asked me not to. And it seemed a harmless lie, because I honestly didn't think I'd see her again. It was only later I realized that what I was doing was somehow..." I stopped there, because I didn't know the word. Was it wrong?

Lily gazed at the vast branches of a tree, the spotlight casting shadows on its golden leaves.

"And so what now?" Lily asked.

I'd had all day to think about it, and I knew the answer. I didn't hesitate, because I got the impression in their world you needed to know what you wanted, and reach out and grab it. After all, if I hadn't hoisted myself up on the branches of the oak tree I wouldn't have discovered Matilda.

"I need a favor," I said. I felt silly even asking it, since here was a woman who had showered me with favors over the past few months. "I want to take her away."

It was quiet for a moment, as Lily contemplated what I had just said. The ice in Lily's drink was stuck together, and she rattled the cubes free.

"I don't know if that's such a good idea," she finally remarked.

"Why not?" I asked.

"For more reasons than you realize."

She was right, of course. But despite the risks, I had determined I was going to run away with Matilda, even though there were infinite reasons to do just the opposite.

"Who is she, Lily?" I asked.

"I can't comment on that. It's a very complex situation," Lily said. "One thing Los Angeles doesn't lack is pretty girls. Perhaps you should cast your net wider."

"So are you suggesting I walk away?"

"It seems you haven't much choice. Besides, the older you get, the more you realize that things that are too difficult are not usually worth doing."

"That's an interesting perspective coming from you, in light of our conversation last evening. What if you were Matilda, would you want me to walk away from her? Is that what you wanted your fiancé to do?"

There was a pause then, long enough to give me hope that I had hit one of Lily's well-bred nerves.

"My father had a little house in Hawaii," Lily said. "David will never think you'll take her there. Even I would have forgotten about it if the estate attorneys hadn't called to ask if I wanted to put it on the market. When you return to Los Angeles, Kurt will be waiting at my house with a key and two tickets to Honolulu."

"What about my job?"

"As you may have surmised by now, Phil and I are close friends. I'll request you take a month-long sabbatical to do a project for me and I'm certain he'll acquiesce. I'll throw a few exclusives his way. Phil's an easy fish to catch."

I stared through the wavy glass windows. The street lamps resembled sparkling diamonds.

"Now *you're* betraying David." My voice was little stronger than a whisper.

"I will deny we ever had this conversation. In fact, I'm going to stay here tonight, so David doesn't suspect our collusion.

When he informed me that you've been sneaking onto the estate to see Matilda, I told him I was horrified by your actions. I have been nothing but gracious to you, Thomas, and look what you've done in return." She said it sarcastically, mimicking the tone she must have given David.

"What if Matilda won't leave with me?"

"It'll mean the end of the affair. David will never allow you back."

"And if I threaten to tell the world David has a hidden daughter?"

"Then I'm certain David will find a way to make sure you never work in the news business again. It will make what happened at the *Journal* seem uneventful. And if he doesn't ruin your career, I will."

Lily's green eyes turned glassy, devoid of emotion. I suddenly realized that her bad side was not a place I wanted to be on.

"I plan to leave on the eleven o'clock," I said, to change the subject back to our plan. "I have an early breakfast meeting and I'll fly out after."

"David and I are leaving at two," Lily said. "That gives you three hours to do what you need to do."

"And what about Hector? Was he fired for what we did?"

"Hector has worked for the family for over forty years. He'll be very well taken care of—I can assure you of that. But I'll tell him you asked after him. And apologized."

I stood up, leaving half of my drink on the table, despite its caliber.

"Thank you," I said. "And thank you for Hawaii. And talking to Rubenstein. Come to think of it, *thank you* doesn't seem sufficient."

"It is, and you're welcome. Kurt will call you in the morning and coordinate arrangements. Enjoy your trip."

I walked through the grand lobby of the hotel and thought of my conversation with Lily. Lily hadn't given anything away, but she had been flustered during our conversation. When I had asked for a comment, Lily had deliberately avoided the question. I had always believed there was a story behind Matilda Duplaine, but now I thought it may have been bigger than I even realized.

I got into the backseat of my cab and took the short trip back to Carole's brownstone. I was beginning to think I had a story here—a big story. But then I remembered Professor Grandy, who always advised us against leaping to conclusions, and I thought of his esteemed Rule Number Four:

Be careful of No Comment. It sounds important, but it may mean nothing at all.

When I returned to Los Angeles, so did the rain. I landed in the early afternoon, among heavy storm clouds. I marveled again at the vast sprawl that was Los Angeles. I still wasn't accustomed to it, but it was finally feeling more like home.

I headed to my apartment first, throwing a few belongings into a duffel. I had been running on fumes since the flight to New York, and it was only now that the gravity of what I was about to do struck. I closed the door behind me, and I contemplated what kind of man I would be the next time I opened it. I didn't know the answer to that, but I knew it would be a man much changed.

I drove across town, taking the now-familiar route to Lily's house. When I arrived I weeded through flowers to find the buzzer. Kurt must have been expecting me, for the gate opened instantly. Before the gates had fully closed behind me, Kurt was standing in the doorway.

I didn't even put my car in Park, such was the efficiency at which Kurt moved. The key marked Honolulu and an envelope with the tickets were slipped into my carry-on. A Louis Vuitton suitcase with a tag with Lily's name and Hawaiian address was placed on the passenger seat. The whole thing took no longer than sixty seconds.

I drove the few blocks to David's property and parked beside the garden. I jogged toward the oak tree and caught a firm grasp of its lowest branch. Unlike the last time, I had worn appropriate clothing for this sort of thing, and the climb went more quickly.

Once I was perched in the tree, I surveyed my surroundings. David probably assumed I was still in New York, so there were no guards. Sure, there were video cameras, but by the time David watched them it would be too late.

I hopped onto the canopy of the tennis viewing area and then onto the court. I walked along the edge of the property, narrowly missing the gaze of two tree trimmers and a gentleman who polished horseshoes, and then I slipped through the back door of the kitchen, which I knew was generally kept open for the staff.

The kitchen was empty, save for a heaping plate of blueberry pancakes and soft scrambled eggs that sat alone on a counter. It must have been Matilda's breakfast, and it had gone untouched.

I crept through room after room. The dining room seated no one and its candelabra was unlit. The formal living room had two crackling fires, but no one to enjoy them. The conservatory was quiet; there was no music.

The first floor was vacant—no Matilda. I sneaked around the back, thinking she might have been bowling. The alley was empty. A single bowling ball sat on the rack, three holes pointed at the ceiling, in the exact position for Matilda's fingers to slip into them seamlessly.

I didn't consult my watch, but I suspected I was running out of time. I had two options: I could head upstairs or to the screening room. I opted for the latter.

I opened a formidable door as heavy as a bank vault and descended the stairs. It smelled of buttery popcorn, and at the bottom of the stairwell I could see the spray of a black-and-white grainy light. I heard an aristocratic voice that I recognized as belonging to Audrey Hepburn. When I reached the bottom of the stairs I saw Matilda's bare feet first—crossed on the back of a deep blue sofa. She had elegant, high-arched feet—the feet of a ballerina.

In the age of digital everything, most screening room owners had abandoned the old-fashioned projector, but David had kept his. Like everything in David's world, screenings were spectacular events. The theater seated thirty, but Matilda and I were always its only ticket-holders. It was a rich and decadent place with plush velvet sofas and curtains.

"Matilda, are you here?" I asked.

There was no answer, so I approached slowly.

Matilda lay on her back, munching absently on a Red Vines and watching the movie with an equal indifference. She was almost unrecognizable as the girl I had fallen in love with. She wore no makeup, and she had eschewed her froufrou style in favor of a sweat suit. Her eyes were hollow and sad.

It took me a moment to realize the movie was *Roman Holiday*, a film about a reporter who falls in love with a princess and allows her to experience, for only a brief time, the real world.

"Dad found out about us," Matilda said. "Hector's been fired, and any minute now I'm sure they'll find you and send you away—for good."

She seemed oddly calm, considering the urgency of the situation.

I approached, and I squeezed her left hand in mine.

"We're going to leave," I said. "I have everything packed. A friend is lending me her house in Hawaii for a month. We have to go, this second. We don't have much time before your father comes home."

She didn't respond and let the silence settle between us. Then, finally:

"Did you see a girl in New York?" she asked.

It took me a minute to piece it together. The car waiting on our block. David must have had me followed and known I had dinner with Willa. I had loaded my own barrel; all he had to do was pull the trigger.

"Yes."

"Who was she?"

"My ex-girlfriend. Nothing happened."

"You just told me you saw her."

"I did, but that doesn't mean anything happened."

"What's your exact definition of 'happened'?" Matilda asked.

What did "happened" mean? I wondered to myself. Did it mean "have sex with her"? Is that how I had justified the whole thing? Because I hadn't slept with Willa?

"It would seem to me that dinner is a happening," Matilda said, tracing the ridges in her licorice.

"You're right. It was a happening. But it wasn't significant."

"Who is she?" Matilda asked.

"She's someone I loved before I loved you."

"Do you still love her?"

"No."

"Not even the littlest bit?"

"No."

"Not even during a particularly sunny day, when the winds are right and the wine is sweet and Lou Reed is playing and she's wearing a pretty dress?" Matilda asked.

"Not even then," I said.

"Does love ever go away?" Matilda inquired.

"I haven't loved a lot of people in my life, so I'm not sure," I said. "In the case of her—Willa is her name—it took a long time for it to disappear."

"I think that love is like a cancer," Matilda said. "It can go into remission and you can think you have it licked, but there's a part of it that always stays inside you. Even if it's so small a microscope can't detect it, and even if it doesn't make you sick anymore—it's there."

"That's a sad way of thinking about it."

"Or it's a beautiful way of thinking about it."

Matilda paused for a moment and then inhaled deeply, the way her father often did.

I was worried, at that moment, that she might break up with me because she believed there was a little bit of Willa inside of me, dark and malignant, ready to begin eating away at me. But then I wondered if Matilda even knew what breaking up with someone meant. She knew what *goodbye* meant, and it was pretty much the same thing.

"Matilda, there isn't anyone else—and there won't be. But our relationship will have to end if you don't run away with me. And if we don't leave now you'll never see me again. Because your dad won't let me come back, but also because I can't be complicit in this anymore. I can't keep you in captivity just because he does. And maybe someday there will be someone else who manages to sneak through, climb over your walls. You'll take him through the sculpture garden and tell him who John Mc-Cracken is, you'll beat him six-love in tennis and maybe you'll even live together here for a while and watch movies like this." I pointed to the screen. "But that, too, will fail. I'll assure you of it. Because love doesn't work like that."

I looked away from her toward the screen. There was a red dot on the upper right corner, indicating the reel would need to be changed soon. It struck me as fitting, the movie was reaching its turning point.

"And what if we're caught?" Matilda asked. "Have you thought that through? Or are we being impetuous?"

"Yes, we're being impetuous, but no, we won't be caught. And if we are, you'll end up where you started. That's our worst outcome."

"The worst outcome is I end up back where I started," Matilda repeated to herself. "That doesn't sound like poor odds."

"All reward, no risk," I said, thinking my odds weren't so favorable. "And just think, the upside is the world."

"The upside is the world." Matilda smiled. "Well, that seems a bet I should throw my chips on, shouldn't I?"

Just then, the reel snapped off the projector and the screen went black. We stood under the chandelier for one last moment. It cast stars on the floor below us, and we were surrounded by so much velvet I felt like a diamond nestled in a jewel box. But the stars weren't real, and I wasn't a gem. In fact, it was only then that I realized that pretty much everything about the gilded life of Matilda Duplaine was make-believe.

We were outside, a mere three acres from freedom. I grabbed Matilda's hand, and we sprinted along the side of the wall. When we reached the tennis court, I saw it on the driveway, in the distance. There was a hulk of an SUV with a man disembarking from it.

David was home.

I wondered how he had got back so quickly. David Duplaine was the only man somehow able to make a six-hour cross-country plane ride into four. I envisioned him prodding his pilot faster, to step on the gas because he had someplace to be.

When I saw him I surveyed our surroundings, quickly formulating an escape plan. The only ways in and out of the estate were the garden, the oak tree and the front gate. It took me a split second to realize that the oak tree was our only option, which was fine, because we were almost there.

"Come on." I prodded Matilda. "Let's go."

There is a difference between pausing and stopping, and in this case, Matilda stopped. She didn't move. Ironically, we were on the tennis court when David reached us. The only thing separating us was the net, erected to the exact regulation height. The large oak tree reached out over us like an umbrella, and I longed to grab Matilda and bring her with me, hoist her onto its branches. But instead, I stood still, beside her.

David was the one who spoke first—to me.

"I suggest you leave here immediately," David said. "Or I'll have you arrested for trespassing."

"I'm not going anywhere without Matilda," I replied with a strength I didn't know I had. "I love her, and I want to take her away with me, to allow her to experience the world. Like you should have done years ago."

"Let me remind you that a few months ago you were covering freeway expansion plans, and before that you were run out of Manhattan because you were a disgrace, a cheater who stole another man's words," David said. "It is solely because of our generosity that you are where you are. And all it takes is one phone call to change that. So I'm suggesting you leave, right now, and alone, or I'll have the FBI on your tail for kidnapping by the time you reach Sunset Boulevard."

"You will do none of those things," Matilda demanded. "Because I'm leaving on my own volition. For twenty years I've been trapped here because of something that happened a long time ago, for reasons you've kept from me all this time. But I can't stay here anymore."

Matilda stepped closer to her father. She was taller than he, blonde to his brown hair, light-complexioned to his olive tone and just plain softer. From their appearance, you would never know she was his daughter. I couldn't imagine all this sweetness being created by this unscrupulous man. I would have said her mother must have been the sweet one, but then again, she had abandoned her daughter to rot in captivity.

"I've given you a good life here, Matilda," David said. "You've had the best tutors, everything you ever wanted. I know you've been confined here—and that it hasn't been easy. And that's why I've done everything in my power to make you happy."

"I'm grateful for what you've given me—incredibly grateful. You've raised me alone, as a single dad, without a mom. I know you've sacrificed so much for me—I'm sure a love of your own, which is the supreme sacrifice—and if it weren't for you I shudder to think what may have happened to me. But I need more than you can give me now. There's a whole world out there I've never seen."

"This is an acute case of the 'grass is always greener,'" David said. "And I guarantee you if you leave you'll not find greener grass than this."

"Maybe not." Matilda scanned the lawn around her. "Maybe it will be brown and dying and infested with weeds and bugs, but it will be grass I've never seen before. I'm a grown woman now, and you have no right to keep me a prisoner here anymore. I will keep your secret. No one will know you're my father, where I have grown up—the odd circumstances of my upbringing. But I am leaving."

"If you leave, you may never come back." David's tone was even, and I thought I caught the slightest bit of impatience in his voice, as if he had somewhere else to be. "Think about the consequences before you make your decision."

There was a moment of hesitation. If Matilda and her father shared one gene in common it was stubbornness.

"Come, Thomas," Matilda said. "We have a plane to catch."

She held my hand as we walked away from David, and I could feel his eyes burning a hole through my back. She led me through the rolling hills of the estate to the driveway. Now that this moment was here, I was terrified. My heart beat so intensely I could feel it in my wrist.

Once we reached the iron gates to the estate, Matilda hit the red emergency release button, and they opened for us slowly. For a brief moment I thought David might follow us. But instead he let her leave.

We walked out between the gates. They were timed to close quickly behind us—they had secrets to keep after all—and when they did I heard the rattle of iron.

Then it went silent.

Twenty

The first thing she noticed about the real world, she said, was the feeling of the air on her face. She was slightly nauseous from driving at fifty miles an hour down Sunset Boulevard. I opened the passenger window. She stuck her face into the wind, and she commented that the air tasted different, that it was faster than she was used to.

It was interesting to see what caught Matilda's attention and what didn't. For example, after we took a right onto Sunset Boulevard, we passed a sprawling college campus and Matilda looked at it with envy, watching girls her age play field hockey and peppering me with questions about the students who studied in its halls. Once the campus was in our rearview mirror, Matilda asked why Sunset Boulevard was so curvy. "Certainly" she said, "there must be a straighter means of getting to the end." And it wasn't the concept of automobiles that amazed her—an invention that still fascinated me, because I didn't understand how gasoline and an engine caused steel to move at fifty-five miles per hour—but how many different models of cars there were.

Matilda's education had been limited to old movies and books. Some pertinent information could be gleaned from those sources, but they, like the estate, were microcosms of the world's vastness. So Matilda sprayed me with questions, and I didn't have the answers to most because they were things that I had long ago accepted and taken for granted. By the time we pulled into the airport parking lot—"All those cars arranged so symmetrically"—Matilda said her brain might burst open with all its new knowledge.

We boarded the escalator to the gate, and while others hurried through the terminal, eager to make their flights, Matilda walked slowly, marveling at all of it. She had known what an escalator was but had never seen one. Ditto with the airport. Matilda had seen airports in movies of course, but in real life she was fascinated by the X-ray machine and the gates that led to faraway destinations like Tokyo and London. For the first time Matilda was realizing that life had unlimited choices. There were different types of everything, from newspapers to candies to bottled water, and she was being introduced to almost all of it for the first time.

At the gate, Matilda couldn't sit still. I lassoed her into a chair beside me, where she curled up, hugging her knees to her chest. She kissed me lightly on the cheek, before glancing around self-consciously.

"Do people kiss in public?" she asked demurely. "Or did I just do something wrong?"

"You did it right," I said, rubbing my lips on her blond eyebrows and combing my fingers through her hair.

"I want every last person to know you're mine—that you belong to me," she said.

I smiled and pulled her closer, whispering in her ear, "I need you to understand that you can go home whenever you want." I don't know why I said it.

"I know." Matilda watched a plane lift into the sky through the terminal's window. "One month, it's already seeming too short, Thomas. I get you for every minute of it, right?"

"It's one month in Hawaii and we still have the rest of it—all ahead of us."

"The rest of it," she said. "I forgot about that part."

I had first flown when I was two years old, and I remembered none of it. Now I reveled in my flight the way Matilda did in hers. The clouds, the seat belt, the safety information card, the bumps when the wind was wrong, the smooth ride when it wasn't: I noticed it all as if this were the first time I was ever in the sky.

Neither of us slept. I kept watch over Matilda, and she kept watch of the skies. She was remarkably quiet, and when we dipped below the dense clouds and descended toward earth, I heard a slight gasp as she saw Hawaii for the first time.

As the plane gently rocked back and forth with the tropical winds, I closed my eyes and felt my equilibrium sway. I didn't know how Matilda would assimilate into the real world. In fact, I knew very little—not even exactly where we were going. All I had was an address and a key. My whole life I had never been one who took risks. And here I was, abandoning my new editor position and betraying the most powerful man in Hollywood. I shivered when I reflected on my conversation with David, what could happen to me when I returned.

The plane's wheels dropped, and Matilda squeezed my arm.

"That was the plane's wheels. It means we'll be landing soon," I said.

The landscape below was breathtaking. We descended over the volcanoes and the mountains, and swung around the ocean again, where people small as dots played on the shore and surfed the waves.

"It fascinates me how a plane this big can land on wheels smaller than a truck's," Matilda said, pressing her fingertips on the window glass and smiling nervously. "I guess we just hope for the best. Generally when you hope for something, it comes true. Right?"

As the plane touched down in Honolulu and the wheels met

the pavement with a thud, I told myself Matilda was right—
hope for the best and it'll come true.

Joel Goldman's vacation house was a rambling one-story midcentury estate perched on acres of cliffs overlooking the ocean.
The roof hung low over the glass walls, and the house was sheltered from the street. Its seclusion seemed a particularly suited
spot for hiding the most reclusive heiress in the world.

Once glorious, the house and grounds had fallen into dis-
repair. The large gate to the property was so rusted it was stuck
in a half-open state, and the metal mailbox must have lost a battle
with a car, for it leaned at a forty-five-degree angle. Exotic and
bright tropical flowers grew wild, and parts of the lawn were
brown from being scorched by the sun. Other parts stayed green
under the enormous parasols of Australian palms that were so
densely planted they completely shielded the sky. There was
a grass tennis court in the front yard, but its net sagged in the
middle and its grass had overgrown its specifications.

I had to jiggle the key a few times before the lock turned. I
pushed the door open, not knowing what we would find.

By the decor, it seemed as if the estate had been frozen in the
1960s. White sheets covered furniture and crystal. The Hawaiian sun had penetrated the filmy white curtains, streaking the
floors almost white. The walls were now bare, save for empty
art hooks.

There was something eerie about this timeworn house, and
I was concerned Matilda would regret her decision to leave her
father's fastidiously maintained estate. But she had already disappeared through one of the back doors.

I followed her outside. Webbed lawn chairs that hadn't been
replaced in years were stacked in a corner and tied together
with rope. A large lagoon-shaped pool with a rusted-out diving board overlooked the roaring waters twenty feet below. The
pool's plaster was peeling, its coping cracked.

Matilda stood at the edge of the cliffs, transfixed by the ocean. The sun glittered on the water the way stars twinkle in the sky, and the waves crashed into the beach, causing the air to fizzle with salt and humidity.

"The ocean is so different in real life," Matilda said. "It feels so fierce, so alive."

Matilda rubbed her arms with her hands. Specks of salt had settled in her wispy blond hairs.

"I feel sticky—good sticky, but sticky."

"It's the salt water," I said.

Down below was a private beach and cove, accessible by rickety wooden steps jutting out from the cliffs. The swirling, foaming water and crashing waves threatened to sweep us out to sea in their undertow.

"Have you ever thought about how beaches are made up of the fossils of sea creatures?" Matilda said, staring down at the beach. "I had always thought of the beach as a graveyard, but now that I see it in person it seems to have nothing to do with death." A sailboat rolled across the horizon. "Look, a sailboat. Let's go on one."

"Someday."

"Someday is such a pretty thing." Matilda leaned back into me, wrapping my arms around her. "Whose beach house is this?"

"My friend's father's. His name was Joel."

"Where is he?"

"He ran out of somedays," I said, contemplating how one man's death had changed my life. It was because of his obituary that I was here, more alive than I had felt in a long time.

"What do you mean?" Matilda asked.

"He died a few months ago."

"That's terrible," she said, resting her head on my shoulder.

"Some people think it's wonderful, that we go someplace much better than this when we die," I said. I thought of Lily's version of Heaven, that place where we could live our lives all over, as a series of happy data points.

"There is nothing better than this," Matilda said, outstretching her arms toward the ocean. "The world is so beautiful it takes my breath away."

The sun had dipped below the horizon. The sky was red and purple and the moon and stars were out. It was the magic hour, as they said in the movies—that brief dramatic intersection of day and night.

"It is, isn't it?" I said, sweeping my gaze across our extraordinary surroundings. It was ironic, because the first time I had seen David's estate it had taken my breath away, but Matilda was right. It was dull compared to the splendid world outside its gates. "I feel sorry for the rest of the world."

"Me, too. I feel sorry for anyone in the world who doesn't have you." Matilda said it with a flourish, as if she was a magician who'd just plucked a rabbit from a hat. "So that makes billions of people in the world to feel sorry for."

I kissed Matilda on her forehead. "Let's go inside and see where we'll be living for the next month."

Darkness descended, and I picked Matilda up by her small waist and carried her inside. She laughed loudly, that idiosyncratic laugh I had first fallen in love with on her tennis court in Bel-Air.

I peeled the sheets off the furniture, and Matilda followed my lead. Before we knew it, it was nine o'clock and we hadn't eaten. Matilda was used to being served at exactly six o'clock every night.

There was no food at the house, and we were on the outskirts of Honolulu by a few miles, too far to walk. I opened the door to the garage, on the off chance there might be a bicycle.

Sure enough, the garage did house a bicycle, but there was also a car: a red Ferrari Dino convertible, vintage early 1970s. Even in its neglected, dust-covered state it was worth a quarter of a million dollars—more money than I would most likely accrue in my entire lifetime, and here it was, abandoned.

"I don't think we're going to get this running tonight," I said.

"We don't need it," Matilda replied. "I have a wonderful idea for dinner. Follow me."

Matilda led me to the front yard, where she plucked an orange off a tree. She did the same for a grapefruit, then an avocado.

We sat beside the run-down pool and ate freshly picked fruit, staring out at the ocean and up at the stars. Our fingers were sticky, our hair wet with humidity and our moods too buoyant for sleep. We listened to the flap of pelicans' wings and the fizzle of the ocean's surface. When we finally walked inside around midnight, our suitcases still sat near the front door where we had dropped them hours earlier.

We headed to the back of the house, toward an ocean-view master suite. It was the prettiest room in the house—a grand room with a pitched ceiling and broad windows that felt like a picture frame for the astonishing view of the water and the glimmering lights of Honolulu beyond. There were his-and-her closets and a large bathroom with onyx walls, vanities with bronze faucets in the shape of swans and a shower big enough for two.

I set our suitcases down beside the bed while Matilda turned on a single lamp and opened the doors to a porch. The surf crashed loudly and powerfully.

She turned toward me, looking at me shyly.

I walked toward her and cupped her neck in my hands. We kissed more passionately than we ever had, as if once we had left the estate we were finally given permission slips to be adults.

"For so many years, I dreamed of leaving the estate, of what the world would be like. So many people and places, the possibilities were endless. But this is beyond even the realm of my imagination."

Matilda touched my jaw. It was still her favorite part of me.

"It's prickly," she said, repeating what she had said that first evening on the tennis court. Matilda rubbed its reddish stubble with her pink fingernails. "Such a man's jaw. I feel like you will always protect me, Thomas Cleary."

Then she pulled her hand away, awkwardly smoothing out the fabric of her skirt. I realized she was just as nervous as I was.

Matilda leaned in and spoke softly. "I've wanted this for so long."

"So have I," I whispered. I paused, fumbling at what to do next. This was a girl who had utterly enchanted me for two months, a girl I deeply loved. I had thought about this moment more times than I could count, and yet I somehow felt paralyzed by my own nerves.

I took a breath, and I started at her right index finger, kissing it slowly, from knuckle to painted pink nail. I did the same with each finger on her right hand, then her left.

I leaned in and kissed the back of her neck—that little crease at the base of her skull, the part where her blond hairs sprouted. I felt her hands grab for me, and she kissed me on the lips. She was still inexperienced, but it was different from those nights on the estate when she would explore me innocently and naively, without understanding what she was moving toward. In the past, before this, our kisses had been end games, acts of affection meant to punctuate an evening rather than extend it. Her kiss was now an opening act.

"Are you okay?" I asked.

She smiled. "Yes, more than okay."

I took her hand and led it to the bottom of my shirt, and she pulled it over my head. She had seen my chest before, at the estate swimming pool, but now she allowed herself to focus on it intensely. Her eyes lingered on the area under my stomach where a patch of reddish-blond hair disappeared into the top of my shorts. She touched the hair lightly, before fumbling with the button on my shorts nervously. She couldn't get it undone.

"Sorry. Do you want to do it?" she asked, a bit of uncertainty in her voice.

"No, you do it," I said gently.

She slipped my shorts down, sliding her hands down my hips as she did.

Then it was my turn. I slowly unbuttoned Matilda's dress, slipped it over her head and put it on the bed beside us. She was wearing a white cotton bra and underwear, and her instinct was to put her arms across her chest, to cover herself up.

I took her wrists in my hands, delicately, and I placed her arms at her sides, looking at her while I did. I unclasped her bra. I had thought of her every minute since I had first met her, but her body was beyond even what I had imagined. The curves of her, her length—they were all somehow too beguiling for her innocence.

"Do I look okay?" Matilda asked, tilting her head downward in a shy manner.

"You're absolutely flawless."

"You're just saying that."

"I'm a journalist. Only facts here."

Matilda smiled, and I laid her on the bed, sliding her underwear off her hips. She pulled my boxers off, and for the first time we were unclothed with each other. She looked at me intrigued.

I kissed her belly and hugged her hips in my arms. I stared at her body beneath mine—her soft stomach pale as a porcelain doll's, the arc of her hips, the muscles in her legs.

"That tickles," she said quietly, under her breath, when I touched a crease behind the back of her knee.

I kissed her inner thighs, inch by inch. I took care to be gentle, as if every bit of her was breakable.

"Are you okay?" I asked again.

"Yes. Are you?"

"Yes. More than okay," I said with a smile.

I was inside of her then, and she took a deep breath like a hiccup.

I whispered in her ear, "You are so perfect. I feel as if everything beautiful about life is in you."

She squeezed my hands tightly, and when it ended, much later, Matilda studied me tenderly, as if she was seeing me for the very first time. She traced my eyelashes with her fingertips. I kissed the back of her neck, and I smelled her perfume, more pungent with her sweat.

"You smell so pretty."

"Thank you," Matilda said. "My father bought it for me. It's my mother's scent."

Matilda turned toward the outdoors, in my arms. We lay on our sides, and in the distance the lights of Honolulu sparkled on the ocean. Above us stars filled the clear night sky.

"Look, the Big Dipper," Matilda said, pointing through the floor-to-ceiling glass at the sky. "Can you see this constellation all over the world?"

"I don't know," I said.

"Let's pretend you can't," Matilda whispered. "Like nobody else can see it, that it's ours and only ours—our secret."

The Big Dipper was brighter and bigger than we were. It was silly to think that we could hoard it, that those pins of light that shone so brilliantly from miles away could be our secret, but for a brief second I believed it.

Twenty-One

Is being in love any way to spend a day? It is, for all I did was love Matilda Duplaine. Our first days in Hawaii were joyous ones. It was a time that I believed in possibility—the most glorious word in the English vocabulary—and that the bliss would never end.

Matilda and I were biased of course, but as we sipped pineapple juice and listened to the rumbling of the sea, we would say that Joel Goldman's Hawaiian estate was even more magnificent than David's in Bel-Air. There was no horseshoe pit, no sculpture garden, no croquet lawn or bowling alley, but none of those things mattered anymore.

In fact, there couldn't have been two more different worlds than David Duplaine's estate in Bel-Air and Joel Goldman's in Hawaii. While Bel-Air was still, stately and impassionate, Hawaii was untamed, beastly and roaring. In Bel-Air every moment was programmed—golf instructors and tutors arrived neither a minute too early nor a minute too late and dinner was served at six sharp. Our time in Hawaii was free and unscheduled— meals were skipped, timetables ignored.

In the mornings, I would pull the sheets off Matilda while she slept and kiss the shoulder blades that had gone erect with the morning chill. She would squirm, and I would kiss the back of her neck. A muffled giggle would come next, and then I would bury my face in her hair, the backs of her knees, the hollows of her elbows. We would then make love—we didn't revel in it, for we had a day to conquer—and then take showers outside in the morning sunlight.

Matilda wanted to pack the hours as tightly as possible, so as not to waste a minute of her new life. We walked down the jetty and cast fishing rods, and we visited the aquarium and watched the fish slither through treasure chests. We took day trips to different shores and went for long walks, listening to the electric sound of the sun and wails of the seagulls. We spent hours in the bookstore—Matilda loved its smell of paper, the fact that you could turn a book's pages without commitment. We drove on Hawaii's back roads and sped through the streets in the Dino, Matilda with a scarf in her hair, like Grace Kelly. We cooked, toured volcanoes and looked at the stars through a telescope. As I had promised, I took Matilda sailing and we moved so fast we felt as if we might defy gravity and end up on the moon.

Matilda devoured it all. She marveled at the simplest of things: the order of the shelves at the grocery store—"Why are pickles kept next to ketchup," she wondered—the *ka-ching* sound of a cash register, the buoyant cacophony of children laughing on the playground. Every one of Matilda's senses was alive. She could spend minutes examining a single rock, a grain of sand or a specimen of tree she had never seen before. The smell of the ocean, the humidity of the air before a storm still intrigued her. And she heard sounds I had long ago forgotten to listen to—the croaking of pelicans, the tapping of a foot, a guitar strummed in a lonely park at night.

Late one afternoon, Matilda and I sat on a jetty overlooking the ocean. Matilda wanted to learn to surf, and we signed her up for a class set to begin the next morning. We watched as the surfers balanced precariously on their longboards, learning the map of the ocean for the first time—whether waves were rights or lefts and the precise timing of a pop-up.

When the sun was beginning its slow descent toward the horizon, Matilda and I pulled ourselves away from the ocean and its intoxicating waves, and we walked across the street for a stroll through our favorite park.

Hawaiian grade-schoolers kicked soccer balls back and forth. Teenage girls in mod outfits gossiped about exams and boys. An older gentleman with weathered skin painted a scene at an easel and lovers walked hand in hand. Matilda watched all of them silently, still enrapt with the idea that the world was full of so many people.

We stumbled upon a little burger place and Matilda ordered a teriyaki hamburger—aptly called a teriburger—something, I explained to her, we didn't have in California.

"How's your teriburger?" I asked.

"The best hamburger I've ever had," she said. She ate a French fry and sipped a chocolate milk shake. "Everything is incredible—it really is. I feel as if I'm walking through a magnifying glass," Matilda said contemplatively. "I don't know if I'll ever get used to seeing all these things you see all the time. And the people. There are so many of them." She paused. "Is it true that God didn't make the same person twice?"

"That's what they say, but I guess there's no way to prove it," I said.

"It's so hard for me to believe—in all those billions of people there's never been the same combination," Matilda said. "You know, Thomas, being here in the world—it's the people who still most fascinate me. I had only met a handful before." Matilda's fingers were dripping in mustard—her preferred sauce for her fries—and she counted on them. "Maybe thirty people, in all those years at the estate."

"No wonder you liked me." I grinned wryly. "Not a lot to choose from. The percentages were definitely in my favor."

Matilda laughed. "If I had met a million people it still would have been you."

"Well, I *have* met thousands of people, and it was still you."

Matilda leaned over the table and she kissed me. She put her fingers up to my face to cup it and then giggled when she realized she had almost painted me with brown mustard.

As Matilda finished her teriburger and fries, she sat for a moment. That was the other thing about Matilda: whereas I would run from this destination to that one, she would take time to experience everything. I thought of David, the consummate multitasker, and again considered how different Matilda was from him.

"Do you miss your father?" I asked Matilda tentatively.

"I do—terribly sometimes, but other times—" Matilda paused. "Well, I guess love's difficult when it's far away. It's so much easier when someone's there, in person. Do you miss *your* father?"

"Yeah," I said. "And more than everything—even more than the missing—I feel like I should be around for him. And sometimes, particularly over the past couple of months, I feel guilty—like I don't deserve to be happy when he's still so sad."

"About your mom?"

I nodded.

"What was it like to have your mom die?" Matilda asked with slight uncertainty, as if she might be prying.

"It's the flip side of falling in love. Remember when we met? And you told me once that I remained in your air long after I had left?"

Matilda smiled and nodded.

"Death is the opposite of that. When you fall in love, the air feels different, like there's more oxygen or carbon dioxide or whatever it is because you feel lighter. When someone close to you dies, the air feels heavier. The world doesn't quite seem the same, but in a bad way." I paused. It felt nice to talk about it, because I had held it inside for so long. "And your thinking is muddled. At first, I thought she was still alive. For months I would look for my mom in crowds, and at times I would think I found her, that the cancer hadn't gotten to her after all. And then, once I accepted that she was gone, I would think that she was reaching out to me from Heaven, to tell me she was still with me. I would see her favorite flower and think she made it bloom just for me, or I would hear a song on the radio and believe she somehow influenced the DJ to play that very song at that very minute. But then, well, I guess reality sank in. My mom had nothing to do with any of those things—they were just random coincidences."

"Do you know they were random coincidences?" Matilda asked.

"I guess I don't know either way," I said.

"But do you *believe* they were random coincidences?" Matilda pressed.

"Yes. I think that's what I believe," I said sadly.

"I don't know which is worse," Matilda said, "a world that was never whole to begin with or one that was."

I was inclined to think that it was worse to have a mom who died, rather than have no one to lose. But then, again, I didn't know.

"Come on," I said, needing to lighten the mood. "Let's take a walk."

We walked back through the park, and I noticed, in the distance, an A-frame structure that looked as if it was built in the 1960s. A few clunky cars were parked in the lot, and a kitschy sign in a pointy midcentury font read Kalekulani Lanes.

It was as if it had materialized just for us: a bowling alley.

I put my hands over Matilda's eyes, blindfolding her. She giggled, and I whispered in her ear, "I have a surprise for you."

"A surprise? I love surprises. Tell me what it is."

"I thought you just said you loved surprises. If I tell you what it is, it's no longer a surprise."

I guided Matilda across the parking lot, and as I opened the glass doors we were greeted with the thunder of bowling balls, children screaming in delight and music. Matilda threw my hands off her eyes.

"Oh, Thomas," she said, "a bowling alley!"

She rented shoes that didn't fit as snugly as they should have and chose a ball that was loose around the thumb but too tight for her ring finger. Our lane was overwaxed and shiny and wasn't prepared according to Hector's strict specifications. But none of it mattered.

Matilda's first frame was a spare. A cartoon appeared on the television screen and Matilda laughed raucously.

We bowled for two hours, and every bit of it delighted Matilda. Matilda helped a group of teenage boys on the lane beside us with their techniques—"Flip the wrist—like so"— and they were as enamored with her as I was. We bowled until Matilda's fingers were chapped and her feet were blistered from the ill-fitting shoes.

After we returned the balls to their racks and the shoes to the rental counter, we started to walk toward the door.

"I don't want to go home," Matilda said.

It was a surreal moment, because I briefly forgot where "home" was.

"Well, there's always the lounge," I said, pointing toward a vacant room that held a circular-shaped bar and a few vinyl booths. The walls were decorated with strings of garishly colored blinking Christmas lights.

Matilda grabbed my hand and pulled me toward the bar.

"Two of those please," I said to the bartender, as I pointed at a lighted Pabst Blue Ribbon sign.

The bartender delivered two plastic mugs of beer, and Matilda studied the carbonation and foam.

"Cheers," I said, lifting my beer up in toast.

Matilda smiled widely.

"This is my first 'Cheers,'" she said. "And it's so appropriate because there's just so much to be cheerful about."

"Don't forget the eye contact," I said, as she raised her glass.

"The eye contact?"

"Yes, you have to make eye contact—for luck."

Matilda locked her eyes on mine and clinked my mug with hers with great enthusiasm.

I took a gulp of beer, relishing its alcohol as it slid down my throat. Matilda, on the other hand, coughed the moment the beer hit her tongue.

"What's wrong?" I asked.

"I've never had beer before. It's terrible."

"It's an acquired taste. They brew this stuff in Milwaukee, where I'm from, so I'm used to it."

Matilda licked the foam with the tip of her tongue.

"I guess I can get used to the foam part—the rest, I'm not so sure."

Matilda forced down a second sip and then a third.

"Tolerable?" I asked.

"Barely."

"You better watch it or you'll get drunk."

"I've never been drunk," she said. "What is it like?"

"You'll see." I had done a reckless thing, stealing Matilda and taking her to Hawaii and now getting her drunk in the Kale-kulani Lanes. But I had no regrets.

"Bartender," I called. "Two more, please."

"More? I haven't even hit the bubbles yet," Matilda said, more to the bartender than to me, and she winked at both of us.

I noticed a jukebox in the corner. We flipped through the catalog of songs, eventually finding what we were looking for: Air Supply's "Making Love Out of Nothing at All."

"Let's dance," I said, despite the fact the lounge was hardly the type of place anyone would dance. In fact, it wasn't the type of place anyone would even *be*, as evidenced by the fact that an hour had elapsed and we were the only ones there.

I leaned in closer and felt Matilda's cheek on mine. Her hands slowly ran down my back. "Did you ever think we'd be here?"

She paused. "I never wanted to allow myself to think about it, in case it didn't happen."

"I remember that night in the bowling alley so well," I said, after the song had ended.

Matilda laughed. "You bowled four gutter balls in a row. That had to be a record of some kind."

"And you threw four consecutive strikes. You always beat me, Matilda Duplaine."

We swayed back and forth long after the song had ended, to the sound of strikes and gutter balls, laughter, and frustration. At the estate, Matilda had worn a nice dress and high heels to go bowling, but here she wore jeans and a T-shirt and no makeup. Her hair was in a messy ponytail, coarse from that magical elixir of salt water, sun and sand. She was, simply, gorgeous.

"Thomas," she whispered against my neck, electrifying me. "Thank you."

"Don't thank me," I said. "I wanted this as much as you did."

"But wanting and doing are two very different things," Matilda replied. "For all those years there were probably people who wanted me to escape—tutors or members of the staff—and maybe they even thought of helping me themselves. But they were too scared of my father, of his power, of what he might do to them. You were the only one who took the risk—and it was a big risk, I know that. I'll owe you the rest of my life for what you did for me."

"Matilda," I whispered into her ear. "I want you to know you don't owe me anything. Ever. No matter what happens to us when we return. If we go back and I've been fired from my job, if they won't let me into Los Angeles because your father has had me banned from the whole city. Remember, whatever the scenario, that there is no debt between us. I'm not a guy who believes in debts."

Matilda brushed my cheek with hers, and I'll always remember it as her first real grown-up moment. She was dressed as a normal twenty-year-old girl, slightly drunk on cheap beer, dancing in a seedy lounge that had probably given birth to hundreds of one-night stands. I moved so close to her I could see the slight sunburn on her cheeks from our afternoon walk and a smattering of freckles under her eyes.

I had spent the year since my mother died looking for her in familiar ways—songs on the radio, her favorite flower, on my childhood baseball field or in our church—but it was only now, in this remote place, that I found her. My mother had never been to Hawaii, but for the first time I felt she was with me, swaying back and forth beside me, enjoying my redemption.

Twenty-Two

The next morning Matilda and I drove to the beach for her first day of surfing school. I parked the car and gathered Matilda's towel, sunscreen and hat in a beach bag. Beside us, teenagers, coppery tan like pennies, walked past holding longboards. It was a scene from a postcard—a scene that, as a boy in Milwaukee, I would have never really believed existed in real life.

We walked toward the surfing school, a tent so rickety I was concerned it would be blown down the beach in a manner of moments. Surfboards, a large bucket of water and a haphazard pile of ratty beach towels sat on the sand, and hanging rash guards swayed to and fro in the wind. A group of about ten students had already arrived, and they stood in close proximity to each other, making small talk. When we reached the rest of the group Matilda stood in the outskirts nervously, shifting in the sand and glancing back at me. I was reminded of early grade school, that game of ring-around-the-rosy where someone was always left out.

"You must be Matilda." A Hawaiian girl of about Matilda's age approached. She was for whom the term *cute* was coined— long dark hair, eager brown doe eyes. It was clear she was accustomed to this role—the task of prodding people into their first day in the surf.

"Yes, that's me," Matilda said with a level of nervousness I had never seen, even when she confronted her father before we left the estate. "And this is my boyfriend, Thomas." Matilda motioned in my direction.

"I'm Lorelei," the girl said to both of us, before focusing on Matilda. "What a cool name—Matilda. It's so old-fashioned."

"It is?"

I could sense Matilda's self-consciousness.

"You have a cool name, too," Matilda remarked. "It slides off the tongue, like a lyric of a song."

"What a sweet thing to say," Lorelei said. "Now, let's get you your rash guard. You're so tall and you look like you belong in a swimsuit magazine. I'm insanely jealous."

Matilda giggled and her cheeks went red. Just then a shaggy-haired guy approached and introduced himself as Isaac, Lorelei's boyfriend and the surfing teacher. Isaac was good-looking in the way men who spend their lives being tossed around in the surf are. His face was already weathered and lined, and his blond mop had a greenish tint from the mixture of sun and seawater. I envied him, though, for his "right now," carefree attitude. Within minutes of meeting Isaac I could tell he was the guy I never allowed myself to be. There were exams to take, races to worry about, parents to please, scholarships to maintain.

Matilda slipped her flowered beach dress over her head and beneath was a one-piece bathing suit. I could tell by her scrunched-up nose that she was aware that the other girls, including Lorelei, wore bikinis and that maybe her swimwear choice was inappropriate. I thought I caught her glance in my direction, in a slightly accusatory manner, as if I should have informed her that one-piece bathing suits were—like her name—old-fashioned.

Isaac called the group together and began his speech on water safety, pointing to an instructional card with pictures of stingrays and jellyfish, explaining what to do in a chance encounter. Lorelei then provided the students with their foam-topped surfboards, and Matilda practiced her pop-ups. With those long and gangly limbs she wasn't the most graceful, and I watched her as she surreptitiously observed the other members of the class, gauging how she stacked up.

Finally, after about half an hour, they were ready to go into the water. The rest of the group walked toward the surf together, and I noticed cliques already forming. There were three single people in the group—two guys and a girl—and they walked close together. The three couples had become fast friends, and Lorelei and Isaac carried the gear.

That left Matilda alone, trailing behind the group.

Matilda glanced behind her, in my direction. "Are you sure you don't want to come, Thomas?" She asked it an almost-pleading manner, as if it wasn't so much a question as a favor.

In truth, I hadn't been one for surfing—all that effort to get twenty seconds or so of wobbly bliss—but, more important, after seeing Matilda with her newfound group, I thought it was important that she go without me. There was the rest of life to think about—the world after Hawaii.

"You go ahead," I said, resisting the urge to kiss her on the forehead because it felt too fatherly. "Have fun."

Matilda headed toward the water, and I grabbed a towel from the pile and claimed a spot on the beach from where I could observe. Matilda fastened the surfboard's leash around her left ankle and then paddled out on her stomach toward the waves. The waves were gentle, and she navigated through the water, pushing through the waves beside Lorelei.

It seemed somehow significant, but I didn't yet know how.

Her first few attempts to get up were futile, but with Lorelei's demonstration and a strong push from Isaac, Matilda finally got up. She excitedly looked toward me, and I gave her a wave of encouragement.

By the lesson's end, Matilda was getting up with regularity. When she finally joined me, she raved about the thrill of the surf, about the bursts of warm air and the cold. As she spoke I leaned in for a brief kiss, tasting the salt water on her lips.

"Lorelei's so nice," Matilda said. "She has the best hair. Beyond shiny. So bright it glitters."

"Your hair is so bright it glitters, too," I said, as I put my fingers through it.

"My hair is terrible compared to Lorelei's. I wish I had black hair." Matilda took my hand and stopped it from coursing through her hair. "And she's so skinny. I wish I looked like her." She glanced at her curves with frustration.

"That's silly. You have a far better body than Lorelei," I said. "Even Lorelei said you look like you belong in a swimsuit magazine."

"I don't know what a swimsuit magazine is," Matilda began. "But it's not true. We're surfing tomorrow, too."

I squeezed the beach towel beneath me, surprised by my sudden disappointment. I had found myself a glutton for Matilda—I was accustomed to having her every moment, all to myself.

"Thomas, is that okay?" Matilda asked for grandfathered permission.

"Of course," I said, shaking off the jealously. "I'm glad you enjoyed the lesson."

Matilda and I stopped at the teriburger place on the way home, and as Matilda ate her fries with brown mustard and spoke adoringly about Lorelei, I thought about that time long ago in the conservatory when Matilda, dressed as Cleopatra, said her life had seismically shifted when she met me. It was Day Fifteen of our vacation, the midway point, and I somehow felt the same seismic shift. I couldn't put my finger on how, but it was as if beneath us there were all these platelets rubbing together, and eventually that friction was going to move the earth, and it was never going to be the same.

Matilda and I drove to the surf the next day. I had come prepared this time—with a book and a few magazines to get me through the day. I parked, and I noticed that Matilda hesitated.

"There's no need for you to wait around, Thomas," Matilda

said, graciously, observing the other surfers, on their own. "Not that I wouldn't love for you to stay, but yesterday you were the only one watching. And I felt, well, I felt a bit like a child. Everyone else is here by themselves—without anyone staying to watch. I'm not going to drown without you there."

"I didn't think you were," I said. "Going to drown."

"Oh, that came out wrong. It's just—"

"Of course," I said, passing Matilda her beach bag. "I should do some work anyways."

"It's not that I don't want you to come," Matilda said kindly. "I would love for you to watch, but—"

"I know," I said. "No offense taken here. Next time."

"Next time it is. It's a date, then. For next time."

"For next time."

Matilda didn't leave right away. Instead, she held her straw hat across her heart, then kissed me sweetly before opening the car door. She touched the sides of my hair, which were growing long.

She got out of the car, and she walked across the wide beach. When she was about halfway to the shore, she turned around to see if I was still there. She waved, then turned away again before I lost her to the ocean.

In fact, it had been a best-case scenario, as my fair skin had burned the day before, and truthfully I had been dreading sitting on a towel for the entire day with a book I wasn't enjoying. But when I drove to the house, I found myself wondering how Matilda was faring without me, and wishing I was there beside her, watching her get up and waving to me on shore after she did. It was odd when I considered it: it was her first moment in the real world alone. And not only that, in my time with Matilda, I had been the one to leave her—for work, for events, for the art opening, for New York. Now, for merely one day, I had been the one confined to home, and I admit, selfishly, I felt left behind.

It was eerily quiet at the house. The only sounds were the wind and the crashing of the waves. I walked outside, and I stared up at the wispy clouds that covered the blue sky like a coverlet of lace. I thought of Matilda, at the beach yesterday, riding the waves among her surf mates.

It was here, in this first moment of quiet solitude I'd had since we arrived in Hawaii, that I began to think about the questions I'd left behind in LA.

Who was Matilda *really*? I wondered. She had been held in virtual captivity—a science experiment of a girl who lived without social interaction for her whole life. And why had she been kept hidden for so long? As a reporter, the second question should have been the one I strove to answer, but I hadn't.

There was a story behind Matilda Duplaine. Of course there was. Here was a child who had been held captive by her media titan father on a vast estate in one of the most exclusive neighborhoods in the world. I thought back to the boy who had been a track star, to those subzero mornings in Wisconsin when I trained mercilessly toward my goal of being one of the fastest men in the five-thousand meter. That boy, the one who ran his way into Harvard, would have never let this story lie. But I had ignored it because I was in love with Matilda, and perhaps, subconsciously, I did not want to face the moral and ethical dilemma if I had discovered her lineage, why she had been kept in captivity for so long. It was a story that would expose Matilda to the world. Her privacy—the greatest luxury the estate offered her—would be effectively destroyed forever.

Outside, under the low-hung roof that sheltered me from the wind, I pulled out a notebook and began jotting notes. I didn't know which facts were relevant, but I scribbled what I had: the note from Lily to Joel explaining he had made a "mess of things" in France; the fact that Lily had been once engaged to Carole's brother, her family's stable hand, but something had gone irreversibly wrong. And then there were the birth records, which seemed to show no evidence of David Duplaine having had a daughter, despite the fact he clearly had. I wondered again if there was anything to my presumption that David and Carole were having an affair. Carole would have been eighteen when Matilda had been born, and there was little chance David would be carrying on the affair twenty years later. He would have married her long ago, but instead she married Charles.

And Lily: *resemblance* might have been too strong a word, but there was one definite similarity between Lily and Matilda. Both had eyes of an unusual shade of green that I had never seen on any other creature. And there was something else vaguely familiar about the two—something I couldn't put my finger on.

Part of me had always believed that Lily Goldman was Matilda's mother, but another part believed it unlikely. Certainly Lily could have given birth to Matilda when she was in her midthirties—that wasn't the issue. Judging from her relationship with Carole's brother, Lily wasn't opposed to younger men, so it was possible she would have fallen for David, who was five years or so her junior. And David and Lily would have known each other at that point through Lily's father. But that was where it stopped making sense.

If Lily and David had a child, why would Lily have abandoned her? Lily was not the type of person to choose to live alone while her daughter lived down the street in David's care. And what was so scandalous about David and Lily having a child that would have caused them to hide her? And, finally, Lily and David were both relatively small, whereas Matilda was almost six feet tall. Besides the blond hair and green eyes, Matilda would have borne little resemblance to either of her parents.

So something wasn't right. Either a piece of the puzzle was missing or it was right in front of me, hidden underneath other pieces.

Professor Grandy's Journalism Rule Number Five: Assumptions are the mother of all fuck-ups.

But there was a distinction between an assumption and a gut

feeling. Professor Grandy insisted a reporter's gut was always to be followed, because gut was generally right. And the moment I had arrived at Joel Goldman's vacation home, I had a gut feeling that it held answers.

I walked to the room I presumed was Lily's. Like her parents', Lily's bedroom faced the ocean; and like her parents', it was decorated sparely. It had yellow bedding, a plain wooden headboard, a vanity and a white dresser. On the dresser was a single crystal bottle of stale perfume.

The closet held a row of hangers and spare linens. The dresser was empty, except for the bottom drawer, which stored clothing that appeared to be a teenage girl's. I went through the clothing, jotting down in a notebook exactly what I found: a dress, two tank tops, two one-piece bathing suits and a shirt. So Lily had most likely spent time here as a teenager.

I paused for a moment, reflecting on the estates of Bel-Air. They had grass sheared tightly as a general's haircut, the foliage was sculpted or deliberately allowed to grow wild and a wayward leaf was a calamity. Joel Goldman and his daughter both had notorious control issues. Lily's world—from the jewels to the shop to her home—was maintained as fastidiously as an accountant's checkbook. Yet despite its claim on one of the most stunning bluffs in the Western world, this house had been effectively left to rot. Why had the family allowed it to dilapidate? Likewise, Lily had mentioned her father's house in the South of France on multiple occasions, but she had rarely alluded to Hawaii, to this sprawling vacation house that had also belonged to her father. I wondered if perhaps there was a reason for this oversight.

I looked around Lily's childhood room again, feeling as if I had missed something. I opened the closet again, rubbing my fingers over the metal hangers that hung in a row. They clinked together and made a soft, but haunting, melody.

There was something about Lily's room that kept me there, that made me want to explore more thoroughly. I opened the drawers one more time, and when I closed the top drawer I felt something uneven under the dresser's lip. I craned my head and saw a small key taped to the bottom of the dresser. I removed it.

It was a tiny-toothed key, the type used to open a safe or maybe a drawer.

If someone had gone through the trouble of hiding the key, it felt as if it was somehow significant.

I still had a few hours before I had to leave to pick up Matilda, so I decided to search the house to see if I could find the lock that fit the key.

I made my way through each room, notebook in hand. I searched for the mysterious keyhole, but while I did I also inventoried the house to see if I could find another clue to Lily Goldman's relationship to Matilda Duplaine.

I could find nothing remarkable about the kitchen, nor the open area that served as both living room and dining area. Joel's office was almost totally bare, which I took as a clue in its own right. There wasn't much left: an empty oversize wooden desk, two tufted chairs and a bookshelf devoid of any books. The bedrooms were next. Joel Goldman's house had six bedrooms. Four were completely empty, save for a bed. Matilda and I had moved into the room I presumed belonged to Lily's parents. I was familiar with its contents and there was nothing of interest.

As I walked through the chambers, I carefully wrote down even the smallest and seemingly benign details, always looking for a drawer or safe but finding nothing.

After a couple hours of combing the house, I paused to regroup. It was possible the key wasn't a safe key or a drawer key. What else could it have opened? Then I remembered: the mailbox.

I walked outside. It was a humid day and by the time I got to the end of the driveway, sweat had settled in the crease in my neck. I thought of Matilda, in the waves, and found myself the slightest bit agitated that she hadn't invited me to join her.

When I reached the mailbox I inserted the key into the small lock, certain it would fit. I jimmied it, wondering if I would garner a secret through years of Joel Goldman's mail.

But the key didn't work. I tried it again and then again. Still no luck.

As I walked through the heavy air back to the house, I rubbed the tiny metal key between my fingers, feeling its sharp edges and dull face. Every key has to open something; it was merely a matter of finding where that something was.

I arrived to pick up Matilda early and was preparing to walk down to the surf and watch her, but then stopped myself. She had clearly indicated she didn't want me hovering around, so I waited in the car.

Surfing class ended at three, and by three thirty there was still no Matilda. I was beginning to get impatient, but then I calmed myself. Surely there was an explanation for her lateness.

When Matilda finally got to the car, just before four, she seemed different somehow. Her gait seemed surer and the sway of her hips more pronounced, like that of an actress on the red carpet. She ran her hands through her hair, disciplining those gorgeous blond strands—another newly acquired habit. Matilda had always worn one-piece swimsuits, but now she wore a bikini that showed off her curvy breasts and hips. Sand stuck to her wet legs and hair, even her eyelashes, and she had a palpable air of lightness. She reminded me of those popular girls in college who sashayed through the Yard, all ego and little substance.

"I got up every single time. And not only that, I surfed all the way into the shore," she bragged when she reached me. There was an unfamiliar arrogance in her tone.

"You did?" I said, a bit taken aback by her boastfulness. "And you also got a new bikini."

"On the beach—at a little bikini shack. Do you like it?"

"It's very sexy." It was an understatement, and I found myself inexplicably jealous. "And you were also late. I did say I was coming to pick you up at three, right?"

"Lorelei and I grabbed a lemonade after class," Matilda said unapologetically. "She's so funny—she was telling me this incredibly sweet story about when she met Isaac, and I must've lost track of time."

Matilda giggled at a story she kept to herself like a secret. Her laugh was more restrained now. It was as if someone had told her to reel it in, because that was how ladies were supposed to laugh. I wondered if Lorelei or someone else had made a comment about it.

I pulled Matilda closer, pressing my lips on hers. She kissed me back, but it felt disingenuous, as if her mind were somewhere else.

As Matilda and I drove to the house, she spoke disparagingly of another girl in her class, and I almost commented that she wasn't being very nice but figured it would be futile. As soon as I parked the car, Matilda ran inside to the kitchen and sliced open a papaya—surfing *famishes* you, she had said emphatically—and then she retreated to the bathroom to take a shower, because Lorelei had insisted the key to keeping shiny hair was to wash it of sand, sea and sun immediately after surfing. We had always showered together, but she seemed to forget that.

We had dinner, and Matilda spoke incessantly of her newfound friends and her day. She never asked me about mine, what I did or how I had occupied my hours. In fact, as we ate dinner, I felt as if she was the popular girl, and I had sat at the wrong lunch table in the cafeteria.

We crawled into bed around ten. It was the first day of our vacation I hadn't enjoyed. Nevertheless, I leaned in to kiss Matilda on the back of her neck, hoping the evening could be salvaged. She had already fallen asleep, though, still smelling of the surf.

I tossed and turned, contemplating the events of the past two days and the mysterious key I had found. I didn't want to wake Matilda, so I quietly got out of bed and went into the living room.

Matilda, usually meticulous, had tossed her wet beach towel so it hung limply on the back of an armchair. It was an oversight, only one act of frivolousness, I told myself, as I blotted the damp armchair with a dry towel.

I didn't go back to our bedroom. Instead, I again pulled out the key.

I walked around the house again, even more slowly this time, looking for a compartment or drawer ripe for the unlocking. I started in Joel's office. There was one drawer with a lock, but it was slightly ajar and empty. There were no file cabinets, nothing else in the office that required a key. I went into the kitchen, but there were no locked drawers there; ditto with the living room and the bedrooms. Most of the art had been removed at auction, but there was one piece that remained—presumably not valuable enough for auction. I pulled the painting off the wall, hoping to find a safe behind it. There was none. I stealthily pulled up rugs and furniture but still came up empty-handed. It was unlikely Joel Goldman would have been storing valuables in a vacation house, so the lack of a safe wasn't surprising. But that still left the question of the key.

I returned to the living room, and I sat in an armchair, resting in that mysterious and hazy space between consciousness and slumber, feeling as though there was something in the house that was significant.

The air was feeling musty and stale, so I opened the windows and the drapes billowed in the wind. The house certainly seemed like a tropical paradise, but there was something about it that felt not right. *Haunted* may have been too strong a word, but from the moment we had arrived, I had felt uneasy.

I wasn't sure what it was, but I still believed there was a clue in this sprawling Hawaiian villa—a clue that would solve the mystery Bel-Air could not.

Twenty-Three

By the time I awoke after my poor evening of sleep, Matilda was already in the kitchen. She was wearing her new bikini under a rash guard and standing over the stove, preparing eggs and toast. Two glasses of pineapple juice sat on the kitchen counter next to open papaya halves sprinkled with blueberries and a jar of orange marmalade jam.

"Good morning, sleepy bird," she said to me, kissing me sweetly on the cheek. I wondered if I had imagined her detachment of the day before. "I was just about to wake you to tell you that breakfast was ready."

"Do you need help?" I asked.

"Yes, I need you to sit down in front of that plate," Matilda said.

I did as told, and the plate was soon full of sunny-side eggs and sourdough toast, almost burned, just the way I liked it. Matilda sat beside me, thigh on mine, and we talked about surfing, work, a book she was reading.

Conversation was pleasant, the banter of old.

I was making yesterday up, I told myself. *Matilda is still Matilda.*

After breakfast, while Matilda and I did the dishes, she asked what I intended to do for the day.

"Just some work." I thought again about the key I had found, wondering what it could open.

"At the house?" she asked.

"Probably," I said. "Honolulu's not exactly the hub of the entertainment business."

"That's fantastic. Because I was thinking I might take the car today and drive myself to my surf lesson," Matilda said. "If it's okay with you, of course."

I was taken aback by the request because it seemed yet another uncharacteristic act of independence on her part. Matilda had a driver's license but her skills had been honed on the driveway that wove through the estate. She had never driven in Hawaii alone before.

Matilda sensed my pause. "Oh, do you need the car?" she asked sweetly. "If it's a terrible imposition, let me know. It's just that I need to learn to drive myself places. I've just now realized what a child I've been. I was the only one at surfing school yesterday who was dropped off. Everyone else drove by themselves."

"No, not an imposition at all," I said. "I can bike anywhere I need to go."

"Are you certain?" Matilda asked.

"More than certain."

I walked her to the car and we stood in front of it for a moment, as if we both recognized the symbolic nature of her leaving for the first time without me. I found myself playing with the door handle to avoid her eyes.

Matilda fiddled with the keys, nervously I thought, and they clanked together. She smiled, and she kissed me long and hard on the lips. She tasted of orange marmalade jam.

"I'll be home soon," Matilda said. "You won't even have time to miss me soon."

Matilda got into the car and revved its engine a bit too strongly. She looked at me, embarrassed. She took a try at it again, properly this time, and the car rattled in place. She sputtered off jerkily and uneasily, and finally the car sped up as she gained confidence. I watched the car as it turned different shades of red in the changing light—a fiery red, the red of molten lava, the red of dried earth—and then finally disappeared, leaving a quiet street, canopied in Hawaii's greens and blues.

Matilda told me she would be home before I missed her, but I found myself missing her the minute her car had disappeared. Six or seven hours loomed ahead of me, empty and lonely, with nothing to do.

I walked into our bedroom to put on a bathing suit, but instead spotted my running shoes in the closet. I hadn't run in months and wasn't even particularly compelled to do so now, but I decided it would invigorate me or, if nothing else, get me out of the house for an hour.

I put on my running shoes and shorts, and I left for the hills.

The first few strides were the toughest. The concrete found its way directly to my shins and hips, and my back tightened under the force. When I was younger, I'd feel the first bead of sweat around the thousandth meter. Now I felt it in the first few blocks.

I almost turned back, but then I thought of my father, how he used to follow next to me in his car, prodding me along with a stopwatch.

Come on, son, he'd say. *Keep it going.*

The weather reminded me of those August days in the Midwest, the late-summer days of my youth. It was neither raining nor sunny, neither cold nor warm, but the air sweated with humidity. There were filmy clouds, but they moved so slowly they appeared to just sit there. It was as if they were glued to the sky.

My stride hit, and then my breath hit, and then my legs followed. Out there on the Hawaiian road, clarity had finally returned.

In the past couple days, Matilda had shown signs of detaching into her newfound independence. I had no idea of who Matilda would be when she inevitably transitioned into the real world. She was no ordinary girl, and my life felt exceedingly ordinary, even dull, by comparison. I thought of my apartment in Silver Lake, the reporter's salary that barely enabled me to support myself, let alone a woman who had grown up in a hundred-million-dollar estate in Bel-Air. I cringed at the thought of having to be dependent on David Duplaine for anything.

When I returned to the house, I took a seat beside the pool to wind down. The water was swampy, but the wind created ripples on the pool's surface, and the movement reminded me of a piece of art I had seen at the estate, in the vast living room. It was a painting of a man standing over a diving board, water rippled with squiggly abstract lines. I thought of the metaphor. I felt like that man, ready to dive in, but I didn't know what I was diving into.

My thoughts widened to David's art collection—and Joel's. The sun-streaked walls in the Hawaiian house were empty, but darker rectangular spots indicated twenty or so paintings had been removed. There was only that one that remained. The evening prior, when I had searched for the safe, I hadn't focused on the painting itself. I had assumed it was the least valuable, but perhaps that was an incorrect assumption. Was it possible that the painting that remained had some other significance?

I went inside. Oddly, the remaining painting hung in Lily's bedroom—another reason I had been led to believe it wasn't worthy of the auction. Most people, I assumed, hung their most valuable art in their living areas.

I entered Lily's room and examined the painting carefully. The painting was colored in pastels and wildly abstract. I was hardly an art aficionado, and I couldn't tell if the piece was priceless or worthy only of a charity drop-off. I studied it closely, looking for some clue. It appeared to be a series of haphazard paint strokes, but upon careful scrutiny I realized it was a painting of a person—an amorphous woman with fleshy thighs who

I was looking at from a side angle. Around her was a tornado of greens, pinks and yellows. And, upon even closer examination, I realized the painting was vaguely familiar. It took me a second to remember where I had seen it: a similar painting hung in Carole and Charles's foyer. If memory served correctly—which it generally did—I would have bet it was the same artist.

If that was the case, my guess was this piece of art should have been auctioned. Carole's estate was full of multimillion-dollar pieces, so this one most likely would have been equally valuable.

The only two clues I had garnered—the key and the painting—had both come from Lily's room. So I decided to comb through the room one last time. I went through the closet again and the dresser. I even pulled the sheets up on her bed. There was nothing else of interest.

I was about to leave when I walked over to the crystal bottle on the dresser. I turned it over and pressed it against my middle finger. I put the scent to my nose. The scent was familiar: it smelled like Matilda.

It's my mother's scent, Matilda had said.

Just as I was no art expert, I was also no women's perfume expert. That said, I knew enough to know that there were an infinite number of scents, and the chance that Matilda would wear the same scent as Lily highly improbable. But, then again, perhaps it was a coincidence, I told myself. Or maybe—just maybe—this was Matilda's mother's room.

I had to tread carefully. Right now all I had was a complicated theorem without a proof.

One of my assumptions was that Matilda Duplaine had been born in the United States. I was befuddled by the absence of a birth certificate. But it was possible Matilda had been born abroad—more specifically, in France, to Lily Goldman.

I knew just the man who could help. I dialed my friend Jacob, my friend from college whose father had introduced me to Rubenstein. Jacob worked for the longtime ambassador to France, and I asked him for "a favor for me…and Rubenstein"—to look into Lily Goldman's whereabouts, to investigate if by chance she was in France in April of 1988. And, while he was at it, I asked him to look through birth records to see if a Matilda Duplaine had been born anywhere in France that same year.

When Jacob asked about the famous last name Duplaine, I said it was a coincidence.

I hung up and contemplated my next call.

I hadn't phoned Lily since we had left Los Angeles, but I was now compelled to do so. My time in Hawaii was leading to questions, but no answers. One of my strengths as a journalist had been opening the figurative doors for my subjects. I would invite them into my room with kindness and my gee-whiz Midwestern smile and hope once they were there they divulged their secrets. Even if Lily wouldn't divulge secrets, at the very least, she would have answers about the painting in her bedroom.

I dialed Lily's cell phone. It went to voice mail without ringing.

"If it's good news, leave a message; if not, hang up."

I didn't know if my news was good or bad, so I ended the call without leaving a message.

Four o'clock. There was no sign of Matilda. Surf school had ended at three, and it was a mere ten-minute drive home. I found myself consulting my watch every thirty seconds. I had no car to drive to the beach. Matilda had no phone.

Four thirty. Still no Matilda. I vacillated between worry, resentment and anger. Matilda's life suddenly seemed to be moving forward while mine was stagnant. We were switching places, stepping into the shoes of each other's lives. I had given up so much for Matilda, and on the littlest hint of freedom she had run off, leaving me alone.

At five o'clock I saw the flash of red coming up the hill.

Matilda drove up too quickly before stopping the car danger-ously close to the garage. She silenced its engine.

"Where were you?" I asked, trying not to betray my anger.

"Surfing class," Matilda said, with the slightest hint of sar-casm. Sarcasm wasn't something Matilda had used before because her father was too frank for it and her staff would have never used it around her. She must have picked it up on the beach, from one of her new friends.

"I mean after," I said.

"Oh, a bunch of us decided to get a drink." Matilda focused on her beach bag as she said it, as if she was covering up a lie.

It was a simple explanation, too simple for the place my mind was going.

"Would you like to have a glass of wine?" Matilda asked, as she collected her straw bag. "I found a fantastic bottle."

I was about to ask how Matilda even knew what a "fantastic bottle" was but then refrained.

"Didn't you say you just went out for drinks?" I responded.

"One—just one. Let me pour you a glass. You could use a little something to take the edge off. Did something happen today?"

I hated her patronizing tone.

"Work stress," I lied. "I'm going to the store. We need food for dinner. Unless you've already eaten."

"We had some apps," Matilda said. *Apps.* "But perhaps I could eat a little something else."

I was not a high-maintenance sort of guy. Had Matilda of-fered to come with me to the grocery store, her indiscretions would have been forgiven. Instead, Matilda tossed a vague wave in my direction before going inside. It wasn't a gesture meant for a boyfriend who had waited all day for her to come home. It was the kind of wave a princess on a float would give to by-standers at a parade.

I opened the car door, relieved at the opportunity to escape for a few minutes. Matilda must have driven barefoot because her sandals, along with quite a bit of sand, were on the floor of the driver's side. More than anything—leaving me alone carless, the drink before driving, the lateness, that flippant wave—those sandals infuriated me. It was as if she was waiting for a member of her staff to pick them up, when the only other person there was me.

Manhattan, the summer after graduation.

I had been naive then and believed that our lives would continue as they did in the golden halls of Harvard. But when Willa and I moved to Manhattan, things had gone off course, quickly and irreparably. It had been a particularly hot and humid summer, and I remember the stickiness as much as I recall the demise of our relationship. The first weekend after graduation it started: I was stuck with a tight deadline, hunched over a proverbial typewriter in a hot and muggy walk-up while Willa went to visit a childhood friend at her family's house in the Hamptons. Willa helicoptered out to the shore on Friday; I took the jitney out Sunday morning. By Monday we were both back in the city, after a terrible argument about my lateness, which I tried to explain couldn't be avoided.

It only got worse from there.

Our lives quickly veered in different directions: mine took the road of the young, working professional who was handcuffed by responsibilities, a tough boss, and the scary and strange realization that this—the world of work and deadlines—would be the next fifty years of my life. Willa, on the other hand, had slid into a comfortable vanity job in fashion with lackadaisical work hours. It was employment specifically tailored to accommodate the schedule of the socialite.

We had moments where our roads intersected, but they were so few I remember them exactly: the time I took her to Central Park with a basketful of her favorite food; the dinner we had with friends at an Italian restaurant in Chelsea. There was also the time I ran into Willa on her way to a party downtown; the evening turned into beer and tortilla chips and a late-night impromptu visit to a seedy underground jazz club, arms wrapped around each other in a dark corner as we listened to the soulful blues. We went back to Willa's place and spent the weekend with the shades drawn, in bed. Our happiness was artificial, though, for on Monday we were back to the real world, to an affair on the brink of the end.

The next few days with Matilda were not as bleak as that painful summer in Manhattan, but there was something about it that felt scarily familiar.

Matilda would return home whenever she pleased. I had bought her a cell phone, but she never picked up. She texted now, but for a girl who had such an extensive vocabulary, her texts were surprisingly short and her words abbreviated beyond recognition. The innocent, singsongy voice was rapidly changing into the voice of a teenager, peppered with adolescent vocabulary and cadences. She was petulant sometimes, and moody. I could tell what kind of evening it would be by the manner in which she drove home: if the car ambled in slowly and gently, it would be Matilda of old, and if the tires squealed on the gritty pavement, it would be Matilda of new.

Every day Matilda would leave for the surf, for her friends I barely knew and activities we had never shared, and I was left alone. For the first three days I stayed at home, scouring the abandoned house for additional clues. There were none. I had begun to think that my premonition that Joel Goldman's house held answers was, simply, wrong. When I considered things objectively, I realized that all I had was a key that opened nothing, a painting that still hung on a wall and a few drops of perfume at the bottom of a bottle. I also realized that my gut, a part of me I would have coined my strongest muscle, had weakened in recent years. In fact, I was beginning to think I could no longer trust it at all.

By the fourth day, I decided it was best to leave the house, for the term *cabin fever*, it turned out, was created not only for cabins in winter, but sprawling Hawaiian vacation houses in fall, as well. Matilda had once again taken the car, so I hopped on the bike. The air was a welcome distraction, proof that there were things still moving, that the world was as it was supposed to be.

I rode to downtown Honolulu, where Matilda and I had spent our days before she had started to spend so much time in the surf. While it was nice to be around activity and people again, every destination reminded me of Matilda. There was the jetty where we fished, the souvenir shop where Matilda had bought a puka necklace, the local café where she had first sipped coffee. I walked around aimlessly, finding myself glancing at my watch every few minutes. Whereas only days earlier Matilda and I had wanted to stretch our minutes longer, now I just wanted them to disappear.

After several hours had passed, I started my bike ride home. In the middle of rolling hills, with nothing around it, I saw a slightly run-down bar with a lit shamrock in front. I realized, just at that moment, that I was homesick—not only for Los Angeles, but for life before Bel-Air and Matilda, life when it had been simple.

On a whim, I decided to stop for a drink. I locked my bike and opened the door to the dark pub. Inside, I was greeted by three generations of fast-talking redheads, who I soon learned owned the bar. Their greeting was as warm and friendly as if I was a long-lost cousin off the boat from Dublin, and their sparkling blue Irish eyes gave off the impression that the day was dull before I showed up. I think they quickly took a liking to me because of our shared hair color and affinity for baseball and good drink, but whatever the reason, it felt good to have someone want to spend time with me again. Rightly or wrongly, I was beginning to feel Matilda was using the surf to avoid me.

A football game aired on the televisions, and it felt nice to watch. I had been away from civilization for so long I had forgotten the real world was moving while I was staying still. The redheads served heavy dark ales to familiar patrons, laughing at a story they had probably told each other countless times before, glancing at the TVs once in a while and commenting on the score. It was ironic, I thought, that I was spending the afternoon in a windowless bar that smelled of yeast and my hometown while Matilda was out in the sun-filled sky. It was symbolic: it signified how quickly and seemingly irreparably my life was diverging from Matilda's.

Around five o'clock, I found myself looking at my watch, concerned Matilda would be home. The bartender insisted I have one last ale and volunteered to drive me home after, as darkness was ready to descend.

We navigated the Hawaiian hills toward the house, making small talk about sports while the city prepared for night. Lights were flickering on, the vivid greens around us were turning black. When I spotted the rusted gates of Joel's house, I pointed out the entrance to the long driveway.

"Here we are," I said. "Take a right through these gates."

"Funny, I haven't been here in a long time," the man said, as he drove past the decrepit grass tennis court and the tall date palms. He stopped at the wide entry, looking at the house wistfully.

"You've been here before?" I asked.

"Just once or twice, when Joel was still coming to these parts."

I perked up. Clues had run dry and I had all but given up. "Did you know him?" I inquired eagerly.

"Nah, not well. We had a few friends in common, so I was invited to the house a couple a times." He smiled again—more like smirked, really. "Whatever happened to the girl?"

"Which girl is that?"

As a journalist I did my best not to lead the subject, but I assumed he was referring to Lily. He stopped the car in front of the house and looked at it nostalgically.

"The dark-haired girl that lived here. I'm not a fan of brunettes—prefer light hair myself—but she was one of the prettiest girls I've ever seen."

My heart fluttered. Lily was blonde. I leaned closer to my subject, hoping he'd tell me more.

"Who was she?" I asked.

"One of his staff, if I recall. Don't remember her name. She spent some time here, house-sitting I think. I only met her once, and it was after Joel stopped coming." He paused. "Or, on second thought, it could be this old man's memory playin' tricks."

I thought back to earlier hours, at the bar. This man recited sports scores and recalled exact goals and touchdowns as if they had happened minutes, instead of decades, earlier. His memory was sharp as a med student's. This was what we call in journalism a reliable source.

"How long ago did Joel stop coming?" I asked. It had been a question I had only considered in a vague sense. This once-majestic property had been abandoned—but for how long, and why?

"Joel hasn't been here in twenty years—give or take. Such a shame, this pretty spot with no one to enjoy it. I'm glad you're taking advantage of it. I always believe beauty shouldn't be wasted on the rich. Now, you come back and visit us, you hear? Football this weekend."

"I will," I said, thinking that questions were leading to more questions, not answers. "Thanks for the ride."

I got out of the car, pulled the bike from the hatchback and walked through the front door, calling Matilda's name as I did. There was no answer. I immediately regretted leaving the bar so soon. I should have known I would come home to an empty house.

But then my mind went to the conversation just moments earlier. A brunette, I thought. But Joel's wife and Lily were blonde. There was a house sitter at the house, or a member of the staff. I wondered if somehow the key was related to her. Maybe it opened something that had belonged to her—a suitcase or a jewelry box—and she had left it behind by mistake.

Mood buoyed with my newfound information, I walked to the staff bedroom in the front of the house. I had searched this bedroom before, and I sifted through its few contents again. There was nothing significant—in fact, it seemed hardly lived in. I peered out the dirt-covered window toward the driveway, thinking I heard the sound of a motor. I wondered if Matilda had come home.

Instead, it was the man who had driven me home. He hadn't left. He was still in the car, staring at the house—with regret or longing, I couldn't tell which—until he saw me watching him and he drove away.

Twenty-Four

The next afternoon Matilda returned home from surfing earlier than usual, two shopping bags swinging from her right hand, car keys jingling in her left.

Initially I thought that Matilda had finally come to the late realization that she had been ignoring me, and that she had come home early to spend the afternoon together. But I was wrong. She leaned in and brushed her lips on my cheek, almost as an afterthought, then focused her attention on her bags, rifling through the expensive tissue.

"We're going to dinner tonight with Lorelei and Isaac," Matilda said, pulling a black jersey dress out of the wrapping by her fingertips, like a charmer teasing a snake out of its basket. She stared at it lustfully. I was wearing an army-green T-shirt and khaki shorts, and Matilda glared at the ensemble.

"I'm going to get dressed. You may want to change into a nice shirt, Thomas. This dinner is really important to me."

Before Matilda disappeared, she bit off the price tag on her dress and tossed it, along with the credit card receipt, onto the dining room table. When she left, I picked up the receipt. The dress was a thousand dollars—money I didn't have.

I did as Matilda asked and changed into the only nice shirt I had brought with me on the trip, while she put the finishing touches of makeup on her face. Her eyeliner was heavy, reminiscent of the way Willa wore it at the art auction, but less artful. She had applied it with an unsteady hand, and it was something like the job of a fourteen-year-old who had dug into her mother's makeup drawer with the babysitter.

"How do I look?" Matilda asked, studying herself in the mirror over her vanity.

Gone was the girl who had left pretzel bits on her lips without a care in the world.

"It's not your usual look," I said.

"What do you mean?" Matilda asked.

"Your eyeliner's usually more pencil than paint, isn't it?"

"Is it bad?" she asked, alarmed.

"Not at all. It's just different." In fact, the makeup application was terrible, but we were running late and I didn't want to start an argument. I already had the feeling this night was one I would soon want behind me.

We walked to the car and Matilda relaxed for a moment, pressing her hair between her palms to straighten it. Our drive was quiet, as Matilda admired herself in the side-view mirror.

"Thomas?" she said, more to the mirror than to me. "I haven't told Lorelei much about, well, where we live. I get the sense she doesn't have a lot of money and I don't want her to think we do."

"I don't have a lot of money. You may, but I don't. You know that, don't you?"

"Oh, Thomas, now's not the time to talk about such things."

"There's never an opportune time to talk about money," I said. There was a pause.

"You know, Matilda, I can't afford dresses like the one you're wearing." It was the first time I had used a tone of admonishment with her, and she reacted with surprise, as if I had no right.

"It was just this once. It's a special occasion."

"It's not a special occasion," I said. On cue, I saw our destination in the distance. It was a dingy little club with its name in neon lights. Matilda and I would both be grossly overdressed. "It's drinks with some friends."

"Let's not get this started on a poor foot, Thomas," Matilda said, misusing the expression. "You've been in a horrendous mood all day."

I pulled into the lot. A few faux palm trees in pots flanked the entry, and the structure's stucco was peeling. An open parking spot waited in front, the first good fortune of the whole day.

"Wait," Matilda ordered, before I could turn the car into the spot. "I usually park far away from the beach so Lorelei can't see the car. If she sees the car—"

"She'll know about the money," I completed her sentence. "Got it."

I drove down the street, toward a slice of gravel. "Here okay? Or would you prefer Kona?"

"This is perfect. I just don't want to screw anything up. I really like her."

Matilda was typically affectionate; she always wanted to hold hands or wrap her arms around my hips. But as we made our way into the supper club, she seemed distant and distracted. I reached out for her hand, but it was already waving in the air toward a girl dressed in all black—boots, dress, eyeliner and nail polish.

Emulation is a form of flattery, or so they say, and if that was the case, Lorelei should have been more than flattered. Matilda had clearly tried to look exactly like her.

"Hi, M," Lorelei said, embracing Matilda in a hug.

"Hey, hi!" Matilda said. She seemed to hold on to Lorelei for an extended length of time, long after Lorelei had let her go.

Lorelei turned to me. "Good to see you again, Thomas. We've missed you at class, but Matilda tells us you've been busy working on an important story for work."

Matilda didn't know about my research, but in her mind it was a lie designed because she didn't want me there. She had never even extended an invitation to me.

"Yeah, I've been really busy," I said, putting my hand out, determined to make the best of the evening ahead.

"This place is really cool," Matilda said, looking around the club with starry eyes, as if she was a teenage girl who had just run into a pop idol on the street. I wondered if she really thought this supper club with sticky floors, paper menus and sullen waitresses was "cool."

"Isaac and I come here all the time." Lorelei squeezed the top of Matilda's arm. "Rockin' dress. Where did you get it?"

"I don't remember. It was forever ago." Matilda dragged out the word *forever* and beamed with the compliment.

I opened my mouth, ready to tell Lorelei that she picked it up at an expensive boutique that afternoon, that its thousand-dollar price tag lay at home in the trash. Instead, the rest of the group sat down at the table, and I excused myself to the bathroom.

The bathroom smelled of urine, cigarette smoke and gin, but it was still a respite from what was going on outside it. I walked into a stall, latching it behind me. I leaned my back against the cold metal door, grateful to be alone. I could feel the metal through the dress shirt Matilda had demanded I wear for the dinner.

For not the first time over the past days, I tried to reconcile the girl I had fallen in love with and the one who had accompanied me to this seedy club. But I couldn't. I wondered if this relationship could be salvaged; and, if it couldn't, what would happen when I returned to Los Angeles without her—literally or figuratively. It wouldn't be decided tonight, I said to myself, emerging from the stall. I splashed water on my face and inhaled deeply, convincing myself I could get through the next few hours.

As I opened the bathroom door, a wave of laughter washed over me. I braced myself for a return to the table.

"We were getting worried about you. Isaac was about to follow you into the bathroom to make sure you were okay."

It was Lorelei who said it, not Matilda. Matilda looked at me as if I was a parent who had come home too soon and broken up the party.

"Phone call," I said, holding up my phone as proof.

Lorelei turned to me. "Your girlfriend is amazing. She knows more about music than anyone I've ever met."

Matilda blushed again at the compliment, and I realized that, besides me, Matilda had never been praised by someone who hadn't been well compensated to admire her.

"I know," I said. "She's an encyclopedia. On our first date we listened to everything from Air Supply to Interpol."

"Air Supply, my God, I haven't heard them forever." Isaac laughed, and Matilda glared at me. In this short time, she had come to realize that Air Supply wasn't cool.

"Neither had Matilda, actually. Air Supply was my choice. Interpol hers."

Matilda smiled at me. I think it was her way of thanking me for taking the fall.

"How did you guys meet?" Lorelei asked.

We were both quiet.

"At the tennis courts," I finally replied, though it was a stretch of the truth.

"How old-fashioned and romantic," Lorelei said.

"It was, actually. Matilda's too modest to say it, but she's an incredible tennis player. I've never beaten her."

"So, was it love at first sight?" Isaac chimed in.

"Well, I can't speak for Matilda, but for me it was. I couldn't get her out of my mind. Still can't." I tossed Matilda an affectionate smile, but she seemed more besotted with her passionfruit mojito, gulping it through a straw.

"That's so sweet. And, Matilda, what about for you?" Lorelei asked.

"What?" she asked, swirling a brightly colored umbrella in her drink.

"Was it love at first sight?"

"I think so, but I had nothing to compare it to," Matilda replied.

She didn't say it maliciously, and she had finished half of her mojito at this point, so it was entirely possible by the glint in her eye that she was drunk. But Lorelei and Isaac glanced at each other surreptitiously, aware her response was odd, if not rude. I considered excusing myself to make another phone call, but then realized it had only been five minutes since my last trip to the bathroom.

The rest of dinner passed uneventfully. Lorelei and Matilda sat hip to hip like Siamese twins and gossiped about a guy at the beach and the girl I quickly gathered was the outcast of their group. Isaac, for his part, peppered me with questions about Harvard, a place he had only seen in the movies.

As we finished our after-dinner cocktails, however, their questions turned dangerously personal. "Matilda, where did you go to school? What are you studying? Thomas, why did you leave your job to come to Honolulu?" My answers were slow and clumsy, and I was entangling myself in a web of lies.

"We should probably get going," I said around midnight. Matilda's eyes were bloodshot from alcohol, and she seemed to sway in her seat.

"I hope you guys don't have a long drive," Lorelei said.

"We don't," I lied, yet again.

"Where do you live?" Lorelei asked. Matilda had obviously refrained from mentioning to her friends that our stay was a vacation, not life.

"In the hills," I said vaguely.

"Are you renting?" Isaac asked.

"Sort of." I thought back to Lily, to that night at Carole's

when she had said we were all just renters. "We're all just renters of life if you think about it."

Lorelei and Isaac exchanged side glances.

The waitress left the check on the table between us and I
tried to get a cue from Matilda to see if she wanted me to pay.

"Let's split it, man," Isaac said, making a poor attempt to
reach for his wallet.

"I'll get it this time. You guys can get it next time," I said,
grabbing the check.

Matilda finally became aware that I had paid for dinner, but
I couldn't read her expression, if she was upset or pleased. Her
eyes were cloudy and unfocused, and she looked as if she might
get sick.

"Where did you park?" Lorelei asked, as we walked outside.
The fresh ocean air felt good. Lorelei and Isaac headed toward
their car, an old model with a broken taillight.

"I missed the lot, so we're right around the corner. Besides,
I read somewhere that if you park three blocks away from your
destination, you lose an extra pound over five years," I said,
making light of the situation.

Everyone laughed except Matilda.

"Do you want to grab a nightcap?" Lorelei asked. "There's a
great bar around the corner."

"Why don't we take a rain check?" I suggested. "I'm beat, and
I have a story due tomorrow. One of my reporters had a death
in the family, so I'm doing him a favor."

As the night was coming to a close, the lies were coming
easier.

Isaac and Lorelei got into their car and angry music erupted
from the stereo, as if it was waiting, all this time, to scream its
rage. We watched the broken taillight disappear over a mountain, and then we walked the three blocks to our car in silence.

I put down the top, thinking both of us would do better with fresh air—for different reasons. My frustration with Matilda was bubbling at the surface, ready to erupt.

I floored the gas and turned on the radio. It was an angst-ridden song, which seemed to suit the mood.

"Can you drive a little more slowly?" Matilda asked as we pulled onto the highway. "Everything's a little blurry."

I didn't answer, I didn't slow down and I didn't speak to Matilda for the entire ride home.

Instead, as we drove through the hills, I couldn't help but think about that dangerous time in a relationship when it teeters on the precipice of disaster. I felt like a bystander on a sidewalk watching two cars about to collide, a coach seeing an interception before his tight end did. I knew things were about to go very wrong, but I was standing on the sidelines, helpless to stop it.

Twenty-Five

Matilda was still asleep when I sneaked out of the house the next morning.

First, I drove to the gas station. I had noticed on our ride home from the club that Matilda had left the car on empty, despite the fact that she was the one who had spent the past five days driving. It might have been my fault, as I had never taught her to pump gas, but it upset me nevertheless.

After getting gas, I drove to the park and took a walk through the grounds, watching an old man feed pigeons and kids shoot soccer balls at a net. My life had become a giant question mark. I had risked everything to emancipate Matilda, and it took merely days for her to forget it. I was not an unreasonable person, but Matilda's growing detachment and her self-entitled behavior were infuriating me. For days Matilda had left me alone—with no car, no invitation to join her at the surf and no interest in how I spent my days without her. I knew the minutiae of Matilda's life, but Matilda barely knew anything about mine. And worse: it didn't seem to bother her.

Later that morning, I returned home to find Matilda, hair done in curls shaped like s's, sitting on a lounge chair in a skimpy black bikini I hadn't seen before. I figured she had bought it with Lorelei.

She was painting her toenails, and black polish was every-where—the chaise, the stone, her fingers. The only place it didn't seem to be was on her toenails.

"Where were you?" Matilda asked, without looking up from her toes. "I missed my surfing lesson. Isaac was upset."

It was only then that I realized Isaac wasn't much different than Matilda's instructors at the estate. He was someone remu-nerated to be nice to her.

"If Isaac missed you, he should have come by and picked you up," I said.

Matilda said nothing, because we both knew why she didn't want Isaac coming to the house.

"Where were you anyways?" she asked again, her eyes trained on her toes.

"You left the car on empty."

"On empty?"

"You left the car with no gas. It was running on fumes. If you drive, you need to fill it up," I said.

Matilda attempted to paint her little toenail, but it was fu-tile. Exasperated, she dropped the bottle on the stone. She fi-nally looked up from her toenails, just now bothering to make eye contact with me.

"Next time you're going to take the car, please ask," she said.

"I could say the same for you," I said.

"If you needed the car, you could have told me," Matilda said. "I didn't get the impression you needed to leave the house for anything. What exactly is it you need to leave for, Thomas?"

I didn't answer.

"Don't get upset with me," Matilda said under her breath. "You're the one who's chosen to sit around the house all day."

"With all due respect," I said. "I don't think you're one to talk about sitting around the house all day. Wasn't that how you spent the last twenty years?"

Matilda's face paled.

"How dare you?" she said.

"I've risked everything for you." I raised my voice. "My career, my livelihood. Los Angeles is my shot—my last shot. I abandoned a boss who rescued me from failure, and betrayed your father, who happens to be the most powerful man in the city. Either one of them could press a button and destroy my life in less than a second. And this is how you thank me?"

Matilda looked away, toward the ocean. Her green eyes were starting to turn glassy with tears.

"You don't know what I'm going through." Matilda's voice was so low it was almost a whisper.

"Actually, Matilda, I spent the past three months understanding you, but have you ever once asked what it's like to be me? Have you ever tried to understand me? I can answer that for you. No. You don't even know me."

"That's the worst thing that you've ever said to me. I love you. Are you implying I love someone I don't even know?"

"Have you ever asked me why I ended up in Los Angeles in the first place? Are you even aware that I live in a shitty apartment in Silver Lake? Wait, probably not. Because you've never heard of Silver Lake. Because you can't imagine what a shitty apartment even looks like."

Matilda hadn't removed all of her makeup from the night before, and the black eyeliner began to run down her cheeks like a pen that had leaked.

"How about my mother? She died only a year ago. Do you know what she died of? I know everything about your dad. Do you know anything about mine? He's at home alone right now with no family and a couple thousand dollars in his bank account. My dad doesn't run a movie studio or newspapers or television networks. He works in a lumberyard. He sits at home at night icing his back watching Milwaukee Brewers games on TV because he can't afford to go in person."

I swallowed a lump in my throat. I was not a man who cried,

because Midwestern men did nothing of the sort. We did not wear our hearts on our sleeves. We kept them in our chests, where they belonged. Even in those terrible months in Manhattan when my life fell apart, I did not shed a tear.

"I would've never taken you away if I had known it would be like this."

It was the worst thing I could have said to her, and I immediately regretted it.

"You could have just told me," she said quietly. "If you needed—or wanted—to talk about these things. I didn't know. And I didn't know you were feeling that way—about our trip. I've been a terrible burden on you."

"Matilda—" I began.

"I'm sorry," she said. "About your father."

It implied she wasn't sorry for the rest of it, or that was how I construed it. I collected myself and raised my chin stoically.

Matilda headed inside, but before she did she approached me and ran her hand along my shoulder blade, as if expecting me to say something. But there was nothing left to say.

An hour later, Matilda emerged from the house. She wore a low-cut black dress over her bikini and a brightly colored silk scarf knotted loosely over her hair. She had bought it at Hermès in town, two weeks earlier, when everything had still been good. She had put it on my credit card, not realizing that I couldn't afford five-hundred-dollar scarves.

Matilda carried her small designer duffel bag at her side. "I'm going away with Lorelei and Isaac," she said, readjusting her scarf so it was just so. It was a rich lady's accessory—something Carole and Lily would wear—and its elegance now seemed out of place with the rest of her.

"Where are you going?" I said, her betrayal washing over me.

"To the North Shore, surfing for a few days."

"Define 'a few.'"

243

"I'll be back on Thursday."

That was four days away.

"How are you getting there?" I asked.

"I'm going to the beach to meet Isaac and Lorelei. Isaac's driving."

Just then, I heard a car pull up and a honk.

"I called a cab so you wouldn't have to drive me," Matilda said.

The cab driver honked again, twice this time.

"I keep trying to feel that glorious thing that we had in the beginning," Matilda said, looking up at the date palms. "But it's disappeared, and I don't know where it's gone. And what's worse is I don't know how to get it back."

It was as if she'd tossed a grenade at my heart. I had thought I was the one tiring of her, but here she was, thinking the same thing. She had used the surf as an excuse to avoid me.

Matilda walked toward the door and then at the last minute turned around.

"Cancer," she said. "That's what you said your mother died of."

She looked at me for another moment, and I made myself look at her, too. I wondered what I would have thought of her had I met her now, in that outfit, with that skimpy bikini top and eyeliner too dark for her skin. I couldn't think of it, though, because I could only remember her as I had first met her that night on the tennis court.

To me, that would always be my Matilda. This girl was a stranger.

I wondered if I was a stranger to her, too.

For the first few hours Matilda was gone, I thought she would change her mind and come home. I turned up my ringer in case she called. I checked my messages hourly. Finally, at dusk, I poured myself a scotch in one of Joel Goldman's crystal highball glasses, and I stood on the front porch, thinking that if I stood there she would magically come back.

She didn't.

I was still on the porch, on my third drink, when my phone rang. I fumbled for it, picking it up without looking at the name on the screen, hoping and believing it would be Matilda.

Instead it was Jacob, my buddy who had been investigating Lily's time in France.

"What did you find out?" I asked, trying not to sound too eager.

"I suspect not what you wanted me to find out," he said. "According to passport records, you were right. Lily Goldman did spend quite a bit of time in France, but she wasn't there in April of '88. You sure you have the right dates?"

I paused for a moment, wondering if Matilda could have thought her birthday was different than it was. The web was getting thicker, but I believed she was twenty. There was no reason for David to lie to her about that.

"Pretty darn sure."

"The reason I'm asking is Lily Goldman was in France, but she left Nice on March 2, 1988. By April 20, your magic date, she was gone."

This wasn't the answer I expected. "Do you have any idea where she went?" I asked, as I traced the indentations on the crystal glass on my lap.

"Back to the US, according to passport records," Jacob said. "Lily Goldman landed in Los Angeles. I have a photocopy of the stamp from LAX to prove it should you not believe me."

"I believe you. And Matilda Duplaine?" I asked, wincing as if I had reached a dead end I hadn't even hit yet.

"Doesn't exist according to the illustrious country of France."

I had been so certain my hypothesis was correct, but this seemed to quash it altogether. Lily wouldn't have been flying overseas while eight months pregnant, and even if she had,

Matilda would have been born in the States, so there would be some record of her. Even the rich and powerful couldn't make a birth certificate disappear.

We ended the call, and for the first time I firmly eliminated the possibility of Lily Goldman as Matilda's mother. I realized how I had subconsciously believed it all along: it was those eyes and Lily's preternatural closeness with David and now the shared scent. But the glue to hold that hypothesis together had always been watery.

I stared in the distance at the dark road where a stray pair of headlights came and went.

I thought of venturing to the Irish pub, to ask further questions about the mysterious girl who had taken care of Joel Goldman's house in his absence, but instead I sat on the front porch until midnight, not wanting to miss Matilda in case she came home.

As a reporter, I was always looking at the clock, trying to make a deadline. It was ironic, because since we'd arrived in Hawaii, time had always been running too fast. But in the hours since Matilda had left, it felt as if it were standing still.

During my run the next day, I kept my thoughts close to me. I didn't turn on my music; instead, I listened to my breath, my feet, the chirps of birds, the slow breeze rolling through the palms. Only a few cars passed, and when they did I focused on the sounds of their motors, the tires that treaded on pavement, squeaky brakes that seemed louder than they were in the quiet Hawaiian air.

I recalled what David had told Matilda about her mother: if someone doesn't want you, you shouldn't want them. It was simple advice really, but advice I hadn't taken. I had loved Willa long after she had reciprocated that love, and I wouldn't allow myself to do the same with Matilda.

Professor Grandy's Journalism Rule Number Six: Never fall in love with your subject.

That had been my first mistake, and the one that had led me to the wrong shore. Here I was, a man who had chosen a different path than my friends at Harvard. I had excelled in school, and I could have had virtually any job I had wanted. But instead I had prided myself on being the only one who didn't sell himself for money while all of my friends had been bought by investment banks, hedge funds and corporate law jobs.

I thought I had chosen the honest path, the path of a reporter. I almost laughed out loud at the thought. A story of the Hollywood century lay in front of me, and I had chosen not to break it.

By mile number four, my shirt was damp with sweat and I could have shaken the water out of my hair it was so wet. I thought about the future—immediate and far. Sure, there were the next few days to consider: how to muddle through the time without Matilda more gracefully than I had after Willa. There would be no counting down of minutes this time, no thinking of how to make myself more worthy of her love. If she was gone for good—a frighteningly distinct possibility—I would begin the rest of my life anew. I would not lie in bed awake for years, sleeplessly reaching for a season that had already shed its leaves.

And if this was to be the outcome, there was the story to consider. I would betray Lily in writing it, and the same for David and Matilda. But of all of the characters in my life, it was Rubenstein to whom I owed the most. And, if I was being honest, myself. If someone had asked me to list my greatest character traits, I would have pegged loyalty at the top, but the older I got the more I realized just how rare a thing loyalty is.

I returned to Joel Goldman's house and took a quick shower. Thoughts of Matilda weighed heavily on me—questions about her past, the dismal reality of the present—and I found myself starting to corrode, like this old house.

I decided I needed to give myself a purpose, and the purpose for me, for as long as I could remember, had always been putting pen to paper to tell a story—to tell the truth. I thought again of the story of Matilda's lineage and decided to start writing it— even if it was for my consumption only.

But I couldn't stay here, in this crumbling estate. I needed to go somewhere else to work. Anywhere. Matilda had been right about that. I had been stuck at home for too long. I decided that the library was as good a place as any.

I drove to the library, feeling more productive and, oddly, hopeful, than I had in the past two weeks. It was a palatial building situated behind an impressive garden. As I walked through the tall doors into an entry that smelled of paper and cardboard, I was reminded of boyhood—of sitting cross-legged on the floor with a Hardy Boys book, of cramming my way through Harvard.

I chose a table in a secluded corner. I turned off my cell phone so I couldn't be tempted to see if Matilda had called, and I spread out three months of research in front of me like a fan.

I had two notebooks of transcriptions, but no story. After all, I was dealing in the world of David Duplaine. He didn't accidentally drop clues; he was too clever for that.

I spent hours sifting through the pieces, and by midafternoon, my head was spinning with facts. I thought of the key that seemed to open nothing, the piece of art that still hung in Lily's bedroom. And who was the mysterious brunette the man from the bar had longingly recalled? Something told me that Joel Goldman had to have known about Matilda. But what did he know? And then there was Lily's fiancé, Carole's brother—that may have been the strangest piece that didn't quite fit. There was no mention of him in the press, and his engagement with Lily had been derailed for no apparent reason. I wondered if his disappearance might have been more significant than I had thought.

I needed to delve further, and so I called the office and asked one of the young researchers to pull extensive background checks on Joel Goldman and Carole Partridge's brother.

It wasn't until the library was about to close that I packed up my bag and left. Once in the courtyard, I lit a cigarette and glanced at my phone. Matilda hadn't called. It was as if we were two boxers bobbing on either side of the ring, waiting for the other to move to the middle first.

My head was spinning with facts, but there was something nagging me. I kept feeling as if the critical pieces of the story were those I hadn't yet touched. There was still something I was missing, but I couldn't isolate it.

Professor Grandy's Journalism Rule Number Seven: Sometimes what isn't there is more important than what is.

Twenty-Six

I woke up the next morning to a text from Matilda. It had come in at one in the morning.

Got here ok, it said. How r u?

A simple text, but it felt significant. Matilda had shuffled into the center of the ring first. I debated about how to respond and then put my phone down without texting back. I was a journalist, too careful with putting pen to paper, or thumbs to keyboard as the case may be.

Still sore from my long run the morning before, I put on my running gear, determined to reprise yesterday's productivity. The sky was covered in wisps of clouds, ethereal and bright white.

The first mile was the hardest, and then it got easier. My legs and hips seemed to remember what to do; they just had to keep going until the adrenaline kicked in, which it did, around mile three. When I returned home after six miles through the green hills, I was invigorated. I picked up my cell phone and texted Matilda.

I'm good. Have fun and enjoy the surf.

I took a cold shower before heading to the library.

Honolulu was three hours behind Los Angeles, so by the time

I sat down at the table in the library, I had two emails from the researcher at the *Times*.

I combed the background material on Carole's brother first. As expected, little was known about Michael Partridge. Michael had been employed as a stable hand of Joel Goldman's for over a decade. At twenty-seven he had moved to Honolulu, but if social security records were any indication, at the time he was still under Joel's employ. Soon after his move to Honolulu, he left his job with the Goldman family, and he appeared to have odd jobs at various ranches. He had been fired on multiple occasions and seemed to have no real consistent employment. This career end coincided with Carole's first movie roles, so my guess was he was being supported by her.

I knew very little about him, but even in the rare photo Michael Partridge didn't seem like the type to live off his sister, so I wondered if something had happened. I thought back to my conversation with Rubenstein months earlier about Lily's failed engagement.

They were supposed to get married, but it didn't happen. He ran off to someplace far away—Hawaii, I think it was—and never came back.

I had learned in journalism that coincidences were few and far between. It seemed too great a coincidence that Michael would have ended up in Honolulu, so close to the estate that belonged to Joel Goldman. But even more of a coincidence— or, I suspected, not a coincidence—was his date of relocation. He moved in the summer of 1988—two months after Matilda had been born.

The email listed a current place of residence. I searched for it on a map and found it to be well inland, far from the coast and civilization. There was a phone number as well, and I started to dial but then stopped. I didn't know if Michael was somehow integral to the plot, but if he was I thought it better to visit instead of call.

I put his information to the side and then opened the second email.

The information on Joel Goldman was vast. After all, he had been one of the most public figures in the history of Hollywood. Much of it I had found before, through my research for his obituary. I searched through photo after photo, news article after news article. Eventually, I decided to look into the Honolulu house, since that was the house that seemed to have a connection, however flimsy, to Michael Partridge.

I flipped through the title reports for information on the house and found it. It had been purchased in 1959. Joel's other real estate holdings included the home in the South of France, a pied-à-terre on the Upper East Side in New York, the equestrian estate in Hidden Hills, and two houses in Bel-Air—one that had been sold and one purchased in the same year, suggesting he moved from one Bel-Air house to another. Nothing out of the ordinary there. It was a typical real estate portfolio for an überwealthy gentleman in Los Angeles.

I was about to minimize the title research on my screen when suddenly two details caught my eye. One was the date of the transfer of the Bel-Air properties: April 1988, the month and year Matilda was born. The second was the address of the property: the current home of David Duplaine.

For a moment everything around me blurred, and then it became sharply clear, as letters in an eye test at the click of a lens.

Joel Goldman had lived in the same house in Bel-Air for twenty-eight years, and then in April 1988, the month Matilda was born, he transferred ownership of his six-acre estate to David.

David's Palladian mansion had once been Joel Goldman's house. Lily said Hector had worked for the family for over forty years. I had thought it was an exaggeration, but perhaps Hector had first worked for Joel and then David—both on the estate.

I thought about my biggest assumption in this mystery, and I jettisoned it. For the first time since I had stumbled upon

Matilda on the tennis court, I abandoned the assumption that David Duplaine was her biological father and considered Joel Goldman instead.

Joel Goldman would have been sixty-one when Matilda was born. He was married, but his wife was long past childbearing age, so there was no way the child could have been theirs. So if, indeed, Matilda was Joel's daughter, he would have had to father her with someone other than his wife.

But why hide her? Why hold her captive?

Had Joel merely had an affair, there wouldn't have been reason for such a dramatic measure. Los Angeles was a city of loose morals, so it had to have been something truly scandalous.

I put down my story. The more I learned, the more holes needed to be filled. It was a leap of faith to consider the possibility of Joel Goldman as Matilda's father. And if I did, it still left the burning question:

Who was Matilda's mother?

I worked at the library until closing. I stopped at a little convenience store on the way home for a bottle of scotch.

Once home I set up a makeshift office on the veranda overlooking the ocean. I sat in front of my computer, research strewn about me, seashells serving as paperweights. The laptop light glowed, and it reminded me of those late nights at the *Wall Street Journal*, writing into that glorious part of the night when everyone else slept. It felt good to be back there, to that place when my life had meant something.

My phone buzzed. It was a text from Matilda.

Surf's good. Miss u.

I walked over to the bar, poured myself another drink and wondered if I missed her, too. Missing her came over me in waves, like the sadness after my mother died. It ebbed and flowed, was unbearable then not. But I also realized how suffocating my love for Matilda had been. It wasn't her fault; it was mine. I had lost myself in her. Ironically, I had needed her to leave in order to find the parts of myself hidden in her, so I could put them back in me where they belonged. Maybe Matilda and I had been brought together to teach each other freedom.

I sipped my scotch, allowing it to take the edge off but not take away my clarity. I needed that. I stepped away from the bar, inventorying its contents.

And then it hit me.

Would you like to have a glass of wine? Matilda had asked me. *I found a fantastic bottle.*

That was it: Matilda had indicated she had "found" a fantastic bottle of wine, but there had never been a bottle of wine on the bar or in the kitchen. So where had she found it?

The logical place for wine in a vast estate like this would have been a cellar, but houses in Hawaii didn't have basements, because it was too expensive to cut into the volcanic rock. And besides, I had pored over every inch of the house—or so I had thought. If there were a wine cellar, I would have seen a door to it.

On our first day of class, freshman year, Professor Grandy recounted a story that had been branded in me since. It was the true tale of a man who made the arduous journey to the West Coast to find gold. He spent years looking for the stuff and eventually gave up, only to later discover that he had stopped three feet from a vast gold mine.

The lesson: *Professor Grandy's Journalism Rule Number Eight: Don't be the poor fool who stops three feet from gold.*

Suddenly I began to think I was merely three feet from gold— I was so close I could smell it. I started my search with the living room. It was unlikely Matilda would have moved heavy furniture to find a cellar, but I did just that. If I was onto something, I had been sloppy and haphazard in my search before. So, I pushed chairs, the sofa, lamps and rugs around, as if they were pawns on a chessboard, finding nothing. I then did the same in Joel's office, struggling to move his heavy desk and rolling his desk chair across the room.

Again, nothing.

I took a breath, deciding to be strategic about the search. Where, I wondered, would Matilda have spent more time than I? The answer was obvious. I walked to Joel's suite and went directly into the closet.

Matilda had taken her new clothing with her, leaving her old clothes behind. I rubbed the nylon of her one-piece bathing suit, the demure dress she had worn the day we had come to Hawaii. Her plump diamond earrings were haphazardly thrown on top of a dresser, a symbol of a life she wanted nothing to do with anymore.

I looked below me, on the floor, at first seeing nothing. I moved aside everything in the closet, finally shifting a laundry basket a couple feet to its left. It was then that I found what I was looking for: a large brass latch on a heavy wooden door.

The latch wasn't easy to open, and it took a couple tries before I successfully swung it toward me. It revealed a narrow ladder. I took each step carefully and eagerly, feeling that I was close to a great discovery.

The ladder led to a small room that at first blush appeared to be a wine cellar. But I knew better. There was no way a wine cellar would have been put inside a closet, and the cost of drilling into volcanic rock wouldn't have justified such measures— even for someone as wealthy as Joel Goldman. It had to be a safe of some sort.

The cellar did contain several decades-old bottles of wine, but the rest of the valuables in the long-forgotten room had been cleared out. I was ready to believe I'd hit another dead end when I spotted it in a corner: a small metal safe built into the wall. It was a key-lock safe, not a combination, and it immediately clicked in my mind. I ran upstairs and retrieved the key I had found taped under Lily's dresser.

My anticipation was palpable as I put the key into the safe and I felt the lock gently give way. I slowly pulled the door open.

The safe was empty, except for a single object: a square-shaped item wrapped in a deep-purple-colored cloth. From the shape I guessed it was a book of some sort. I peeled away the layers of cloth, my heartbeat increasing with each fold.

It was an old white photo album that had gone yellow, the kind with a slightly cushy cover and nylon sleeves. In the age of digital storage, it was a relic from the past. I opened it up tentatively, still feeling Joel Goldman's breath on me. He was buried an ocean away, on the hills of Forest Lawn Cemetery near the back lot of the movie studio that he had built, but I felt him watching me from the grave, warning me to turn around.

I flipped through the pages of the album and examined the pictures closely. It took me only a moment to realize that Carole Partridge was in nearly every one. The first photos were of her as an infant. She had wisps of brown hair, cheeks so full they could have been hiding chestnuts and a wide smile. There were photos of her playing hopscotch and tennis, and one of her beaming behind a birthday cake, just before blowing out the candles. In another picture, she stood at the top of a high diving board, child's legs—lanky even then—crossed nervously.

At around age ten, pictures of backyard birthday parties were replaced by pictures of her with Thoroughbred horses at the Goldmans' equestrian estate. By the time she was fourteen, her body had changed. She didn't look like a teenager at all, but a woman. Her sole companions appeared to be her older brother, Michael, and Lily—who at the time was a striking blonde in her thirties. Like so many staff of the rich, Carole and her brother seemed to be absorbed into the family Michael worked for. In the early photos there had been a woman who must have been Carole's mother, but there was never a father pictured. And in later pictures, the woman seemed to vanish like a ghost. The only family Carole seemed to have were her brother and the Goldmans.

I paged through the photos, enthralled by a life that had started so ordinary but turned extraordinary almost overnight. I turned to the last page of the album, and it was then that I saw it. The photo was so haunting the hairs on my arms stood straight up. It had been snapped somewhere along the Mediterranean. Carole was around seventeen or eighteen, and she sat on a rocky beach. Beside her, leaning into her and whispering into her ear, was Joel Goldman. He was sixtyish, but handsome in the way powerful men of that age are. Carole was looking away from him slightly, head tilted toward the rocks. Despite the coquettish body language, she had the smile of a girl basking in the bright light of a man's attention. That photo was the only one of Joel and Carole together, but it told me everything that I needed to know.

I considered taking the album with me, but instead pulled the photo of Joel and Carole out of its sleeve, and I blanketed the book in its coronation-purple cloth, returning it to its hiding place. I locked the safe behind me, putting the key in my pocket. I crawled up the ladder and again went to the bedroom that I had assumed was Lily's—with more purpose this time, because I had a strong hunch the room hadn't belonged to Lily at all.

Once in the bedroom, I opened the bottom drawer of the dresser, sifting through its clothing. There was a formfitting floral dress made of an inexpensive rayon fabric, a tight skirt in cinched jersey and a one-piece bathing suit with a cleavage-baring V.

Lily's closet in Bel-Air had been filled with couture. Valentino, Yves Saint Laurent, Chanel and Hermès. Even as a teenager Lily had dressed in a way that implied she was a girl who would never come cheap.

The clothing I was sorting through, on the other hand, was made of inexpensive fabric, with labels I had never heard of.

And not only that, the size of the clothes would have been too big for a teenage Lily Goldman. In fact, it would have been too big for the Lily Goldman of today.

This wasn't Lily's clothing.

The perfume bottle still sat on top of the dresser, and I again dabbed my finger into its scent. It smelled like Matilda's mother, and like Matilda.

The breeze had picked up, and heavy tropical rain clouds were moving in over the ocean. I went out to the veranda, collecting my research and computer and bringing them inside. The doors slammed against their frames, and I shut all but one, locking them.

I looked at the photo again. Carole's smile was unmistakably Matilda's smile. Her lips were Matilda's lips. Matilda's body had Carole's length and curves. They had the same pointed nose, the same square face.

Joel Goldman had been blond and so was Matilda. And then there were the eyes. Lily and Matilda shared the same striking emerald-green eyes, which had thrown me off because I had believed Lily to be Matilda's mother. In fact, those eyes were Joel Goldman's eyes, too.

I had now come to figure out that the bedroom had belonged to Carole Partridge, not Lily Goldman. And I was just about convinced Matilda Duplaine belonged to Carole Partridge, too.

I didn't sleep at all that night. Instead, adrenaline as thick as syrup kicked in, and I was brought back to the days of frenetic research and the nights of burning the midnight oil, to deadlines barely struck, to running across the newsroom with a piece of paper in hand to make the next day's paper in time. All that was missing were the celebratory beers with friends.

Early the next morning I began substantiating my facts. I first called Carole's high school to confirm the dates of her attendance. Sure enough, Carole had been a student there, but she'd never graduated. She had dropped out, never to return. They could not provide a reason for her departure, but according to some old biographical pieces on Carole I had dug up, she'd said she had dropped out to pursue her acting career. It was worth noting that there had been two years between when Carole dropped out of school and when she starred in her first picture—a film produced by Joel Goldman. As Willa had aptly pointed out, I had always had a good memory, and I cataloged the pieces I had pulled together over the past few months. I thought back to the letter I had discovered in Joel Goldman's coat pocket from Lily, referencing the "mess" he had left in France. I remembered the photo of Joel, Lily and Carole on the red-clay tennis court. My bet was the fourth double's player was Carole's brother—Lily's fiancé. And then there was the brunette who had once been a house sitter or member of the staff. It was certainly possible the striking brunette had been Carole.

I called Jacob for another fact check, and he called me back within minutes this time. A Matilda Partridge was born in Nice, France, to Carole Partridge on April 20, 1988. The father was listed as unknown. Anticipating my next question, Jacob had already researched Carole Partridge's return to the States. She had come back on May 30, 1988, and her destination had been Honolulu.

The pieces were falling into place, but I was still tormented by the thought of Joel and Carole as Matilda's parents. It was strange, but at first I had blamed Matilda for her lineage, as one might blame a loved one for dying. When I got over that irrational line of thinking, I simply felt sorry for her. She had been raised by a father who wasn't her real dad; in fact, David Duplaine was, in a sense, the highest-paid actor in Hollywood. And Matilda's mother had not only abandoned her, but was apparently having an affair with the man pretending to be her father. That, in my opinion, had almost been a worse sin than leaving her entirely.

Those were the facts, but there was a lot I was still missing.

Carole was eighteen when Matilda was born, Joel sixty-one. Had the relationship been consensual? Was there even a relationship? Or had Joel Goldman raped Carole Partridge and then covered it up? Why hadn't Carole had an abortion?

I didn't know what I was going to tell Matilda. I didn't know if I was going to publish this story for the world to read. I had been unjustly fired from the *Journal*, and the possibility of breaking this story seemed my due reward. But it felt wrong. I suspected there was one person who had the answer to my questions, one person who could tell me if I should bury my story or break it.

And the next day I was going to see him.

My destination was about an hour away. I swiveled inland, through the hills of a dormant volcano. I had the top down on the vintage car, and I felt strange driving it now. Not just because it wasn't mine, for I had always known this life of shiny things was temporary, but because everything related to Joel Goldman—his house, his car, the papayas plucked off his trees, even the birds that flew over his yard—now felt immoral.

It didn't make sense, and I knew that.

It was almost four months since I had first walked into Lily's shop. I had been swept into this world like the tropical winds sweeping in from the ocean. I didn't know the stakes then, but now I did—and they were high.

The ranch was nestled into the hills. There were two structures: a modest bungalow and a barn that could probably shelter three or four horses. In between the two, a single horse grazed on dead grass. He was a stunning animal, all muscle and grace. His coat had a recently brushed sheen to it, and he looked as if he belonged at a derby rather than in these humble surroundings. Beside him were a few bales of hay, dead and yellow, stacked one on top of another.

It was a flawless day, and the sky was blue as far as the eye could see, uninterrupted by a single cloud.

I turned off the car. The beast of a racing engine seemed gauche in this quiet and rustic setting.

The front door was open, with only a screen door between the living room and me. I knocked, and the whole house seemed to rattle. The siding was rotting, half a rain gutter sat on the dirt and the screen was ripped where someone had cut it open near the lock.

"Hello," I called. "Anyone home?"

The wind whistled. It wasn't strong, but it felt like a warning. I headed back toward the car, and the horse gazed at me lazily. The streak on the crown of his head was white like baby powder.

I heard the man's footsteps behind me, crunching on the dirt. I turned around and tried to reconcile the man in front of me with the one I had seen in the photographs. I tried to pick out the light eyes, the mischievous smile, the blond hair, the broad shoulders and arms.

But there was nothing of that guy left.

"Is there something I can do for you?" he asked in a voice that sounded as if it was filled with years of cigarettes and drink. He sideswiped the car with his eyes, and only then did I realize that he had probably figured out the matter I was here for. It was, after all, Joel Goldman's car.

"I'm not sure," I said, looking down at the dirt, suddenly feeling selfish for being there. "My name is Thomas Cleary, and I'm a friend of Lily Goldman's."

I tried to detect something in Michael's face, but there was no reaction. It was silent, except for the sound of the horse rubbing his back hoof on the ground.

"I'm sorry to intrude like this," I continued. "I'm just looking for some answers. Not that I expect you to give them to me."

"There aren't any answers here. I think you should leave." His tone was firm but not hostile.

I opened the car door, and I felt the antique lever in my grip. It was so exact in its design—it was from an age when things were crafted by hand, with hands in mind. I thought of my story: I couldn't complete it without this interview. There were too many holes to be filled.

"I'm in love with a girl by the name of Matilda Duplaine," I said. "And I know that Carole and Joel are her parents."

I am not an expert in human behavior, but I fancy myself pretty close by nature of my occupation. And I believed that Michael Partridge had chosen these hills in order to escape the exact story I was crafting. But he was also a man from my father's generation and my father's stock: he was a man who gave nothing away. His emotions weren't readable. All he did was squint at the sky as if looking for something in it.

"What do I have to do with it?" he finally asked.

"I know you were supposed to marry Lily."

"So what do you want to know?"

"I want to know what happened," I said.

"It was a long time ago," he replied. He didn't elaborate, but I could tell he wanted to open up. When subjects want to keep things hidden, they retreat and grow defensive, but Michael had not. He stood his ground and I stood mine, waiting for him to continue.

"I hear Joel died," he said. "Funny, because I waited for so long for him to die. I don't know why—I don't know what I was waiting for. It wasn't going to change anything. And I can say whatever I want about it now, because the truth is buried somewhere in Los Angeles six feet under."

I nodded. "I know. And I also realize that it's intrusive for me to be coming here. But I didn't know where else to turn. I thought you would understand."

I felt the brilliant sun warm the tops of my shoulders, my sunburned neck and face. Suddenly I felt as if we understood each other. I saw the creases on the sides of Michael's eyes relax. He trusted me.

"I'm an honest man," he said, and I believed it. "It was his fault—of course it was his fault. She was seventeen years old when she got pregnant and he was sixty, so he should have known better. But my sister was born with stars in her eyes. She wanted to be famous since she was a little girl. She believed she loved Joel—she really and truly believed that, and even to this day she does—but it wasn't him she loved. It was his life, his wealth, his fame."

Even now, years later, Michael shuddered at the thought. "It only happened that once, and she got pregnant. Of course he wanted her to have an abortion, but Carole wouldn't hear it. Our family was Catholic, and on top of that I think Carole knew that with the baby she would always have a part of Joel—that stardom she desperately wanted. You never met him?"

I shook my head no.

"Joel was a man who took care of things. That's what men like him do. A problem comes up and they find a way to solve it. So here was this baby that he didn't want and a girl who wanted to be a star. And then there was David, who wanted to be Joel—in pretty much every way. David was Joel's protégé. At the time he was starting his production company, and he needed money to get some movies going, and he was best friends with Lily. So the solution became simple—give the baby to David to raise, fund David's company and pay Carole for her confidentiality.

"Simple enough, right? But there was a hiccup. Carole had the baby abroad and didn't want to give her up. She was incredibly attached to her. She fled France and moved to Joel's house in Hawaii. That's when I came to help her out. It was clear it wasn't going to work, though. Carole was eighteen and broke. She couldn't be a mother. After six or so months she gave in to Joel's demands, and he cast her as a lead in one of his movies. He made her a star, but she stayed a star because of what had happened to her. She brought the sadness and anger of her life to her roles."

The evening in the swimming pool when Matilda had reflected on her past, she had told me that she had dreamed of the ocean, wide and gray during a storm. She had dreamed of salty air and of a woman whom she believed to be her mother. Matilda must have been thinking of Hawaii, of her time with Carole.

"Carole had it written into her contract with Joel that she could spend three hours a day with Matilda. And she did, religiously, always. She visited under the guise of Matilda's tennis coach, and she loved those hours—they were the jewels of her day. It was known in Hollywood Carole wouldn't shoot in the late afternoons, and she very rarely would travel for roles."

At first I wasn't sure I'd heard it correctly, but then it sunk in. Carole Partridge was Matilda's tennis coach. It had always struck me as odd how much Matilda adored her coach, but now it made sense.

"Didn't Carole want to tell her the truth?" I asked.

"Carole promised Joel she wouldn't tell Matilda. She almost did, once or twice, but she thought it would have been worse for Matilda. Matilda would have never been able to live a normal life, and Carole knew it. And after so many years in captivity on the estate, how would she possibly explain it? Not just to Matilda, but to the world. It would be a media circus. They were trapped in the lie."

Michael went quiet and looked at the sky again contemplatively.

"How's Lily?" he asked tentatively.

"That's tough to answer," I said honestly. "I don't really know. She seems sad."

"Did she ever get married?"

"No." I shook my head.

Michael's body language relaxed slightly. "We used to ride for days, Lily and I. She's great with horses, you know."

"I didn't."

"Yeah." He smiled. It was Matilda's and Carole's smile—wide and off center. For just a flash, I saw the guy from the photograph, the man Lily had fallen in love with. "That girl wasn't scared of anything. Life was so good then, so fun."

I couldn't imagine Lily ever having fun. She seemed so serious now. My heart ached being there—for Matilda, for Michael, for Lily. For all of those loves and lives gone awry.

"I'm not going to say I see a lot of women up here, because I don't, but to this day she was the prettiest girl I've ever laid eyes on. I couldn't ever believe she was mine. And maybe she wasn't really." Michael looked down at the dirt after he said it, as if he was somehow ashamed.

"Why did you leave her?" I asked.

"I blamed the wrong person for the wrong thing," Michael said.

"You blamed Lily for her father?" I already knew the answer, but I asked it anyway.

"It was the easier thing to do—or maybe it was the cowardly thing."

"Maybe you can call her?" I suggested, thinking of Lily sadly holding that photograph.

Michael smiled wryly. "You're still young, but you'll learn as you get older that the thing about life is that it hands you these golden moments, but every one of them has an expiration date stamped on the bottom of it. If you don't use them, they go bad."

Michael retreated a step. It was my cue to leave.

I opened the car door and glanced one last time at Michael's humble ranch. It was then that I noticed the hibiscus tree. Its magenta flowers were in bloom, brilliant and full with fertile golden centers. The tree was incongruous with its surroundings—the dirt, the man weathered from the sun and life.

I turned around to see Michael, his hand on the battered screen door. I thought he was going to say something else, but the words seemed caught in his throat. Instead, he walked inside, and behind him the screen door gently bounced back once, then twice, and the third time it latched and I heard it lock.

Twenty-Seven

Thursday morning I finished my story. There were still holes, but it was tight. Facts were substantiated, the prose brushed, commas and periods in their correct positions. Whether I broke it or not was another story, but for now I had twelve double-spaced pages of the best writing of my career.

It was my ticket to the moon, my vindication for everything that had happened in New York. I could take it to *Vanity Fair*, to the movie studios, to a publisher. I could walk into Ruben-stein's office with it—the supreme act of gratitude for what he had done for me. I could use it to blackmail David Duplaine. After all, what was a million dollars to a guy who had a hundred? My father could retire from his minimum-wage job at the lumberyard. He could move to Los Angeles into a little house David would buy him, and we could run through the sunny hills of Bel-Air in the mornings as we had during those snowy days in Milwaukee.

But the decision wasn't as easy as that.

I needed to clear my head, so I changed into my running clothes and set out for my morning run. It was my longest one yet, and I could feel the strain in my lungs, but it felt good. It started to drizzle by the seventh mile, and the rain refreshed me. As I ran up the driveway, my pace hadn't slipped at all. My breathing was still in tune with my music.

As I neared the house, I noticed a figure at the front door. I had been living in a world of ghosts, and the figure was an apparition at first.

Matilda stood with her suitcase resting on the pavement beside her. The door was open a crack, as if she had gone in but then opted to wait for me on the covered front porch. My mom used to do that with my dad—wait for him outside. It was as if she couldn't stand to be without him, even for the minute it took for him to walk into the house.

We just looked at each other, as if we were strangers meeting for the first time, not quite sure what to make of each other.

Matilda's blond hair was straight and her face free of makeup. Gone was the black nail polish; in its place was a pale pink. She wore a conservative one-piece bathing suit beneath a long floral cover-up.

I had spent days writing about her, but I had forgotten how beautiful she was. Forgetting must be a defense mechanism to lessen the hurt of losing someone.

I caught my breath, still quickened from the run. Sweat had seeped into my eyes and they burned.

"Hi, Thomas," Matilda said softly, unsure.

I didn't say anything. The suitcase sat on the ground beside us, reminding us what had happened. That she had left.

"Did you go for a run?" she asked carefully.

"Eight miles on these creaky legs." She smiled that wide crooked smile. It was her mother's smile, her uncle's.

An uncomfortable silence fell between us. Matilda looked at me repentantly.

"What do you do after a fight? Just make up?" she asked.

"Most of the time," I responded.

"And the other part of the time?"

I didn't want to think about the alternative, so I didn't re-spond.

"What happens in the other part of the time?" Matilda pressed.

"The other part happens when people aren't sorry."

Matilda stared into the distance. There was a slight breeze and the trees swayed gently as it swept through their branches. It was still drizzling, but it felt as if heavier rain was coming.

"I'm sorry," she said. "I feel as if I've been terrible to you. I *have* been terrible to you. And I wouldn't have blamed you for leaving me here to fend for myself. I was worried I would come back and you would be gone."

"I'm not that type of man—you know that."

"I know, but I haven't been thinking clearly," Matilda said reflectively. "This isn't going to make sense, but I'll say it any-ways—I was so happy that people liked me. Not because they were being paid a king's ransom, but because they really liked me. And it made me question a lot about my life. I finally started to feel resentment. I wanted to hate my father for keeping me imprisoned for all those years, and my mother for leaving me. I know it's not fair, but I took it all out on you."

I thought about my unjustified anger toward Matilda when I learned of her lineage, how I had at first blamed her for it, as if it was somehow her fault. We were both placing blame on the wrong people.

"But when I was away I realized I missed you—horribly missed you," she continued. "The world is a terrible place if I can't share it with you. I dreamt of the world for so long, but I realized it's only worthwhile with you in it. "

"I'm sorry, too," I said. "I've thought about it as well, and I think I took you off the estate for my own selfish reasons. I knew we couldn't really be in love there. I mean, we could be, but it wasn't real."

"I wanted to leave. Desperately. Do you think I would have

been better staying there? You can't think that. If that's what you're apologizing for, then your apology is not accepted."

Matilda reached up and took the back of my head in her hands. I was self-conscious because my hair was drenched in sweat while she was so pristine, but she didn't seem to care.

"You were my salvation, Thomas Cleary, and I'm sorry it took leaving you for me to remember that. But sometimes it takes distance to make things clear. You've given me the whole world, and look what I did in return. I wouldn't blame you if you never accepted my apology."

She kissed my forehead tenderly.

"You taste salty—" Matilda licked her lips "—like pretzels."

It was an intimate gesture. I brushed her lips with mine, and it brought me back to that magical night at the estate bowling alley when I treaded carefully with my lips.

"You taste sweet," I said. "Like sugar."

"Like guava." Matilda grinned playfully.

"I missed you." It came out before I could think about it.

"I missed you squared, times seven, plus four," Matilda replied.

It reminded me of something Matilda would have said at the estate—childish in a way. She was a completely different woman than the girl I had met on the tennis court, yet in some ways still the same. I needed to love the woman she was becoming, not just the girl she had been.

The breeze rippled through the trees, and Matilda scanned the sky. "I think a storm's rolling in."

We walked around the back and sat on the veranda, looking out at the ocean as the storm arrived with a flourish. Gray clouds filled the air and the winds swept in from the west. The ocean roared and the flapping palm fronds fooled the ears into thinking it had already started raining, when rain was still only a threat.

We ate lunch under the overhang, watching the raindrops bounce off the swimming pool and the lightning rods strike the ocean. We didn't get thunderstorms like this in Los Angeles, and Matilda was still fascinated by them. It was warm and muggy, and there was a film of perspiration on her skin. She smelled of baby powder and rain.

I kissed the back of her neck. She turned around and put my arm around her protectively. She studied my fingers.

"I love you so much. Every part of you," Matilda said, pulling me close to her. "There's no inch of you I don't like—down to your knuckles."

We listened as the rain crashed against the overhang and the thunder rumbled in the distance. The air smelled of wet plumeria blossoms and a few hours later the sun peeked out from behind the clouds.

Later that evening, after we had made love, I walked outside under the parasols of the date palms, and I looked out in the distance, at the twinkling lights of Honolulu. Thirty days had seemed an infinite amount of time, but now it was almost over. I wondered what would be next for us in Los Angeles, and I wondered if Matilda was wondering the same thing, too.

I woke up the next morning to the glorious spray of sunlight after a storm. Matilda sat on the side of the bed, dressed in a frilly white tennis dress, hair pulled back in a ponytail with a bright white ribbon. She carried two glasses of freshly squeezed pineapple juice.

"Good morning." She handed me a cold glass, and I noticed she had her mother's long, muscular arms. "I squeezed you pineapple juice. Fresh, pulpy—just like you like it."

I took a sip of the juice and brushed the soft fabric of her dress with the back of my fingers. "Am I going to beat you in tennis today?" I asked.

"I've been dying for a game." She set her gaze in the general direction of the court in the front of the house. "I thought we could play for old times' sake."

She gave me that seventy-five-watt smile, the one that lit up everything around her.

We made our way to the tennis court later in the morning. Matilda's court in Bel-Air was clay and sheltered by an ivy fortress. Here, if not for the net, the grass court would have disappeared into the grass around it. There were no fences, no ivy, no viewing area.

Matilda bounced a ball and it died. I had played on grass before and was prepared for the odd bounce, but Matilda was not. We hit back and forth, and the playing field was more level than the one in Bel-Air. Without Matilda's requisite three-hour daily practices, she was atypically errant, and she had trouble bending low enough for the ball.

I couldn't stop thinking of Matilda playing tennis with Carole—her mother. I imagined Carole proudly watching Matilda from her side of the net, using a grip or stroke adjustment as an excuse to be closer to her, to touch her daughter's hand. It was at once sad and comforting.

When the first set came to a close, we retreated to the cove down by the beach, the place where Matilda's toes had first touched sand.

The cove was its own paradise, shielded from the rest of world as if nature had created this special spot millions of years earlier for our sole enjoyment. Matilda and I sat facing each other, knees to the sky and feet to the sand, my hands around the backs of her calves.

Sweat sparkled on our arms and legs and the napes of our necks and I couldn't help but think of the first time we met, the droplets of sweat that hung off Matilda like seed pearls, and the electric moment when her fingers learned my jaw for the first time.

She stood up and removed her tennis dress, tossing it onto the beach.

It was miraculous how, in just a few short weeks, every part of her had changed. It wasn't just her arms. Matilda's shoulders had always been broad, but now the broadness continued down the top of her back. Her shoulder blades were lined in muscle, and her pre-antebellum waist appeared less tiny because her hips had lost most of their flesh. Her legs had been coltish before, but now they seemed very much in her control—as if they belonged on her.

Matilda glanced over her left shoulder seductively, then waded into the water, stopping when it reached her ankles and then again at her knees. She finally dived forward in the water so I could only see the bottoms of her feet. She disappeared below the surface. Matilda was changing almost hourly. Admittedly, at first I had resisted the changes, but now it was exciting for me to wonder who Matilda would be. She was like a gift still waiting to be opened.

When Matilda returned to the beach a few minutes later, she sat down beside me, wrapping a towel around her torso and looking out at the horizon. She squinted at the distance, at the unknown.

"I know we're due to go home in a few days." There was sadness in Matilda's voice when she said it. "Do you want to go home?"

"I've loved being here with you," I began. "Really. In a lot of ways it's been the most memorable month of my life. But as much as I don't want to, I have to get back to life—to real life. I'm nervous about my job and money. And I'm starting to feel isolated from the world—which maybe is the reason I started to feel isolated from you." I wrapped my arm around her and pulled her in closer to me. "What about you? Are you excited to go back?"

"I don't think I have anywhere to go home to."

"I'm sure your father will allow you to come home," I said, but I knew that plan didn't include me.

Matilda leaned her head on my shoulder.

"Don't you see, Thomas? It's exactly what Daddy said to me. *If someone doesn't want you, you shouldn't want them.* I can't go back there for that very reason. Let's pretend for a moment I went home," Matilda said. "What's going to happen with us? My father's most certainly not going to welcome you with open arms. And what if he doesn't let me leave the estate again? What if everything just goes back to the way it was?"

"You'll come stay with me, then." It was an impetuous thing to say.

"I'd be an imposition," she protested.

"You could never be an imposition," I insisted. But then I imagined how Matilda would react when she saw my apartment—a place as different from her estate as real life is from a fairy tale.

"What am I going to do all day when you're at work? What am I going to do about school? How am I going to make money?"

"I'm not going to lie to you, Matilda. I don't know the answers to any of it. We have to take it day by day. We've made it this far, right?"

Matilda played with a seashell and grew pensive. "Sometimes I miss things as they were before. It seemed so easy then."

"It's only hard if we make it hard," I said. "I've been through much more than this before, and I've made it out the other side."

"You're right. There are so many things to look forward to. We have it all in front of us, don't we?"

"We do. There's all of Los Angeles ahead of us, and the entire world. Look at that sky."

Matilda followed my gaze upward.

"See all that blue—it's not the limit. It's only the beginning. There's infinite sky above that, and infinite sky above that, too." I brushed the top of Matilda's ear with my lips, feeling the soft, delicate skin. "We have so much ahead of us, limitless opportunity. And I want you to know that I'll take care of you. You have nothing to worry about."

Matilda smiled. "I know. From the moment I met you on the tennis court, I believed you would take care of me. Even when I told you you couldn't come back, that night after our first tennis game, I believed you would. But you must promise me one thing. Promise me that whatever happens with our lives—if they're infinitely glamorous or we're broke and struggling, if it's a honeymoon or a goodbye—someday you'll bring me here again."

"We'll come back here. I promise."

Matilda curled herself up in me and I buried my head in her damp, tangled hair. It was an easy promise, because I believed Matilda and I could make it through anything. I had an amazing job to go back to, I was returning to real life with the woman of my dreams. I didn't believe the sky was the limit; my plans were much grander than that.

Twenty-Eight

The flight back to Los Angeles was uneventful, yet bittersweet. The car ride from the airport to my apartment was generally quiet, only punctuated with occasional small talk. Matilda scanned the radio from one station to another until she settled back in her seat contentedly, her eyes falling on the road ahead of us—both figuratively and literally.

There was an accident on the freeway, so Matilda and I were forced to take Sunset Boulevard, and as we crept closer to Bel-Air, I found myself with a pit in my stomach that reminded me of those evenings in Manhattan after I'd lost my job at the *Journal*. I was suddenly afraid Matilda would change her mind, instruct me to take a left into Bel-Air's gates.

As we approached the grand pillars, Matilda set her eyes on the sign.

"It looks like the *E* burnt out when we were away," she declared.

Sure enough, Bel-Air's cursive *E* was black, and a gentleman scurried about, working to fix it. Another man stood beside him, carrying a lightbulb in his right hand.

"B L-Air. Doesn't sound nearly as romantic, does it?" Matilda said, smiling wryly.

"It sounds like the name of an oil tycoon," I said.

Matilda laughed. "Or a bandit," she added.

"A stockbroker."

"A regional airline."

"Or someone heading to San Francisco for the Gold Rush."

Matilda giggled, and then Bel-Air was behind us.

For the rest of the drive Matilda peppered me with questions about San Francisco—a place she had only read about in books. When we finally arrived at my apartment building, we walked up the grungy, narrow steps to my apartment and I pushed the key in nervously. I opened the door, concerned that Matilda would be disappointed with the meager accommodations a reporter's salary afforded. Matilda had never been successful at hiding her emotions, and I tried to read her thoughts.

The apartment was worse than I remembered it, if that was possible. I had left in a rush, so there were a few dishes with food remnants in the sink, and the bedroom was littered with clothes. The only plant in the place was nearly dead, its leaves wilted toward the floor. The balcony door was open a crack, and it had blown piles of papers around, creating the look of a place just ransacked.

Matilda stood frozen, taking in the mess.

"That bad?" I asked with trepidation.

"This is my new home?" Matilda asked.

"It would appear that way," I said, concerned she would demand I drive her back to Bel-Air, to the estate.

"I love it—absolutely love it. It's so—bohemian. Is that the right word?"

"That's the nicest possible way of putting it," I said, making a futile attempt to pick up the papers and then deciding it would have to wait until the weekend. "You're very kind. I'd offer you something to drink, but—"

"We'll go to the store tomorrow," Matilda interjected, finishing my thought.

Tomorrow, I thought. We had an eternity ahead of us.

Matilda walked around the small space, examining every detail. She put her few belongings in a top drawer beside mine, and I loved the intimacy of our T-shirts side by side, my boxers beside her underwear. She picked out her side of the bed—the side away from the door because that was where she had heard girls were supposed to sleep—and she put her toothbrush beside mine in a glass. Even more than Hawaii, this felt grown-up, the beginning of our life together.

Once she was settled in and unpacked, Matilda walked out to the balcony and leaned over its edge. I followed her. My neighbor's holiday lights were finally appropriate. We were a few days away from Christmas.

In the distance, Matilda spotted fluorescent lights that shot into the air in between the mountains.

"What's that?" she asked, pointing. I followed her finger out into the distance.

"That's Dodger Stadium," I replied.

"What's a dodger stadium?"

I laughed. "A baseball stadium. Where the Los Angeles Dodgers play."

"You mean people play baseball so close to you? Can we go? Now?"

"It's not baseball season. There must be something else going on there."

"When can we go to a baseball game?"

"In April. I'll give you a rain check."

"A rain check." Matilda looked contemplatively at the lights. The fluorescence reminded me of the evening on the tennis court, when I had first met her. "You know this past month was the best month of my life. You may not think that's saying much, because my life was so dull before I met you, but it's the truth."

She leaned over and kissed me, sweetly and passionately. She wore a summer dress and it smelled of Hawaii—of the ocean, sun, teriburgers and plumeria. I squeezed her dress in my hand, wanting to be back there.

"Remember when we only had Fridays?" Matilda whispered. "Life in between Fridays was like the wire between lanterns, and Fridays were the parts that glowed."

"But now we have every days," I said. "Every day we have each other."

She smiled, and we stood side by side, overlooking the decrepit swimming pool and the sliver of mountains beyond. In the distance, the lights of the baseball stadium illuminated the sky, and I thought of everything we had to look forward to. It was as if our pockets were full of rain checks, and all we had to do was cash them in.

Twenty-Nine

I returned to work the next morning to find my cubicle had been emptied.

Panic set in initially, but then I remembered that a perk of my new assistant editor position had been an office, and to say mine had been prepared for me in my absence was a gross understatement.

Gone was the cheap metal desk that had probably been purchased from a wholesale office supply store. In its place were a hand-carved antique walnut desk worthy of David Duplaine, two guest chairs upholstered in luxurious fabric, a bronze desk lamp that looked as if it had been won at auction at Christie's, and a small bar with crystal glasses and bottles of top-shelf alcohol. Above the bar, across from my desk, hung a drawing I recognized from Lily's shop. It was a modern chalk art that featured the face of a woman with a large halo of kinky hair.

My computer had been left on, as if waiting for me to type in my password. An orchid adorned the desk—pure white, perky and seductive.

It took me a moment to register that this office was mine, and another to reconcile the fact that Lily Goldman had spent the month I was away designing it just for me.

A linen envelope leaned against the computer monitor. I opened it to find a note in Lily's well-bred penmanship.

Congratulations on your new position, Thomas. Your mom would have been very proud. The desk belonged to my father. I trust it will bring you the same success it brought him.
Love, Lily.

"Good morning, Cleary." I knew the voice instantly, and I looked up to find Rubenstein filling the door frame.

"Phil," I said, "thanks for—"

"Nice tan," he interrupted. "I trust you got your project done for Lily?"

"I did. Thank you."

"Stop with the thank-yous. They embarrass me," Rubenstein said. He glanced at his oversize gold watch in a meaningful manner. "I'll let you get settled in, and then you're needed in the conference room for a nine-thirty meeting. The entertainment industry doesn't sleep while you're on holiday."

He turned to leave, then hesitated. "And, Cleary?"

"Yup?" I was waiting for a quip about my expensive office furniture, which he was examining with a bit of a smirk.

"It's good to have you back," he said.

"It's good to be here," I replied, because it was.

It was a day of meetings and getting caught up. Darkness rolled in around five o'clock, and I had avoided calling Lily all day, partly because a total office design required more than a phone call to express gratitude, and partly because I didn't know how I felt about it. A thirty-day sabbatical at her father's vacation house was extravagant, but the office—and especially her father's desk—somehow felt more intrusive and, well, presumptuous. Not only had Lily chosen my furnishings, but she also must have paid for them, and I couldn't afford to reimburse her. And, of more importance, I felt like an intruder in her family's secrets. Lily had invited me into her world, and I had proceeded to dissect it and open it up, leaving its guts on the table. I didn't know what I should tell her or what I should keep to myself.

I decided I would pay Lily a personal visit over the next couple days, after I had sorted out exactly how I felt about things.

I dialed Matilda instead. Her cell phone had a Hawaii area code, and it made me wistful. It was nice to be back at work, but I longed to be back there, drinking freshly pressed pineapple juice on the veranda and making love to Matilda on the beach.

"Oh, Thomas, it's you. It's delightful to hear your voice. I love the telephone," Matilda declared, without even saying "hello." She still wasn't accustomed to phone etiquette. "I hear the sounds of frenetic typing in the background. Are you creating the news?"

"Or writing about it. Creating makes it sound so important."

"You *are* important, and I miss you so. I've become a glutton for you—a terrible fate," she said, giggling to make it sound not so terrible.

I smiled. It had been so long since I had been loved like this. If I was honest, I had never been loved like this.

"Well, if that's the case, I'm calling with good news. I'm leaving now. So I'll see you soon—what is it you say? 'Way too soon to miss me soon'?"

"Yes, that's exactly it. And I still don't want to hang up, because having you on the phone feels like I have a real part of you. Even the crumbs of you I like."

"I'm on my way," I said, looking out at Los Angeles, lit for the night. The sky was crisp and clear.

I returned to the apartment to find Matilda at the door, dressed in blue jeans and a gray T-shirt. Her hair was done in the messy after-bed look girls of Los Angeles preferred, and she wore a touch of makeup. It was the first time I found myself eager to come home to my shabby apartment. The route hadn't been quick enough. There had been too many stoplights and they all seemed to be red.

And then I had a sharp realization: perhaps Bel-Air was only glorious because it was the place I had fallen in love with Matilda. Maybe it had nothing to do with the sheared lawns, the exotic birds, the vast walled estates with swimming pools and croquet lawns.

"Hello, stranger," Matilda said, whisking me back to the present. "Penny for your thoughts?"

"Dollar and we have a deal."

"Oh dear, I'm unemployed," Matilda said, smiling. "But I'll owe you for it? I'm good on my word."

"You seem like a woman of your word, so deal. Did you miss me?" I asked, kissing the side of her neck, smelling her perfume.

"Ridiculously so. I'll tell you all about missing you over dinner. I'm starving," Matilda declared, as she wrapped one of my sweaters around her.

I had made a reservation at an Italian restaurant in Hollywood. It was a quaint neighborhood joint with red vinyl booths and checked tablecloths. We sat down in a dark corner with a red votive candle to light our table, and Matilda cupped it, warming her hands.

When we were in Honolulu, I had feared returning to Los Angeles. I didn't know if Matilda would assimilate into the real world. Yet at dinner I realized, among the young Hollywood set, Matilda was just another one of the girls. She had come from a castle in the hills of Bel-Air, where she had been kept captive her whole life, but biology is a powerful thing. A person has to adapt for survival.

After dinner, we took a walk down Hollywood Boulevard. The street was paved with the stars of Matilda's favorite actors: Audrey Hepburn and Lauren Bacall, Humphrey Bogart and

John Wayne. She traced their names with her pink fingernails, and she recited the history on each.

We walked past the Mann's Chinese Theater, big and bold and colorful and swarmed by tourists. There was a movie playing there Matilda wanted to see, and we made plans to go Friday after work. After, Matilda made me promise to take her to the Griffith Park Observatory and its planetarium, a giant domed structure that loomed above us on the crest of the mountains. I was already excited for Friday, and it reminded me of those early days, when Fridays were all I had to be excited for.

I put my arm around Matilda, pulling her tightly into my side. The dizzying lights of Hollywood Boulevard projected onto Matilda's face, and she smiled widely and crookedly and joyously. We ducked into a souvenir shop, picking out a postcard for my dad, and I pointed out the Capitol Records building—round like a turntable—which Matilda had only seen in movies. We laughed at jokes that seemed tailor-made for only us, and as Matilda and I walked down the famous street, I realized I loved Los Angeles, that glorious city of second chances. It had given me another shot at a career, at love. I had been newly orphaned, broke and disgraced when I had first landed here, but Los Angeles hadn't cared. It had made every one of my dreams come true.

After we returned home from our walk down Hollywood Boulevard, Matilda and I fell asleep on the sofa. I carried her into bed around two and immediately fell into a deep dream. It was still dark out when I awoke for no apparent reason except that I knew something was wrong. I turned on my side toward Matilda, but I found only an imprint in the pillow where her head had been. She was gone.

I walked into the living room and found her sitting on the floor in her purple nightgown, the twelve pages of my story lined up in front of her, in three symmetrical rows of four. Beside it was the photo of Joel Goldman and Carole Partridge in the South of France I had brought back from Hawaii.

She kept her eyes on the pages and the photo.

"I didn't mean to open the drawer," Matilda said repentantly. "I couldn't sleep. I thought I would help by cleaning up a bit. There was a layer of dust over everything."

I didn't know what to say.

"There were also a few dishes in the sink, as well. And I kept thinking before we went to sleep that you had given up your life for me—that you hadn't even had time to do your dishes because you had been busy taking care of me."

Matilda bit her lip. She stopped speaking.

I had fallen in love with Matilda for so many reasons, but the biggest of them all was because she was so pure and good—so full of hope. Even in the darkest days of her captivity, Matilda had somehow managed to be hopeful. Now, in an instant, that part of her was gone.

"Matilda, it's not what you think. I was never going to publish it. I promise you. I promise, I would never do that to you," I said. "I wrote it when we were apart from each other in Hawaii. I did it to make you seem real, when I thought you had left me."

Matilda traced the words on the pages in front of her. "I had sometimes wondered if Ms. Partridge was my mother. She would look at me in a way that felt too affectionate for just a tennis coach, and I couldn't help but think there were parts of us that looked alike. Dad was rarely around during my lessons with her—he was always working—but when their paths did cross, the way he looked at her, I thought maybe he loved her. I didn't know what that look meant until I met you. Those nights, alone in my bedroom, I'd imagine Daddy, Ms. Partridge and me as a family.

"But then I would scold myself because I thought it was the grandest and most delusional form of wishful thinking. I studied genetics and I knew it was impossible that I would end up with light green eyes from hazel and brown. I have such blond hair, but both my parents would have had dark. 'Oh, Matilda,' I would say to myself, 'you're such a desperate girl. She couldn't possibly be your mother.' I was grasping for something that wasn't there. I wanted love so desperately—and to be loved— that I believed it was somewhere it wasn't."

There were tears in Matilda's eyes now.

"You're probably writing this down," Matilda said. "You've probably written all of it down. I think about all of the things I said, and it's enough for a whole book. I should stop talking now. My father says the best businessmen stop talking a full sixty seconds before they think they should."

I walked over to Matilda and I knelt beside her. I put my hand on her arm. She brushed it off.

"Matilda, I know you're not going to believe me, but I promise you—"

"The funny thing is," Matilda said, interrupting me, "I should be angry at my father, but I'm not. I should be angry with Ms. Partridge, but I'm not. The only person I'm angry with is you."

It took Matilda a moment to untangle her long limbs, and then she stood up. She collected the pages and put them back on the desk, in the order in which she'd found them.

"Matilda—" I begged.

She ignored me. She walked to the bedroom and collected her things. She got dressed in the bathroom, and through the door I heard her call a cab.

She walked toward the door without a word, suitcase in hand.

"Where are you going?" I asked.

"I'm going home. Which is probably the only place in the world where I belong."

Matilda put her hand on the doorknob. She rotated it a quarter of a turn and then faced me.

"There were so many moments," she began. She was crying now. "The bowling alley, the swimming pool, that week on the estate when we would lie on our backs in the grass and look at the stars. And Hawaii—when we made love for the first time. I'm afraid of the answer, but I need to know the truth. Were all of those moments make-believe? Was there a single minute— even just a smidgen of time as brief as a blink of an eye—that you ever liked me, too?"

I walked over to her, and I placed my hand over hers on the knob, stopping her from turning it any farther.

"Matilda, I have loved you—absolutely loved you—from the second I saw you on the tennis court," I said.

Matilda didn't say anything. The cab honked outside, and I suddenly felt the moment slipping away from me, as if it was already in the past, even though we were still in the present.

"There wasn't the smallest fraction of time when I ever second-guessed my love for you. Ever. You were never a story to me. I need you to believe me, Matilda. I can't imagine going a minute without you, let alone the rest of my life. I couldn't make those moments up—fabricate them from nothing. I'm not an actor who could play a part and pretend to be in love with you. I'm a good person, and I would never play a charade like that. Please stay, and give me a chance to prove to you that what I'm telling you is true."

Matilda didn't react. I hoped she believed me because I always stood for the truth. But she didn't know that. For all she knew I had lied once before at the *Wall Street Journal* when I had stolen someone's story, and here I was doing it again.

She stood at the door for a moment longer, then turned the knob and exited my life.

Thirty

She didn't call.

I showed up to the planetarium on the Friday of our planned rendezvous, and I gazed at the stars alone, staring at Orion's Belt, wondering if she was looking at the same constellation from inside the leaded-glass windows of the estate. I went to the Mann's Chinese, too, and I arrived early so I could see moviegoers as they walked down the velvet aisle. If I caught a glimpse of a blonde girl, my heart would flutter, but it would never be her.

I would think of Matilda every moment, dissect my days according to her schedule. I imagined her waking up to her old-fashioned bedside alarm clock and selecting her outfit for the day before sitting down alone at the long dining room table and eating her preferred breakfast of pancakes and extra syrup. I'd see her walking across the grassy knolls of the estate, small heels getting caught in the grass as she stumbled to the auditorium for biology class. At precisely three o'clock every day, I would think of her playing tennis on the ivy-drenched court where we met. She knew Carole was her mother now, and I wondered if she had told her.

I would never know, because weeks went by and Matilda still didn't call.

Work progressed uneventfully. If Rubenstein had known anything, he didn't let on. He still fed me stories and we lunched, weekly at a dimly lit private club, slurping down martinis and chatting about the most glamorous business in the world—the business of entertaining. No one had come to dismantle my office. The priceless Cy Twombly drawing of the woman with frizzy hair watched over me, and I still worked on the desk that had once belonged to Matilda's biological father. The bar was drained of top-shelf alcohol at this point, but that was my doing.

I avoided Bel-Air. On the rare occasion I had to drive in its vicinity I skipped it altogether, taking the circuitous route around Sunset Boulevard, the road that led there. The only time I allowed myself to pass through those pillars was in my dreams, and sometimes those dreams were so vivid it would take me minutes after I had woken up to realize I wasn't actually there.

Three weeks after Matilda left my life, I heard that David was having a party for the president of the United States. It was a ten-thousand-dollar-a-head affair, and, surprisingly, David was hosting the party at the estate, a place previously closed off to the rest of the world. This raised the obvious questions: Had Matilda told him what I had found out? Was he no longer worried about keeping the secret? And perhaps most important, was it possible Matilda would attend the party?

Under the guise of covering the event for the paper, I finagled a ten-minute visit for the *Times* photographer. My instructions to him were clear. He was to return with a photo of each and every guest; not a single soul could be skipped.

I couldn't bear to be away. I parked as close as possible and stood across the street from Bel-Air's East Gate. For security reasons, the entrance to Bel-Air was guarded with dark-suited gentlemen with clipboards cradled in their arms and wires in their ears, and it was closed to everyone except residents and partygoers. A line of luxury sedans and sport utility vehicles with tinted windows drove through the illustrious white pillars.

As I watched the cars from under the canopy of a large date palm, the realization was sharp as a blade: Bel-Air was a place that had never been mine. It was merely a holiday in my life, like a family vacation to Disney World. I remembered my dream of Matilda and me living in her father's pool house with our smiling strawberry blond children. It had been a worst-case scenario in my mind, but in fact it was quite the opposite. It was a fantasy that would never come to pass.

As Lily had said, we were all just renters, and Bel-Air was never mine to own.

I walked away from the gates and I returned to the *Times* office downtown. I waited nervously until the photographer returned with the pictures. He was still high from being in that tornado of power, and I wanted to shake him, to tell him that it wasn't real, that I had been where he was, too. I asked to be alone with the photos, because I didn't know how I would react if I saw her. The familiar faces were there, in familiar expression and familiar attire. Lily in refined black silk and an ivory-and-diamond necklace, Charles with a drink in his right hand and a sullen expression on his face, Emma in plumes, and Carole with her cherry-red lips and regal purple dress. George and David chatted in a corner of the croquet lawn—George wore his saber-toothed grin, and David seemed bored at his own party.

But there was no Matilda.

"Where are you?" I said aloud, as if the photos were available to answer my question.

But of course I knew where she was. She was back in her life behind iron gates because the real world had broken her heart expeditiously, within weeks. It had made promises of a future, and then it had taken it all away.

It didn't matter if she was upstairs in her room listening to Jim Morrison and watching the party through filmy drapes, or if she was practicing serves on the tennis court hoping to snatch that extra mile per hour. It didn't matter if Matilda was lounging in the screening room watching old movies and munching on Red Vines or knocking strikes by herself in the bowling alley. All that mattered was the world had betrayed her.

And so had I.

Thirty-One

Carole had been right about everything that night in the aviary. I had never been good at endings.

I never forgot about Matilda. I didn't know if I wanted to shake her loose or hold her tight, and I found myself in that terrible gray place I had been in after Willa. I did not sleep; I did not eat. The highlight of my day was five o'clock, an hour I convinced myself was an acceptable time to have the evening's first drink.

Almost two months after that dreadful morning when I'd found Matilda with my story in her hands, I was on a plane to San Francisco to interview an actress about her Academy Award nomination. Once in the air I realized I had forgotten to bring music or a book to keep me occupied, so I combed through the seat pocket to find another distraction. Buried deep was a copy of the *Wall Street Journal*, a paper I didn't typically read for obvious reasons.

I absently fanned through the Marketplace and Money & Investing sections, recognizing names in the bylines as colleagues from my past, and then stumbled upon the Real Estate section. I paged through ski chalets in Switzerland and vineyards in France before spotting a one-column story accompanied by a grainy photo. I looked closer to see it better, and my equilibrium faltered.

It was an aerial shot of Joel Goldman's vacation home in Hawaii. I could see the pool, the low-slung roofline, the webbed lawn furniture, the date palms.

The house had sold for land value, the article said. A gentleman who worked in the world of hedge funds had purchased it, and speculation was it would be torn down to make way for a bigger and more modern estate.

The news was like a wrecking ball. I had promised Matilda I would take her back there, to that crumbling house that had been our sanctuary. Even in her absence, I still believed somehow we would reunite, and I had found comfort in knowing that the house was still vacant, waiting for our return. I hadn't even given Lily's key back, because I wanted to feel as if that door was open to me, even if it wasn't.

I landed in San Francisco, and I drove to Hillsborough, a tony, hilly suburb of turn-of-the-century mansions that were once inhabited by kings of industry and now by kings of technology. I did my best to stay focused and engaged during the interview, for I was careful this time, after what had happened at the *Journal*.

After the meeting, I drove to San Francisco and retreated to my hotel room in Union Square. It was a big hotel full of tourists, a place that may have been chic when it was built in the early twentieth century but was now dingy and old, with worn carpets and pipes that hummed. I had stopped by a liquor store and bought a bottle of scotch, and I ripped open the paper bag, sat on my bed and drank straight from the bottle. But it did the opposite of what it was supposed to do. It sharpened the pain instead of dulled it.

In the months without Matilda I had never called her. I had dialed seven or eight digits of her number, but I always stopped short. This time, from an unrecognizable hotel number in San

Francisco, I dialed the full ten digits, hoping she would pick up, and I could tell her that I would bring her back to Hawaii one last time before our house was torn down, that I was a man who would never break a promise.

Instead, I could say nothing. The number had been disconnected.

The idea that Joel Goldman's house was to be torn down haunted me. Matilda never strayed from my thoughts for more than a minute or two, but this news, in particular, felt as if it was demanding I do more. As I sat on the plane on a runway in San Francisco, surrounded by water and precipitous hills, I realized that I had let Matilda go too easily. Willa Asher hadn't been worth fighting for, but I would fight for Matilda Duplaine.

So when I landed in Los Angeles I decided to reach out to Matilda, to tell her how I felt. I arrived at my apartment, more excited and determined than I had been in a long time. I pulled out a pen, and I began to write.

For a man born with a talent for words, I struggled through the first paragraph—the lead, as we say in reporting. I wrote and rewrote, littering the floor of my apartment with pages of futility. Finally, I got it right. I told Matilda everything, from the beginning: how I had fallen for her on that enchanting evening on the tennis court, how I hadn't been able to stop thinking about her, and that the rest of my life would be empty without her in it. I told her how I had longed to see her, that I had never stopped loving her. I asked her for one last chance to prove that love, for I had given her a chance—this girl who had never once seen the world. She had been a gamble, I told her, and she was worth every chip I had laid down. I told Matilda that if she had ever loved me even a fraction as much as I had loved her, she needed to let me explain. I asked her to meet me at the planetarium the following Tuesday night.

I knew Matilda was the one to retrieve the mail every day—

she would walk to the end of the driveway and peek out the mail slot at the world right beyond her grasp—so my hope was she would receive the letter. I put the note in a linen envelope— the type of letter dressing that seemed suitable for the world in which Matilda lived. I wrote the name Miss Matilda Duplaine in my nicest penmanship, and I closed my eyes as I put it in the postbox, hoping she would open it and give me a second chance.

I woke up the following Tuesday morning with a flutter of excitement in my stomach, and the air was crisper and clearer than it had been in weeks. I dressed carefully, in a blue checked shirt that had been Matilda's favorite and a dark pair of blue jeans. I had shaved, so my face, for the moment, was smooth, the way she preferred it. I went without cologne, because Matilda had always said she liked the smell of me.

I showed up to the planetarium early for the 8:00 p.m. show. I stood near the entrance and combed the crowd eagerly, hoping she would come. Matilda was always five minutes early to everything, so I knew she wouldn't arrive late. But even after the lobby had cleared out and everyone took their seats for the show, I still fooled my mind into believing she would meet me.

I sat through the show alone, spotting Orion's Belt from beneath a dome of stars. I had convinced myself that Matilda had hit traffic, that somehow she would still show up. The planetarium was a long way from Bel-Air, I told myself, so she would come eventually.

But she never did.

I returned home late, again after too much to drink, and fell asleep on my floor, hoping the past two and a half months of my life had been a nightmare. Hoping I would wake up in Hawaii and my life would once again be good.

I went to work the next day, muddling through my day, trying to grasp the fact that Matilda was gone. I had a lunch scheduled with Rubenstein, and as we sipped—or in Rubenstein's case, gulped—martinis, I inexplicably had a false sense of delusion. For no reason at all, I suddenly believed—or tried to convince myself, whichever the case may be—that Matilda hadn't received the letter at all. David had intercepted it or the postman hadn't delivered it because he'd never heard of a Miss Matilda Duplaine. Or maybe, just maybe, Matilda had received the letter and had desperately tried to leave the estate, her plan thwarted by David.

I was sure she wanted to see me, but a force beyond her control had ruined her every best effort.

So I decided that the next day I would make the long, sinuous journey to Bel-Air.

I drove through the pillars and took the familiar turns, hazy with delusion as if I was under some sort of spell. I drove past Emma and George's house, remembering the dinner party that had first led me here. I made the single turn, and my heart raced when I saw the grand entry to the estate.

I turned right into the driveway, facing the tall, impenetrable gates. They loomed above me. I buzzed and waited patiently for an answer.

"May I help you?" a male voice asked after a pause that seemed to stretch on for minutes.

"I'm here to see Matilda Duplaine," I said.

There was a brief silence, and then the gates opened.

It was the fifteenth of March, a glorious early-spring day. As I drove up the long driveway, the giant specimen trees wept green leaves that fell to the ground with a gust of wind, gracefully and slowly, like snowflakes. Invisible sprinklers watered the grounds, creating an eerie mist that looked like fog over a lake. There was something mysterious about it.

I arrived at the motor court, and the valet opened my car door and took my key. He ushered me toward the front door, and I was greeted at the entry by a good-looking gentleman in his forties dressed in a crisp suit. I thought, regretfully, of Hector, who was the last person to greet me here.

"I'm Thomas Cleary," I said, reaching out my hand to his. "A friend of Matilda's."

"I'm told to have you wait in the parlor." The butler led me to the waiting area and motioned me toward a chair with the flip of his right hand. "Would you like a bottle of water?"

"No, thank you."

I had prepared for the worst but she hadn't turned me away. Instead, here I was, in the parlor. I couldn't sit, I couldn't stand, I couldn't have waited a single extra moment to see her.

I paced beside the two Jasper Johns paintings, and I glanced at my watch. It was two forty-five. I wondered if Matilda was surprised by my visit, if she was hastily brushing her hair and slipping on a dress she knew I liked, excited I had finally come to get her as I should have done so long ago.

"Come, this way," the butler said a few minutes later, leading me down a long hallway with wooden panels covering the walls.

As I followed him I wondered where we were going. Perhaps Matilda would want to meet on the tennis court, the place where we had first made each other's acquaintance, or maybe in the sculpture garden or the bowling alley. It didn't matter where he was taking me, for all I wanted to do was see her.

I was escorted to a closed door. The butler pulled it open and gestured for me to go inside. My heart swelled with anticipation, but the only person in the room was David Duplaine.

He should have been at work, but instead he sat on an armchair in front of a low-lit fireplace. He focused his gaze intently on me and motioned me with a graceful fan of his fingers to take a seat in an empty chair that faced him.

I felt deflated. All that hope quashed so expeditiously.

I sat down across from David, in a chair situated neither too close nor too far. David's office was paneled in walnut, with floor-to-ceiling French doors opening to the grounds. Its pale-wooded furniture was upholstered in light fabrics, and on the coffee table sat a small pot of freshly sheared moss, still wet with dew, and a single book on the history of the motion-picture business. The walls held bookshelves filled with volumes on art and film, and three Academy Awards glistened gold under pointed lighting. Above the fireplace was the painting I recognized from Carole's bedroom in Hawaii—the abstract painting of the woman.

I focused on it for a second too long, flashing back to that glorious month Matilda and I had spent together. Then I turned to face the man who sat across from me. He seemed more complicated than he had before, now that I knew the facts. David had never married, and he had been in love with a woman he couldn't have. He had devoted his life to a girl who wasn't even his child. I felt sorry for him, until I remembered that everything in his life had been funded with blood money.

"I'm here to see Matilda," I finally said, cutting the silence.

"The irony," David began, "is that if you had been up-front all along, man enough to ask my permission to see her, I may have allowed it. I don't want Matilda to be deprived of love—that's life's ultimate tragedy. It was how you did it, sneaking behind my back. Lack of courage is a terrible weakness."

"And so you're punishing Matilda for what I did? That hardly seems fair."

"You took that into your own hands, didn't you, Thomas? By writing that story. As predicted, you created your own undoing. All I had to do was sit back and watch it happen."

"I would have never published it," I said with candor. "I was so in love with Matilda I just wanted to know more about her, and once I started investigating, I couldn't stop. If I wanted to publish it I would have done so already, especially now that I have nothing more to lose."

"I believe you," David said. "That's why I left you alone."

"That couldn't have been the only reason. You've never struck me as a passive guy."

"In your time away I realized that you gave me something, too," David said. "I didn't have to show my daughter how hard reality is because you did that for me. You kept whispering in her ear that the world was so perfect, so grand. But it's not. Matilda knows that now. In thirty-two short days you taught her how terrible life can be. You can say I'm the bad guy because I held her captive all these years, but imagine a life where you never have to worry about money, having your heart broken, betrayal, pain or even something as simple as a bad day. I gave Matilda a perfect world. So, now Matilda's back here, of her own accord this time—with her parents, who love her." David emphasized the word *love* as if I did nothing of the sort.

"Parents?" I asked curiously.

"Yes, Carole and I are going to marry," David said. "Carole and I have been in love for a decade. But we couldn't marry while Joel was still alive."

"You're going to live here, then? The three of you?"

David Duplaine had always been a stoic man, and for the first time I saw a glimmer of emotion pass through his eyes. I indulged myself and imagined it for a brief second: Carole, David and Matilda sitting beside the swimming pool, eating scones and drinking lemonade with mint.

"What about Charles?" I questioned.

"He was Joel's financial advisor. It's been more of a burden for him than anything. He loves Carole but..."

David's voice faded as I diverted my eyes, again looking at the painting. In the glow of the lamp, I realized now the painting was of a mother and child, and suddenly it became clear: Joel must have left it for Carole. That was why it hadn't been auctioned with the rest of the art.

"I sent a letter to Matilda," I said, returning my attention to David.

"She never received it," David responded matter-of-factly, and I had a brief flicker of hope, like the flame on a match. Matilda hadn't seen the letter. It was still possible we could have our happily-ever-after.

"Why not?" I asked, knowing the answer.

"Because it's over, Thomas."

"That's not your decision," I said. "I need to see her."

"In life we seldom receive the same opportunity twice." David leaned into me, propping his elbows on his thighs. "You had your opportunity, Thomas. You chose to squander it. There are no second chances here."

"Does she miss me?" I asked, hoping the answer was yes. Hoping I could convince David that we were destined to be together.

"Matilda has never mentioned you. Not even once."

Not even once. She had forgotten me.

Just like that, the flame died.

"It's fortuitous you decided to pay me a visit today," David remarked, as if he hadn't just destroyed something in me for good. "Just yesterday, I received a call from a friend of mine at the *New York Times*, and it turns out they're looking for an entertainment editor. It's a big job, and I recall you always had an affinity for Manhattan, so I told him I knew the perfect guy. I think we'll both agree—all three of us would, I can speak on behalf of Matilda—that New York may be the best place for you. Don't you think? Sometimes a fresh start is in order."

I stood up and walked over to the leaded-glass doors that opened to the vast grounds.

"I was once in love with this girl," I began. "She was the one I saw in New York. And I bought her these emerald earrings for her twenty-first birthday. They were tiny. Barely a fraction of a carat. But I had saved six months to buy them, so in my mind they were bigger than they were."

I looked to David, to see if he was engaged in the story. He was listening, but his face was impassive.

"And so finally her birthday arrived and I couldn't wait to give them to her. They had been sitting in my drawer for a few weeks by this time. I remember I had wrapped them in a paper decorated with zebras—rewrapped them twice, in fact, so the presentation would be perfect. And when it came time for the girl—Willa was her name—to open them, I waited for her face to light up. But it didn't. It went dark."

Just then, in the distance, outside, I saw Matilda. She was walking across the vast lawn wearing a frilly white tennis outfit, a ribbon in her hair holding a ponytail that swayed back and forth with her girlie gait. The sun sparkled off her hair, and my heart stopped.

I wanted to throw open the doors, to call out for her, to run to her—anything, just to show her I hadn't given up. But I did nothing.

"'I don't deserve these,' the girl had said to me when she saw the earrings. And that phrase haunted me for all these years and I hated her for it. She was rich, so of course she felt she deserved nice earrings. But I hadn't given her the benefit of the doubt. She had known I had saved months for that present, and she had known she was going to eventually break my heart. That's why she didn't deserve them. What she was trying to say is she was trying to do the right thing."

I paused as Matilda walked farther into the distance, down the croquet lawn. The sun haloed her, so she looked filmy instead of real, as if she were already a ghost.

"I don't deserve Matilda," I continued. "It's not that I'm not rich enough for her, or not good enough looking or smart enough, or any of those things—although maybe all that is true. But she deserves for her first love not to be her last love. Matilda deserves fifty first dates and fifty first kisses, and she deserves to be looked at with longing from across a room, to blush under someone's stare. And, most of all, she deserves to grow up without being tethered to someone who she feels indebted to. Maybe it won't be me, but it would break my heart to think of her alone—loveless—for the rest of her life."

Matilda passed the horseshoe pit and then rounded a bend and disappeared.

I watched out the window for a moment longer, before turning my back to the outdoors.

"I'll go to New York. But you must make me a promise in return. You said yourself that lack of love is a tragedy. Don't do that to her."

My words hung heavily in the air. I would not leave until I got my promise, and David knew it. Finally, he nodded.

"I promise that," he declared. "You have my word."

I leaned over and shook his hand. "Thank you. Goodbye, David."

"Goodbye, Thomas. I wish you the best of luck at the *Times*."

I considered David's choice of words. It was exactly what he had said to me the first night we had met, when we had dropped him at the estate after his driver had fallen ill and the single upstairs window had been lit. It was a different *Times* he'd referred to then, and I reflected on how life had changed in such short order.

I walked to the door, and then I turned around, looking at David one last time. He suddenly seemed tired. His life had been made up of a series of dramatic decisions, and I wondered if he ever regretted them, if he wished he had lived life differently.

The butler escorted me down the hall and then outside, where I was greeted with the bright cadence of birds in spring. My car idled in the motor court, and I inhaled one last time, taking in the sadness—or was it glory?—of the estate.

I got into the car and slowly pulled away from the house. I drove down the driveway and when I neared the tennis court I stopped. I heard the crisp sound of a racket hitting a ball. I heard her idiosyncratic laugh and the light pitter-patter of her soles on clay before she hit the next shot.

She had already forgotten me.

I paused, briefly considering stopping and walking down to the court. It was the city of the motion-picture business after all, and that's what would have happened in the movies. On-screen, everyone seemed to get their happy ending. Instead, though, I continued onward, finally making my way out the gates. I took a left, weaving my way down the tight roads of the rich. I passed between the grand white pillars of Bel-Air and allowed my eyes to linger in my side-view mirror long after they should have, long after the sign had disappeared.

Thirty-Two

Two weeks later, twenty-four hours before I was to leave for Manhattan, I stood on the street where it had all begun. I needed to say goodbye once and for all, to let go of Los Angeles so I could embrace New York and embark on the rest of my life.

The tinkle of an antique servant bell announced my arrival.

The place was still a well-crafted mess, and I waited a few moments for Lily to appear magically from behind a piece of furniture.

She didn't. The shop was quiet. It was regular business hours, but there didn't appear to be anyone there. It had always seemed to be a place light on customers, for those who did come were heavy on the wallet, but it was unusual for it to be totally empty.

"Ethan? Lily?" I called out, to no answer.

I glanced to my left and saw the candlestick in the shape of a bird. It pointed north. It felt as if it had been so many migrations since I had met her.

I was about to leave when I decided to walk through the store, to the back. There was a small garden, some gravel and a single chaise with a table beside it. Lily stood in garden gloves, with clippers in her hand, carefully removing thorns from a pale pink rose.

She didn't look up from the flower.

"Darling, Thomas. I missed you something terrible."

"How did you know it was me?" I asked.

"The sound of your footsteps. You're wearing the shoes I brought you from Boston."

Lily turned around then, and she first focused on my shoes, to be sure she was right, which she was. She then took a long and hard look at me. I wore an outfit crisp as bills from the bank, and her face registered satisfaction with it.

In the months since I had last seen her, Lily Goldman had turned larger than life, as a dream often does. But now, in person, I remembered how slight and small she was, with the lightness and frailty of a bird.

I avoided her eyes, because they were Matilda's eyes, too, and they were painful to look at.

"Did you miss me?" she asked.

I didn't respond because I didn't know the answer myself.

Lily put five roses in a vase of water so their flawless tops shot out in different directions like a star.

"I'll take that as a yes," she said, abandoning the roses for a moment and stepping closer to me. She made a small adjustment to my collar. "You look pallid, Thomas."

"It hasn't been the easiest of months," I said, as an understatement.

I tried to read Lily's face for emotion, to see what she knew. As always, she gave away nothing, so I continued, "I'm here to tell you I've decided to take a job with the *New York Times*. I wanted to say goodbye, and I wanted to thank you for all you've done for me. In so many ways you've changed my life, and for that I'm very grateful."

"Manhattan can be a very intoxicating woman, Thomas. Just remember she breaks the hearts of even the best of men."

"So does Los Angeles," I responded.

Lily snipped a thorn off a final rose and it pricked her finger before falling to the ground.

"I am aware that you know our secret. And before you leave, I think it's important that you understand something," Lily said. "It was a terrible secret that grew and grew. It was never meant to happen this way. My father fell for Carole when she was a teenager. She was the sister of the man who ran our stables."

When Lily spoke of him, even now, she seemed overcome by sadness.

"The whole thing was terribly inappropriate, but complicit. There was nothing illegal or forceful about it, and Carole would say the same thing if she were sitting here. Carole adored my father—she was absolutely besotted with him. He was very handsome and very charming, and he had this uncanny ability..." Lily stopped herself then and gazed into the distance.

"Some men—powerful men—make you feel like the world revolves around you, like you're the brightest star in the sky, even if it's just for a moment. My father wasn't like that. He kept you in the waiting room, with no food or water or compassion until you scraped and clawed at his doors, dying to be allowed in. My father kept you thirsty, that was his secret. He did it in his business, with my mother, with Carole, with me."

"How could you look at him after what he did?" I asked. "She was seventeen, for God's sake."

"My father and I had a very complex relationship," Lily said. "He could be a tremendously good person, though he was capable of evil. I grew up in a world of powerful men who were very fallible, and I loved them anyway."

"And what about Carole?"

"Carole ruined my life just as much as my father did. We were incredibly generous with her. Her mother was an alcoholic who had given birth to Carole's brother when she herself was sixteen. Carole has never even met her father, and Carole's mother abandoned her children and my father took them in. They lived at our equestrian estate. Carole knew her brother and I were very much in love and supposed to marry. My father was inappropriately older than she, certainly, but she was manipulative, even then. She knew my father wanted anything he couldn't have, and she used it to her advantage. Girls nowadays grow up getting it wrong. It's the women who have the power in a relationship."

"Why did you remain friends with Carole? You must have hated her for what she did to your family."

"I'm older than you, Thomas, and much wiser. No offense."

"None taken. I prefer to be younger without the wisdom."

"Carole may have seduced my father, she may have destroyed my greatest chance at love, but there was never a single day I would have traded places with Carole Partridge. Imagine." Lily caught her breath, and her eyes turned glassy. "Imagine the terrible sadness that burdens her every single day. Her whole life has been bound with confidentiality clauses, and she lives blocks from a daughter who never knew she existed—until now. I know Carole well, better than anyone else knows her. I think in the beginning she thought her daughter was a fair trade for the extraordinary life my father gave her in return. But quickly she would've given every penny, all the fame, the beauty, just to have Matilda back."

"She does now," I said. "Right?"

"Yes, so you've done a good thing. Inadvertently perhaps, but wayward intention never diminishes a good result in my eyes."

"You know I never would have betrayed you like that. I wouldn't have published that story."

"I know," Lily said. "You're far too good a man for that."

It was a brilliant blue day, no clouds. I looked up, toward the heavens and my mom. I thought of how much my life had changed since the first time I had walked into Lily's shop. The past few months had been the most difficult of my life, but they had been preceded by the most glorious.

"Thomas, love. Is there something you'd like me to tell Matilda? A message before you fly off to Manhattan?" Lily asked. At the mention of her, still, I felt as if the sky turned a bit less blue.

All I'd wanted those months without her was a chance to tell her that I loved her, that I would always love her. But I had made a promise, and I was a man who kept my promises.

"You can tell her goodbye for me," I said. "If you wouldn't mind."

"That's all? That seems rather brief for a man of words."

"Yes, that's all. And thank you again, for everything."

"You're very welcome."

I walked toward the tall French doors into the shop. I placed my hand on the brass knob, then turned back in Lily's direction.

"Lily, there's one last piece of the story that needs answering," I said. "I know you invited me to that first dinner party because you wanted me to write a flattering piece about your father. But what about after that? Why did you invite me to dinner parties and the art opening? Why did you orchestrate stories for me with my boss? What was it? Was it all an elaborate plan to bring Matilda and me together?"

"It was nothing of the sort. I never thought you'd meet," Lily said. "The truth is that you reminded me of the man I was supposed to marry. You were both so innocent, so sweet. I know plenty of men who were born into wealth and have no potential. You were both the opposite—born into little means but with so much ahead of them. I felt when I was with you—well, that I still had a part of him. He was twenty-seven when he left me. And he reminded me so much of you."

"Do you still love him? Even after all these years?"

"I've never loved anyone since him, not even a little bit," Lily said. "You know something? I haven't so much as uttered his name since the day he left. I never once asked after him, and Carole never brought him up. Michael—that was his name. Such a strong name."

For a moment, Lily seemed to drift away in a daydream.

"There's a part of me… It's a terrible thing to say, but there's a part of me that hopes he's dead at this point, because it seems an easier cross to bear than thinking of him someplace in a world without me in it."

I could have told her Michael was alive, that he lived in a decrepit and lonely ranch tucked into the side of a volcano in Hawaii with a single horse. I spared her, though, because Lily Goldman didn't deserve that. Lily had once told me her father had been a gambler and Lily had been, too. She had bet on me, and now it was up to me to decide if her wager had been a winning one.

"I'll call you from Manhattan," I said.

And with that, I walked out.

The servant bell announced my departure.

Thirty-Three

When the plane took off, we headed west, over the ocean, and for a moment I fooled myself into thinking I was on my way back to Hawaii. I glanced beside me, hoping to see Matilda, but there was only a vacant seat with a television that played for no one. I ordered a beer and pulled out the morning's *Los Angeles Times*.

We took a U-turn then and we headed over the city. I could see the expansive green lawns of Bel-Air—a place where the houses were as fastidious as movie sets, the cats were exotically bred and where Matilda was at this very moment. We passed over the compact downtown area, and there was the Hollywood sign, perched regally at the top of its mountain, a beacon for dreamers as I had once been. There were the movie studios; the hills of Forest Lawn Cemetery, where Joel Goldman was buried with his secrets; and the grassy knolls of Hidden Hills, where Lily Goldman had once ridden her horses and fallen in love.

We passed the mountains and it all disappeared behind us, just like that, as if it had never been there to begin with.

Somewhere over the Rockies, I closed my eyes and fell asleep. My dreams transported me to a memory so vivid I would have bet my paltry savings it was real. It was a fall evening, and the hot Santa Ana winds blanketed Matilda and me between the cashmere throw below us and the twinkling stars above. Matilda leaned close to me—so close I could smell her shampoo—and she pointed to Orion's starry belt buckle flickering in the sky. When she did she whispered in my ear, so her breath tickled the back of my neck:

Someday you'll know exactly where to find me. I'll be twinkling for you.

The dream played over and over again in my mind like a motion picture, and I was so deep into slumber I only awoke when the pilot announced our final descent. I peered out the window and saw Manhattan below us, once again inviting me into her wide and seductive embrace.

My apartment was a modest walk-up in the East Village. It was a worse place than Silver Lake, if that was possible. There was no view of the mountains in the distance; instead, I faced a brick building. There was no swimming pool here, and even the sky seemed at a premium. I found myself homesick for Los Angeles.

The next morning I woke up to the unmistakable sound of a city. I dressed in an outfit that Lily had given me, and I headed for the subway. In Los Angeles people look you in the eyes, straight to your soul. In New York people avoid your eyes. They looked around you.

It was a font recognized around the world, and when I arrived at the *Times* building, I was awestruck.

The *New York Times*. It had been my dream from that ripe age of fifteen when I had decided I wanted to be a journalist. It was what I had gone to Harvard for, why I had been studying on the Charles when I had met Willa. The *Wall Street Journal* was supposed to have been a stepping stone to it, but instead, what had happened there had quashed the dream of it completely— or so I had thought.

I imagined Phil Rubenstein standing beside me, encouraging me forward, and I smiled.

I walked through the lobby and then was escorted up the elevator. The editor in chief approached me dynamically, hand out, as if I was the important one.

"Thomas Cleary," he said, shaking my hand with authority. "David speaks so highly of you—which is a compliment of the highest order, since we all know he's stingy in the compliment department. Welcome to the *New York Times*. We sure are glad to have you."

"Thank you, sir," I said. "Glad to be here."

I was taken to my office. I had a window, albeit small, and Manhattan lay before me, as if it was there for conquering. Unlike my office in Los Angeles, this one had no antiques, no priceless drawings or desks that had belonged to studio heads. Instead, the only personalized touch was the most stunning bouquet of cabbage roses, in eighteen shades of pink. I smiled, thinking of Lily. She'd probably cut them in her garden and had had them shipped in water from the West Coast.

The day was a hectic one, full of introductions and meetings. I'd had not one but two second chances, and I wasn't going to let this one pass me by. I worked late into the night, compiling research for an article on the opening of a new Broadway show and briefing one of my reporters on a digital-music conference in San Francisco.

The cabbage roses sat on my desk, a flourish of color in a business that was still black-and-white. It was around nine when I was ready to turn out the lights and go home that I opened the note that accompanied the flowers. It was dated the day before.

Dearest Thomas,
I spoke with my dad this morning, who told me you had come to find me, but he had kept you away.

Oh, Thomas, I have thought of you every moment for all these months, too, and I kept hoping you would come to me, because isn't that what men in the movies do? I play tennis late at night, and I look up at the oak tree, hoping you will be there watching. Nothing has been the same without you here.

I know you are in Manhattan now, which seems so far away from me. I thought you might want some flowers from the estate to get you through your first week at your new job. I cut them from the sculpture garden, beside your favorite John McCracken sculpture, so you know exactly where they came from.

By the way, I couldn't believe it when I learned about this thing called Federal Express. It seems nothing short of a miracle. I wish I could Federal Express you back here because I miss you, and Hawaii, and those days on the estate, and absolutely all of it.

There's no need for fifty kisses if you know the first one is the right one.

Let me know if you want more flowers, because Daddy says they don't have flowers in Manhattan. Why would you want to live in a place with no flowers?
Miss you to infinity,
Matilda

I read and reread the note so many times the words blurred together.

Matilda had once told me that she could imagine things so vividly that she could believe she was in another place. This, she had said, was her way of escaping those years of lonely confinement on the estate. I closed my eyes and I was once again beside Matilda in the old-fashioned bowling alley. She was whole, and complete, of green eyes and crooked smile. She was the high scorer and I was the low, and we were drinking tins of pineapple juice, eating pretzels and listening to Air Supply. I put my hand on hers, and she laughed her idiosyncratic laugh. I pulled her closer, and I whispered something in her ear, something that only she could hear.

When I opened my eyes all was quiet at the *Times*. Reporters had gone home to families or to business engagements and I closed my office door. I stood before the window, taking in the vibrant city before me, miles of sky that glistened bright and never went dark. I set my gaze beyond Manhattan—west, toward Bel-Air, where the nights were black and mountainous and starry, where palm trees swayed in the wind, where dreams were never too big to come true and where Matilda Duplaine waited for me to someday come home.

★ ★ ★ ★ ★

Acknowledgments

Not so long ago, when this book was in pieces on my floor, locked in a drawer or almost forgotten about, there was one person who believed in it absolutely. Andrea Walker, thank you for your patience, your kindness and your friendship. Working with you was a true gift, and it changed my life.

Andrea delivered me to the fabulous Michelle Brower at Folio Literary Management. Michelle, you are the most incredible agent and friend. Sometimes you have to have enough belief for both of us, and you are always up to the task.

Erika Imranyi, my superheroic editor: Thank you. Thank you for acquiring the book and for slaving over it so many times, sentence by sentence, word by word. You never dialed it in. You always pushed me to be a better writer, and you sprinkled fairy dust on the world of Matilda and Thomas and made it glow in the dark.

To Leonore Waldrip, Emer Flounders, the marketing, art and sales departments and everyone at Harlequin/MIRA: I appreciate your belief in the book and in me. Publishing is a collaborative effort, and the book is only the beginning. It is the people who deliver it to the world who change its fate.

There are so many people who make my real life gilded, and a few deserve particular mention. Blair Rich, Mark Cohen,

Christina Bing and Margaret Swetman, thank you for years of friendship. Thank you, Kelly Schwartz, for your ear and your invaluable editing help, and Weston Armstrong for my gorgeous artwork. Layne Dicker and Rob Mandel, you have been so supportive of me in my business life, and that support has made my personal life infinitely better. And a very special thank-you goes out to John Chernin. You inspired me to write again.

Thank you, Family—the Brunkhorst part of it and the Novack part of it. Thank you Mom, Dad, Vanessa and Austin for too much to mention here. Debbie Novack, Martin and Cheryl Novack, Helen Novack and all the Novack kids—you are as much my family as my own. And, finally, Brian Novack, my best friend: you have never once put a ceiling on what I can do, so it is because of you that I keep reaching higher.